John Trenhaile lives in Ashdown Forest with his wife and two children. *The Tiger of Desire* is his tenth novel. His first, *The Man Called Kyril*, was adapted for television and shown in 1988 as *Codename Kyril*. His most recent novels are *Krysalis*, *Acts of Betrayal* and *Blood Rules*.

## BLOOD RULES

'Taut suspense . . . horribly convincing.'
*Daily Telegraph*

'An exciting tale of obsessiveness and retribution.'
*Sunday Press*

## ACTS OF BETRAYAL

'Shocking . . . the suspense, woven by a British writer hailed as the heir apparent to le Carré, is killing.'
*Today*

'This is a novel full of lies and moments of truth; none of the truths is palatable and all of the lies are deadly.'
*Evening Standard*

## KRYSALIS

'A tighly paced tale of manipulation and deception.'
*Today*

'Tense . . . moves forward smartly all the way. Most impressive.'
*Independent*

*Also by John Trenhaile*

JOHN TRENHAILE

# The Tiger of Desire

Fontana
*An Imprint of* HarperCollins*Publishers*

Fontana
An Imprint of HarperCollins*Publishers*
77–85 Fulham Palace Road,
Hammersmith, London W6 8JB

Special overseas edition 1993
9 8 7 6 5 4 3 2 1

First published in Great Britain by
HarperCollins*Publishers* 1992

ISBN 0 00 647313 X

Set in Linotron Meridien

Printed in Great Britain by
HarperCollinsManufacturing Glasgow

For John and Jenny Howard,
and James, too.
(And Kelmscott Road an' all.)
With love.

## AUTHOR'S NOTE

Mr W J Abbott not only allowed me to visit HM Prison Pentonville, of which he is Governor, but in the course of a long conversation gave me some feeling for what a life sentence might mean to the prisoner himself, his family, and those around him. I am deeply grateful both to him and to the prison officers who gave up their time to explain much that would otherwise have remained obscure.

Thanks are also due to the staff of the National Library, and also of the National Archives, Hill Street, Republic of Singapore, for their tireless assistance in helping me to map the Singapore of 1971–1973.

Finally, I want to express my gratitude to the various citizens of Singapore who gave up their time to describe to me what the atmosphere in the Republic was like at the outbreak of the Gulf War with Iraq in January 1991, particularly Mr Khoo Hye Tin and – as always – Teri Lin.

I

# ONE

EDR stood for Expected Date of Release; that was one of the first things you learned when your husband was convicted of murder and given a life sentence. Alison had kept it marked on the calendar for three years, transferring the letters each New Year's Day as a way of countering the near-suicidal depression that Christmas generates in lifers' wives, but without much success. Three years, two years, one . . . what difference? EDR was like death: coming but unreal.

Then it did make a difference. Hard to say when: but suddenly finite and hard. Two months from now. Next month. Next week.

*Tomorrow.*

She felt a fool and wallowed in it. Her fingers were shaking, tears stung her eyes, but she managed to pick up the red pen and cross through October 4th, 1990 on the kitchen wall calendar. She was laughing and crying and she wanted to be sick, and it was all too wonderful for words. She looked a wreck, didn't care. One more day and Iain would be home, having paid his penalty, his debt to society. One more day – but even now she did not dare say to herself, 'We've made it.' She wanted to. She longed to beat her breasts and shout, 'For seventeen years I've stood by him and supported him and I've raised his child, and I love him, and we've done it.' But she was afraid. EDR was tomorrow. Tomorrows did not always happen.

'I'm so sorry,' he'd said on his last night of freedom, 'I forgot to make the bookings for Bali, I'll do it tomorrow.'

11

Whereas tomorrow three Singaporean policemen had come to arrest him, sending her husband back to England and a limbo where they'd kept him for over seventeen years. During that time she'd aged on the outside and he'd aged on the inside of a succession of prisons, sinking through the system, Categories A to D, open prison, hostel . . . no, no, no, my dear, don't think about that. Wipe your eyes. Kate will be home soon, oh God, don't think about that either, do something.

Alison unpacked her string bag, putting each article away at once; in a kitchen this small, this old, this damp and drab, it was necessary to be methodically tidy. There was hardly enough room in the tiny fridge for more than a couple of cartons of milk and a tomato, but she made space for the steaks. She hadn't eaten steak for such a long time, and the *price*, well. He'd asked for corned beef hash, because that was his favourite, but she'd protested that they couldn't celebrate the end of his sentence with hash, and so then he'd said in that special, bitter, jailbird voice, 'What then – porridge?' But he wanted something fresh, and green. A salad, crisp lettuce, oil and vinegar. Or vegetables: courgettes, French beans. Then he'd pounded the table and said he wanted hash and he should have the right to choose. Then he'd cried. So she didn't really know what he wanted. She was used to making the decisions, though. Steak, salad and baked potatoes.

She wondered what she would say to him next day when they met, her first words. She'd never had a pet name for Iain. No love-name . . . Just as well; how futile it would sound after all these years apart.

As she folded up the last plastic bag and stuffed it in a drawer she noticed that her hands had not stopped shaking.

She heard a key in the lock and her shoulders stiffened. Sure enough, Kate's voice twanged down the narrow hallway, counterpointed by Darren's whine. What was he complaining about this time, Alison wondered as she tried to compose her face, dole money short again? Had that little DHSS cow – I think it was little cow, it may have been fat bitch, or was she his probation officer? So hard to keep track – had that little cow tried to get him to work? No, it was the Tories; ah yes, the old songs, always best.

As they loped into the kitchen she wheeled around, compressing the lines of her tired face into a smile. Do not, under any circumstances, make a fuss tonight, she told herself, for tomorrow is EDR.

'There you go, then.'

Kate was holding out a bottle of red wine, on her face that smug smile, the one she'd learned when she was, oh, seven. Gauntlets were out of fashion nowadays. Too much trouble to throw them down, perhaps; not that you'd ever be called upon to pick them up afterwards. Kate, too, was aware of EDR, and here was her contribution to the festivities. Chateau Batailley – expensive. How nice. Alison thought about melting, and waited instead.

'Darren nicked it down at Tesco's.'

Never melt, not with Kate.

'What am I supposed to say?' Alison enquired. 'Thank you? Isn't one jailbird enough for you?'

She felt a mounting desire to lash out. Within her lay this streak of violence that had always terrified her, never more so than when Kate was little. She hadn't given way to it, not once. And now if she did use her fists Kate would fight back. So leave it. *Leave it.*

Tears, such a waste of time. She dashed them away and turned to the sink, ignoring the bottle of wine.

'Suit yourself, then.' A clink as Kate put the bottle down.

'It's okay, Alison.' Darren's voice, soothing but with a hint of laughter in it. Laughing at *her*, at the murderer's

13

moll, and why not? 'No one saw me do it,' he went on. 'Clean as a whistle, we was.'

She swung around to look at him, ready to deliver some tart reply, but she couldn't. They looked so pathetic, both of them. He, with his razor-slit jeans, six cod's mouths gaping to reveal white flesh, and leather jacket and hair slicked back above a high-shaven neck; Kate slovenly as ever in her dirty trainers, black woollen tights, black skirt and lipstick, black, unwashed hair . . . even their matching earrings, blasphemous in intent, served only to highlight how pathetic they were. A big gold female symbol, with Jesus crucified upside down on the cross, dangled from Darren's left ear, its counterpart swinging from Kate's right.

'Will you come with me?' she said abruptly. 'Tomorrow?' *God! To think I have to ask . . .*

'Definitely.' Darren gave her the thumbs-up. 'Car to the door, eight o'clock sharp. Stretched limo's got a problem, but the van's in A1 nick.'

Not you, she thought. I didn't mean you, Darren. You're not his son.

'Kate,' she said. 'Will you come with me?'

'Yuh.' She kicked the skirting board a couple of times with the back of her heel, not looking at Alison. 'Course I will, Mum. Got something I want to show you, Darren, c'mon.'

Alison had forbidden them to make love in the house, but they'll do it anyway, she thought, as they clumped upstairs. And why not, because everyone else their age did it? She operated in a vacuum where standards were soggy. Iain could have backed her up, but he lodged in a place that did not have standards at all.

She'd decide what to do about the stolen bottle of wine later, but now she was tired and must lie down. She would pretend to sleep while with half an ear she listened to the subdued noises and scuffles next door. She would

14

remember when she had last made love to a man, seventeen years ago, and wonder, in the most secret, fearful recess of her heart, what tomorrow would bring.

She climbed the stairs with heavy steps and lay down on the bed. What a hovel, she thought dully. What a place for him to come home to . . .

Alison closed her eyes. Next door, things were surprisingly quiet. After a while she fell into a trance-like state, aware of her surroundings but unable to move. Behind her eyelids, a familiar scene began to unfold.

She was in London, it was cold, wintertime, she was walking along darkened streets, towards the river, looking for Iain. She approached the apartment block where she was supposed to meet him, Gerry Reynolds' apartment. Gerry was Iain's boss, mustn't offend him, mustn't be late. She was going up in the lift, nearly there now . . .

Stop. Stop. Stop.

Alison opened her eyes. She swung her legs off the bed and went over to stand by the window, looking down at a street bright with sun and peace. Her pounding heart slowly steadied. She took half a dozen deep breaths. Iain would be home tomorrow and things were going to be all right.

She lay down again and closed her eyes, willing only good thoughts. And her brain was merciful; after a few moments she sensed the comforting presence of another person, not yet here but close: someone who'd promised to come but was late, almost at the door now . . .

In her dream the man she had been waiting for all these years came to lie beside her, but his face wasn't Iain's and Alison felt glad.

*

Verity Newland had always liked high places, although her concept of 'high' continued to evolve. She had spent her first year in Singapore in a sixth-floor office

15

overlooking Collyer Quay, which, according to notions prevailing in what was then just the tip of Malaya, amounted to a skyscraper. Now she perched in an eyrie just beneath the Pinnacle Restaurant on top of the Overseas Union Bank Centre, with a breath-stealing view of the Singapore River, Parliament House, the Supreme Court; a view that extended to the airport at distant Changi, enabling her to watch the planes climb silently into a royal blue night sky, until their winking lights merged with the stars.

It was after nine p.m., but most of the windows in the OUB Centre were still illuminated. Behind them the dealers wheeled and hunted and went without sleep, like so many restless sharks in an aquarium. Workloads became heavy with the onset of war, and that there would be war in the Middle East Verity Newland did not doubt. She welcomed the prospect. War was profit.

The woman raised her eyes from the screen for long enough to register another set of lights as they lifted off from Changi, and only when they had climbed out to the south-east did she resume work on the analysis she was preparing for Emil Barza. He would arrive from Baghdad sometime soon and she did not like to keep her clients waiting for bad news, any more than Barza would have delayed his master, whose name was Saddam Hussein. Certain resources needed to be moved, secretly and in great haste; this was her forte. The hours were long, commensurate with the rewards. In her vast white office, kept almost as cold as the Arctic it resembled, Verity Newland toiled through the tropical night, her tailored grey suit as pristine as when she had put it on at five o'clock that morning.

Her eyes grew tired. She reached into a drawer and took out a packet of wipes. Mechanically she polished the screen, as she did on the hour every hour, not trusting the cleaning-woman near her computer any more than a heart patient would have allowed some student nurse to change his pacemaker.

Professional enough to acknowledge the law of diminishing returns, she acknowledged it was time to quit for the night. She removed the diskette and went to lock it in the safe she kept behind her reproduction of Malevich's painting, *White Square on White*. One last thing to do . . . she seated herself again before the screen and brought up tomorrow's diary.

Steven Lim, her secretary, had added one entry since her last check. 'You asked me to keep an eye open for Iain Forward's release; according to my source, it's fixed for tomorrow.'

'No.'

This single word, the first human sound to have been uttered in the room for so long, lingered like an after-echo. She bit her lip, angered to find that her composure could be so easily shattered, and cleared the screen with a flick of her hand. She stood up purposefully, then realized she had no purpose in mind. She went to stand by the window, looking out through the triple glass at Singapore, seeing only another time, other places.

*They could not let him out. He had been sent to prison for life. Could not, could not . . .*

An old woman, with her hands held up to cover her mouth, was staring at her. Verity Newland stared back, appalled by her own reflection. She was old. Not yet forty-eight, and old.

'No,' the ghostly woman in the glass mouthed silently. 'No.'

\*

The shape on the bed stirred slightly and Jay Sampson's mind came back from where it had been wandering, lithe and free. 'Sal,' he murmured. 'Sal, you all right?'

His wife moaned and swallowed: a dry sound. Jay

17

poured a glass of water from the jug and held it to her lips, supporting her dead weight with his other hand, before easing her back horizontal and arranging the pillows in an attempt to make her comfortable.

She would never be comfortable again, and it could go on like this for a long time.

Jay sat limply in the bedside chair, hands clasped in his lap. His thoughts strayed, scared to linger anywhere long. Time had a habit of slipping away from him. Sometimes he would spend hours by the bed and they would pass like minutes. Other times, seconds ticked by real slow. He guessed most death-watches were like that, but this was his first and he had no comparisons.

After a while – he had no idea how long – he went to fetch a Crodo mineral water from the refrigerator and stand for a while on the back porch. The little town of Eccles (pronounced like the first two syllables of Ecclesiastical, to the surprise of nobody but the occasional lost English visitor) closed down around nine in the evening, and now it was midnight so all was quiet. There was a nip in the air. Tomorrow maybe they'd see frost, and the children would palette the streets with bright woollens for the first time this year. Jay smoked a Salem Light, enjoying silence broken only by the sporadic mew of a cat. Once he heard an owl hoot, far away; Breaky Hollow, maybe. Some place like that.

The phone rang.

He thought about letting it go. Wrong number, more than likely. Then again . . .

Jay went back in the house and picked up the phone. 'Hello,' he said.

'Jay? Neil.'

He was glad he'd answered, then. 'Neil, hello. How's things?'

'Not so bad. You?'

'Breathing.'

'Sal's asleep?'

'Yes.' Sal was Neil's sister. Neil was Jay's best friend. Neil's question made Jay realize he must have been whispering, but that was how he usually spoke these days.

'Any change?' Neil asked.

'Sinking real slow.' A pause. 'I'm sorry.'

'Yeah. Me too.'

The long-distance line seemed somehow comforting, a link to the outside world where people lived and laughed and got on with real lives. Maybe a whole minute went by.

Jay said, 'Well.'

'Yes.'

'What's new on the Beltway?'

More silence. 'Gonna have ourselves a little war,' Neil said at last.

'Yeah? When?'

'Third week January looks a good bet.'

Jay half laughed. 'You're kidding.'

'Oh, man . . . I wish.'

Now when they did not speak it seemed less of a link.

'Doctor says she could go any time,' Jay said. 'You maybe want to . . . '

'Yeah.'

'Like, say something to your boss, you know? About . . . '

'Make arrangements. Well . . . Jay, I have some news.'

'I'm listening.' But really his ear was attuned to the bedroom, where Sal might have moaned.

'Iain Forward gets out of jail tomorrow.'

For an instant Jay's mind continued on its well-worn track. Then he said, 'Say that again.'

'Forward's out. Tomorrow.'

A long silence.

'Jay, you still there?'

'I have to go now, Neil. Sal needs me.'

He put down the phone while Neil was still speaking, not because he meant to be rude but because he had no choice. Catastrophes were like that.

Jay hadn't touched alcohol for many years, not even when they diagnosed Sal's cancer, but there was a bottle of Jack Daniel's in the cupboard that he kept for rare visitors and now he went to pour himself a large glass of it, pouring with fingers that shook, making the bottle clink against the glass, and he swallowed it down like the Crodo of half an hour ago, but maybe whisky lost its potency once opened, as perfume did, because it left him feeling as cold and dead as before, but with this ugly addition: he was frightened.

*

The news of Iain Forward's imminent release did not frighten Terence Grindle. The intensity of his own anger did.

He sat with his head well back, holding a letter at arm's length. The darkness outside was reflected in his face. He did not curse, or pound the desk, or stride about; like most civil servants aligning with the runway for their final approach to retirement, he prided himself on a certain *gravitas*. To betray emotion was to betray the inner self. Grindle specialized in betrayals, but always other people's. For his own part he kept faith not only with his country and the government that employed him, but also with himself. He had integrity, from the Latin *integer*, whole. Wholly smooth, wholly seamless, wholly impervious to criticism, Terence Grindle possessed precisely the kind of integrity the British government required from a Regional Director of its counter-intelligence service, MI5.

He was also given to fits of nightmarish temper. Tonight, sitting at his desk in perfect stillness, man and object forming a composite statue hewn from one stone, he felt the demon's presence and shuddered.

He pursed his lips and brought the letter close to his eyes. He permitted himself a smile, to show the demon who was in charge here. He read.

'My dear Terence, My thanks for a most pleasant lunch. Your dedication to the catering committee has, if I may say so, generated more improvements to the club's table over a six-month period than any of your predecessors managed to achieve in a decade.'

New paragraph.

'I had intended to confine myself to an expression of thanks, but I fear I must intrude into the realm of the confessional. Upon my return I discovered, with distaste, that this department has been guilty of a lapse from grace. You will recall that some years ago your then ADD(A) submitted a Standing Watch Request on Iain Forward which, among other things, asked for advance warning of his release date. This was overlooked. I now have to tell you that Forward will receive his discharge, from HM Prison Leyhill, on 5 October.'

Third paragraph.

'I also have to submit my most profound apologies for this oversight, on behalf of myself and of the Department. In mitigation, I can only draw your attention to Alan's unfortunate domestic contretemps, of which we are both painfully aware, and trust that in the goodness of your heart you will on this occasion – an isolated one – see your way to taking the generous view.'

Conclusion.

'Again, my thanks for hosting such a stimulating interlude in an otherwise tedious week. Yours etc . . . '

An artful composition, Grindle reflected as he allowed the Home Office letter to fall from his fingers. The writer knew him to be a Roman Catholic, of course, 'confessional', 'grace', the concluding appeal to higher notions of mercy. And he was – had been – a friend.

Grindle would keep this letter. Sometime before his

21

retirement in 1993 he would use it to good effect, but cleanly, showing the mercy sought by dispatching the letter's author into some outer swamp, instead of visiting on him the destruction he deserved.

Grindle reached for the phone. When his wife answered he told her he would not be back until late, maybe not at all. That done, he stood up and moved across to the window. Rain slanted down on Gower Street, flecks falling through the lights to make a pavement of dark gold and black. There were still a few people about, hurrying along behind the largely psychological protection of their umbrellas. Normal life went on. As he watched, Grindle found himself wondering how the normal life of October 1990 would strike Iain Forward on his release after seventeen years in prison.

There had been a few changes.

As Grindle returned to his desk and sat down his eyes lighted on the old-fashioned stand-up calendar facing him. The date was framed in a red square that moved around the face of the monthly sheet on a plastic strip. Tonight the frame encased the figure '4'. Forward came out tomorrow.

# TWO

Each double seat was fastened to the floor of the train by eight bolts. Unlike the one-way kind you found in prison, these could be unscrewed. One double seat each side of the aisle – sixteen bolts. Iain Forward had counted the number of seats in a carriage before the journey even began, multiplied by the number of coaches, come up with a completely useless number of bolts, projected the number of InterCity trains on this route between Bristol and Paddington, multiplied again, endlessly, getting it all straight in his mind before they reached Bath. 'Inside', you counted everything because it passed the time; perhaps it helped that he'd been trained as an accountant. A refinement: bet on the outcome. How many birds would seek refuge from hawks within the razor wire? In an hour? In a morning . . .

A man pushed a trolley down the centre aisle, selling refreshments. Iain toyed with the idea of buying something, not because he was hungry or thirsty, but just for the hell of it. He decided not to, afraid of entering into transactions here, where everyone was free. In prison, a couple of spliffs would get you five pounds (not that he'd ever sold cannabis, or bought it, either) and you could flog a cheap tranny for a pail of hooch, but people did not buy cups of coffee inside. There were four wheels on the trolley, and the steward's waistcoat was fastened with six buttons. Iain had £39.64 in the trouser pocket of the suit his Clothing Board had allowed him to buy: three tens, a fiver, four one-pound coins, three 20p pieces, two tuppenny bits. His discharge grant. Perhaps he'd give it all to Alison; she'd know how to manage it. Perhaps he'd keep it.

As the steward with the trolley passed by he turned to stare at Iain, who gazed back expressionlessly. They'd never met, but the guy realized he was an ex-con, you could see it in his eyes. Iain knew exactly how he must seem: a shrunken man in his mid-fifties, although in fact he was only forty-six, with a sallow-complexioned square face that appeared waxy by the carriage's artificial light, the result of poor diet and too little fresh air; a man with a scrawny neck, cheeks that once had been flat and now were hollow; a mouth too long and with lips too thin to be attractive; bad teeth; spiky bushes sprouting out of his ears, pepper-and-salt, same colour as what was left of the hair on his head. A con. A lifer. Wasted.

He gave up counting things in the carriage and stared out of the window. The train was travelling fast. Frighteningly fast.

Alison.

She'd wanted to come to Leyhill, where he'd spent his last night in the system, but he'd said no. He wanted time by himself, to cast off the shadows. The final hours had passed slowly enough to make him almost regret his decision. Discharge Board: wing governor, chaplain, MO. A caution about the restrictions imposed by his release-licence, reading the Firearms Act prohibitions, a reminder that for the rest of his life he would have a probation officer who could send him back to jail just by filling in a form. A sleepless night. Then being signed off: they'd given him his scant possessions and his grant, they took a photograph of him, gave him a shower, and breakfast. A final check in Reception by a Principal Officer, who'd logged him off the computer for the last time. Somebody, somewhere, had pulled the chain, flushing Iain Forward out of the pan, into the sewer outside. Categories A, B, C, D, hostel scheme and out. The lifer's long, long drain.

No, he did not want Alison to meet him at the gate.

They were speeding through open countryside now — wide, soggy plains stretching to the horizon with only an occasional tree to check the monotony. He felt his bowels stir with apprehension and sat more fully upright, appalled by himself. She had stood by him for seventeen years, borne the burden of raising their child alone, never lost faith in his innocence, in *him*. How could he not want her?

He was dreading the sight of her, and what kind of bastard did that make him?

For many prisoners, you could say the majority, the worst punishment wasn't loss of liberty, it was the knowledge that your nearest and dearest on the other side of the wall *had* liberty. Freedom to fuck around with other men, namely. (It's wives, girlfriends we're talking here: *possessions*.) So if, just occasionally, a man's wife kept faith, it caused comment. Envy — yes, you could say that: the kind of envy that drops a turd on you from the 'fours', as the fourth-floor landings were known, when you're walking along the ones on your way to slop out; a turd falling three storeys becomes quite a little dum-dum by the time it hits you . . .

But mixed in with the envy was admiration: of the woman and of the one who'd inspired such love. A lifer, in particular, whose woman stood by him to the end, became a big name. 'Well respected', in the jargon. But if the lifer did dirt on her, people turned on him. Iain had seen it happen. While still on the Scrubs' D-wing, awaiting dispersal after conviction, he'd been in a cell next to Rocko. Rocko celebrated the end of his ten-year stretch by letting the girlfriend know on her last visit that he'd turned queer, and he was sorry. But not nearly as sorry as when a week later they got him in the showers . . . Heart, the MO said cause of death was heart, because there was this little difficulty over where the landing

25

officers had been at the time and nobody wanted to risk his pension for an animal like Rocko . . . As Iain's table-tennis opponent put it at that night's association, his time had come, he had to go.

'He had to go.'

He heard the words as clearly as if the speaker were sitting next to him, but he was not in Wormwood 'the Scabs' Scrubs any longer and he was not on the train. A woman's voice, light and low; subdued but firm. Iain felt tired. The dreary plain outside flickered, and gave way to something brighter; he realized his eyelids were drooping. Nineteen seventy-one . . . sunshine everywhere, sunshine and warmth. *He had to go, I'm afraid, it was inevitable* . . .

\*       \*       \*

Rain brought blessed coolness, giving Iain the first good night's sleep he'd had since landing in Singapore a week ago. It was taking him a long time to acclimatize to life ninety miles north of the equator. At eight o'clock a car had brought him down to Clifford Pier where his boss, Gerry Reynolds, was waiting by the bumboat, ready to take him on what he styled 'the grand tour'. They'd chugged out to Sudong, the island south-west of Jurong where Harchem was building its new plant, and Reynolds had held forth on tax breaks, rent-holidays, the cheap, disciplined labour, all the commercial glories of Singapore, while Iain mopped his forehead with a tissue.

At lunchtime he got back to the Prince Hotel on the corner of Orchard and Bideford Roads in a muck sweat. Amal, the old Malay-Indian behind the desk, was slower than ever with the room-key, but Iain was happy to stand beneath the overhead fan while the clerk short-sightedly hunted through his little wooden lockers. Iain accepted the key without looking at it. He took the lift up and walked along the corridor before noticing that he'd been given the wrong key. He swore, wondering if he'd been smart to take this job, if it really was the gateway to wealth and prestige he believed, if he could stand another day in this sweltering heat. He retraced his steps to the lobby. He tried to be polite to Amal, remembering all they had taught about life in the tropics – never lose your temper, it costs you face and you sweat buckets – but he was short with the old man and it showed on Amal's face. Armed with the right key, Iain went back upstairs.

The room was as he remembered leaving it, except in one respect. His suitcase, which had been lodged inside a closet, lay on the bed, open, empty. Iain distinctly recalled locking his traveller's cheques inside it. He took a step forward, then stopped. Visions of the police, questions, form-filling, unreeled themselves before his tired eyes. He could not go on. Harchem would have to find themselves another chartered accountant for the Far Eastern posting, because 1971 Singapore was impossible. He was going back to England.

He lifted the phone and asked for the manager. A woman answered, quite young by the sound of her. She quickly came up to his room, and with a start he saw she was European.

'I'm Alison Cowper,' she said, in a light, low voice. 'Let me see what I can do to put the pieces together again.'

He continued to gaze at her without speaking. She was one of us! After days of trying to make sense of Sing-lish – 'So late still don't come, lah!' – he knew a gratitude that was almost pathetic in its intensity.

'I've been robbed,' he said, gathering himself at last. 'Your clerk downstairs gave me the wrong key . . .'

'We do have a safe-deposit that we advise clients to use . . . however, spilt milk needs cleaning, not crying, I know.'

She was a bit younger than he; twenty-one, maybe.

And oh God, she was beautiful! After all those yellow, brown, near-black skins, that raven hair, here was light and grace and *beauty*. Beneath her cool cotton dress he could see that her figure was his idea of perfect: slim and athletic, a tennis-player's figure with a tennis-player's tanned complexion complementing a sprinkling of freckles. Honey-blonde hair, cut short for the heat. Small, refined features, the nose rounded at the tip, cheeks that dimpled when she smiled, and eyes that had been made simply to look into his . . .

'Are you all right, Mr Forward?'

He felt a little giddy. He wasn't drinking enough to cope in this tropical heat. As if divining the problem she went to the bathroom and fetched him a glass of water. Then she picked up the telephone and got busy.

She was, he discovered, marvellously effective. She arranged for the police to interview him in the hotel's conference suite, and when they were through he found an American Express representative waiting outside with replacement cheques. Afterwards he could not remember the bureaucratic details. What he did remember was the rijsttafel lunch she laid on, courtesy of the hotel: all those deliciously spiced Indonesian dishes served around a mountain of rice and washed down with glacially cold beer.

They talked about themselves. Her father, a lawyer, had settled in Singapore not long after the War; this was the only home she had known. She lived with two other expat girls in a small, traditional Chinese house on Tosca Road: it had green shutters that fell off unless you knew the knack of closing them, a stone bathroom with no hot water, and a number five iron kept on the porch to thwack cobras in the nuts. Yes, there were cobras, about one a year; also rats and flying squirrels and a gutter that leaked into the roof space when it rained. A nice neighbourhood: on the left, Dr Francis P. Ang, a secondary school headmaster who lived alone and liked to be called F.P. (no one knew what the P stood for); to the right, the Chans, nine of them if you included the grandmother who never emerged from her room and was reputedly two sticks short of a satay dinner. The Chans were *Teochew* Chinese, wont to conduct machine-gun arguments late at night in the belief that this passed for family conversation. Mr Chan owned a gold shop on North Bridge Road and couldn't stop talking about it, with a loquacity and an enthusiasm that did not extend to giving away samples. F.P. and the Chan males had developed a keen interest in gardening, Alison said, since she and her pals had come to 'mess' in the neutral territory between them, but only when the members of the mess were sunbathing in the back garden, beneath an angsana tree that was getting too big for its roots. Then F.P. and the Chans, suspicious neighbours for many years, found much to discuss over their fences, batting the Sing-lish (they had no other common language) small-talk to and fro across the prone, swimsuited female flesh that both divided and united them.

Iain could see everything. She painted it for him with her hands, eyebrows, lips, laughter. There was a Singapore beyond the heat and dust; he wanted to be part of it.

'How come you're doing this job?' he asked her as they left the restaurant. 'I'd have thought someone so efficient could have her pick of hotel work here.'

'Thank you, kind sir. Yes, this hotel is middle of the range, I know, but then there's the politics. I'm European-white, you see. Immigration's getting tighter all the time; local staff for local jobs.'

'But you've obviously been well trained.'

'I served my sentence in Switzerland.' She laughed. 'But that only counts for so much. You don't want to hear about Singaporean in-fighting, you're not ready for that yet. Can you see yourself settling here?'

It was on the tip of Iain's tongue to say no. Then he thought of the Chinese house with its wonky shutters and the words stayed unspoken.

When he went to collect his key, Amal wasn't behind the desk. He'd been replaced by a Chinese girl. Iain glanced at Alison with a smile and said, 'Siesta? Or is Amal lying low?'

She rested against the desk and returned his smile, her gaze direct and clear. 'He had to go,' she said. 'I'm afraid it was inevitable. You see, you weren't the first . . .'

\* \* \*

The train braked suddenly, throwing Iain forward in his seat, and he opened his eyes to see Acton sliding past the window. Nearly there.

He wanted to go to the toilet; too late for that now. He'd spent weekends at home, that was part of the pre-release softening up, but when he got off this train he'd be as free as any lifer ever could be and he'd have to start making something permanent. She'd stood by him through seventeen years of hell and he owed her. Swapping one prison for another. All life was a prison, then.

He closed his eyes again and mentally recited the Lord's Prayer. Funny thing about prison; there were no agnostics there. You were pro or anti, but you couldn't be a don't know. Iain had tried both points of view and belief was marginally easier. He prayed because he wanted somebody to hear; therefore somebody did.

When the train stopped Iain was last to get up. He collected his brown paper parcel from the rack and made for the door. A stream of people was flowing along the platform towards the barrier. He took a deep breath and joined them.

He knew his wife and daughter would be waiting for him at the barrier. He'd wanted to go all the way home alone, Alison had pleaded to come to Leyhill; this was their compromise. All he could see ahead was a blur of backs moving at different paces. Then a couple of brief-case-toting businessmen moved aside and he caught sight of Alison.

Before Iain could register emotion – fear, delight? – he saw something else.

There were about half a dozen people clustered behind his wife: two had cameras slung around their necks, one of the others had recognized him and was taking a note-pad from his pocket. Iain stopped dead. For a moment he longed to have high walls around him again, remembering his fear when he'd first gone into a hostel and felt it was safer inside prison than out. Then his face hardened. So. They wanted a convicted killer, did they? Right.

He marched on, looking like a man who'd tasted vinegar and couldn't forget. His stare drilled into the lens of the front camera, now less than twenty yards away. A reporter edged nearer to Alison, said something to her. The gap was closing now. Iain reached out to grab his wife. For the first time he noticed Kate standing beside her, hand in hand with someone he didn't know but already resented . . . words surged to his lips, 'Fuck off, cunts,' that's what he would say; and if that didn't work, he'd pitch into them with his hands, knowing those lay-abouts hadn't a chance against a man who'd learned all he knew about fist-fighting 'inside'.

But as he seized Alison's arm, ignoring the words that came pouring out of her, it fell apart. He couldn't say the things he yearned to say, couldn't perpetrate the violence that had become second nature to him. Not because of her, but because a stroke of the pen was all that was needed to send him back; he had no rights except to

31

breathe. And life would always be like this. So get used to it, repress, endure.

He raised the parcel to shield his face from the cameras and urged Alison on. Until then she'd been wooden as a puppet, but suddenly she lashed out with her foot, catching a reporter on the shin. Kate shouted, standing in for her father with the obscenities he could not afford to utter. He moved relentlessly, ignoring the hubbub, the passengers stopping to stare. Flash-guns blinded him with their diamond sparkles. Then a voice cried out from the mêlée, a voice he thought he recognized.

'Iain! Over here. It's Ted Smurfitt.'

His stride did not falter, but he remembered the journalist who'd wanted to write the series of articles about life inside, who'd promised money and been rejected because he'd come along at the wrong time in a circular, endless loop of time. Smurfitt: a kind, well-meaning man, interested in penal reform, pleased to discover an intelligent, educated lifer he could relate to. Well *fuck you, Smurfitt. Cunt!*

Looming up ahead, a grimy Bedford van. Alison was urging him to get in the front seat but he threw off her arm and piled into the back, slamming the door behind him so that Kate had to open it again before she could join him. Iain sat hunched with his back against the van's wall, covering his eyes with both hands. Then they were moving. He heard a crunchy change of gears and felt the van gather speed.

He lowered his hands. Slowly, methodically, covering all the angles, he swore. When at last he stopped, there was a silence. In that silence he became aware of two things: Kate's wide eyes studying him with unblinking intensity from across the van, and Alison quietly crying.

'Sorry,' he said.

Alison hastily wiped her eyes, swivelled in her seat and reached out for his hand. But he threw himself against the back of the seat and kissed her clumsily, missing the mouth she turned to him at the last second, his lips ending up against her ear. Then Kate scrambled across the thin rug that covered the metal floor, putting her arms around him, crying a little but not so much that she couldn't say, 'Oh, Dad, *Dad*, welcome home, I'm so happy, so happy . . .'

Everyone felt good. Things would be all right. Marvellous. But then Darren said, 'Hi there, Iain, my name's Darren,' and Iain said, 'Who *is* this?'

Inside, you never acknowledged anyone until a third party had given him credentials.

'He's my boyfriend,' Kate said.

Iain surveyed as much as was visible of Darren. He looked like a cocky stoppo, doing his first remand. You could always tell a getaway driver by the way he cornered, that's what they said inside; on which basis Darren was a stoppo but an ignorant one. Needed sorting.

The silence continued. Iain knew, in a confused way, that the two women expected him to express gratitude to Young Hopeful in the driver's seat. Bit early for that. We'll see.

'Good journey?' Alison asked.

'Yes.' Her voice told him all about the effort she was making. He should respond. 'Quick. Long time since I've . . .'

Yes, that's right, make it worse. *Dickhead!*

'Those new trains are great,' he said. Then he remembered they were new only to him. He went quiet for a long time after that.

Things were slipping away from him. First the train journey, now the last mile home: final sector of a journey he wanted never to end. Clapham. A run-down house between the commons, on a hill; three up, two down. God knows he believed her when she said that was all she could afford on a hotel night manager's salary, and he knew full well she'd never get a better job.

Murderers' wives received dead rats through the post, were spat on in the street, ostracized. Alison had been lucky to avoid the worst horrors, but his name followed her around whenever she went looking for work. Twelve hours a night, six days a week, in an Earl's Court hotel owned by Arabs, that was her lot. Like his, a life sentence, one from which she'd never be released. Even he got out on licence and he was the guilty one. Or so the jury said.

Darren pulled up outside the house. Iain scuttled in, anxious for the illusory security of being behind a locked door again. He perceived no irony in this. He knew the layout from weekend visits and went straight to the kitchen, where he poured himself a glass of milk.

'Don't fill yourself up,' Alison said brightly. 'Lunch will be soon.'

Iain looked at Kate. 'Shouldn't you be at school?'

'I got the day off, to bring you home. And it's sixth form college.'

He knew that. Art. Christ, as if art mattered a rat's fuck . . .

'What's that?'

Alison turned around from the gas stove to see he was pointing at the bottle of wine Darren had stolen the day before.

'It's to celebrate.'

Iain peered at the posh-looking label. His eyebrows shot up. 'Can you afford it?'

He sensed the aggro his question caused. He was alive to nuance; in prison you only survived by knowing which corners not to turn when.

'Just this once,' Alison answered.

Iain grunted. The cost of trying to clear his name had ruined them. He wanted to pick at this scab that would never quite heal. He needed to hear, in some shape or form, the words: 'It's all your fault, Iain,' because then he could go in with fists flailing. But she knew him better than to rise to it.

He'd expected his home-coming to be on a par with previous weekend visits, but it wasn't. The atmosphere was different. Worse.

'Don't want to hold you up,' he said to Darren. 'Thanks for the lift.'

'Dad!'

Kate was holding on to Darren's arm, but the boy merely smiled and disengaged himself before saying to Iain, 'It's all right.' He pecked Kate on the cheek. 'See you.'

She went out to the hallway with him; Iain heard her arguing, Darren's laughter ... then the front door slammed and footsteps crashed up the stairs.

'Is she always like that?'

'No.'

'I don't remember that Darren creep being here at my weekends.'

'He's new.'

'He's pig shit.'

Alison left off scrubbing the potatoes. She uncorked the wine and fetched a couple of tumblers and sat down at the table opposite Iain. She said, 'I know it's hard. I do know that, darling. But here, right here, is where we start to go up again.' She lifted her glass. 'I love you, I always have, I always will.' The last word was almost lost in her tears, but she fought on. 'Now I want you to drink to *us. Please.*'

Iain's flinty eyes contained only assessment. When, after half a minute, he still hadn't replied, she snatched her handbag and rummaged for a pack of cigarettes.

He said, 'You never used to be on the burn.'

Alison's hands were shaking as she lit the cigarette. She folded her left arm across her chest and used the hand to support her right elbow; that way, she could hold the cigarette in front of her face as a partial shield from his gaze.

'I started years ago. Supermarket own brand, cheapest, five a day. I didn't want you to worry.'

'What else haven't you told me because you didn't want me to worry?'

Silence.

'Iain, I —'

'Men. Were there men?'

She shook her head. 'Not one. You?'

'Me what?'

'Did you have men, in prison? They say you do, you know, they say prisoners turn gay.' She picked up her glass, spilling wine down her front. She gazed down at the stain. Then with sudden brutality she smashed the glass down on the table, breaking it. As the shards scattered across the table she screamed, 'You never made love to me once, on your weekends, not once. Are you gay, then?'

His mouth fell open. 'You . . .'

'Bitch,' he'd meant to say, but suddenly the horror of what they were doing overwhelmed him and he burst into tears, burying his head in his hands amid the broken glass, sobbing his heart out. He heard the scrape of her chair as she came around to comfort him and he flung her off, only to collapse into her arms next moment. He hugged her tight, filling his nose with the scent of her body: warm, aromatic, clean. He took breath after breath, wanting to gorge himself on her, the sensuousness of her woman's body.

'I'm sorry,' he heard her say; and he burst out, 'No! It's me that should say sorry, not you.'

'I understand. It's all right, my love, I understand, I do, I do . . .'

'I thought I could take it. After the weekends here, I

36

thought it would be just another weekend, only longer. And it's not. It's not.'

They held each other like that for a long time, until at last his sobs were stilled. She disengaged, ever so gently, and pushed his glass across the table. He raised it. 'To us,' he said in a choky voice. 'To all of us. We three.'

Alison fetched another glass from the dresser and filled it. 'We three,' she said.

The first wine he'd tasted in seventeen years . . . he marvelled at the colour, the aroma rising from the glass as he savoured the first, cautious sip. Inside, he'd tried hooch and it had made him ill; when they'd started to let him out for a few days at a time he'd drunk the odd half pint of beer, which was all he could afford. But he'd never been a beer-drinker. Wine took him back into the past, and a time when life had meaning.

That one sip was all it needed to make him feel drugged. His head buzzed with incoherent lightness. His own hand slid over the table to pick up Alison's pack of cigarettes. Then he remembered something: he said, 'May I?'

'Help yourself.'

He lit up and inhaled. Within seconds he wasn't feeling so good: not used to mixing wine and tobacco. A ripple of nausea floated into his stomach. He was going to be sick. He blundered towards the door, and that was where the panic attack hit him. The door was open and he could not pass through it. He stood there, awaiting permission to proceed – 'One on, sir,' 'One off, sir,' – but nobody said anything, the landing officer wasn't there, stay still, *you there! stay still!* or they'll knock you back three months, Governor's report, Good Order and Discipline, Forward, eight double four five six nine . . .

Iain vomited on to the floor.

Alison helped him back to his seat. She mopped up the mess, gave him water. She squeezed his hand and said,

'Never mind, don't push yourself, it'll be all right.' And when his head trembled in despair she said, 'It *will*.'

'I want to lie down,' he told her.

She helped him upstairs. Their room was at the front, bare of all but essentials: a double bed, a veneered wardrobe and dressing table, a chipped wash-basin. He took off his top clothes and lay down, shielding his eyes from the light with a forearm. After a while his breathing deepened and Alison drew the curtains shut before tiptoeing from the room. He waited until the sound of her footsteps on the stairs had died away. He counted up to fifty. Then, with the silence taught by years of incarceration, he swung himself off the bed and knelt down beside it.

All the papers relating to his trial for murder were in a cardboard box that had once contained bottles of cider. He'd made Alison swear not to throw them away, and on each of his weekend releases had checked the box to see that it was still intact.

He lifted the box on to the bed and removed the bundles. Together they stood some fifteen inches high. The flyleaf, 'Queen against Iain Forward', was thick with dust. He flicked it away almost lovingly, like someone unearthing a treasure long since buried.

There'd been a time when he'd known the case papers almost by heart. At first all his attention had been focused on the appeal; every day was spent poring over the evidence, trying to find the weak link that would show how he'd been framed, fitted up for the murder of a man called Reynolds, his old boss at Harchem. But the papers were mum.

Eighteen months later, when his appeal had been turned down, the psychiatrist had told him he had a choice: to accept his fate, acclimatize himself to prison life, and work his way through to the end of his sentence day by tortured day; or to protest his innocence, refusing to conform. In which latter case 'they' – governors, screws, fellow inmates — would make his life hell. 'Ours is a conservative society,' the shrink said. 'We do not like those who stand out from the crowd.'

Iain realized then that the legal system he'd been brought up to believe in had betrayed him. He'd resolved to have the worst of both worlds. He lived a good if useless life in prison. He made no enemies, broke no rules, shirked no work. Unusually for a convict, he did not complain. But every day he made a point of telling somebody that he was innocent and that he'd prove it.

Iain sat down on the bed and placed both hands on top of the trial bundles. He felt like a man conferring a blessing, who by his own act is himself blessed. He felt reverence, in this tatty room. Reverence and, for the first time since leaving Leyhill, a kind of inexplicable joy; for now his life's work could begin.

He had already begun his mission, in a small way. He'd convinced one governor that his conviction had been a miscarriage of justice. This man, the head of Iain's Category D prison, had not been explicit in his acceptance of the story, but he'd said, 'Well, Forward, I don't know: either you're a hell of a liar, keeping it up for twelve years, or you're innocent.' And this, the nearest he'd come to a vindication, proved to be Iain's glimpse of the Grail. If he could persuade one man, he could persuade society. It was then that he'd started praying again.

He took a ballpoint pen from his jacket-pocket and turned over the flyleaf. At the top of the page he wrote '1. Anthony Powis.' Then, giving each entry a new line, '2. Terence Grindle. 3. Verity Newland.'

He arranged himself more comfortably on the thread-bare rug, using the bed as a table. There were three people, at least three, he had to find. How?

'What are you doing?'

Kate had sidled into the room without making a sound.

Before he'd even identified the voice as Kate's he'd scrunched the paper into a ball and let the pen fall inside his shirtsleeve, though the rest of his body didn't move. 'What are you doing, Forward?' 'Nothing, sir.' 'Well don't hang about here.'

Then he remembered: this was freedom.

He put on a smile for his daughter's benefit. His daughter, he must remember that. How nice to meet you, stranger. We must have a conversation sometime, get to know each other. But not now.

'Thinking about my trial,' he said. 'You weren't even born then.'

'I'm sorry about . . . you know.'

She'd edged across to the window in a series of loopy, dropsical movements and now was staring out through the gap in the curtains.

'We weren't at our best, were we? I'm sorry, too.'

She turned into the room. 'Are we going to be friends?'

'Yes,' he answered cautiously.

'I've never had a dad before.' She grinned at him, showing yellow teeth, one of them crooked. 'You're kind of new.'

On his weekend releases they'd circled around each other like animals discovering a new species, and he'd sensed Alison must have instructed Kate how to behave.

She came to sit down on the bed, shoulders hunched, hands folded in her lap. 'You didn't do it, did you?' she said. 'It was a fit-up.'

She knew the jargon, too. What a wonderful thing education was.

'That's right.'

'Tell me about it.'

'Not now.'

'Please.'

If she had been a fly he'd have swatted her. She did in fact look like a nasty black insect that had crept out of its

40

fetid lair; did Darren insist she wore black or was that a misguided whim of her own? Her slutty appearance made it hard to accept her as a creature sharing common flesh and blood. But then, what do you expect of a killer's daughter? – that's what the neighbours would ask.

'Why do you say it was a fit-up?' he asked.

'Alison says so.'

Alison. Not 'Mother'. But he'd let that go on his first weekend pass; a situation beyond retrieving.

'You always do everything she says?'

Kate laughed. 'Leave it out.'

He spent his rage in silence: a thwarted ejaculation left to drain away through every nerve in the body. 'All right,' he said at last. 'I'll tell you about it.' As far as he could read her face, she wanted to hear his version but was afraid of not believing it. 'You're going to hear this a lot,' he went on. 'Over and over again, until you know every last detail. Because I'm going to clear my name and I need help, see?'

She nodded, but the fear remained.

'The jury found me guilty of murdering a guy called Gerry Reynolds. I was supposed to have stabbed him three times. Bit of legal education here, Kate: stab once and it's manslaughter, stab twice and it's definitely murder. Now you won't hear a brief say that, but what do they know, eh?' He laughed, in the way that substitutes for 'Fuck *that*!'

'Reynolds had been my regional boss while I was working for Harchem Pharmaceuticals. Finance Director Far East, that was me.'

'In Singapore. Where you and Mum met.'

He hurried on, not wanting to be distracted by trivia. 'Reynolds was on a visit to London. We'd gone over, Alison and me, because he'd called me, said he had something hush-hush, couldn't talk on the phone. Big problem, he said. I went to his flat one evening. No sign of

41

Reynolds, so I pushed off.' He paused. 'We were going to the theatre that night, your mother and I.'

'Oh.'

'We met up at Covent Garden, she'd been shopping.' He looked down at his hands. 'Next day, we found out Gerry had been murdered. We had to answer lots of questions, but they didn't seem interested in me at all. They let us go back to Singapore. A week later, the police came to our flat and arrested me. Handcuffs. Out through the lobby, everyone watching.'

'God.'

'Yeah. Anyway, they'd found Reynolds' appointments diary, my name there all neat and tidy in block capitals: his last appointment. And by then they had a story, too: Reynolds had been selling industrial secrets to overseas buyers. I was in it, got fussed about the size of my cut, came over to haggle, ended up killing him.'

'What kind of secrets?'

'You tell me. Of course, Harchem had secrets, any big chemical combo does. We had a paint that was fantastic for protecting the bottoms of ships, I remember that one. Pesticides: cockroach cocktails, we used to call them. Snake repellent. Not the sort of thing you'd stick a knife in someone for, eh? – "Ooh, I'd do anything, anything at all, to get my hands on your cobra crap; let's kill Reynolds, why don't we?"'

Kate giggled.

'Funny, isn't it.' Iain smacked his hand down on the pile of papers. 'Well it gets a damn sight funnier, I can tell you.'

'I wasn't laughing at you, Dad.'

'I know, yeah. There was a real murderer; Gerry didn't fall on the knife three times. There was a killer and he had to be protected. So somebody made sure there was a scapegoat. Me.'

He could see that something troubled her. He waited.

'Why couldn't it have been just a thief who panicked? I mean, why does it have to be so, y'know . . . organized?'

'Ask the Home Office. They put their oar in at my trial. No details of the secrets that Reynolds was supposed to have been selling were to be put before the jury. "Not in the national interest", those were the words. "Details touching on the security of the state." End. Of. Quote.'

'And the judge bought it?' she scoffed.

'Like somebody begging to be sold a duff motor.'

'So who do you think really did it?'

He noticed something that interested him. Her diction was improving, as she forgot to coarsen it for his benefit. She'd been trying to make the poor old lag feel at home, now, had she?

'Who do you suspect?' Kate said. At the same moment, fingernails scratched the bedroom door, irritating Iain, because he knew it could only be Alison, unsure whether she should knock or just barge straight in, and although he didn't know which was best, she ought to have done. After seventeen years of having decisions made for him, he liked it.

'Who do I suspect?' he grated. 'Everyone.'

He raised his gaze to Alison's face. She looked tired and drawn; her complexion was pale but there were red blotches in her cheeks. For the first time he noticed that her left cheek sprouted a tiny mole with a hair growing out of it. Was that recent? Had it always been there?

'Lunch is ready,' she said. 'How are you feeling?'

'Better. Thanks.'

Her eyes lighted on the papers. 'Oh,' she said.

The awkward silence was broken by Kate saying, 'I asked Dad to tell me about everything.'

'Couldn't it have waited? No, forget I said that – come on everybody, let's eat.'

Iain tapped the pile of papers on the bed. 'You should

read these,' he said, eyeing Kate. 'Then we'll talk again.'

As he reached the head of the stairs he hesitated, struck by an unusual smell: real food. Meat and fresh vegetables that hadn't been left to stand and chill. He breathed in deeply. It took time to adjust to a new atmosphere. The air he'd breathed for seventeen years had been tainted with sweat, sperm and shit. Wholesome scents brought their own sweet delights.

He followed the two women downstairs. As he passed the half open door to the small front room, a series of sounds brought him up short. Two clicks, a beep, a distorted voice.

'What's that?' he asked.

'Oh, just the answering machine,' Alison replied. 'Ignore it.'

'You have an answering machine?'

'For the dressmaking.'

He went into the kitchen and sat down. 'Why do we need an answering machine?' he said.

She began to dish up, while Kate poured the wine. 'I do a lot of dressmaking now,' she said. 'It helps pay the mortgage. But most of my customers are at work during the day, so they want to be able to leave a message in the evenings, when I'm at work.'

He knew how much she hated these conversations about money, but he could not leave it alone. 'It must have been expensive.'

'A fiver.' She put a plate in front of him. It smelled so wonderful that he felt giddy. 'Police auction.'

'What?'

'They have an auction, at Brixton, each month.' She finished serving up and took her place opposite him. 'They sell things off to pay fines and so on. That's where I got the fridge, when the old one went kaput.'

She stared him down until his gaze drooped and he began eating.

44

'I'm glad it's Friday,' Alison said. 'We've got the weekend.'

'Mm.'

'Steak all right?'

'Great.'

'You've got an appointment with your probation officer on Monday, ten o'clock.'

'I know.'

'She's nice, I like her.'

'Good.'

'Jenny Clinton. She's found you a job.'

Iain made a face, said nothing. He realized he was making a lot more noise than the other two, and slowed down.

'What kind of job?' he asked.

'With a talking newspaper. They make tapes for blind people.'

He chewed a piece of steak for a long time, extracting every last scrap of flavour from it. Then he said, 'Where?'

'Near Clapham Junction. You can walk there easily. Eight thirty to five, Monday to Friday. They're a charity, so they can't pay much. It works out at just under a hundred pounds a week.'

'After tax?'

'Before.'

Seventeen years of nothing and then back into the swim at a few quid more than his first salary. How time did fly when you were enjoying yourself.

'What sort of a job is it?'

'General clerical.'

'Making the tea, in other words. They know about me, of course?'

'Yes. And they are apprehensive, Iain. Look, I'm sorry, but –'

'Oh, leave him alone, why don't you?' Kate's voice was gritty. 'He knows the score.'

45

Silence – the kind that heals.

'Alison.'

She looked at her husband, sitting hunched at the table, his eyes cast down, and she tensed. 'Yes?'

'That was a fabulous meal. Thanks.'

'I'm glad you enjoyed it.'

'And I'm glad to be home.'

She stood up and busied herself stacking dishes in the sink, not trusting herself to speak.

'What's for pud?' said Kate.

'Ice cream and tinned peaches.'

'Wonderful,' Iain murmured. 'You must have read my mind.' Throughout the first course he'd been taking cautious sips of wine. Now he emptied his glass and pushed it across to Kate with a smile. 'You be mother?'

She poured. 'Mum and I thought you might like a walk on the common this afternoon,' she said. 'While it's sunny.'

A twisting tornado of fear whipped out of nowhere. 'Go out?' he stuttered.

'Needn't go far. Just a breath of fresh air.'

'No,' he said. 'Not today.' He stood up, pushing his chair against the radiator with a clang. 'Going to lie down now. Tired.'

He stumped upstairs, ice cream and wine forgotten, seeking the haven of their bedroom, and lay down on the bed. When the trial papers collapsed against him he thrust them aside, not caring that they landed on the floor in a disordered heap. He closed his eyes and tried to sleep, but he was tinglingly wakeful. Ten minutes later the front door slammed; he heard light footsteps, the creak of the rusty gate, and knew he was alone in the house with his wife.

She came to him almost immediately, not knocking this time. He opened his eyes, managed a smile.

'Mind if I lie down for a bit?' she asked.

46

He patted the bed. She slipped off her shoes and smoothed her hair in front of the mirror before coming to join him. Like Iain, she lay there staring at the ceiling, hands folded across her breasts, a stone virgin on her tomb. Her smell drove him crazy, but not nice-crazy. He could distinguish deodorant, talc, perfume, shampoo and sweat; they didn't jell. He glanced obliquely at her arm. It was mottled with tiny goose-flesh: red pinpricks. She was wearing out and all she had to show for it was a wayward teenager, and an ex-con for a mate.

Iain haltingly reached for her hand. She let it lie in his for a moment before trying a cautious squeeze.

'Alison,' he said.

'Yes.'

He continued to seek inspiration from the ceiling. Some plaster near the central light-fitting was cracked. He could see the clumsy brush strokes around the rose, a splodge of paint on the plastic.

'I'm sorry I'm not back in the swim yet. It's going to take time.'

'I know.'

'But what I . . .' He tried again. 'I'm trying to say that I'm grateful to you for sticking by me. Thanks for loving me that much.'

She squeezed his hand again, more strongly this time.

'But I can't repay you,' he added.

'Please don't try.' Now it was her turn to hunt for words. 'If I stuck by you and came to those dreadful places week after week, it was because I love you, just you, no one else. ''For better, for worse,'' that's what we agreed, isn't it? Well, the worse is over now. You're only about halfway through your life and it's going to get better, and go on getting better, and . . . '

She could not finish. Great sobs spilled out of her, she turned into his body and wept against his chest until she could weep no more. Then it was his turn. A cry of grief

47

and remorse and anger burst out of him, flowing in uncontrollable spasms that left him limp. He, too, turned on the bed, until he could put his arms around her and hold her close. He looked into her tired eyes, saw the love there, and for the first time kissed his wife properly.

'Kate's gone out?' he asked; and when she nodded he slowly began to unbutton her blouse. She looked down at what his hands were doing and blushed, as if she could not conceive of such a wonder. She undid the top button of his shirt. It took time, they were out of practice. And they were shy: this business of revealing your body, the whole of it, to a stranger, could never be easy. At last they managed it. There they lay: two skinny, worn-out people on the verge of middle age, with white skin that no longer glowed, not much muscle, thinning hair, early wrinkles.

Slowly, Alison reached out a trembling hand to touch him between the legs. She stroked him, ever so gently, as if afraid of hurting him. She firmed her touch, loosened it again. She went on like this for five, ten minutes, longer. She stopped.

With a slowness that matched hers, like her, not wanting to give hurt, he rolled over on to his back and lay as limp as the funny, useless thing between his legs.

# THREE

Three days after Iain Forward's release, Sal Sampson died. The certificate spoke of various carcinomas but omitted the real cause of death, which was cancer of the will.

'The first,' Jay murmured, kicking aside a pile of fallen leaves.

'Of many.'

'Are there leaves in Kuwait?'

At some point in the walk from Sal's grave to the parking lot, Neil Robarts had slipped his arm through Jay's. Now they halted. Neil removed his arm and placed both hands in his pockets, hunching his shoulders against a wind that, despite the day's bright sunshine, felt raw.

'Will it happen?' Jay asked; and Neil nodded.

'It'll happen,' he said. 'The drums sound. Voters have cars, autos need oil, Kuwait has it; there will be a war that isn't ours and young men will die.'

He thrust his arm back through Jay's and walked on, easing him away from where they'd just buried Sal: the first 'leaf' of many that would fall this winter. Every so often he'd use his free hand to rub the socket of his right eye, the one the Viet Cong had shot away in 1970: another poor year for leaves. The glass orb that replaced it sometimes gave trouble in the cold.

'What are you going to do?' Neil asked Jay as they reached the car.

'Nothing, for a while.'

'Don't waste too much grief. Listen: she was my sister, I loved her, but she wanted to die and she did. Okay?'

'Thanks for trying.'

'She had a drink problem, personality problems . . .'

'Which she didn't always have.' Jay looked at the ground. 'Not at first.'

He'd married Sal, an old schoolfriend, on the rebound from the great love of his life. He'd stayed with her, sunk in near despair, for the mutual support that two damaged animals can sometimes give each other. As the basis for a relationship, it lacked a certain something.

'You coming back to the house?' he asked.

'I'd better hit the road.'

Nearby, someone sounded a horn, but softly, almost apologetically, and they turned. A man and his wife waved from their Oldsmobile as they drove away. Jay waved back. Good of the neighbours to come. There'd been twenty or so mourners around the grave and Mr Richards, the Presbyterian minister, had said some nice things.

'Well,' Jay said. 'Okay.'

He got into the driver's seat of the Pontiac Le Mans and set a course for Wyoming County Highway, route 19, heading north. The drive to Buffalo took over an hour, but for most of the way they sat in silence. The two men had been friends since the fifties. In those days, emotion was something you shared – flaunted, even. Now was different, because every time you thought of something meaningful to say you discarded it unspoken, believing it not to be worth much.

'Those who refuse to learn from the mistakes of history are condemned to repeat them. Or something . . .' Neil grunted. 'You'd think one Vietnam would be enough.'

A couple of miles disappeared beneath the Pontiac's tyres. Jay said, 'You sound pretty convinced about this war.'

'Where I drink, they're convinced. CIA, FBI, NDA,

50

Army Intelligence, Pentagon, White House . . . and they are *loving* it! Hey, man, party time again! Let's see if those ninety-thousand-buck-a-piece screwdrivers some contractor sold that dumb major really *work*!'

'What's Saddam Hussein got to throw against us?'

'You should know. You helped us sell him most of it.'

'That was a long time ago,' Jay said quietly. 'What's he got?'

'Scud-Bs. No air force worth shit, no navy; half a million raw recruits in green overalls. Oh yeah, and enough chemical shit to wipe out the corn belt. And maybe, just maybe, the odd nuke or two.'

'Who's arming him?'

Neil laughed. '*You* ask *me*?'

Jay barely smiled. He'd devoted part of his life to the service of the United States government, usually delivering to the back door the instruments of death that certain regimes could never acquire via the front. He'd been a good employee, a true company man, unlike Neil, who'd been invalided into Army Intelligence when he lost his eye and thereafter drifted from murky to murkier agency, making his living as an analyst, until someone in the FBI had taken pity on him and steered him into a port where he could lie out his days.

'You should be careful,' he said, causing Neil to look at him sharply.

'What?'

'I mean . . .' But Jay hesitated, realizing he'd been drawn into saying too much. 'I mean, war's a testing time. No passengers. Be a team-player.'

Neil snorted. 'Me, a team-player? Oh, come on, Jay! I'm anti-war, anti-government, and passionately concerned about the fate of my fellow men. What kind of US team do you suggest I hit for?'

They scarcely spoke again until they got to Buffalo

airport. Neil came over from the check-in counter to join Jay by the news-stand. 'Holy shit,' he muttered. 'Our guys were supposed to be dug in by today.'

'It's delayed.' Jay held his newspaper so that both of them could read the front-page lead article.

'I guess nobody really believed all our troops would make it into Saudi on time,' Neil said at last. 'Thank God for England – at least *she's* there.'

'Will she fight?'

'Like you wouldn't believe.'

Jay, listening with half an ear, continued to scan the news-stand. He hadn't read a paper for about a fortnight; the headlines made only partial sense to him. 'Friends again?' he said. 'England and the US, I mean?'

'They know everything there is to know about Arabia. We don't know shit. How does this grab you: a post-war Middle East peace conference. Soviet Union crippled by *perestroika*, right? Iraq a heap of smoking rubble, right? Room full of English public schoolboys who could pass for an Arab at high noon, telling Stormin' Norman where to stick his little flags.'

'And where's Israel?'

'South of Lebanon. I want a beer.'

Jay bought *Time*, the *Christian Science Monitor* and a day-old *Washington Post*. He knew he was into the business of delay, now – spinning things out until he could no longer hold Neil, and would be truly alone.

'I'm all yours,' Jay said; but then his eye lighted on an English paper and he added it to the pile because the more he had to read back at the house the better, and he'd always enjoyed the London *Times*. So he paid for his purchases and as he walked across to the bar with Neil he tucked most of them under his arm, taking only *The Times* to look at while Neil fetched a couple of Buds. His friend came over, put down the glasses, and Jay, anxious not to let beer spill over his papers, hastily folded *The*

*Times* so that its back page was face up. He reached out for his glass, at the same time looking for a clear stretch of table-top, and that was when he saw it: 'FORWARD RELEASED.'

He read the piece twice. Only then did he surface enough to hear Neil say, 'Hey, can you hear me, or what?'

'What did you say?'

'I said: d'you mind making some space here, or do you want me to sit at the next table?'

'I'm sorry.' Jay made room and pushed *The Times* across. 'Forward's out of jail.'

'Yeah. I told you.' Neil swallowed half his beer, wiped his mouth and said, 'Listen, my friend, I have some advice for you. Forward is so far back in history he predates the Ice Age. Forget.'

'I can't.'

The words were out before Jay could check them. He wanted desperately to retrieve the slip but Neil forestalled him.

'Forget Forward, forget Singapore, forget *her.*'

'Who's "her"?'

'Oh, for God's . . .' Neil threw himself back, gripped the edge of the table with both hands and looked down to one side. Then he stared straight at Jay and began to talk, but Jay wasn't listening. He had reverted to the secret place everyone carries inside himself, the place called Happiness.

\*     \*     \*

Singapore, September 1971 . . . At dawn he'd been woken by the sound of a servant rhythmically sweeping the drive outside his bedroom with a bamboo broom, that perennial wake-up call of the East. He felt wonderful, having just returned from a short break, rock-climbing in the Himalayan foothills. He'd gone to the office at seven thirty, before the heat became unpleasant; he'd sorted through his correspondence, signed a few letters and one important contract, phoned South-East Asia while she was still waking up with a yawn.

His heart was as light as his schedule. The Malaysians were arriving tomorrow, but it was playtime: the hard work had been done months before, in Kuala Lumpur. They were coming down to get a drink and a girl or two before flying back to the jungle and their impeccable Muslim lifestyles. Jay could take care of that. In a strait-laced society where everything had its place, he knew just where everything was. The Far Eastern way meant flowing with the river: when you came to a dam, you went around it; when you found a space, you filled it. He believed, passionately, in the Chinese adage that everything has its true owner and eventually will find it. Some planes he owned had found a home with the Malaysian Air Force and his world was in perfect balance.

On impulse he asked his secretary, Li Lin, to find a new hotel where he could entertain the Malaysians, somewhere offering big discounts and bigger portions, because he wanted a change from the Raffles Grill, and rich men could indulge their whims, especially when they meant saving money. His name went before him in the Singapore of the seventies; hotel managers would compete for the account of Trader Sampson, the property king, the expat king.

Try the Prince, she'd suggested. There's a new under-manager there, a woman; she's good. So at noon Jay went to see what the Prince Hotel could offer. He bounded up the steps into the lobby, whistling a tune. As he took off his Panama hat and looked around he caught sight of a European woman standing by the house-phones. At first he could see only her back: a white cotton blouse with a collar low enough to reveal her lightly tanned neck. Then she turned.

He snatched in breath and unconsciously held it. The skin of his face tightened. His hands tingled, his heart gave a big thump before racing off without the rest of him, he felt giddy. Without realizing what he had done, he took a few steps towards her. She was perfect, perfect, in all respects perfect. She held her head just *so*, and what a face! That mouth, those eyes, oh God! those green eyes . . .

Not quite perfect.

He came to a halt within three feet of her. She was aware of another presence now, and looking at him oddly. By turning her face towards Jay she'd enabled him to see how one drop of sweat had rolled from her hairline (perfectly carved in exactly the right place), down her left cheek, almost to the jaw. Too small for a tear, too big to be called a bead, it described a runnel across her immaculate skin and culminated in a droplet of pure fluid that he had to taste if he were to save his life . . .

He moved closer. The woman, conscious of the tiny flaw that drew him, reached up with her left hand to dash the moisture away. Looking at the fourth finger he saw that she was flawed in another respect, married, enslaved by some animal from whom he would, must, now free her.

Her eyes widened in fright, then narrowed. Her lips parted. They stared at each other on the border of somewhere awful. One step, that's all it would take, salvation this way, damnation that, but no real choice. *She saw him exactly as he saw her.*

'It's hot today,' Jay murmured. 'Isn't it?'

Not taking her gaze from his face she replied, 'Are you talking to me?'

Slowly, very slowly, he looked to the right. He looked to the left. Apart from them, the lobby was empty.

'Do you know,' he said, turning back to face her, 'I rather think I must be . . . don't you?'

And so his one great love began.

*       *       *

'*Don't you?*'

Jay Sampson came to himself, and the bustle of Buffalo airport, with a start. 'What?'

Neil heaved a sigh of exasperation. 'You know what I'm saying makes sense, don't you? War's on the slate: with your inside knowledge of the Iraqi set-up you could walk into any one of a dozen offices in Washington DC and have them fall over you shedding tears of gratitude.'

'I'll think about it,' Jay muttered.

'Jay.' Neil reached forward to grip his hand. 'Tell me straight. Do you need bread?'

A pause preceded the lie: 'No.'

'Great. When can I have the money back I lent you?'

Jay had borrowed from Neil to pay Sal's medical bills; Blue Cross insurance hadn't covered everything. But lies beget lies. 'A week from now?'

'I don't believe you.'

'Okay, then I'll sell the house in Singapore. The land must be worth something.'

Neil gazed at him in disbelief. 'You still *own* that ruin?'

Jay shrugged. 'I know it's there, anyway.'

'What else do you know?'

'I keep in touch.'

'With *her*?'

Jay looked away. 'Not with her. I know where she lives, that's all.'

'It's over,' Neil said emphatically. 'A lot of very powerful people want never to hear that story again, so let it rest. Especially if you plan on getting back into Washington.'

No reply.

'Jay, did you hear what I said?'

'I heard. Maybe I will sell the Singapore place. I need a break. Fly out east for a while, put it all to bed.' Suddenly he laughed without humour. 'I could look up Verity, ask her to find me a buyer for the house. It's fair.' Again that empty laugh. 'I beat her to it on that bungalow plot in 'seventy-one, maybe it's time she –'

'*Jay!*'

When Jay fell silent, Neil went on more quietly. 'Perhaps I was giving you bad advice. I was thinking you'd like to get back into the old game, how I could help. But that isn't the problem. Seems the real problem is how to save your life.'

Jay looked at him. 'My life?'

'Verity Newland was always bad. She's gotten worse, much worse, since you . . . knew her.'

Then the real message did dawn and Jay sat up straighter. 'You mean she's in your line of fire?' he said incredulously.

'Let's say she's in the Middle East frame.'

The two men continued to stare at each other while Neil's flight was called. Jay kept his face expressionless, but inside he was bracing himself for the moment of abandonment.

'You're right,' he said. 'I'm not thinking straight. Bereavement . . . does that.' He reached out to lay a hand across one of Neil's. 'To everyone.'

Neil placed his other hand on top of Jay's and they sat for a moment, not speaking, until with one accord they rose.

They did the parting quickly, walking away without a backwards glance, and that was good, because somehow it prevented the loneliness from hitting immediately. Jay meant to head straight out to the parking lot, but then a strange thing happened: the beer he'd drunk staged a rebellion, he wanted to throw up. He turned towards the men's room. For a while he stood bent over a basin, resting his hands on its sides. The sickness slowly passed. He splashed water over his face, then washed his hands, running them through his sparse hair to dry them while he stared into the mirror at a stranger. Who was this gaunt, paunchy, middle-aged sonofabitch?

Nature hadn't been able to do much about his big frame, but what it supported, the outer spectacle, had changed beyond belief. The man in the glass was hunched, beaten: nothing like the fine figure that had shouldered its way through South-East Asia a lifetime ago. His black hair had lost most of its body and was thin enough to let streaks of white scalp show. The eyes, formerly challenging, had sunk into their sockets. Jay saw these things and, because hope had left him, failed to register the good features that remained.

He moved away from the mirror while his hands were still damp, keeping his eyes lowered. This had become a natural posture for him: over the past decade he'd seen most of the ground he had walked on.

He found his car and navigated out of the airport, out of town. While he drove he thought about his situation and wondered how he could survive.

He was really and truly broke, although he'd kept the full extent of the disaster from his friend. It wasn't just the medical bills, though they'd hardly helped. Post-Singapore he'd made what he hoped would be a clean break with the past, travelling extensively, playing a lot of golf, investing here and there. But investments had a habit of deteriorating if you didn't monitor them, and he started to lose money – this was round about the time he began to drink, seriously, as the quickest road to amnesia.

Jay drove through the bad backlands of Buffalo before turning east. After a while the electricity pylons gave way to trees, the densely built houses to copses of fir and larch. The transition was swift and stark: he was in deep countryside and it was as if Buffalo, just a few miles up the road, had ceased to exist.

Eventually, tired of wandering and nearly broke, he'd come home to America, met Sal again, married her. Remembering how in Singapore he'd done work for the US government, he'd phoned around his old circle of grizzled colonels to see if there was anything he could do for them now. Working for the Pentagon, he soon discovered, was like being baptized a Catholic: the tentacles never quite relaxed their grip on your soul. His life developed a routine. Quiet men would call him out of the blue, shoot the breeze, make a proposal. A few days later Jay would be in the first-class cabin of a plane, heading for some country against which the United States had imposed an arms embargo, with a stack of brochures headlining the merits of the latest fighter-bomber, the newest missile-detection radar, the best anti-personnel carriers this side of Jo'burg. Weeks later, a cheque would be deposited in an account somewhere sleepy, where audits were few and taxes nil; and Jay could afford to carry on for a while longer, swearing this had to be the last time . . .

But the first-class visits became more frequent, not less. Within ten years of leaving Singapore his private fortune had all sort of just . . . gone. Leaving him with Sal, and a grey-and-white house she'd inherited from an aunt, in a place called Eccles. Eccles, with its general store and its newish McDonald's and a nice old colonial porticoed church . . .

He'd sunk the last of his money in a business renting out agricultural equipment, and for a while he'd done okay. Then came the offer of some land: a pine plantation, other side of Warsaw, the biggest town close to Eccles, and he'd taken it with help from a savings-and-loan outfit that was about to go belly-up. Everything got called in, and Jay went belly-up too. The Pentagon hadn't called in a long while; the war-machine, so long exempted from the laws of economics, was feeling the same chill wind as everyone else. Jay sold his agricultural equipment business for what he could get, and had been living on a lean mixture of income and capital the day Sal died.

He had a little under four thousand dollars in the bank and owned a place in Singapore called *Rumah Anggerik*, the House of Orchids.

There had been a dwelling on that site overlooking the Strait of Johor since before anyone could remember. Its name originally was *Sentosa*, which in Malay means 'tranquillity': the right name for so lovely a house in so peaceful a setting. But after a while the Singapore government renamed an offshore island known as Blakang Mati, calling it Sentosa too, and the man who owned the house in those days had changed its name, not wanting to risk confusion; although the possibilities of confusion were slight, for Sentosa Island was destined to become a tacky resort, whereas the house remained a paradise on earth.

It was there that Jay had lived through the great love of his life. He had given his soul to a woman, only to lose both it and her; and from that day to this he had not set foot inside the house again.

Memory drew him on like an invisible magnet, down the highway, through Warsaw, right past Caesar's diner, two blocks down to the Eccles Village Offices, right again by the Atlantic gas-station into Hoover Drive and thence to the cluster of houses that nestled on the edge of Breaky Hollow. He parked his car in the drive and walked up the path to his front door, not noticing the unkempt lawn, not bothering to check a mailbox that had gone unopened for days. He let himself into the grey-and-white, timber-frame house; he shut the door behind him, leaning against it and closing his eyes against the knowledge that he was at last entombed in a silence without end.

He took off his coat. He wandered through to the kitchen, not bothering to switch on the light, even though it was dusk. He thought about a Jack Daniel's. No: the sensible thing to do was make tea, so he would do that. The long distance runner's first training session in loneliness.

He took his tea through to the living room and sat down in his favourite chair with its view of the back garden. He flicked his way through the TV airwaves. Cartoons, the Oprah Winfrey Show, George Bush rejecting linkage of the Kuwait crisis with Israel's withdrawal from the occupied West Bank . . . Jay turned off the set.

He washed up the tea-things and changed into more comfortable clothes. By now the house was almost dark, but still he did not turn on the lights. He let the memories tug at him until he could fight them no longer. Without knowing how he'd got there he was standing beneath the trap-door to the attic. He climbed up into the roof-space and here he did need light because he was afraid of treading on plaster and falling through the ceiling; with no one else in the house he might die there, trapped and alone.

The single light bulb showed him a lifetime's mess and muddle. Gingerly he picked his way past two cardboard boxes. They were, he knew, full of LPs. It was many years since he'd owned the means of playing them, but he'd kept them, because they were a memento of Singapore, of dancing on the terrace beneath the moonlight . . . Jay pushed on. In one corner lay a number of suitcases. He knew the one he wanted.

Albums lay stacked inside. They were wrapped in cloth to protect them from dust, but even so, as he removed the first bundle a spider fell out and scuttled into the darkness, making him curse with fear of what he was going to find. When he took off the cloth, however, he saw no signs of damage.

He carried the albums downstairs. He put them on the big, roll-top desk he'd inherited from his father, who'd used it every day of his working life until he'd quit practising law at the age of sixty, vowing never to look at a brief again. He switched on the lamp and pulled a chair close to the desk.

The first page of the first album, charcoal in colour, heavy and thick, contained just one large photograph. It was so old that darker parts of the monochrome image had faded to the hue of weak tea. The photographer had been standing halfway down the drive, facing towards the strait and the artificially created beach with its patches of delicate flowers: sea morning glory, oxeye, screwpine. The left third of the picture was dark and smudgy: a clump of feathery bamboo, thick angsana trees, monkey-puzzles, with the jungle behind. Emerging from this foliage, melting out of it, was a tall white house: *Rumah Anggerik*, the House of Orchids.

Jay took up his father's magnifying glass and pored over the photograph, which he'd acquired with the house; it had been taken around 1910, or so the seller said. Black-and-white striped awnings hung down along the two visible sides, shading the verandas from the sun. Square white columns supported the house, leaving space beneath for air to circulate except where the kitchen was. With his forefinger he picked his way along the upper floor, counting rooms, until he came to the corner nearest the strait and there his finger hovered. His bedroom, its rattan chick-blinds lowered against the glare outside. Beneath that stood an open-topped Rolls-Royce, its trunk in the shade afforded by the house's east wing; apart from that, there was no sign of human occupation.

The image taunted him. A second of time, frozen for ever, with innumerable secrets before and ahead of it but nothing to say to the man who sought its message eighty years later. Who had lived there then? How had he made his money? Did he have a wife? Children? Was he happy?

When he lived in Singapore Jay used to lie on the bed with this album propped up on the pillows and as the fan revolved soundlessly above his moist body he would interrogate the photograph, finding no answers but each day inventing more questions . . . was it a widow who had owned 'Sentosa' in 1910; who kept a Rolls-Royce parked half in shade and half out? A sultan, perhaps? Who had taken the photo, why had he chosen that day, that *hour*, to encapsulate a corner of paradise here on earth?

Had he (or she) won it at *fan-tan*? Was this the day before a big wedding, meant to be the start of a dynastic pictorial record? *Had he – or she – loved in this house?*

It was the most beautiful home in the world. It belonged to him. And it was there that he had lived his magnificent abiding love, the joy of his existence, his reason for having been born.

After a while tears began to fall. Jay wept for a house where he had known happiness, and grief, and laughter; he wept for a wife who was newly dead and had been his only source of comfort, and in the end he let his head droop forward on to the cradle of his arms and he cried for another woman who had been his world and his life and his soul.

This monsoon of sorrow could not last. He came back from the margin to find himself still half-lying across the desk, the album clutched to his chest.

He was alone now. If he wanted to eat he must cook; if he wanted company, he had to seek it out. But he wanted nothing, except to curl up by himself and forget.

He rose and went in search of the Jack Daniel's. But on his way to the kitchen he had to pass a dresser on top of which stood a snapshot of Sal, taken in happier times. Even though it was partly obscured by a vase it snagged his gaze. She was smartly dressed, her hair looked great, her mocking smile teased and seduced as only she knew how. Jay stopped. The dead woman seemed to be saying to him, 'You jerk!' As she had often said it in life – with an upward lilt that took away offence.

Her name was Sally. He'd known her by that name when they were kids together. Yet after he came home from Singapore he'd never called her anything but Sal. It took him two years to realize that Sal and the first syllable of his great love's name – Alison – rhymed.

This was a photograph he knew about, unlike the one of *Rumah Anggerik*. He knew what secrets preceded it and what came after. It was part of the life he had lived. He gazed at the snapshot for several minutes. Then he reached out, perhaps with the idea of turning it to the wall, and his fingers brushed against something beside the frame, a half-finished pack of Merit Menthols. Sal's cigarettes. Jay screwed up the pack, screwed up his eyes, too; he tucked the crumpled mess into his pocket, wondering how many more mines lay hidden around the house to ambush him.

He stood there a few moments longer, poised between two worlds. At last he picked up the frame and, very gently, kissed the glass over her lips, before replacing it almost where he had found it.

He should go back to Singapore. And the House of Orchids.

The idea took hold, sending down roots, pushing out branches, with the tenacity and speed of some exotic tropical creeper. Strange how he'd held on to *Rumah Anggerik* for so long, even when everything else had been sold . . . it wasn't just the advice he'd received at a time of falling property values, there was the sentiment, the love . . .

He could rot or he could grow; those were the only two options. *The only two!* Slowly he went back to the big desk. He stood there staring down at the pile of albums for a long time, while inside his brain the exotic plant extended its tendrils, finding new holds. He could rot or he could grow . . .

He sat down. He pulled a sheet of airmail paper towards him, uncapped his pen and began to draft a letter. The words came easily.

My dear Verity,

You will be surprised to hear from me, I know, after all this time, but I have decided to come to Singapore and thought I would give you advance warning of my plans. Sadly, I am now a widower. I need money. It is time for me to sell the House of Orchids and, while I am about it, realize my investment in the Occydor group of companies.

I know that this is not something that can be achieved overnight. You are now the majority share-holder and you may wish to explore different ways of buying out my remaining ten per cent. But candidly, my dear, I am in trouble and I need to have something in the bank soon.

I did think about approaching our mutual contacts in the Pentagon to see if they could help, and it may come to that yet, but in times like this I naturally turn to my friends first. It is my dearest hope that negotiations can be opened and concluded swiftly. Please share your thoughts with me on this.

Sincerely . . .

Jay addressed an envelope, inserted the letter and placed it on one side. He drew a yellow legal pad towards him, and picked up his pen again. But then he faltered. For a long time he looked at the empty sheet of paper, and his eyes were as vacant as the sheet. At last, hesitantly, he began to draft another letter.

It was an odd letter for a man to write: it commenced with the words, 'My darling Johnny, dearest love'.

Jay got as far as that and laid down his pen. How unlike the first time, years ago . . . Then, because he had never written a love letter before, he'd expected to find it hard, but the pen had seemed a live thing, a demon with a life of its own. Now, nearly twenty years on, his fingers were numb, like his brain.

He picked up the pen again. At first he composed slowly, then with greater fluency, but without ever finding the right words. Hour after hour he wrote, tearing up endless versions. At some point the light changed, causing him to look up and blink in surprise when he saw how dawn had come to soften the sky. By the time he'd finished it was day. He turned off the lamp and went to make coffee. Refreshed, he took a sheet of airmail paper and began to make a fair copy of his letter.

Do you remember, darling, *Ching Ming* festival of 'seventy-two? We were lying naked on the bed, you and I, with the fan going strong, your body tucked into mine, soldered by so many wetnesses: of sweat, and seed that had dissolved in the heat, and the juice from your insides all sticky and spent. My hand lay squeezed between your thighs and you pretended to be asleep while I worked . . . but then you amazed me and my hand stopped, for you had quoted poetry in that quiet murmur of sated love which always made my limbs burn; you said this . . .

'The moon over the royal palace looks down
    upon their parting
The parting of those who go to the east
From those who go to the west.'

And in that moment I knew you were sad beyond expression, because you loved me . . . as I loved you, but there was a parting, a separation, to be endured. We both believed it would be days. And see how the days have become years.

I love you now as I loved you then: beyond the line that makes us rational and human. You will know the things that are happening to my body as I write to you, just as I know the effect my words will have. Yin and yang do not change – the spear's work is to thrust inside, the body's to open, the lips to yield . . . so it will always be, my love, my dearest love.

'Every banquet must end', your last words to me. Every day I speak them aloud, with bitterness and sorrow. But there is another banquet. Those who go to the west sometimes return.

Count the days.

He addressed an envelope to Alison Forward before putting both that and the letter into the desk's secret drawer. He rolled down the top, locked it and sat there to savour the first moment of peace he'd known since the funeral, before slowly mounting the stairs to bed.

# FOUR

On the first Sunday after his release Iain woke up early, still finding it strange not to be jolted back into reality by the harsh notes of a prison-landing tannoy. The minute he opened his eyes he remembered: today he was going to begin his search for the truth by finding Anthony Powis, the first name on his list of three.

He left the house without waking Alison and took a bus to central London. It was drizzling. The streets had a greasy, littered look to them. He rode on the top deck. Some of the windows that he passed at eye level were lit. As a child, he used to wonder what was happening behind those windows; in prison, likewise. In prison he reminded himself (or someone did it for him) that every second a man was screwing a woman, or a woman was conceiving, or giving birth, or lovers were splitting up, or meeting, or taking off their clothes for the first time, or worming a Durex out of its wrapper. And it was all going on without you; the world of the senses was passing you by. You and me, mate; and the old faggot in the next cell, an' all.

He got off the bus in Trafalgar Square and decided to walk the rest of the way, through a part of London he'd once known well. The Strand was different. He didn't like this gaudy new style, all pot plants and cream lah-de-dah. Even the banks looked plastic.

He was early for his appointment so he didn't mind when his memory led him astray. He walked through Covent Garden, which had changed out of all recognition, before cutting across to Cambridge Circus and so on up Shaftesbury Avenue, the less salubrious end, until at last he ducked down a narrow alley near the cinema. At the back, obscured by a wheelie dustbin and three crates of empty bottles, was a door. He knocked. Nothing happened. Then some automatic device wrenched it open, showing Iain a flight of ill-lit steps leading down into darkness. He slipped inside, knowing a moment of familiar, lost peace as the heavy door slammed shut – 'One on, sir! One off, sir!'

Iain ran down the stairs and found himself in a drab waiting-room. Nobody else was there, but the moment his feet touched the bottom step he knew instinctively that someone was watching him.

Closed-circuit TV, eh.

The room was illuminated by a single, sixty-watt (he checked) bulb on a flex. No shade. Opposite the stairs, a steel door, edged with rivets; no keyhole or handle visible. On the wall, a coat-rack, fastened by two screws, one of which had come loose. Iain wondered what had caused that. A blow? Had they hung something too heavy from it, causing the screw to work loose?

What was heavy enough to do that . . . ?

It was neither hot nor cold in the room, but it felt damp. The seconds ticked away. Iain's eyes kept reverting to that row of hooks. He was starting to feel edgy.

A small room, lino, a chair, a door, some stairs . . . a coat-rack. What had happened in here? He began to enact mental scenarios, none of them pleasant. The coat-hooks were those upwardly curling metal kinds, lengths of rod bent into the shape of a crooked finger. By the light of sixty watts they looked vicious.

The steel door swung open without warning and a man came through it. Shambled through it, was how Iain described the event to himself. He'd been tall, once, but now his shoulders were rounded in a hunch and his feet scarcely lifted from the floor as he walked. His carpet slippers made a soft-shoe shuffle on the lino. When he held out his hand, Iain saw that he was old; late sixties at least. His go-between had said the Guv was old, but it somehow came as a surprise, all the same.

'Mr Forward?' A soft, oily voice.

'Yes.'

'Sorry to have kept you waiting; come in, come in.'

The old man went back through the door and Iain followed. In keeping with this area of London, the cosy little office beyond was of the kind much favoured by theatrical agents and their ilk: red wallpaper, a table covered with a velveteen cloth, multitudinous photos in gilt frames, some bowls of faded flowers, a big silver ciga-rette-box on a cluttered desk, next to a matching lighter that smelled of fuel – the old fashioned, liquid kind. What illumination there was came from a standard lamp in one corner and, on the desk-top, an anglepoise with a broken spring, sagging sideways. The room was full of shadows, dark corners, unseen things. It stank of stale smoke and a penetrating chemical odour that Iain couldn't identify. Ratsbane, perhaps, or something for an old man's bowel complaints . . . There was one other door, this time with-out armour-plating: an ordinary door, with a china knob-handle.

'I don't get in so early Sundays as I used to,' said the Guv, shuffling to take his seat behind the desk. He low-ered himself into it with a 'humph' of relief. He leaned forward to fold his hands on the desk and regard Iain through big, round, NHS-framed glasses. His rheumy eyes blinked slowly. A few strands of hair lay smoothed across his pate. He looked a kindly soul, did the Guv; a careers master of somewhat advanced years, or an under-taker's assistant. In fact he was a gang-leader, a violent man who ruled his patch through terror. Mo Brown, Iain's last long-term cellmate, had told him how to con-tact the Guv, who was his uncle, and had given him a

70

'reference'. Mo was doing a fifteen stretch for grievous bodily harm. He was a hard man, was Mo; when he warned Iain to take care over how he handled the Guv, Iain paid heed.

'I'm in the habit,' Iain said, 'of getting up early'; and the Guv smiled.

'Where you've come from . . . odd hours.'

'Yes.'

As Iain spoke, his attention was drawn upwards and to the left. Behind the Guv's chair it was very dark. Now something was oozing out of the blackness, like a slug uncoiling itself into the half-light. Something that glistened moistly . . . a face, a *black* face.

Iain wanted to say something, but his tongue stuck to the roof of his mouth. A mountain of a man slowly advanced to stand with one hand on the back of the Guv's chair. He was about six feet nine, muscular, and he did not smile or speak. He stood there like the Guv's guardian angel, and waited.

'Certain people would like me to be good to you,' the Guv began. 'Well-respected people who approached you for advice and assistance, over the years.'

Iain said nothing. It was true that in prison he'd used his accountancy skills for a variety of purposes, none of which would have met with the Institute's approval. This was his pay-off. He hated the feeling.

'A passport was mentioned. Also, a list of names that needed addresses fitting to them.'

'Yes.'

'Yes. Would you like a job?'

Iain's eyes widened; he hadn't expected this.

'Our Far East operation.' The Guv continued to sit with his hands folded in front of him, shoulders hunched, head slightly to one side, while he peered at Iain through his thick glasses. 'Bangkok. You're familiar with the region, I think?'

71

The black man took his hand off the Guv's chair. He walked around the desk – floated would be a better word, his feet made no sound and he exhibited a dancer's grace – until he had disappeared out of Iain's range of vision. As the man passed, Iain detected another smell: pungent cologne, heavy as corruption.

After the silence had extended itself to unnerving length, Iain said, 'What kind of work?'

'Accountant. You are an accountant? Chartered?'

'They struck me off.'

'But you kept abreast in prison? Or so those *very* well-respected sources I mentioned earlier have insinuated. You studied. You gave assistance and advice. The lack of a qualification wouldn't bother us, you know.'

Another silence, while Iain studied his shoes. 'Drugs,' he said at last. 'Heroin, and that?'

'And . . . that.'

'No thanks. And I do mean thanks, Guv – thank you very much indeed.'

Be careful with your manners, Mo had warned him.

'Yes, well. Think it over.' If Iain had gone down in the Guv's estimation, he gave no sign of it. 'Now. Have you travelled on a false passport before?'

'No.'

'Do you speak a foreign language?'

'I get by in French.'

'Perhaps French Canadian, then?' The Guv regarded him doubtfully. 'Think about language, think about disguise. You can't grow a beard overnight; you can't shave one off without it showing. Hair dye . . .' He lifted a hand and patted the side of his head. '*Very* troublesome.'

'What do you suggest?'

'The simplest way of disguising yourself in a hurry is to change your hairstyle and the colour of your eyes.'

'And how should I do that?'

'Get a decent wig. And tinted contact lenses. Again, not something to be mastered in a hurry. Immigration officers are trained to detect disguise, but these things work. Smoke?'

'No, thanks.'

The Guv took an untipped cigarette from the silver box and lit it. He resumed his former position, hands folded on the desk in front of him, but now smoke curled up towards the ceiling from between his wrinkled, nicotine-brown fingers. When he took a drag he sucked in his cheeks before opening his lips wide and blowing the smoke out through clenched teeth.

A whiff of that strong, somehow putrefying cologne assailed Iain's nostrils. He could sense the black man moving behind him, coming closer.

'I can fit you out with wig and lenses,' the Guv went on. 'And we'll need a passport photo with you wearing them. After that, let me know what nationality you've decided and the passport will be yours within a week.'

Iain shuffled in his chair, unconsciously shrinking away from where he believed the Guv's black familiar to be. 'Thanks.'

'Don't mention it. And now, you wanted an address?'

'You've got it?' The words broke through Iain's controlled façade despite himself. 'Powis?'

'Sir Anthony Powis, OBE, founder and former chairman of Harchem plc, now retired.'

'Retired *where*?'

The Guv did not move. He continued to gaze at Iain through the same benevolent eyes, a tortoise-smile on his lips, the smoke gently rising.

'I'm sorry, Guv.'

Still no reaction from across the desk. But something was happening behind Iain, something to make his flesh creep. The black giant was there, somewhere . . . nobody had warned him about the black.

73

Iain said, 'D'you know, I hope you don't mind me saying this, but I could really fancy a fag after all.'

The tortoise's face cracked into a wider smile. The Guv passed over the silver box, following with a light. He had lung cancer, still in an early stage; he was jealous of healthy people. 'Tap him for a cig,' his nephew had advised Iain, 'if things get a bit rough.' And now Iain could feel the presence behind him start to dissolve. Movement . . . The bodyguard, secretary, whatever, was returning to take up position behind the Guv's chair. The Guv's fleshy features remained expressionless, but his eyes never left Iain's face.

'You've been under strain, Mr Forward,' he said, his voice climbing to a sympathetic whine. 'As has your dear wife. A legendary lady, your wife.'

'Alison. Yes.'

'Woman trouble is the fate of most. That, and ulcers.'

Iain kept quiet. He was thinking of visiting days at the Scrubs, where he'd served so much of his sentence, when they used to cheer him off the landing on his way to see Alison, clapping, whistling, laughing. Even the sex things they shouted out were only awkward, not bestial – 'Give her one from me, then!' – because nobody ever stayed by them for so much as a year, let alone ten. Let alone seventeen. A life stretch. People joked about marriage being a life sentence and thought it was funny.

'Above rubies,' he muttered distractedly. 'That's what they say.'

'Above rubies,' the Guv agreed sagely. 'A good woman. Like my Elsie. Fifty years come Christmas. Golden indeed.'

'Congratulations.'

'*Thank* you, Mr Forward; that's civil. Mo told me you were civil. We seem to have got away from the business. Powis lives in a village called Leigh, near Tonbridge in Kent. His house is called "Outerbridge".'

'I'll find it. Thanks, Guv.' Iain hesitated. 'Guess I'm in your debt.'

The Guv took a last drag on his cigarette and squinted at Iain as if the smoke hurt his eyes. 'No,' he said eventually. 'I don't know what you did in prison, Mr Forward, but you're a very well-respected individual. Know that?'

Iain shook his head, and stood up.

'Come again tomorrow, eight o'clock in the evening. Can do?'

'Yes.' Iain's eyes could not help straying to the black. As if in response to Iain's glance, the man's head now swivelled slowly, with robotic smoothness, until his two deep-set eyes could focus on the whitey who'd come to disturb their Sabbath calm. Not agreeable eyes, those.

The Guv stood up also. 'Goodbye, Mr Forward,' he said, extending his hand. 'Lovely meeting you, really lovely. I do mean that. I do.'

His hand was damp, slightly sticky. As Iain climbed the stairs, the electronic door opening before him, he held his right hand to his nostrils and sure enough, the smell he'd noticed earlier seeped up.

Harchem used to be like that: all bright administrative corridors and stink: a paradoxical environment.

It had stopped raining. Iain stubbed out his cigarette and looked around for a phone box. He telephoned Alison to reassure her he was all right, saying he needed time to be alone. He couldn't tell what she thought and, to be honest, he didn't care. He ought to care, though. He should pay her back for all she'd done for him, over the years, and he *would*, once this business was out of the way.

When he'd left the house earlier that morning he hadn't intended to do more than contact the Guv. But the thrill of actually holding Powis's address in his brain proved too much. He had to go and see him this instant, today, *now*. Besides, he was due to start work tomorrow, after he'd met his probation officer; no time to waste. And he knew exactly what he wanted to ask Powis, because he'd had seventeen years to think about it.

Iain took a bus to Waterloo, where he caught a train to Tonbridge, glad now that he hadn't given his discharge allowance to Alison after all. He got directions for Leigh and he walked, saving bus money for more important things, although after a bit he regretted that. Walking down a wet country lane gave him the creeps. The notion of being able to go anywhere he liked brought on panic attacks, sometimes. And today he was nervous: first the Guv, now Powis . . .

There was a church, with people coming out of it, and a village green and a pub. Iain noted the Vicar's name, painted on the signboard by the church. He asked one of the congregation for directions to 'Outerbridge' and received the information coupled with a strange look, reminding Iain that he didn't resemble your typical Sunday lunch guest.

He walked on, but at a slower pace. This notion of rushing in to see Powis didn't make a lot of sense, he realized. If he announced himself under his real name, chances were that Powis would throw him out, call the police even. In prison he'd made a list of all the things he wanted to say to his old employer, but he'd never bridged the practical gap between finding him and gaining access. He'd never thought about the mechanics.

Go back, come again another day? No – too expensive, and besides, he'd be working after tomorrow. Improvise. Think.

What did he know about Powis? A religious man, by all accounts, though Iain hadn't had anything to do with him while in Harchem's employ. His time there had overlapped a period of ill-fated American expansion, which meant Powis spending most of his time in Delaware and no strong hand on the helm. Ah, yes – he was a religious man, and had a weakness for cigars. Iain couldn't buy cigars on a Sunday, out here in the sticks. What else did he like?

He sat down on a bench beside the green and thought. Reynolds had described head office to him, once. He'd been laughing on account of what he'd been offered. Not coffee, not tea, but . . .

Fruit.

Powis used to keep a huge bowl of fresh fruit in his room to offer guests, fresh spring water and soft fruits . . . That's it, that's it . . . he never drank tea or coffee, said they over-stimulated the brain, which was rich when you thought how much alcohol he got through in a week.

Nowhere to buy fruit on a Sunday, not here. He'd have to wing it.

Iain waited until the last of the church congregation had disappeared before getting up. He found what he wanted down an alley running parallel to the high street: his second dustbin of the day. Beside it stood a pile of empty cardboard boxes, neatly stacked. On the top one was printed the name of a well-known fruit importer. Iain skimmed off a few items of rubbish from the bin and packed them in the box, covering everything with a more or less dry newspaper plucked from the same source. Not perfect, not even good – but the best he could do.

'Outerbridge' turned out to be a mock-Tudor mansion all by itself down a potholed lane, surrounded by unkept lawns and a hedge that hadn't felt a trimmer in a long time. A beech tree lay on the grass, its crown clipping one of the hedges, blown down (he guessed) by the great storm of '87. No attempt had been made to clear it away. As he walked up the drive he noted other signs of neglect: a gutter dangling from the roof where its fastenings had rotted, peeling paint, an overflowing plastic water-butt. When he pressed the bell he heard no corresponding chime inside the house. The wrought-iron knocker landed on bare wood: its sounding-piece had fallen away, leaving a hole where the screw-fastener once had been.

No one came. Iain stood back and surveyed the frontage. All the windows were closed, and filthy. Heavy drapes prevented him from seeing inside when he made his way along the wall. Don't say the old fucker was out . . .

He went back to the door and knocked again. What had happened here? Powis used to enjoy a reputation for elegance, full of energy, going out of his way to pick up litter. 'Cleanliness is next to Godliness' was his watchword, it had even filtered down to Singapore: somebody would be eating a curry lunch at his desk, sauce dripping on to papers, and – 'Cleanliness is next to Godliness,' Reynolds would guffaw on his way out to the club.

Iain raised his hand to knock again. As he did so, however, the door opened a crack and he paused.

'What?'

The house's interior was gloomy, but he could make out a wizened face obscured by spectacles. The person inside stood back from the door, which remained fastened by two chains.

'Could you tell Sir Anthony Powis that I'd like to see him, please. And Lady Anthea, too, of course, if she's in.'

Silence.

'I've come from church,' Iain said. He remembered the Vicar's name from the signboard. 'Mr Trafford asked me to step by with this . . .'

Still no response from inside the house. Iain wondered uneasily if he'd got the wife's name right. Anthea. Alethea . . . ?

'What's your business?' The voice rippled with fear and hostility. Some crazy old retainer, presumably.

'I want to see Sir Anthony.' Iain raised his voice, deliberately sending it in search of more intelligent ears. 'I'd like a word with him.'

The door began to close. Iain shoved his foot against it and pushed, hard. He heard heavy breathing, followed by a grunt. The loon inside was trying to fight him.

'Where . . . is . . . *Powis*?' No reply. The absurdly ill-matched contest continued for a few more seconds before the weaker party gave up. There was a long pause.

'I'm Anthony Powis,' said the voice. 'What is it that you want? State your business quick, or I'm calling the police.'

This wasn't right, it couldn't be. Powis had been a powerhouse of energy and intellect, a mover-and-shaker before the expression was invented.

'You . . . you're Powis?' Iain said.

'What's wrong with that? Who are you, anyway? What do you want? What does that buffoon Trafford think he's doing? Isn't once enough for him? Eh? I said, Isn't once enough for him? Are you *deaf*?'

'He's sent you some fruit,' Iain said, feeling stupid. 'Here . . .'

He pushed the box against the door. For a moment nothing happened. Then Powis stuck his face in the gap, his eyes blinking evilly behind his spectacles, and Iain saw that all his attention was on the box. The old man was so eager that he knocked his head against the door-jamb, dislodging the glasses from his nose. A hand came through the gap, wrinkled and skeletal. Iain snatched the box away.

'I've been asked to give this fruit to you personally,' he rasped. 'So if you'll open the door . . .'

'Who are you?'

'My name's Johnson. I'm the new churchwarden.'

A long silence followed, while Powis stared at Iain through the gap, the box temporarily forgotten; and Iain prayed that the old idiot wouldn't recognize him. At last, however, he heard the sound of chains being released. The door swung open a few inches. Powis grabbed the box with astonishing force and pulled it backwards, into the house. Iain, anticipating what he meant to do, barged in before Powis could slam the door.

The old man was kneeling on the floor, drooling over the box. He scrabbled inside, scattering newspaper and other rubbish.

'Where is it?' Powis's voice rose to a wail. 'My fruit – where is it? *You've stolen my fruit, damn you!*'

Suddenly he was up and running towards the back of the house. Iain raced after him. The place reeked to high heaven, God knows what could have made such a stench. Powis had reached the kitchen. He was standing by the back door. His arm was going up, up . . . Iain followed the action, saw where it was aimed and launched himself forward.

His hand gripped Powis's skinny wrist a second before he could punch the red alarm button by the side of the door.

'That's *enough*,' he snapped. 'I'm not going to hurt you, not unless you're stupid.'

'Who are you?' Powis croaked.

Iain felt the resistance drain out of his prey, but he kept hold. He edged backwards, drawing Powis with him, until they were well away from the alarm button. He allowed his eyes to roam, absorbing grisly details. The plates in the sink, the mess on the floor, the dirty clothes, grease, broken glass . . . Jesus, save me from old age.

'My name,' he said quietly, 'is Iain Forward. Remember me?'

For a moment Powis remained still while his watery, narrow eyes flickered over Iain's face. His gaze fell, his face became vacant. 'No,' he whispered, 'oh no, no, no . . .'

Iain dropped his wrist, glad to be free of the old man's

touch. Suddenly, without warning, the antique wreck slumped to the floor in a heap. Powis was weeping. He held his hands up to his glasses, two withered fists used to block out truth.

'Don't kill me,' he whimpered. 'There's no money here. No jewels.' He lowered his hands. 'You're a killer, aren't you? But I'm an old man, I never hurt anyone. Leave me alone. Please. Please.'

His voice died away. Iain reached down and helped Powis to his feet. There was a chair tucked underneath the table. As Iain pulled it out he saw a plate of congealed cat food lying on it. Did cats explain the foul smell? But there was no sign of any pets. He repressed the ghastly notion that the cat food was for Powis and said, 'I'm not going to hurt you. I've got no quarrel with you. Here, sit down . . .'

'Toilet,' Powis breathed. 'Please . . .'

Iain hesitated. 'No tricks.' But the words were redundant; Powis hadn't a trick left in his antiquated bone-bag of a body.

He was gone a long time. Iain listened at the kitchen door for sounds of a phone being used, but all was silent. He realized that his carefully prepared list of questions was useless now. He'd just have to do the best he could.

When Powis came back he was wiping his hands on his trousers; there were traces of spittle around his mouth, and a stain had materialized by his crotch.

'Sit down,' Iain grated. 'And listen.'

He eyed Powis, not sure if his addled mind was capable of understanding. Shit that, in for a penny . . .

'You founded Harchem,' he began. 'Remember?'

After a pause, Powis nodded. 'Harchem,' he said wonderingly; and then – 'My company.'

'Right. In nineteen seventy-three, I was tried for the murder of your regional managing director. A man called Reynolds. Remember *that*?' Now Powis looked at him, and there seemed to be genuine recognition in his eyes. 'Trial. They found you . . . guilty.'

'They did. You gave evidence, yes?'

Another pause. Powis nodded.

'You were cock of the roost, then. Rolls-Royce to court every day. Fancy house, fancy flat in town. Nice wife – where is she, by the way?'

'Wife?' Powis's face had turned blank. But after a while his brain engaged again, and he said, 'Died. Heart. Long time ago.'

'You've been living here, alone, ever since?' It was off track, but curiosity was getting the better of Iain.

'Alone. Retired. Hated all that . . . stuff. City slickers. Bums.' He seemed to like that word. '*Bums!*' he yelled suddenly, and he grinned. 'Sacked the servants, thieving little cunts. Told that bloody vicar . . .'

Here he looked up at Iain, and for a second there was a flicker of the former sharpness, the acuity they used to write about in the finance pages. 'You mentioned Trafford,' he said slowly. 'That's what told me you were a wrong 'un. Can't stand Trafford, can't bear the cut of his glib.' He cackled at his own weak pun. 'Haven't been inside a church for years. Shit-suckers, the lot of 'em. Can't step inside a church without I'd vomit, now.'

What had happened, Iain wondered, to take away Powis's faith?

'The trial,' he said. 'They found me guilty, but I never murdered Reynolds. I'm going to clear my name, and you're going to help.'

Powis's mouth twitched. There was a long pause. 'Good,' he said at last.

Iain was floored. 'Good . . . ?'

'You never did for Reynolds, *I* knew that.'

He sat upright at the table, hands by his sides, and he looked like a human being, instead of the scarecrow that

82

had answered the door. The stimulation of human contact, Iain realized, was having an effect.

'Tell you what,' Powis said suddenly. 'Got a smoke, have you?'

Iain shook his head.

'Fuck. All right. Go on, then.'

'At the trial –'

'I always liked you, Forward. Bright sort of chap.'

'We never met.'

'Did so. Singapore Hilton, May 'seventy-two. Bloody good lunch. You, Reynolds, Thompson from Hong Kong. Talked about the rain forest, I remember. God-awful Beaujolais; never could travel. I had a beer.'

Like a shock-wave the memory jolted into Iain's mind. He was *right*! How could he have forgotten that, all these years? A quick meeting, just to introduce him to Powis; he'd come late, only time for one course . . . *Jesus Christ, how could he have forgotten that!*

'Can you remember my trial?' he asked.

Powis gave his lips a good chewing-over. 'Bits.'

'I'd come to London, at Reynolds' request. The prosecution said he'd been selling Harchem's industrial secrets to competitors, and that some of those formulas had military value. Yes?'

'Balls. They couldn't even say who'd bought the fucking things.'

'*Right!*' Iain knew his first glimmer of hope. 'The Crown's case was that Reynolds had been selling our stuff, that he was the head of a conspiracy and I was part of it. They said that I fell out with Reynolds because he wouldn't pay me my cut, that he panicked, was going to blow the gaff on me, and that I killed him to stop it all coming out.'

'Bloody idiot.'

'Reynolds?'

'*No!* Not Reynolds . . . that little creep of a prosecutor,

83

what was his name? Can't remember. Told him so. Pissed the judge off.' Powis giggled shrilly. 'Gave me a bloody rocket. Stupid fart.'

'Do you remember an argument the lawyers had?'

Powis's eyes filled with tears. 'I'm just a poor old man, I can't be expected to remember . . .'

'It's okay. Take it easy.'

But Powis was sobbing now, as far from reality as he'd been when he first opened the door. Iain wondered how much longer his mental see-saw would take to steady, on which side it would come down. 'Take it easy,' he repeated mechanically.

But then – 'What was it like?' Powis asked unexpectedly. 'Prison?'

At first Iain thought Powis's brain had gone off on one of its trips again, but then he caught a glimpse of the eyes glittering beneath his hooded brows and knew this for a ploy. 'Shitty,' he said. Must have time to think. *What was going on here?*

'I'm afraid of prison,' Powis muttered.

'Why?' Iain asked. 'You've never done anything wrong.'

But Powis was eyeing him surreptitiously again, while his fingers locked and unlocked on the table and his leg knocked against the wood in a steady, nervous rhythm.

'There was an argument in court,' Iain went on slowly. 'The Home Office wanted to prevent the jury learning what I'd been selling in the way of your secrets. Remember that, do you?'

Powis's leg jiggled up and down, up and down.

'They had a certificate from the Home Secretary, all about the national interest. And the judge went along with it. Nobody ever told the jury what I was supposed to have been selling. But you must have known.'

Powis's leg became still. Somewhere in the distance a chain-saw started up, noisily unzipping the silence.

'*You* must have known, because they were your secrets. *What was so deadly that even the jury couldn't be told?*'

Powis's eyes widened, a spark of intelligence showed in them. For a moment Iain dared to hope; but then Powis said, 'I'll tell you something, I gave up the drink. Foul muck. And do you know something, Forward? I felt better for it. *Instantly!*'

'No you don't,' Iain said through gritted teeth. 'You're not fobbing me off.' His hand darted forward to grab Powis's wrist and the old man squawked. 'Now,' Iain said, leaning across the table. 'You fucking well tell me, Powis, or I'll let you know what it's like in prison, all right. I'll give you a taste.'

Powis shook his head. It wasn't a deliberate gesture, he couldn't help it; his head kept on shivering to and fro as if in the throes of a seizure. Saliva dribbled down his chin. His pupils had shrunk to pinholes. Suddenly a nasty smell wafted across the table and Iain dropped Powis's wrist. 'Oh, Jesus,' he said, standing up with such force that his chair tipped over. He walked across to the sink and stood there staring out of the window at the bedraggled lawn. More of a jungle than a lawn.

'Go and clean yourself up,' he said to the glass. 'Go on, get out.'

He heard shuffling noises but did not look round. He continued to gaze out of the window until, minutes later, Powis said from somewhere behind him, 'Why don't you go?'

Iain turned round then, and surveyed his host. 'Because I've done seventeen years inside for a crime I didn't commit,' he said bleakly. 'Because you know why they did it to me, and how, and if you say you don't, then you're lying. Sit down.'

But Powis remained standing. 'I don't think you did that murder,' he said at last, and his voice had firmed

85

somewhat. 'Everyone in the company had you down as an honest man. And it all seemed so ridiculous: you were just an accountant, you didn't have a key to the safe where we kept the formulas, you had no motive.'

'I had a Swiss bank account,' Iain grated. 'It was news to me, but I had it, didn't I? And they found the knife that killed Reynolds in my flat.'

'An account that never held more than a measly thousand pounds and wasn't opened by you but by somebody else. And who would have been so stupid as to hide the murder weapon in his flat? Not you. All a lot of nonsense. But I can't help you, Forward.'

Powis stumbled over to the table and rested his weight on it until he could once again lower himself into the chair.

'It's too long ago. I've . . . changed.'

'Yeah,' Iain said. 'I can see.'

'I don't believe you did it, but the jury thought you did, and there was other evidence, wasn't there?'

'Some.'

'Your fingerprints were on the knife, and on the formula safe in Reynolds' office. You were seen going to visit Reynolds, before he died, that awful bitch Newland said so.'

'Of *course* I was, you stupid . . .' Iain wiped a hand across his face and tried again. 'He'd set up an appointment, hadn't he? But if you think —'

'And there were those letters, weren't there? The Sonja letters.'

Powis's face had undergone a change. No longer frightened, or even merely senile, he was displaying the malicious glee of a decrepit and impotent man who recalls a scandal which brought down another. A sex scandal . . .

'They said there was a code,' he went on, and then he giggled. 'Didn't need a code, if you ask me.'

'Well I'm not fucking asking you.'

'Temper, temper.'

Powis cackled. Iain launched himself forward to bang both hands on the table. He reached out to snatch Powis's cardigan, ripping a hole — one more in a garment that was already falling apart. Powis looked up at him without flinching. He didn't seem frightened any more. *Why?*

'Never mind the letters,' Iain said thickly. 'Just tell me two things. Two, and we're finished. Where's my old boss — Newland, where is she?'

'Singapore. She stayed on, after leaving Harchem. The Chinkies are welcome to her. What a cow.'

'Agreed. Who's she working for?'

'Can't remember.' Powis stared into the distance. 'Oxy-acetylene. Oxy- something. Damn stupid name, anyway.'

'You were making chemical weapons at Harchem Far East, weren't you? And selling them on the quiet, to people who weren't gentlemen, not like you and me, *Sir* Anthony Powis, KMA, Kiss My Arse. *Eh?*'

Iain shook the old man back and forth but without passion, as a bored dog might worry the corpse of a rat.

'In prison, people learn how to think for themselves, Powis. They work things out. You were making some-thing nasty in the woodshed *and I want to know what*!'

But Powis closed his eyes; and all he said was, 'I can't remember anything. It's all so long ago.'

The voice was wrong. He should have been tremulous, pleading even; but he sounded as calm as if he were calling redouble against a bridge tyro who'd had the rather amusing nerve to take him on. Everything was suddenly wrong, wrong, *wrong*.

Iain stepped back. He turned to face the window, not wanting Powis to read his expression. And there outside was a policeman.

Iain's panic lasted less than a second. He smiled at the PC. He waved. The policeman did not respond. He made for the back door instead.

'Rape alarm,' Iain said conversationally. 'Neat. Congratulations. In the toilet, was it?' But his heart beat fast and he was cursing, because this was the end; they'd put him back in jail for this, revocation of licence, maybe even fresh charges. How could he have been so stupid? *How?*

Somebody knocked on the front door. At the same moment, the back door opened and the policeman walked in.

'Good morning, constable,' Powis piped. 'Is that another one of you around the front?'

'It is.' The policeman looked young, also tough. He stared at Iain, committing his features to memory; then he said, 'I'll go and let him in.'

'Please do.'

The policeman walked through to admit another, similarly young and tough constable. Not pigs, Iain thought to himself; piglets. Boys in blue.

The two policemen entered the kitchen. 'Now, Sir Anthony,' said the first one, the one Iain had seen through the window. 'What's this about?'

Powis blinked. 'Thought you were going to tell me,' he said, all owlish innocence.

'Your alarm went off in the station,' the policeman replied. 'So we came. This gentleman is . . . ?'

'I never rang my alarm. Did I?'

'You did, sir.'

'Must have been when I was in the loo, doing my number twos.' Powis giggled. 'What a pity.'

He treated Iain to a long, rancorous look. Iain kept his face still, reluctant to give Powis the satisfaction of begging. Everything hung on the old wretch's next words. Well, fuck him. *Fuck him!*

'This?' Powis made a meal of the word, drawing it out, savouring it. 'This is . . . my godson, I think. Goodness, it's hard to remember when you get to my age.' He

88

blinked furiously. 'You are my godson. Aren't you? And you were going to bring me a box of pineapples. Lots of pineapples, isn't that what you said? And a box of Fidel's finest. Cigars,' he added, as if sensing the two policemen were too young, and thick, to follow that.

There was a silence. Iain started to speak but something got in the way. Gall. He cleared his throat. 'That's right, sir. We knew you always loved fruit, Nancy and I. Her suggestion, actually.'

As if through muffling he heard his vowels smooth themselves out, losing their ex-con's metallic whine. 'Thought you'd given up,' he added with a forced laugh. 'Cigars, eh?'

'Cigars.' Powis chortled at Iain. 'Got it?'

Another long silence, while the two men weighed each other under the speculative gaze of the law.

'Certainly,' Iain said. 'I'll tell Nancy.'

'Yes, you do that, and give her my love. Well, constable –' Powis jerked his head around – 'what was it you said you wanted? Eh?'

'So everything's all right, then, is it sir?' The man kept his eyes on Iain while speaking. He'd know him again, oh yes.

'Of course it's all right. Why did you say you were here?'

For the first time the representatives of the law seemed a little less sure of themselves. 'We couldn't get you on the phone,' the second man said.

'Cut off,' Powis crowed. 'Couldn't pay the fucking bill. Arse bandits.'

It was impossible to tell whether those last words were intended to denigrate British Telecommunications plc, or the two uniformed visitors who continued to study Iain as if preparing to draw him from memory.

The senior copper now said, 'We'll be on our way, then,' in a cold voice.

'Right. Cheerio. Pip pip.'

At the front door the second man delayed a few seconds, sniffing the air. 'Had an accident, did you, sir?' he enquired, and his tone was sarcastic. 'Funny smell in here.'

'You must have brought it with you,' Powis shouted. 'Take it away when you go.'

The door closed. Powis looked at Iain and he said, 'A box of cigars, another of pineapples. Send them, I don't want to see you again. Ever.'

'And if I don't?'

'They'll remember your face. Won't take long to put a name to it, once I get my memory back, and that's what'll happen if *you* forget, Forward.'

He followed Iain to the front door, keeping well behind him, out of reach. But as Iain reached the threshold Powis's hand descended on his arm with surprising force. Iain looked down. The claw was wrapped around his sleeve so tightly that its arthritic fingers had turned white.

'I want to help you,' Powis said softly. 'But I can't. I . . . daren't.'

To his astonishment, Iain saw tears start to trickle down his cheeks.

'It's not that I've anything against you,' Powis said, shaking his head. 'But if I say one word . . . *one word* . . .' He paused. He dropped Iain's sleeve and stepped back. 'I live here,' he whispered, 'like a pig in shit. Not much of a life. But I don't want to die, you see. I want to . . . to hang on. And if I talk about the things in Reynolds' safe . . . if I say *one word* . . .'

With unexpected gentleness he gave Iain a little push, shooing him out of his house, his life; but as he closed the door Iain could see how the tears were running thick and fast now.

He could see something else, too. No one who'd done time could ever fail to read it. Terror.

90

# FIVE

The supervisor at Toa Payoh looked out of the Mass Rapid
Transit's Station Control Room and saw a bespectacled
Chinese boy, say fourteen years old, dressed in neatly
pressed white shirt and shorts. The boy was slight of
build. On his back he toted a cello-case several inches
taller than himself.

The supervisor watched with supercilious suspicion.
For there was a problem here: the boy possessed a peach-
coloured student travel card, but the MRT system did not
cater for cellos. It had not been designed with cellos in
mind. The teenager evidently recognized this, for he
unslung the instrument (not without difficulty) and cast
around for a way to get it through the automatic gate. In
the end he heaved his burden over the barrier.

The supervisor, a Malay with no love for the Chinese
race, consulted the regulations. There were fifty-six
things that passengers on Singapore's MRT system might
not do, such as eating, or bending their tickets, but the
list did not enjoin the carrying of cello-cases. Gloomily
he watched the boy vanish up the stairs to the platform,
bent almost double under the cello's weight. There must
be a new bye-law. He would submit a draft.

\*

The boy's name was Robinson Tang. He lived with his
parents and Chao Grandma (his mother's mother) in a
fifth-storey government Housing Development Board
apartment off Lorong 6, Toa Payoh. He attended a good
secondary school and was clever. He enjoyed his lessons,

especially English. But as he struggled to get his cello-case on to the train he would have given anything not to be made to study music.

It wasn't just the inconvenience of lugging the thing to and from Dr Lee's music rooms in Serangoon, though that was bad enough. Robinson stood his cello-case against the train-doors and gazed morosely out at the passing scenery. It was all his mother's fault. She insisted he learn an instrument. The school took things in hand for her and submitted him to a computer-driven suitability test. 'Cello,' said the computer, so cello it was. Robinson had been hoping for drums. And now his mother was nagging him to go in for prizes, take grade exams, because that was the way to prosper. School in the morning, homework in the afternoon, tuition or practice three hours every evening. Robinson sighed. He was allowed to watch TV on a Saturday night, for one and a half hours. Big deal.

He checked his watch. This evening he had a job to do before going on to his weekly music lesson. Six ten. Plenty of time.

At Raffles Place, the heart of Singapore's business district, he heaved his cargo on to the platform and made for the escalator. He liked riding the MRT, which was air-conditioned, but according to a cunning plan, so that the platforms were cooler than the ticket halls, and the trains were coldest of all: the idea being to keep loitering to a minimum. He liked the glass, steel and marble architecture. He enjoyed the escalators, so smooth and effortless; sometimes the lift at home didn't work and he had to hump his cello up five flights of stairs, but nothing ever broke down on the MRT.

He emerged into the tropical dusk, wondering if he had time for a quick smoke. This, his only vice, would amount to a sin in his parents' eyes if ever they found out, although he was far from being alone. His friends all puffed away like so many uniform little chimneys. But oh, the peril of being caught! Perhaps that was why he liked it so much – danger in an ultra-safe city.

He decided to wait. Too many people about, and in Singapore there was always someone who knew you, watching. He would save it up for later, after he'd discharged his duty, as a special treat.

Robinson sought bearings. Where was OUB Centre? Over there . . .

It was the end of the day and office workers were streaming out in search of buses, the MRT, the nearby Satay Club and dinner. Robinson fought his way through the tide like an eager young salmon. He had one of the OUB Centre's elevators to himself. As it whizzed upwards he imagined himself to be an astronaut, striving to overcome the monstrous G-force of lift-off; the bank of buttons became a console and he wished he'd brought his computer joystick with him.

For the first time he felt glad that First Uncle had entrusted him with this important mission. He did not like First Uncle, largely on account of his temper, but Robinson's attitude changed along with his altitude. A trip to the top of the OUB Centre made up for a lot.

The lift stopped. He got out and found himself in an empty foyer. Ahead of him he could see a big pair of doors, made of what looked like burnished steel. High tech: ace! – his mission had brought him to the planet Zog, where even the people were made of steel. He approached the doors cautiously. They were bare except for a discreet plaque which read: 'The Occydor Group of Companies.' Yes.

Robinson laid his cello-case down on the floor and opened it. Inside, apart from the instrument itself, were an algebra textbook, a pocket calculator and a wad of paper, along with Philip Jeyaratnam's latest paperback. Also, a big brown envelope. He fingered the novel and sighed. Tomorrow was the weekly maths test. Dutifully he selected the textbook, and began to improve the shining hour with a series of abstruse calculations which his mother could never have understood but which she would unstintingly have revered.

Every so often the doors opened and employees emerged, heading for the lift. On seeing Robinson they would stare. He kept his eyes glued to the page. First Uncle had briefed him on what he was to say if challenged: that he wished to see Miss Verity Newland in person and could not confide his business in another party. All the same, he was glad that no one spoke to him.

He couldn't understand what he was doing here. If Uncle wanted to talk with this *ang moh* ('red-heads' was what most Chinese called Caucasians when no Caucasians were in earshot), why couldn't he just pick up the phone, or make an appointment like anyone else? But every time such thoughts surfaced Robinson stuffed them back in the part of his brain where he kept all his un-Singaporean sentiments, such as irreverence for his parents, and love of nicotine, and lust for Daisy Chan in the next highest grade.

It was gone seven o'clock when the doors opened and an *ang moh* lady came out, holding a bunch of keys. Robinson's heart quickened. Uncle had told him only one white woman worked here, so this had to be Miss Newland. She locked the doors and approached the elevators, dropping the keys into her handbag. She caught sight of him and her eyebrows rose. He waited for her to speak, too nervous to take the initiative. But she merely pressed the call button and turned her back on him.

Robinson struggled to find some way of breaking an impasse that wasn't in his uncle's script. But then a soft 'ping' announced the arrival of the elevator; the lady was passing through, any second now the doors would close . . .

The lady, aware of a voice behind her croaking an approximation of her name, blocked the doors. 'Did you say something?' she asked Robinson.

'Miss Newland?'

'Yes.'

'I have something for you.'

She came out of the lift and stared down at him.

'A letter. From my uncle.'

'Well, why didn't you leave it with my secretary, then?'

'He said I was to give it to you personally.'

'Who is your uncle?'

'Tang Gui Wen.'

For a moment she just stood there, her face void of all expression. Then her eyes narrowed, as if some far-off memory had crystallized in her mind.

'You'd better come in,' she said.

She unlocked the double doors and stood aside, one hand extended in what was meant to be a welcome. But Robinson felt his heart beating faster and faster now; he did not want to pass through those doors, however high tech they were.

'Come along,' she called, in a voice that brooked no denial. Robinson felt his feet dragging him along the corridor towards her. Just in time he remembered to pick up his cello-case.

Miss Newland switched on some lights to reveal a reception area done out in pale wood. Beyond that was a huge room filled with banks of computers extending as far as the distant windows. She crossed to another door on the far side and unlocked it. Once inside her office she switched on more lights, making Robinson blink. He had never seen such a white room: white everywhere, enlivened by only the merest touches of colour.

'Sit there,' she said, walking over to sit behind her desk.

Robinson lowered himself on to the sofa she'd pointed out. The cello-case rested awkwardly half on the cushions and half on the floor. He opened it. This time he ignored the novel and his maths homework, concentrating solely on the big brown envelope, bearing neither name nor address. His fingers told him that there was an enclosure; from its shape and thickness he guessed another letter, but couldn't be sure.

'Give it to me, then.'

He looked up with a start. He hadn't heard Miss Newland approach across the soft white carpet. She took the manila envelope and slowly walked back to her desk. She seemed in no hurry to read the letter, turning it over and over, feeling it with her fingers, even holding it up to the light. She appeared to have forgotten him. Robinson found his attention straying. There were two portraits on the wall behind him, directly opposite the *ang moh* lady's desk. He swivelled around in an attempt to see them.

The left-hand one was of a woman, with no discernible expression, wearing the sort of clothes he'd seen in European history books.

'She's pretty, don't you think so?'

He jerked around with a guilty start, his face full of the blood of embarrassment. 'Yes,' he agreed politely; although he didn't think so really.

'She was a witch,' Miss Newland said, watching to see his reaction. When he said nothing, she went on, 'They burned her. In sixteen-eighty. During the reign of Louis XIV: you've heard of him?'

'Oh, yes.'

'Her name was La Voisin. She poisoned people. The other picture's thought to be a portrait of Gerardius Brazet. An Italian.' She paused. 'He poisoned people, too.'

96

She went back to examining the letter. Robinson again squirmed around to examine the pictures above him. La Voisin was particularly fascinating. He didn't believe in witches, of course, but if there were such people then she would indubitably have qualified, with her cold, blank eyes. To be burned alive, how horrible! And they said *Chinese* people were superstitious!

He wished he could go. The sofa was dreadfully uncomfortable. It sagged in all the wrong places, and every time he shifted position the cushion covers made a slightly rude noise.

He found his eyes drawn to one of the few traces of colour in this white tomb of a room: a large ornamental plant, with dark green and maroon leaves, and little spiny green fruits dangling from its branches.

'You see those fruity things?'

She was watching him again, Robinson discovered. He nodded.

'You can make castor oil out of them.'

How extraordinary that Miss Newland should have an oil-producing plant in her office! And portraits of poisoners, too. She was like a character in a Jeyaratnam novel, all contradictions and dark corners. But what on earth could First Uncle's business be with her?

He stood up, glad to be off the sofa, and trotted over to the plant.

'*Don't* . . . touch it.'

Her voice stung him. He stopped dead. When he turned he discovered her stare transfixing him like a beam of bright light. Suddenly she seemed cruel and old.

'It's poisonous,' she explained gently. 'The whole plant. All of it.'

There was a silence.

'You can go now,' she said, rising.

He slung his cello-case over his shoulder and followed

her across the big office to the double doors. She pressed
the lift-button. As the quiet 'ping' sounded through the
foyer she said, 'I have no message for your uncle.
Goodbye.'

Panic suddenly gripped the boy. Suppose Uncle Tang
expected a reply? How could she know there was no
reply when she hadn't even bothered to open the outer
envelope? In his apartment First Uncle had a *teng tiao*,
a bamboo cane, hanging from a hook on the wall;
Robinson had never felt its weight across his back,
but . . .

He really needed that smoke now. He stepped into the
lift; the doors closed. He pressed the button. Down,
down, down . . . Spaceman Tang was descending
through the heat of the Earth's atmosphere to what he
hoped would be a soft landing on a planet where the
people weren't made of steel . . .

*

Verity Newland locked the outer doors before going back
to her own office, which she also locked from the inside.
She sat down at the desk and for a while allowed herself
to contemplate the boy, wondering how much of a threat
he posed and what she might do about him. But she
couldn't put off opening the letter for ever. With a series
of decisive movements she snatched it up and slit it with
a stainless steel *kris*.

*My dear Verity*, she read. Her hand shook, the paper
quivered and was still. *You will be surprised to hear from
me, I know, after all this time, but I have decided to come to
Singapore and thought I would give you advance warning of
my plans. Sadly, I am now a widower. I need money. It is time
for me to sell the House of Orchids . . .*

The paper slid from her hands. She rested an elbow on
the desk's plate glass and let her forehead fall against her
palm for support. Her eyes closed, her heart beat fast;

her face turned the same bloodless hue as the walls that encaged her with wild memories.

* * *

'Trouble is, Singapore's a dump,' Gerry Reynolds said, with the comfortable assurance of a man who has the exclusive Tanglin Club's rich, expatriate membership solidly on his side. 'It's nineteen seventy-one out there, brave new world a'coming, and everybody still thinks of this place as the nipple on the twat of Malaya.'

Verity Newland knew better than to attempt to staunch her M.D. in full, self-righteous flow.

'And they're right,' he continued, leaning back in his swivel chair, resting his neck back against clasped hands and putting his feet on the desk. 'We're both wasting our lives here, my dear, in this sink of ineptitude. Take you, for instance: chartered accountant, managerial qualifications and, as of last month, deputy regional managing director, Harchem Far East. A pleasure working with you, no, really. But we're not going to reinvent the wheel.'

They were in Reynolds' office at Harchem's HQ, not far from Raffles Quay, keeping as still as possible because it was July, the hottest month, and the air-conditioner was rudimentary. She'd requested a meeting to discuss product development; they'd started at three, now it was almost six thirty, and they'd been skating around an illusory issue because the real one, the Humpty Dumpty 'Who's master?' issue, was too frightening. Reynolds, a stocky man in his mid-forties with a nice line in lightweight tropical suits, would not give way, and he had the board on his side. Things had changed; Reynolds hadn't. He and Verity both lived in the same Singapore, but on different planets.

'Product ninety-three twelve,' she said wearily, 'could be a gold mine for us.'

99

'Could, but won't.' Reynolds sat up, taking his feet off the desk and smiled at her. 'I spoke to Anthony Powis last week and he's adamant. Bugs 'n' Gas are for the other fellah. Won't have chemarms at any price.'

'Ninety-three twelve,' she persisted, 'is a fertilizer, should anyone ask.'

'Which, with a touch of the right engineering, kills more than it grows. And I don't need it, my dear, I really do not. Not with the Singapore inspectorate sniffing around my heels every blessed Monday morning, not with tax breaks to forfeit and key personnel to be shipped home without reason assigned. To come back to where we started: Singapore is one, big bloody dump.' He leaned back in his chair, holding the tips of a pencil between soft fingers, and he smiled at her. 'No new products. Not this year. Not any other year. Wrong time. Wrong place.'

'So it's back to paint?'

'Maritime paint, my dear, is one of our biggest markets. *Right* time and place. Now there's something Singapore's good for: shipbuilding, ship repairing, chandlering. Did you know that last year we sold exactly twice the amount of marine paint for ships' bottoms as Europe Division, and it's nearly *sixteen times larger than we are*?'

She did know that.

'Lot of money in ships' bottoms,' he said sagely. 'Bottoms is the name of the game, here in Singapore.' He chortled, and she knew he was already editing this conversation for a replay in the club later that evening. She looked at her watch. She could fancy a drink herself: something long. Fruit punch with a punch in it. She was tired, she was thirsty, she felt frustrated, and not only with Reynolds the Complacent. Her body craved attention.

'It's late,' she said, her voice cracking with fatigue. And then, because she was a political animal, she added,

'Thank you very much for this opportunity to let off steam, Gerry. It does make such a difference.'

Old-style gentleman that he fancied himself to be, Reynolds stood up to show her out – she knew they'd taught him things like that at Wellington and regretted intensely they hadn't gone the whole hog, instilling knowledge of when to commit suicide. She left without bothering to go back to her own office because there might have been calls to return and she couldn't face that. She picked her way through the building site that this part of the quay had become to find her car, parked next to the water, overlooking Clifford Pier. Her needs were growing now, expanding inside her like a virus. She pulled away with a squeal of tyres, and headed north.

She was out of the city in less than no time, her headlights picking up only the occasional sarong-clad worker trudging home through the jungle, or perhaps some lithe animal scuttling across the road. Signs were few and far between, but Verity knew where to go. There was light at the end of this particular tunnel, beautiful, intense light, that drew her on like a magnet, so that her foot pressed ever harder down on the throttle and she took chances that somehow seemed less chancy in the dark.

Lim Chu Kang Road petered out into a track, causing her to slow a little. But she knew that a hundred yards further on there was a turning, and once she had made that turning she would find herself on a well-made drive. A couple of paraffin lanterns winked away to her left, where the servants had their own *kampong*-settlement, a final turn . . . and there, lit from top to bottom like a monument, was *Rumah Anggerik*, the House of Orchids.

She screeched to a halt beside Jay's Aston Martin, already reaching into her handbag for the silver-plated *risis* orchid brooch, a gift from Jay too good to be worn at work. Tubby old Ibrahim was at the front door to greet her, a smile splitting his homely face, with its luxuriant, curly moustache and round pimple of a nose; as she adjusted her brooch she spoke a few words to him, scarcely conscious of what she said, because the virus had her in its grip now and she could not contain herself. She rushed up the stairs, along the landing to the corner suite . . . but Jay was not in his bedroom. Splashing noises told her he was taking a shower.

Verity flung herself down on the wide bed, relishing the feel of cool, crisp linen against her skin. Above her, the fan turned and turned, soothing her into a state of calm, each mahogany blade visible as a blurred wing-shape, reminding her of old bioscopes, better times.

She loved this room almost as much as its owner. It was unmistakably oriental in character, with enough Thai brass, and Indonesian silver, and bamboo-framed photographs on iroko-wood dressers to satisfy the most demanding tourist in search of the gorgeous East. But Jay had softened it with touches of Western comfort. There was his rocking-chair in the corner, the one he'd had made by a local craftsman, because (he said) he liked to make love to a woman on a rocking-chair. The sturdy sofa by the window had come from San Francisco, but it blended with everything else, even the light cotton curtains swept back in French style, with ties, so as not to obstruct his view of the strait. Amidst all the delightful clutter, the occasional tables with their floor-length Japanese cloths; the vases full of rose myrtle, and flame-of-the-forest and the beautiful orchid known as Bangsaen beauty; the small, cut-glass decanters containing his aftershave and cologne in their solid teak frame; amidst all this, only two things irked her, reminding her, as they did, that here was the room of a man who merely camped out in Asia: a portable typewriter on a desk placed before the second window, shaded from the early morning sun by a huge rain tree in the garden outside; and an electric coffee-making machine beside the bed.

She rolled over to look at the machine. The pot contained dark brown dregs: his favourite blend of mocha and Kenyan, no doubt. She made a long arm, opening a drawer in the nearly white Jelutong-wood cabinet on which the coffee-maker stood, and pulled out a packet of condoms. Verity counted. Five. She made a face. She was almost certain that there'd been five left after last time, *almost* . . . but some of his other women would be on the pill, some wouldn't give a damn anyway.

Verity stripped a condom out of its foil wrapper and tucked it under the pillow. When Jay emerged from the bathroom she was smiling.

'Hello,' he said. 'I didn't hear you come in.'

'You were sterilizing your equipment.'

He grinned. He had on nothing but a towel, and he wasn't even wearing that in a conventional sense: it lay slung over his shoulder, the visible end hanging almost, not quite, to his genitals. He leaned against the door jamb, arms crossed over his chest and folding one knee so that the toes of his right foot rested on the floor. Verity sat up. She took a long, hard look at what was on offer and found it perfect.

His dark skin always looked as if it had recently been oiled, lightly, even when he'd just stepped out of the shower. He had a wonderful head of hair, the same black-lacquer tint as Chinese hair, well cared for and neat. Tanned and muscular men had always appealed to Verity, but she'd never had one who so closely met all her requirements. His hard stomach was indented at the sides by two vertical clefts, a couple of inches long: they fascinated her, and he said they were natural, he'd had them since after his first year's weight-training, when he was eighteen. The skin around them was soft, but the insides of the clefts were rubbery-hard; her tongue knew that.

'It suits you,' he murmured, gesturing at the *risis* orchid brooch.

'It suits you,' she mimicked, her eyes drifting below the level of his waist. 'Come here, I want to explore.'

He allowed the towel to slide from his shoulder and advanced. He lay down beside Verity, took her in his arms and kissed her. All the troubles of the day seemed to lift off her shoulders when she gave herself up to that kiss. After a while she pushed him away and held his face between her palms, seeking to read his eyes. They were friendly, amused; nothing more. But when her gaze strayed down his body they found the evidence she craved. Whatever his eyes might say, the body could not lie. Jay still *wanted* her, even though she'd been his mistress for three years now.

She freed herself from his embrace and slipped out of her clothes. When she came back to bed she artfully made sure that her head ended up by his feet, which she proceeded to kiss, toe by succulent toe. She began to work her way up his legs, sampling a black hair here, a brown one there. But when she neared her goal she backed off, teasing him, making him laugh, while he played gently with her behind.

Using her toes, Verity felt beneath the pillow for the condom she'd unwrapped earlier. Jay's mouth was on her thigh now and she knew he couldn't see what she was doing. She folded back her leg until she was able to reach behind her for the condom clasped between her toes. She slipped it into her mouth, as he had taught her. She clutched him firmly, enjoying his gasp of surprise, and used her mouth to unroll the condom down his shaft, taking him into the back of her throat . . .

'Armed,' she said drowsily, as she withdrew, 'and ready to fire . . .'

*

Afterwards he lit cigarettes for them both and they lay side by side on the bed, watching the fan mingle their smoke before sucking it up into nothingness.

'You've been away,' she said. She'd worked on her delivery, but still it came out as an accusation. 'I called,' she went on. 'Ibrahim was vague.'

Jay laughed. 'Good old Ibrahim.'

'Anywhere exciting?'

'Baghdad.'

'Business?'

'And a little pleasure.'

She took a vicious drag on her cigarette. 'How nice. Pass me that ashtray, will you?'

He got up and handed her the ornate brass ashtray he'd brought back from Calcutta the year before, after one of his trips. She expected him to come and lie beside her again, but instead he picked up his towel and headed for the bathroom. Moments later she heard the swish of the shower. Cleanliness was next to obsession, with Jay.

Spurred by jealousy she tiptoed across to his desk and opened the central drawer, where she knew he kept his passport. It was furry around the edges, battered by much use. Saigon, Baghdad, Damascus, Bahrain, Baghdad . . . she flicked through the pages . . . Baghdad, Oman . . .

Why this fascination with Iraq? she wondered, putting the passport back.

She had a mental picture of Jay, but it was like the passport: fuzzy around the edges. All she really knew about him for sure could be distilled into two propositions: first, he bought and sold industrial secrets as other men might buy and sell sheep; secondly, she was hopelessly in love with him and had been since the day they'd met.

Of course he did not advertise the fact that he was an industrial spy; as far as society gossip went, he was known to be 'in property', he traded extensively with Vietnam and Cambodia, he enjoyed a grand lifestyle. All of which was true. He'd based himself in Singapore for the last six years; before that, Hong Kong. He was close to the Pentagon, or so people said; certainly she had seen him around with men in crew-cuts and starched, bottle-green uniforms and dark glasses they never took off. And that was it, really. She'd long ago given up asking him direct questions which he knew how to skirt, effortlessly. So funny, in Singapore, where everyone knew every-thing about a newcomer within a month of his arrival. But Jay always had to be different.

He knew all there was to know about her, of course; that white was her favourite colour, she hated dogs and loved cats, her mother's name had been Bertha but everyone called her Bertie . . .

'Hungry?' he said, and she turned, startled, to find him standing by the bed, sorting through underwear.

'So-so. I'd love a drink; something strong.'

'Bad day?'

'Grim. Let me wash . . .'

When she came out of the bathroom he was fully dressed, standing with one hand in his pocket, staring out into the night, smoking.

'I've got something for you,' she said, trying not to betray her fear. 'It's in my bag, the envelope . . .'

While she dressed, trying hard not to steal constant glances at him, he examined the contents of her precious envelope.

'I nearly got caught,' she said. 'That idiot Forward. He's too keen, that's his trouble; always poking around late at night . . . I was using the copier, in the dark, and sud-denly the lights all came on, and –'

'This is a nutrient?' he enquired thoughtfully.

'Yes. A new kind of animal foodstuff. Cattle-cake, we think.'

'Chicken feed.'

She had been putting up her hair, but on hearing his words she stopped, transfixed by her expression in the

106

mirror. Terror. Stark, raving terror. She pulled herself together.

'In a way.'

He was smiling. He put the papers back in their envelope and dropped it into her bag. 'I'm afraid,' he said, 'the chicken-feed market is awfully quiet, right now.'

For a moment she remained silent. Then – 'Bottoms,' she burst out. 'In Singapore, that's the name of the game, right?'

'I'm sorry?'

'Oh, it doesn't matter, it doesn't matter a damn, here, help me with this, will you, I can't get my ribbon straight.' She stood there helplessly, letting him do a better job than she ever could. 'Forward's a berk,' she said to her reflection. 'Always having to be wet-nursed, always wanting my advice. He's sick- . . . sick, what's the word?'

'Sycophantic?'

She nodded. 'Ow!'

'Don't move your head. Keep still. There. Now . . . a drink. I'll fetch something upstairs. Pimm's?'

'Mm, lovely. Make mine strong.'

He came back ten minutes later, bearing a silver tray on which stood a pitcher of Pimm's No. 1, ice and a soda siphon.

'If it's too strong I can change it,' he said, handing her a glass.

But it was just right. Jay knew about drinks. He knew about simply *everything*. Except love. Verity felt tears sting her eyes. 'I'm thinking of moving,' she said brusquely, dashing them away.

'I promise not to gazump you this time,' he said, sitting down next to her on the sofa and reaching out to stroke the back of her head.

In spite of herself, she smiled. They'd first met three years ago at the Urban Renewal Authority's downtown

107

offices, both checking whether a particular site in Serangoon had residential zoning permission. They'd stood at the counter, side by side, him going first, and she'd heard him ask for the plot-plans she herself intended to requisition, and there, in front of the clerk, they'd had a fine old row, which ended with him taking her to lunch at Raffles Hotel. By three o'clock, they were back at the House of Orchids and in bed. At five he excused himself, saying he had to make a phone call. At five thirty he'd come back, looking smug. He'd arranged to buy the site on which she'd set her heart, the perfect place to build a bungalow for herself, and for Bertie whenever she came out. And by then Verity simply did not give a damn. That was Jay.

'So why are you moving?' he asked, continuing to stroke her hair.

'Oh, I don't know.' She let herself rest back against the pressure of his hand, but tonight it somehow served only to enhance her malaise. 'I need a change. I might even go home to England.'

His hand did not break its regular rhythm. He doesn't care, she thought, and felt sick. To give up three years of your life to a hero and find he was the villain after all.

'What's in England?' he said. 'Apart from the cuisine and the weather?'

She shrugged and then, after a pause, said the one foolish thing she knew she should avoid: 'Will you miss me?'

'Of course; Singapore won't be the same without you.'

'Won't,' she thought bitterly, not 'wouldn't'. I'm already history. A single light moved across her field of vision, ploughing the Johor Strait that cut Singapore off from Malaysia, followed seconds later by the chug-chug of an engine. A *tong kang* lighter, threading its way through the bamboo *kelong* fishing-traps: for an absurd moment she wished she were aboard, were anywhere but here.

If it must end, let it be broken.

'I've done everything for you,' she said. 'I've sat by the phone night after night, cooked meals you never showed up to eat. I've brought you Harchem's secrets, sold myself to you. I'm your bondwoman, Jay. Won't you even fight for me a little?'

The final words ended in a sob; she buried her head in his chest and wept while he continued to stroke her hair. At last she sat up and dried her eyes. 'I love you,' she said.

His silence told her many things. Most important: that she was not loved in return.

'What would I have to do,' she said, 'to make you open your heart and take me in? Only I'm asking, you see. It's not a rhetorical question. Tell me and I'll do it.'

He grunted, embarrassed perhaps, and for the first time his hand faltered. 'Oh, darling . . .' he began.

'No. None of that. Listen: you've never written me a love letter. Not one.'

'It's not something I do.'

'Why not? Afraid of putting it in writing?'

He smiled, but made no other reply.

'Tell me,' she repeated. 'What is it you want?'

When he stood up she grabbed him, because by leaving he made her not tragic but pathetic.

'It doesn't work like that.' He removed her hand. 'I'm sorry.'

'Is there somebody else? Is that it?'

He moved away from her, his cloth-soled Chinese shoes making scarcely a sound on the polished teak floor. Verity wanted to scream. It couldn't be ending like this, *couldn't*, because that would kill her. He was, she realized, saying goodbye. He expected her to leave quietly, not disturbing the servants, allowing his beautiful house with its impeccable routines to resume its even tenor: she was nothing more than a stone that had broken the surface of a lake, causing ripples for a pitifully few moments.

'What do you know,' she heard herself say, 'about defoliants?'

In the silence that followed she became aware of her heartbeat ramming blood through her veins. She felt faint. With all the intensity she could summon, she listened for sounds.

He was sitting down beside her.

'What kind of defoliants?' he asked.

'The worst kind. What they tried to make out of Agent Orange and failed. Something that can strip a sixty-foot-high tree's top canopy in twelve hours.'

'You know of such a thing?'

'We have it in the safe. Reynolds's got the key. But I know the formula.'

He said nothing for a while. She stole a glance at his face from under her eyelashes, but could read nothing there.

'How?' he said at last. No warmth, just light curiosity.

'Out at Sudong, we have a research laboratory. There's a man there called Raj, we call him Reggie. He's brilliant. Reynolds keeps him working at pesticides and paint, but he's only interested in poisons. He got a PhD in toxicology. From Russia.'

'Russia?' And now, yes, there was a tremor of interest in his voice.

'The Institute of Microbiology and Virology at Kiev. His thesis was on the biosynthesis of T2 toxins, derived from grain.'

'Go on.'

'He'd won some kind of scholarship and the Indian government let him take it up. After he came back he tried to get a job in America, but they wouldn't accept him. So he ended up with us, developing marine paint and domestic household cleaners. But nobody really knows what Raj gets up to in that laboratory of his. Back in nineteen sixty-eight, he was working on plant nutrients that could be absorbed through spraying.'

Jay stirred restlessly in his seat and was still.

'We had terrific interest from all over South-East Asia.'

'I'll bet,' he said impatiently. 'What happened?'

'Reggie came up with an effective but highly unstable defoliant. What made it so different, and so brilliant, was his discovery of the perfect delivery agent: something that would "weight" the chemical as it fell, keeping it all together, enabling it to be targeted to within a few metres. Do you understand me, Jay? Do you see where I'm leading?'

'The US stopped defoliating in Vietnam earlier this year because –'

'Because the Ranch Hand pilots weren't getting the stuff to target, yes, but also because when Agent Orange, Agent White, all the crap they were spraying, when it hit the trees, it stopped. It stopped right there, in the upper canopy, leaving thirty or forty feet of dense leaves below. And the Viet Cong, on the jungle floor, laughed at them. But Reggie's toxin was so heavy that it *sank*. It went right on penetrating, impervious to wind and sunlight, until it hit the soil, and when it got there *it went right on sinking*.'

When Jay stood up this time it was to pace around the room, cracking his knuckles, pausing to pick up some object or bang a fist against the wall.

'Why haven't I heard of this?' he said, suddenly rounding on her.

'Because Reynolds suppressed it. On orders from Powis himself.'

*'Why?'*

'He would not soil his hands with it. Nothing military, and besides, they didn't have a market open to them. They didn't know where to start. It would all have been too much like hard work. Gerry would have had to cancel his bridge evening at the Tanglin, out of the question.'

She stood up, and advanced slowly towards him. 'Product ninety-three twelve,' she said, 'is . . . *inconsistent* . . . with plant life.'

He stared at her, but she knew he could not see her. His mind was elsewhere, in a land of opportunity that she had never seen. Her heart beat strongly, but not from fear. From hope.

'Raj told you all this?' he said at last.

'Everything. He was breaking up. His life's work, thrown out with the trash. Reynolds had him in, told him that he was locking the formula and the research papers away and he wasn't to talk about it to anyone.' She spat out the next words. 'He was to get back to *paint*!'

There was a long silence. Verity broke it. 'What would they pay for ninety-three twelve,' she said quietly, 'in Washington?'

Slowly his eyes refocused on her. He chose to answer her question with one of his own. 'Do you know,' he said, 'how many bullets it takes to kill one Viet Cong?' When she shook her head, he went on: 'Fifty thousand. Fifty thousand rounds, just to put away a little guy in pyjamas and shoes made from worn-out tyres. All because the US doesn't have a defoliant that works.'

She stared at him, awed into silence.

'You'll have to start thinking globally,' he said, with a strange smile on his face.

The heart that had been thundering along so recklessly missed a beat. Verity held a hand to her chest. 'Me?'

'We'll need to form a company,' he said, and now he was brisk. 'Fifty-fifty: the Caymans, I think, or maybe Netherlands Antilles. And start working on Raj, but softly, darling, softly. I need time to plan.'

He came towards her, opening his arms. For a moment she just stood there, gazing at him stupidly. Then she let

112

herself fall into his embrace with a little sob of relief. All the tensions that had racked her during the past half hour dissolved away. She would be ill after this, she knew, but that was tomorrow's problem. What mattered for now was that she had turned despair into triumph with a sort of mystical alchemy of which Reggie Raj himself might have been proud.

And the best thing, she thought, as Jay carried her over to the bed, was that she hadn't had to tell him how Reggie was developing product ninety-three twelve: a realm so frightening that it gave her nightmares. She'd keep that to herself for a while. Just in case Jay got any wrong ideas.

# II

# SIX

Martin Heaney had an office to himself on the first floor of an imposing building in South Audley Street, not far from the American Embassy. The building itself was all that could be desired: a dignified composition of orange-red brickwork and white stone facings with an air about it of having been designed by a man who wrote Dungeons and Dragons fiction in his spare time. The ground floor housed one of those art galleries so discreet that nobody could ever be certain whether it was open or not, or whether the *objets d'art* inside were for sale or merely part of the décor.

On the first floor, however, things changed. Anyone who entered Martin's room knew at once that this wasn't the inner sanctum of a fine art professional. Numerous touches told the same story: the metal desk, somewhere indefinably between green and grey in hue, the matching chair, DIY shelving, dusty files on the floor, telephone that hadn't been cleaned in months, Grundig dictaphone (1970s vintage), strip lighting, yellowing net curtains. Gumment, as Martin's father would have said. (The Heaneys originally hailed from Bradford; his dad got a job driving the new diesels into King's Cross and they'd moved to Camden Town.) Government service. OHMS. Overtime Hoodwinks Misery 'n' Shite.

It being eleven forty-ish in the morning, Martin was at his desk. Those who knew his routine made a point of calling him between eleven thirty a.m. and twelve fifteen, because he was usually in then. He worked flexi-hours, but usually came to work around ten, carrying a polystyrene cup of weak, sugary tea from the Italian place around the corner and a pack of Bensons. By the time he'd cleared away yesterday's files he'd be ready for elevenses: more tea but this time around the corner, without the need for polystyrene, since 'Vanni had picked up this job lot of really very decent china in Petticoat Lane. Between eleven thirty and twelve fifteen, Martin worked. Lunch at one of several nearby pubs followed. Two to three was siesta-time, although being in gumment Martin did not actually sleep, he did the *Daily Telegraph* crossword. The rest of the day varied, but if there were phone calls to be made, for example, he'd make them post-crossword, cheap rate, in accordance with current guidelines, and if there were analyses to be dictated this would be the time for them also.

He was forty-two and most people would have said that, what with London weighting, flexitime, guaranteed holidays and index-linked pension, he was doing all right. Martin Heaney didn't see it that way.

At eleven forty this particular morning, Martin's desktop was covered with eighteen typewritten reports and a page from a gay newspaper called *Boyz*. He was matching the reports to the advertisements in the paper, all of which were for masseurs. Lee, beautiful young oriental, will relax you like never before . . . now who had drawn *that* lovely little short straw in last week's raffle . . . ah, yes. Tony. Our Tone. And what did he have to say . . . ?

Martin rummaged among the eighteen reports until he found Our Tone. Our Tone, of course, had not actually sampled the goods, but he'd kept them under surveillance to see who did. Martin's highlighter hovered anxiously, ready to peck down at a misbehaving MP or a married judge who should know better. No luck. Ah well, what's next? Troy, Australian, knows you need a firm hand . . .

At least his present job was seasonal; there would be

something else to do next month. It used to be much worse. Once upon a time, Martin Heaney serviced the night-club run, sitting in a radio-car down an alley off Charing Cross Road with a thermos of sweet tea and a Browning automatic, waiting for his sweepers to report in or get into trouble. That wasn't seasonal, that was eternal. Things had improved a little since then. Now when he went home April no longer sniffed and asked him why he'd taken to wearing scent. She no longer cried at weekends. A good girl, was April. He really ought to think about marrying her sometime. He should.

He used to ask himself: how did I arrive at this terminal pass, what am I doing, why should I live? Now he got on with his analyses, taking raw material supplied by the likes of Our Tone and shaping them into prose fit for perusal in Gower Street. The 'Our' in Our Tone stood for MI5's.

His phone rang. Without looking up, Martin lifted the receiver. 'Hello.'

The voice at the other end spoke. Martin sat perfectly still. He'd not heard this voice for seventeen years, had expected, confidently, never to hear it again. When at last the voice ceased, he waited a moment before clearing his throat.

'I don't think this is a good idea, Mr Grindle.'

The voice snapped a dozen more words. The line went dead. Martin held his free hand to his forehead and rubbed it gently a few times, the telephone clasped to his chest. Slowly he replaced it. He stood up and lifted his Marks and Sparks suit jacket from the back of his chair. He tightened his tie. He went through to the washroom at the back and tidied his ginger hair, running a comb through it a few times while he surveyed his pale, heavily freckled reflection and tried to impose a little order on his feelings.

He sloped off down the stairs, heading for Gower Street and a past he'd thought was buried.

*

At about the same time, Iain Forward was doing the washing up at Aural Sightings' Lavender Hill offices. He worked quickly. Everything he did, he did well. He kept his face to the wall, even when somebody came to dump another cup in the sink, though on those occasions he always smiled and, if the person spoke to him, he replied politely. Years in prison had taught him how to conceal; nobody knew he was nursing his rage.

'Iain, would you mind cleaning a few tapes, once you've done that?'

Simon's voice. Simon was the man in day-to-day charge; the production manager to whom Iain 'reported'. For this was a properly run charitable organization: a limited company, with a chief who 'combined the roles' of chairman and chief executive, and a managing director under him, and a production manager equal in the pecking order with an editorial manager. And unpaid volunteers who came in each day to record the newspapers and magazines on to tapes which then were copied for dispatch to blind subscribers. And a commercial 'arm', which recorded in-house magazines for trade unions and banks, for 'profit', which somehow never quite materialized. And Iain loathed all this with a passion. Especially he loathed Simon: the liberal-minded arsehole with a kindly smile who'd pushed his chairman and chief executive to employ the murderer, Iain Forward.

'Certainly, Simon. I'm just finished . . . '

Keeping the same tight smile on his face, Iain folded the dish-cloth, placed it over the rail and walked over to the other side of the large, open-plan industrial unit where Aural Sightings did good works for the visually challenged. Against the wall, on a table, was a wooden box with a grooved formica top. Above it was posted a warning: 'IF YOU HAVE A PACEMAKER OR WRISTWATCH DO NOT COME NEAR THIS MACHINE'. Iain pressed a switch on the side of the box. It began to hum. He lifted a carton of cassettes on to the table and began to pass tapes over the top of the whirring box, from right to left. This blanked the cassettes. Blanked his brain, too.

Light manual work; the sort of thing they loved 'inside'. He'd hated it then and he hated it now. He was an intelligent professional with a contribution to make, yet here he stood . . . one tape, two tapes, three, four . . .

He thought he'd be invited to make recordings for them. He didn't realize how his voice had lowered and coarsened during the years inside. Funny: as a con, he'd been something. A lifer, a killer, a well-respected villain. Here he was nothing.

He wasn't the only ex-con here. There was a girl who'd done three months for shoplifting. And there was a man who'd been inside, Iain could tell, but nobody else knew. He'd often felt an urge to come up behind young Kenny, ram a finger into his spine, say, 'You're under obbo, my son.' Watch him jump. Watch him shit his pants.

He erased a hundred cassettes, maybe more, before Simon suggested he might like to change to the Graff multi-recorders, machines which could make eleven copies from a single master tape, all at high speed. Iain shifted to the benches where the multis were set up. He arranged blank cassettes in stacks of eleven and selected one of the masters from the heap awaiting copying. He put it on the top left set of spools and checked for sound-level: music blared out, followed by: 'Hello, and welcome to the *Independent*, brought to you by Aural Sightings . . .' That's enough. Using one hand, he dealt a stack of eleven cassettes on to the machine and set it going. He glanced up at the clock. Another five hours of this. Lunch soon, though.

He daydreamed a lot. There was no brain-work, nothing intellectual about it. Today, his mind was on Singapore. Harchem had been a bit like this, in its emphasis on corporate structure and routines: who was 'reporting' to whom, whose responsibility was this and whose that . . .

Lunchtime.

Iain wanted to smoke, so he had to go out; smoking was forbidden on the premises, the fire risk too great. On his way to the door he passed the room where staff took their coffee-breaks. Linda was there, as usual. Linda had her knitting out, as usual. Iain didn't know what Linda was supposed to do at Aural Sightings, unless perhaps she was employed to knit cassette-covers. She wore white-rimmed spectacles in an attempt to make her dowdy face interesting, and she was a right old jewellery queen. Every one of her fingers sported at least one thick ring, many of them set with precious stones, and on her left ankle she wore a gold-link chain. Who does she think she is? he thought in a burst of anger, as he passed the door and heard the click of needles.

'. . . got to be a bit careful, with them around.'

Linda's voice. She looked up quickly as Iain passed, and fell silent. Iain heard another woman say, 'Mmmm,' all long and drawn out, as if she were anxious not to take sides. Or maybe she was frightened of the murderer they'd been discussing a moment ago, before they'd woken up to his presence?

He didn't care. Sod them all. There'd be a war soon, see how they liked that! On the telly he'd seen 'No Blood for Oil' demos in Kensington, but chance would be a fine thing: there *would* be a war, killing would come back into fashion, murderers like him would be at a premium. Name his own price, he could . . .

He'd smoke his burn and take a breather before eating his sandwich and getting back to work five minutes before time; he'd show 'em up. Lazy bastards, all. Five minutes shaved here, ten clipped off there; call that *work*?

He walked up the hill to the traffic-lights, then turned left, making for the common. In the Singapore of 1971, they'd worked. Even the expats. Alison had been rushed off her feet most days, she'd confided in him while they were eating dinner a week after his mishap in the Prince Hotel . . .

*     *     *

He'd seen a lot of Alison in one week, enough to know he was falling in love with her. She didn't seem to mind. It was nice, she said, to have a stranger to show all the sights to, it made a change. They borrowed a car and drove around the island, visiting places the tourists never saw. She showed him the Ice Palace, off Lower Serangoon Road near the junction with Bukit Timah, where she would go to skate lazy circles and figures of eight: a cheap, fun way of keeping cool. One evening they popped over the causeway for dinner in Johor Bahru: Iain had never had to take his passport out to dinner before, it felt a touch risqué. Tonight they'd arranged to meet at the Jumbo Seafood Restaurant off the east coast road.

'I shan't be able to do this next week,' she said, as they prowled between the tanks, sorting out what to eat. 'Night shift.'

He felt a twinge of pain. Not disappointment, pain. Life with Alison was . . . well, just that: life.

'I'm sorry,' he said. 'When will we be able to meet?'

'Do you like Drunken Prawns . . . oh, during the afternoon, if you're free before six. That's when I start my shift.'

'Oh.' He left the office at six. Verity Newland had caught him slipping out at a quarter to, once. (He'd been on his way to meet Alison, naturally.) They'd had a row, right there in the corridor, for all the staff to hear. In local parlance, Verity had caused him to lose face; more straightforwardly, she'd cut his balls off.

'Then it's going to be difficult,' he said. By now they were seated at their table, waiting for the freshly cooked seafood to be brought to them. He poured Moselle. 'I'm going to miss you.'

'It's only for a week,' she said. 'I get three days off then.'

'I'm going to miss you,' he repeated, gazing into her eyes. She smiled sweetly, but he couldn't tell what she really felt.

'You're a busy man,' she said. 'You'll find a way to kill the time.'

He'd already told her that he planned to be head of Harchem one day. Funny, you could tell this girl anything and she wouldn't dream of laughing. She knew he was ambitious enough for ten.

'Overtime,' he said morosely. 'I'll impress the boss . . . if anything's *capable* of impressing her.'

Dinner came. For the most part they ate in silence. Every time Iain thought of something to say it struck him as otiose: making noise for the sake of it. Alison had no need of small-talk. She was a self-contained person, he reflected. Perhaps she didn't want a man in her life. So it surprised him when, after dinner, she said, 'Have you got time to come and visit my place? We could walk, Tosca Road's not far.'

Oh, yes, my dear: time enough for that.

The house was as she'd described it to him that first day (was it really only a week ago?), though of Dr Francis P. Ang and the Chan clan there was no sign. He fingered the number five iron, the cobra-basher, while she unlocked the various Yales and Chubbs and threw open the steel shutter-gate. No one else in, then. Accident? Or had she arranged for her 'mess-mates' to be elsewhere tonight . . .

The house was 'wee', as she put it, but comfortable, too: there were squashy cushions on the sofa, and Indian druggets, and a lot of photos in frames: snaps of horses, and brothers, and polo-players gathering on the veranda for gin-fizz. While she made coffee he stepped out into the garden, curious to see the place where the girls sunbathed while the neighbours chatted across their nubile bodies. He stood there looking at the lawn, as if it might tell him something. But then she crept up to slip an arm through his; he turned, startled, but already raising his other hand to her face, and so they had their first kiss, beneath the famous angsana tree that was 'getting too big for its roots'.

She stepped back a pace, looking archly from left to right. 'Better come in,' she whispered. 'Walls have ears, but neighbours have night vision.'

While he was outside Alison had placed scented candles around the small living room. She poured coffee for him. He deliberately chose the sofa to sit on, and when she handed him his cup, patted the cushion beside him. For a few minutes they sat there, listening to the cicadas. He wanted so much to kiss her again; he was experienced to a degree, but not with women he'd wanted to keep, and the notion of simply taking this one in his arms scared him.

She put her cup down on the table and sat forward on the edge of the sofa, half turned towards him. When he tried to smile at her, his mouth was trembling so much that the spasm spread into his cheeks; God, he must look dreadful! But she reached out to embrace him, at the same time leaning back. Because she was on the lip of the seat her neck sank down into the cushions, and her legs uncurled in front of her. As Iain moved down for the kiss his hand could scarcely avoid brushing against

125

them. She shuddered, a whimper escaped her lips, and he kissed her into silence.

'Why?' he said at last, withdrawing gently.

'Why?' She smiled. 'Why what?'

'Why this wonderful luck? What have I done that God should make me so happy?'

'You make your own luck,' she said quietly. 'Perhaps that's why I want you.'

'*Do* you want me?'

She smiled again, and at first he thought that was all the answer he'd get. But then she said, 'You're different. I don't know any men like you.'

'But surely . . .'

She shook her head. 'Expat males in this part of the world can be pretty grim. Not a brain between them, crazy about sport, no manners, no culture.'

'And me?'

'Sensitive. Intelligent. Everything I'd despaired of finding here. And . . .'

'Yes?'

She shrugged. 'You're you. That's all.'

They stayed on the sofa for about an hour. He did not know what he was doing, quite. He wanted her; she was saying as plainly as a body could speak that she was his, she wanted him, too. But this was not like anything he'd experienced before. This was *special*.

His lips felt raw. His muscles ached, both of them were hot and sweaty, the sofa grew more uncomfortable by the minute. He seemed incapable of solving any of it, so in the end it was she who sat up and said, 'Come to bed.'

'Your friends,' he whispered; 'won't they . . .'

'Out,' she said. 'Leave. Long, long leave . . . Come . . .'

'But the candles . . .'

'Come . . .'

His last words before falling asleep, some time in the

small hours, were: 'Will you marry me?' And hers . . .
'Oh, yes. *Yes!*'

\*       \*       \*

The Grand Hotel might have been grand once, but by
1990 it was no longer. It sat wedged in a kind of arm-lock
between Philbeach Gardens and the Exhibition Centre,
bounded at the back by the District Line. Five storeys tall,
it had once been the gracious town residence of a wealthy
engineer in days when an Earl's Court address still possessed a certain cachet. Now its high, generous rooms
had been divided, and sub-divided and, in the case of 'en
suite facilities', sub-sub-divided, reducing the building to
a down-at-heel beehive. On exhibition days it did good
business for the Tunisian duo who owned it; otherwise
it was quiet. Out-of-town representatives provided the
mainstay of the Grand Hotel's clientele; they were its
backbone, as it were, but an average evening would see
a few casuals making up the numbers. The place was
something of a favourite with transvestites who'd left it
too late to book a room in the Philbeach around the
corner, and occasionally the odd trick could be turned,
depending on the identity of the night manager. Mostly,
however, that was Alison Forward; because the tarts
knew her, they stayed away.

It was nine thirty in the evening when she put on her
coat and came down the shallow steps outside, pausing
to push one of the dustbins further back behind the privet
in a vain attempt at concealment. She stripped the cello-
phane off a pack of cigarettes and lit up with a match
taken from a garish pink booklet: one of the Chekib
brothers' other enterprises was a night-club called the
Pink Pussy and, unlike the Grand Hotel, that did suffici-
ently well to warrant personalized matchbooks. The reception area – well, more of a hole in the wall, really – was

plastered with fliers for the Pink Pussy, and sometimes its matches found their way in as well.

The street was quiet. Alison drew smoke deep into her lungs, mentally going over the night's figures so far. Sixty per cent occupancy was okay: above break-even. The pathetic little attempt at a French bistro in the basement had done half a dozen covers: captive audience only, that, and no more tonight. Six repeat-business, nine off the street, one with a reservation made a month ago, which was record-breaking. No single women, thank God. Alison relaxed a bit. Just let the Chekibs stay away and she'd be laughing. Ahmad had got her in the kitchen early one morning and . . . stuff it. Forget.

A man was coming down the street towards the Grand, but he had no luggage and she didn't rate him as potential trade. He wore a raincoat with its collar turned up. When he walked under a streetlight something about him seemed familiar, but she didn't recognize his face. He came to a halt at the foot of the steps and he said, 'Alison?'

For a moment she couldn't believe her ears. Then – 'Martin!' she cried. 'Is that you?'

He smiled at her. 'Yup.'

Something hard came into contact with Alison's backbone; she'd unconsciously leant against the pillar by the front door. She felt dizzy with surprise, and something more positive than surprise.

'May I come in?' Martin said.

For an instant Alison saw the hotel lobby through his eyes: the faded wallpaper, the carpet with a half-inch lining of dust where the Hoover couldn't reach . . .

'Best not,' she said; and then, hesitantly – 'Let's walk.'

She fell into step beside him. They headed for the main road, taking it slowly and keeping side by side so that neither need look at the other. After a while he slipped his hand through her arm. She didn't protest. She felt blood rising into her cheeks, and the cat that had got her tongue tightened its grip. Martin always had this effect on her.

She remembered their first meeting as clearly as her wedding day. They'd been hustled through Heathrow, she and Iain, he to one car, she to another. In the back of hers this callow young man was waiting; as she'd got in beside him he'd smiled; 'Hello,' he'd said, holding out a hand. 'I'm Martin Heaney. I'm going to be looking after you for a bit.'

Which was a fib, because his job was to interrogate her while his fellow MI5 officers worked on Iain, but even then she had liked him a little. His narrow, innocent, freckled face underneath that shock of undisciplined ginger hair always conveyed sympathy, a readiness to help, while the little bulge of tummy pushing against his shirt somehow rendered him less of a threat. His manner was a front, she realized that now of course. But at the time she'd felt he understood, that he too knew Iain was innocent of murder. He wore a troubled look that said, I don't like any of this; and as the days passed that look had deepened into genuine unhappiness.

It surprised her when he came around to visit, a year after Iain's conviction. He'd explained, gently, that 'they' had sent him to keep an eye on her; but the way he said this, his openness about it, had made her warm to him again. She'd offered him tea, suddenly remembering the way he liked it: milky, almost white in colour, barely tepid, with three sugars. She heard herself teasing him about his mini-paunch and wondered why she was making such a fool of herself.

He'd come again, twice that year, and then he'd sent his first Christmas card. She started to look forward to his visits. One year she'd received an anonymous Valentine. Was it his? She never knew, never dared ask. She tore it up that same night, afraid to leave it lying around in case she forgot it and one day Iain would get out, and perhaps find it.

After the Valentine he'd stopped coming. No word, no explanation. She'd been sad, yes; but also, in a funny kind of way, relieved.

Throughout Iain's sentence, seventeen years of hell, Alison had never been to bed with another man. But she'd looked at another man. And now here he was again, all unexpected, like a good deed in a naughty world.

'What brings you here?' she asked him brightly. 'Thought you'd given up on me.'

He said nothing.

'How's April?' She remembered he lived with a lady called April, remembered it very clearly, in fact.

'Fine.'

'So to what do I owe the pleasure?'

He merely smiled.

'Tell me,' Alison said, this time in an agitated voice.

'Alison, I'm sorry, but it's business.'

She withdrew her arm, then, and stuck her hands in her pockets. 'Business?'

'Iain. We're keeping an eye on him, of course. How are you, Alison?'

She bit back the retort that sprang to her lips. *Think of Iain.* 'I'm doing okay.'

'Nice, seeing you again.'

They'd reached the main road. They stood there, undecided, and she guessed that he didn't know how this meeting was supposed to run, he was coming in blind.

'Grindle sent you,' she said. 'Didn't he?' He'd told her early on that his boss's name was Terence Grindle; later, she'd seen Grindle give evidence against Iain at his trial.

'Sort of. Let's walk back. Cross over.'

They began to retrace their steps, keeping to the other

side of the street, out of sight (she prayed) of anyone looking from the hotel.

'What's Iain done? He's been home with me, how could he –'

'Last Sunday.'

'He went out, yes, he said he needed space.'

'He went to see Powis.'

Alison stopped. Martin took another three steps before perceiving himself to be alone.

'It's all right,' he said. 'Powis doesn't intend to press charges.'

'*Charges!* Why should he? What did Iain *do*?'

'First he went to see a villain, in London. Then he took a train, got into Powis's place. The police came. Powis must have protected him; anyway he walked out of it. Alison –' He took her by the arm again and she didn't have the strength to resist. 'You've got to put a brake on him, love. That's the message. They thought I'd be the one to get it across to you. Because of . . . before.'

'Before?'

'You used to listen to me. Do you love your husband?'

'*Yes!*' The word jetted out of her like high pressure steam.

'And Kate – you love her, don't you?'

She wrenched on his arm, making him stop and turn. 'You leave Kate out of this,' she hissed. 'Understand?' When he said nothing – '*Understand?*'

He nodded slowly, not quite meeting her eyes. 'Well, then . . .' he said, 'better have a word with Iain, love.'

'You touch his daughter and he'll kill you!'

Too late, too late: the words were out. Iain had done a life stretch for murder. He said he was innocent but her words indicted him afresh, corroborating the jury's findings. Heaney stayed silent, letting her replay the tape in her head, letting her do his work for him.

'I'm not handling this very well,' he said suddenly. 'Am I?'

'I don't know what you mean.' She was walking half a pace behind him now. 'Ruin's your job. You haven't lost your touch.'

'I've always had a soft spot for you, Alison. You got dumped on.'

All trace of the warmth she'd once felt for Heaney had gone; I wish I could see your soft spot, she thought savagely: I'd stick a knife in it.

'I don't want you hurt again, love. And they can hurt you, you know that, don't you? You . . . and others.'

'They,' she said, in a small, flat voice. 'You never used to be part of "they". You told me once you hated them.'

'I did. Do.'

'So why –'

'Because they pay the rent.' His voice had an edge to it.

'And they still harass me, don't they?'

Something about the hunch of his shoulders emboldened her. He hadn't known about the harassment.

'Every time I get a job, someone always tells them about Iain. About prisoner number 844569. Killer. Lifer.'

'Yeah?' His voice was non-committal.

'Why the *hell* do you think I'm working in a dump like *that*?' They had stopped opposite the Grand; she jerked her head at it. 'You think it's Sheraton's latest acquisition? *Do you?*'

'You can't blame me,' he said, after a pause. 'I'm an analyst now. Desk job.'

'*You?* A desk job? I don't believe it.'

'It's true.' His voice was thick.

'I used to like you,' she said bitterly, after a long pause. 'I used to like you a lot.'

Alison turned around and crossed the road, not looking back. She went up the steps and entered the Grand's foyer, turning to ensure that she'd closed the door properly. Through the glass panel she could see that the street was empty. She leaned against the wall with her eyes closed, breathing hoarsely. Every breath carried a tiny, tobacco-filed rasp.

She opened her eyes to find Jacqui, the receptionist, standing in front of her, unconcerned. Nothing fazed Jacqui, unless it was a cracked fingernail.

'You said you wanted to do the pay-packets at ten,' the girl said. 'They're all in the kitchen.'

Alison pulled herself together. She went behind the counter and opened the safe, taking out the staff pay-packets she'd checked earlier. They did pay in the kitchen, because nowhere else was big enough. She followed Jacqui down the back stairs. In the kitchen the night staff were standing around, not talking, gazing into space: two Chinese, a Thai, a Moroccan boy with a harelip, the night-maid. Alison sat down at the table, still damp from the grey cloth the Thai had used to rearrange the grease, and opened her book.

'Okay,' she said. 'Happy days are here again.'

No one laughed. The Moroccan boy came forward, wiping his hands on his trousers. Alison glanced at him, then sorted quickly through the brown envelopes: Imad, where was Imad's . . . ?

A grey spot materialized on Imad's pay-packet, quickly followed by another. Alison looked at it. Something dripped and a third spot emerged. She was crying. Through a blur she became aware of them staring at her in embarrassment, awe, contempt, who knew?

There were no happy days, not now. There had been, but too long ago to matter. Strictly once upon a time . . .

\*　　　\*　　　\*

Once upon a time – the autumn of 1971, to be exact, although in Singapore it made little sense to talk of seasons – Alison Forward, née Cowper, had been almost happy. Oh, there were flaws. She was a hotel under-manager who'd recently been passed over for promotion to manager, because expats no longer commanded the best jobs. The reverse was true, in fact: a white skin and blue eyes counted for less than an ethnically suitable background, in the Singapore seventies. She no longer occupied a delightful old house, sandwiched between F.P. and the Chan clan; Iain had bought them a swish apart-ment in rapidly up-and-coming Holland Village, with underground parking and a pool. She ran her own little green Ford, nicknamed Sarah Jane. Marriage . . . well, she'd always known, practical girl that she was, that the honeymoon couldn't last for ever. But it would have been nice if it had lasted a *bit* longer.

She had no complaints, not really. Iain was a good man, caring, tender, expressive of his love. All the things she'd thought she'd seen in him were there in truth. Only . . . Well, all right then, be honest: only he seemed to have got what he wanted when he married her, and now that he didn't have to worry about making sure of her, there were other things to think of. Career things. Boring things. She hadn't married him for his wit, but he could, just sometimes, be a wee bit boring.

Life's okay, she thought, turning away from the house-phone; the Prince was running sweetly, all rooms cleaned twenty minutes before deadline, what did she fancy for lunch . . . ?

A man stood watching her from the middle of the lobby. Funny: the Prince was usually full of people at this time of day, there was no reason why she should think of this individual as being interested in her, except that he was, oh he *was*.

He seemed to have moved right up to her, without her

134

noticing. He filled her vision. Her eyes widened in fright, then narrowed. Her lips parted. He was going to speak to her, and she couldn't move, didn't *want* to move.

'It's hot today,' the man murmured. 'Isn't it?'

Alison swallowed. 'Are you talking to me?'

Slowly, very slowly, he looked to the right. He looked to the left. There was nobody else around at all.

'Do you know,' he said, turning back to face her, 'I rather think I must be. Don't you?'

For a moment longer their stares interlocked. Then she smiled and made as if to move away. 'Excuse me,' she said; 'I'm rather busy today.'

'But not every day. And . . . are you the manager? It's about a catering contract. I need to organize a banquet.'

The Prince had its own catering manager, of course; a portly Japanese gentleman with a degree from Switzerland and scant command of any language save his own. Alison weighed things up, but these scales were loaded. She recognized danger and felt alive.

'Perhaps I can take care of it for you,' she replied, in what she hoped were businesslike tones. What a dish, what a simply scrumptious dish . . . not that Iain wasn't dishy, too, but in a different way. This man came at her with the openness of a streetfighter who'd never lost. She wanted him to lose. He thought he could have any girl in the house, but he could not have her.

*Prove it!*

'Come to my office,' she said. 'It's just down the hall. Mr . . . ?'

'Sampson, but please call me Jay: all my friends do, and you and I could never be anything but.'

She asked him politely if he would like coffee. No, he said, it was time for his glass of champagne. And things got all mixed up after that, because with the effortless expertise of a sorcerer he somehow arranged for a bottle of chilled Laurent Perrier, 1964 vintage, to be brought to

135

her office in an ice-bucket; she did not know that the hotel stocked Laurent Perrier, or that it tasted so wonderful, true nectar, or that this man was on first-name terms with Bertie Lim, her head barman. She watched in a kind of daze as Bertie pocketed five dollars and floated off with a smile, and all she could think of to say was, 'No tipping. It's a house rule.'

He winked at her and she jumped, physically. Bedroom eyes, a naughty wink: *stop!*

'Of course,' he said. 'But all rules are there to be broken, aren't they?'

*No!*

'I suppose so,' she heard herself agreeing politely – Never offend a guest, the first rule of the innkeeper, even more important than the second, which was Never drink with them.

'We're going to do it,' he said. 'Aren't we?'

Her head was about to burst. Perhaps he saw how desperately she needed rescuing and took pity on her – *reculer pour mieux sauter?* – for he added, 'This lunch, I mean. I've got six Malaysians to entertain and we're not going to haggle, are we, we're just going to do it, yes?'

Her glass was empty. She had never tasted such wonderful champagne: surely what God drank while he listened to Mozart. It would be too much to bear if he refilled the glass, so she helped herself, thrilling to the jolt of joyful wickedness that rippled through her.

'We'll see,' she said archly. She felt giddy with pleasure, also with drink. He fancied her like crazy – if he stood up the evidence would be there, inches away from her nose, ballooning for anyone to see. She squeezed her thighs together, trapping the moisture. Why didn't this happen to other happily married girls? Young ladies weren't supposed to be sex-mad.

Alison recognized, through a fog of mild anaesthesia,

that this had gone far enough. She pulled paper towards her and uncapped her fountain pen.

*Suppose he did stand up. How . . . how big would it be . . . ?*

'Now. That's six plus you, is it? Wives, pick-ups?'

He laughed. Oh, how she wished he wouldn't! He had such a sensual laugh; it sent shivers along those tightly clenched thighs of hers.

'Say, you really know this business,' he said admiringly.

She felt a first wave of disappointment. Mere flattery, fizz and fornication – that was the name of his game.

'Tell you what . . .' He leaned forward to rest a forearm on the desk. 'I've been looking for somewhere to entertain guests in town. I can't get through to Chinese hoteliers. They tell me what they think I want and then they do that. I budget twenty thousand Singapore a year for entertaining, and that doesn't include overnight room bills.'

Flattery, fizz, and now bribery. *Bought* fornication. What are the first two rules of innkeeping, just remind me again . . . ?

'Lunch,' she said with sudden briskness, 'will cost you much less than that. Seven covers, yes?'

'They may pick up girls, as you acutely pointed out. By when should I let you know the numbers?'

'Oh, that's all right, we're very flexible. Keep them in the bar for ten minutes and they'll never notice the seam.'

He grinned at her and she wanted to keep a stony expression but her face was splitting from ear to ear and she couldn't do a damn thing about it. She wished her heart would quieten down; it felt as though she'd been running a marathon in the midday sun.

'Chinese food?' she enquired. 'Malay? Rijsttafel's our speciality.'

'Rijsttafel.'

'Alcohol?'

'Let 'em order as they go along. No bar limits.'

She switched on the calculator and pressed a few keys. The machine grumbled a bit, then printed out a row of figures and advanced the paper-roll. She tore off the end and passed it across to Jay. His eyebrows rose.

'Impressive,' he said. 'And accepted. Do you mind me asking, Alison: is that a realistic figure, or a come-on-down price?'

'Both. As under-manager, it's one of my responsibilities . . .'

At least, that's what she *meant* to say. She was under the impression, brought on by the superb Laurent Perrier, that today she could talk with exceptionally rapid fluency; but both she and Jay heard, 'As unna manager, it's vonne my respectability . . .'

He slapped the desk with a roar of laughter and Alison joined in. She hadn't had so much innocent fun in a long while; and yes, it *was* innocent, she decided as she saw him out. One of the pleasures – she nearly thought 'compensations', swerved in time – of being a married matron was that you could flirt without fear.

She stood boldly in the foyer, not caring who saw her extend her hand to Jay in the knowledge that he would raise it to his lips for a kiss.

'Goodbye,' she said.

'*Au revoir,*' he replied, with *just* the right note of insistence.

It did not last, this gargantuan high. On her way home the bus bumped and jarred, sending her now against the window, now into the steel-rivet elbow of the Chinese girl next to her. Alison felt nauseous the way she did before her period: background sick. The incomparable Laurent Perrier (where *did* he find that?) had evaporated, leaving only residue. Jay had worn off, too. She was

138

looking forward to getting home to her husband, with his comfortable familiarity and solid lack of jeopardy. Then she remembered. They were going out tonight.

As she inserted her key in the latch she could hear Iain in the shower. He wasn't singing; how unlike him, and thank God.

Alison made herself a cup of tea and carried it to the lounge. Iain came out of the bathroom, a towel wrapped around his waist. He caught sight of her and said, 'Hi,' before disappearing into their bedroom. I see, Alison thought; and I hope *you* had a nice one too, darling. Iain came out again, this time wearing only underpants. 'Where's my shirt?' he said. 'South Sea Island cotton, that one.'

'It's in the wash.'

He glared at her, but then he smiled, rather tightly. 'Sorry, love,' he said. 'Rotten, rotten, rotten day.'

'So I gather.' Her heart wasn't in a quarrel. 'Me, too. I made a big mistake: drank at lunchtime.'

'Poor thing.' He came to sit beside her. She was aware of his wet-baby smell, the Johnson's talc he always used, and a whiff of something stronger and rather disgraceful: she wished he wouldn't use Eau Sauvage, it didn't suit him. He gave her a quick kiss on the lips, and then transferred his attention to her neck.

She was tense at first, but after a while felt herself relax. She needed to be cuddled, even if it was by a Sauvage. After a while, however, they both lay back on the sofa, with only the sides of their little fingers touching.

'What about your day?' she enquired listlessly.

'Slog. I was in by six thirty this morning, but the Viper beat me to it.'

Viper was his pet name for Miss Newland: Verity the Viper.

'Quarterly figures, *plus* management accounts, *plus*

cash-flow, *plus* bank reconciliation. I just can't get it across to them that a regional outfit like ours doesn't need to use two banks.'

She turned her head to study him in profile. 'I love you,' she said fiercely. 'My God, I do.'

Without quite knowing what drove her, she swivelled sideways so that she could cup his dear, dear face between her hands and lick his mouth, the outside, the inside, everywhere. He was so appealing, like a lanky little boy! Those big hands and feet, stuck on the ends of long, thin arms and legs, the prominent ears, the shambling walk: so English, so embarrassed. Indeed his narrow eyes always seemed a trifle apprehensive, as if he dreaded doing the wrong thing. He had thick and lovely light brown hair, swept back at an angle of forty-five degrees from his high forehead, unfashionably short at the back. Yes, he was a little boy, *her* little boy, right down to the smooth, pink skin that needed shaving only one day in three, and the silky hairs that grew in his ears until she got around to plucking them out, overriding his protests much as his mother might have done, years before.

Not everything was boyish. There was something compelling about his male form, hard in those places where she was soft, as if her little boy had become callused by the effort of becoming and being a man. Without quite knowing what drove her, she let her hand stray to the white-draped hillock between his legs, using the tips of her fingers to stroke it oh so gently, and she was seeing Jay Sampson's face . . .

'What's the matter?'

Iain sounded alarmed, resentful even; for she had suddenly jumped up off the sofa and was already disappearing into the bedroom.

'Got to shower,' she called through the door. 'Don't want to be late for your Viper, do we?'

'We've got time.'

But she was already more than halfway to the bathroom, a shower-cap stuck on her head and a towel wrapped around her middle: dumpy, she looked. Not sexy, not alluring; just a sweaty mess.

Half an hour later, however, as they were bundling themselves into a taxi, she felt better. She wore a long black skirt beneath a white pleated shirt, very chic, with a gold necklace her father had given her as a wedding present and a gold butterfly brooch under the left collar. She wished she'd made time for a perm, but too late to worry about that now, and anyway, her hair always looked better when it hadn't been over-handled. Iain showed up well in a DJ, of course: all men did, but tonight he really looked dashing. She was proud of him.

'Clifford House,' Iain told the taxi-driver. 'Quick as you can.'

They had a quick run down to the Central Business District, virtually deserted at seven thirty. As they pulled up outside Clifford House Alison sighed and said, 'Did it *have* to be the Singapore Club?'

'Venerable institution,' Iain murmured, leaning forward to pay the driver. 'Anyway, it doesn't cost *us* anything.'

A Chinese steward escorted them up to the private dining-room hired for the occasion by Gerry Reynolds. As they entered, Alison noted with satisfaction that they were neither first nor last. Iain led her across the carpet to where Gerry was holding court. 'Don't think you've met my wife Alison,' he said in a reasonable attempt at Gerry's own relaxed drawl. 'Darling . . . Mr Reynolds, his wife, Daphne . . .'

'So glad you could come.' Reynolds, a benign colonial uncle, enjoyed these 'dos'. Held twice a year, the idea was to 'let people get to know each other', 'mingle a bit', and – the Big Lie, this – 'give the wives a bit of a treat'. Nobody, not one single person (except possibly Daphne

Reynolds, and it was impossible to tell what she thought about anything) enjoyed these evenings; nobody seemed to have the power to stop them.

'So Alison . . .' Gerry fairly beamed at her. 'Iain tells me you're in hotel management. Fascinating, that. Daphne, don't you think that's fascinating?'

'Oh, yes; and so young, too.'

Reynolds' wife spoke in low, worried tones; she had the kind of voice movie directors cast for communicating terminal diagnoses. Alison smiled at her, wondering what it was like to live behind such a face, so ugly and tired. She felt sorry for Daphne.

Where, she wondered, looking around while Reynolds droned on about this hotel they'd stayed in last year, perfectly awful . . . where was the Viper? Maybe she wouldn't come. No, you had to come; everyone did. And the place was filling up now; the chaps all had their silver tankards, the girls were forming Gin-and-Itty coteries . . .

Something caught her eye. In one corner a tiny Indian man was dazzling several guests with a pack of miniature cards, shuffling them, letting them fall between his hands, retrieving them, sending them up in a cascade towards the ceiling. He wore a baggy dinner-suit, his bow-tie hung at a sloppy angle and his shirt was like his irregular teeth: not quite clean. But his face made up for these deficiencies. Alison had never seen a human countenance so imbued with fun. The eyes behind his rimless spectacles fairly crackled.

'That's Reggie Raj,' Iain whispered in a voice tinged with respect. 'Our scientific miracle-worker. Let me go and bring him over.'

As Iain departed, Alison felt somebody pluck her arm. She turned to find Jenny Morton-Smythe at her elbow, looking flushed and stretched, as people do when they have big news to confide. Alison had already met Jenny at a party, and liked her.

'Heard the news about Dolly?'

'No. Oh dear, not . . . ?'

Jenny closed her eyes and nodded solemnly. ''Fraid so.'

Adolphus Cartwright pre-dated GOD, or the Good Old Days everyone always droned on about here. No one was quite sure what he did, if anything, but he lived quietly in a colonial bungalow on Bukit Timah Road with a Pomeranian called Bouncer and a couple of Chinese houseboys who never seemed to age beyond eighteen. Everybody understood the situation of course, but you didn't talk about it and you didn't criticize either; because the whole shooting-match depended on expats having standards superior to those of the natives, and a single aberration like Dolly couldn't be allowed to undermine the system. So Dolly, sixty if he were a day, went on leading the quiet life with his dog and his Chinese boys and in streets from Sumatra to Suez not a horse had ever been frightened. Until now.

'What . . .' Alison muttered. 'How . . . ?'

'He's out. Tomorrow's plane to London.' Jenny looked right and left, then faced Alison again and silently mouthed, 'Government.' Which is what you did, in Singapore, in 1971.

'No prosecution, thank God,' she went on in a low tone. ' ''Totter'' McAlister was officer in charge; Rodney got the story from him at the Tanglin this lunchtime. Apparently the police were chasing some drugs smuggler through the back gardens. They lost him, got fed up, decided to root around – all quite aimless, Totter swears, but they must have *known* . . . Anyway, Dolly was sleeping on the back porch that night, the heat . . . and he was, well . . . *en famille*, you know.'

'I'm so sorry.' Alison wasn't being platitudinous. Dolly, a friend of her father's, had been a sort of honorary godfather to her . . . or godmother, she supposed was nearer

143

the mark. Being queer somehow made him the perfect confidant. He was quiet, and charming, and very wise. A gentleman.

'Who'll look after Bouncer?' she asked.

'Totter's taking her, bless him.'

'Can't Totter do anything? I mean, Dolly's lived here so long, never hurt a fly, poor lamb.'

'Forty-three years, according to Totter.'

'Is he dreadfully upset?'

'Philosophical. Apparently he told Totter he always knew it'd end in tears.' Jenny again darted quick looks to right and left. 'Ali, do you want to hear something awful?' But her face didn't say awful.

'Tell.'

'After all the hoo-ha was over, Totter took Dolly back to the house and they had a few snorts. And Totter said, "Why couldn't you have stuck to one, old man, maybe I could have done something if they'd found you in bed with *one* boy, but *two* . . ." And do you know what Dolly said? He said, "Well, Chief Inspector, you know how it is: you nibble on one of these delightful Chinese dishes, and half an hour later you've just got to have another . . ."'

The two women exploded into laughter. But when Jenny caught someone else's eye and breathed, 'Must go,' the laughter died out of Alison very quickly. She was losing a friend in a world where she felt friendless. Today hadn't been her day for misfortune; the goddess had passed her by, seeking other prey, seeking Dolly and his two darling houseboys. Funny: she'd thought to ask Jenny about the dog, not the boys. Now she wondered about them. What would *their* lives be . . . ?

'Darling,' Iain said in her ear, 'I can't get near Reggie, so I'll introduce you to Miss Newland.'

She came to herself with a start and smiled at Iain, glad to remember she had a husband who was straight, that she could feel safe on the raft. He took her by the hand and led her towards Gerry Reynolds' court. Two people were standing directly in front of him, blocking her view of Reynolds; the woman must be Verity, of course. She wasn't married, didn't sound the type for a boyfriend, so who could the escort be? Surely she hadn't rented someone for the evening . . . oh my God.

For the man, hearing voices behind him, had turned around, and he was Jay Sampson.

Alison shook hands with Verity in a blur of shock. She was vaguely aware of the woman saying something nice about her dress and she fought to recover, but it was all so dreadful and her social skills had deserted her. Jay was smiling. His smile sucked her inside of him; she could not take her eyes off his gorgeous face.

'Thanks, Verity,' she managed to get out. 'I do so love your bracelet . . .'

'This? Oh, they sold it to me as jade, but it's hard to tell unless you're shopping with an expert. This is Jay Sampson, by the way.'

Alison panicked, not sure whether to admit to a previous encounter. But Jay took things in hand. 'We met earlier today,' he said. 'Coincidence is a powerful thing.'

Alison was aware of two pairs of eyes that suddenly homed in on her, flashed over to Jay, and then set into a smooth radar-beam pattern from face to face. Iain and Verity wanted details, now, this instant, told with conviction and reassurance. They had to be lied to, she realized.

'Mr Sampson has just become a client.' She addressed herself primarily to Iain, but made sure that Verity was included in her glance. 'He seems to think the Prince has got something: a tribute to his good taste, I'd say.'

'What made you try the Prince, Jay?' Verity, for her part, made no pretence of including Alison; her gaze transfixed Jay much as a pin skewers the butterfly to its board. 'Isn't it a little . . . well, past its prime?'

'The Prince,' he replied with a laugh, 'is like a certain kind of woman; it improves along with maturity.'

Alison giggled. Verity's sharp eyes turned in her direction and studied her for a moment of silence.

'Is that how you see yourself?' she enquired. 'As . . . a certain kind of woman?' She paused. 'Not you personally, of course. Your hotel.'

'Hotels *are* like people, actually; each has its own personality.'

Fortunately the head steward saved the day with a discreet beating of the gong and announcement of dinner.

Reg Raj bounced in at the head of the procession, oblivious to the demands of rank, with a pretty girl on each arm. 'I hope they're not a couple of his tarts,' Iain breathed disapprovingly in Alison's ear.

'Tarts?'

'He only likes tarts. God knows where he found those two.'

They were walking behind Verity and Jay, giving Alison an opportunity to study, critically, Miss Newland's attire. She sensed that the other woman was wearing stand-bys, one of half a dozen outfits she kept in the wardrobe for 'occasions' such as this, with 'matching accessories' to serve any combination of circumstances. A woman who shopped once a year, then, and without joy. Emerald green *certainly* wasn't her colour; who on earth had told her it was? No, of course: Verity Newland made up her own mind, about clothes, about men, about Iain Forward's performance in the office.

And, presumably, about Jay Sampson's technique in bed.

A hard nut of bitterness scraped its way through her entrails, mingling with the after-taste of too much champagne and all-round fatigue to make her feel thoroughly wretched. She resented Verity, not just because the Viper

146

dominated Iain, but because of her pulling-power over a dishy man called Jay Sampson she in no way deserved. Alison found herself constructing nasty little fragments of conversation, all of which ended in put-downs of Verity Newland.

Alison took her seat. Prawn cocktail, she saw with sinking heart. Prawns with pink sauce, tomato segment, bed of lettuce, wedge of lemon. She could have bought this in Durham, where Pa had sent her to university. Half a hundred yards away, Singaporeans were sitting down to vegetable samosas, exquisite bird's-nest soup, satay. Had anyone actually enquired whether the Harchem staff liked prawn cocktail, done badly, when they could have supped on the delicacies of the Orient? And at a quarter the price – the professional in her *would* bring that up. Steak next, of course . . .

She picked up her spoon, then became aware that she was alone in doing so and quickly put it down while Gerry said grace. When the twitter of conversation resumed, 'It's fate,' a voice accosted her from across the table. 'Joss, as the Chinese say.'

Alison shot a quick smile at Jay. 'Think so?'

'Know so.'

She felt a foot knock against hers and instinctively moved it. The other foot followed. She shot upright, glaring at Jay. But he smiled back at her with the ghost of a wink. The foot pressed against hers and was still.

Alison coloured. You did not do things like this at a Harchem dinner . . . *suffer* them, she hastily corrected her verb. And yet . . . the foot was comforting, as well as stimulating. She needed an ally down her quarter of the table, her theatre of war, and the foot said: Here I am.

Her eyes roamed speculatively over what she could see of Jay's body, while he made conversation and she seemed to listen but did not. He was well tanned; she liked that. Iain was a pale fish. Jay's movements reminded her of a panther's: utterly smooth. And, also like a panther, he seemed to have coal-black eyes that glowed.

God, he was dangerous.

Alison suddenly resolved to have no more to do with Jay Sampson. But even as she framed that resolve her treacherous foot pressed against his, transmitting a different message, informing both her and him that one day soon they would sleep together.

Her hand jerked against the bowl, sending half a prawn cocktail tumbling into her lap. Amid the consternation, the expressions of sympathy, she found herself looking along the table at Verity, drawn by instinct to where the unpleasantness would be, the condemnation ... and, looking into that woman's cold eyes, Alison read there something beyond amusement. Yes, those eyes were saying, you'll be lovers. *But you'll regret it.*

'Tomato ketchup doesn't really *go* with blue,' Verity Newland drawled; and everybody laughed.

# SEVEN

Iain knocked on Simon's door.

'Come in!'

'Excuse me . . . they were wondering if you had perhaps got the intro music for *Reader's Digest*.'

Simon assumed his beatific smile, the one he reserved
for ex-cons. 'I don't think so,' he said.

'I don't know why they thought you'd have it.'

Simon was flushed with the need to set Iain's mind at
ease. 'Have you tried the music library upstairs?' he said.

'Music library . . . ?'

'First floor, last room at the end. There's this big rack'
– Simon painted excitedly with his hands – 'and it's full
of intro tapes.'

'Oh. I didn't know. Sorry.'

'Not your fault *at all*. Please . . .'

Iain shut the door. You learned something every day,
he reflected as he trudged upstairs. On one side of the
corridor that ran the length of the prefabricated building's
first floor were the studios: tiny rooms with just enough
space for mixer, tape-machine, cassette-player, two
readers and someone to work the controls. On the other
side were offices. He'd only been up here once, his first
day, to meet the chairman and chief executive. After
that it had somehow become understood – an unspoken
understanding – that he was *persona non grata* above sea-
level. Iain knew why. Upstairs was where they kept the
petty cash. The vonga, in prison slang.

Out of habit he slowed his pace as he reached the upper
floor, and shaped his features into an enquiring look. In

prison you always needed to be able to account for your-self. 'What are *you* doing here, Forward? Get back in your cell . . . I'm watching you.' You had to slap the screw down: 'Reporting to the Governor, sir. On my way to association, sir.' You looked him in the eyes and you got the words out smooth, stripped of sarcasm. You never went anywhere you couldn't give an account of yourself. Never.

The upper floor seemed deserted. He could hear mur-murings from the studios, but no one emerged. He slowed to a crawl.

The first office he came to had its door half open. This was where he'd met the head honcho, that first day. (What a prat!) Iain poked his head in, knowing from the silence that the room was empty. (And if it wasn't? Why – 'Looking for the tape library, sir!')

By the far wall sat a small, square safe, a 'peter' as he'd spent the last seventeen years thinking of such things. This one was a breeze: single key, no combination, no fancy electronic-chippery.

Iain went on his way. You never rushed anything if you were a lifer, because for a man who might spend the rest of his days inside, everything could wait. The urgency went out of every human activity – except having a shit during those vital ten minutes each day when you were in the place God meant you to do it. He'd be working here this week, next week, next year. So push on and find the intro music to *Reader's Digest*, sonny; invest a bit of thought in that safe and keep it for later.

But as he mooched down the corridor his accountant's mind was going over the figures. Aural Sightings had an appeal on just now, with collecting boxes and four-year covenants and payroll giving, and all that. A good response, he'd overheard Simon say. Now what pro-portion was in cash, and what in non-negotiable paper?

Somewhere they would keep a record, an *account*. He

was good with accounts; while inside he'd kept abreast, he'd read the mags, studied the exposure drafts, mugged up each year's tax tables. Perhaps he should remind Simon of his talents. Perhaps he should offer to do a little more . . .

It wasn't only the appeal. To keep bank charges low, they paid wages in cash. Once a week there was a lot of dosh in that safe. Come Friday, someone would be sent down the bank to collect the weekly pay. But that went out immediately, it wasn't left in the safe overnight. So if anybody had an eye on the wages, he'd have to do a daylight job. Not so easy.

Iain came to the last door. He knocked, waited, and when there was no answer, went in. Once he'd got his hands on the appeal's accounts, he'd know if the risk was worth taking. Not that he'd do the safe himself, that'd be stupid. He'd look up a few of his prison contacts and put the job out to tender in exchange for a cut. Might even ask the Guv. He needed a grand for what he was planning. If the figures came out right, and he could negotiate a grand plus, he'd do it.

But first he needed to get his hands on Aural Sightings' accounts. And that needed thinking about.

The room he found himself in was scarcely an office at all, more of a store-room. Most of the space was taken up with filing-cabinets and cupboards; he could see a typewriter, several piles of magazines knotted with twine, a corkboard with a three-year-old annual planner stuck to it. At the end furthest from the door was a rack labelled 'Music', with tape-cassettes in it. But there was nothing under *Reader's Digest*. He ran his finger along. *Personal Computer, Radio Programmes, Royalty Monthly* . . .

He'd done his best. As he stood upright his eye lighted on something he hadn't noticed before: a thin cable draped over the desk. He sidled across to it. The cable led inside one of the drawers. Iain opened it. A telephone!

151

Eagerly he lifted the receiver. No dialling tone: *shit!* But then he thought to look for the other end of the cable. He followed it down to the floor, trailing it through his hands, and began to rummage behind the stacks of magazines. Yes, a phone-jack, there, on the skirting-board! Iain jammed the end of the cable into the jack and again grabbed the receiver. This time he could hear the buzz of a connection.

He quickly lowered the receiver back on its cradle. Somewhere along the corridor a lavatory flushed, followed by the sound of a door opening and closing. Who was that; who worked up here? Chairman, his secretary . . . He heard footsteps going downstairs, the kind a woman makes when she's wearing high heels. Chairman out, secretary out . . .

Iain wasted no more time. He closed the store-room door and shot back to the phone. How long before Simon or somebody came in search of him . . . ?

He got through to directory enquiries, not bothering to write down the number they gave him but remembering it, instantly, as you learned to do in prison. He dialled again. When the operator answered he said, 'Home desk . . . Ted Smurfitt.'

Iain gnawed his nails to the accompaniment of 'Greensleeves', rendered on a tape that stuck now and then.

'Hello! Ted . . . it's me. Iain Forward.'

A pause. Then a slow voice said, 'Well, well. How's life on the big outside, then?'

'Not bad. Listen, I'm getting somewhere. I went to see Powis last Sunday, and –'

'Who?'

'Tony Powis. You know: ex-Harchem chief.'

'Oh yes?'

Smurfitt's indifference was like poison gas; it seeped along the airwaves, getting into Iain's stomach, churning his guts.

'You used to think there was a story in me, Ted.' Iain struggled to keep the rage out of his voice, but it was hard. 'Exclusive exposé; remember?'

'Well, Iain . . .' There was another pause while Smurfitt cupped his hand over the receiver and spoke to someone in his office. '. . . That was then, this is now. I got the feeling at Paddington that you'd lost interest. Frankly.'

'Well *frankly*, so did I.' Iain took a deep breath. When next he spoke it was in Prisoners' Whine, though he did not know that. 'Ted, look, I'm broke. I'm going to clear myself. I can do that. But I need dosh, Ted.'

'Don't we all? Hadn't you better be a bit careful, old son? I seem to recall that *you* can be recalled, unless you're a good boy.'

'So what? In for a penny . . . if I make waves, it's to clear my name, see? And if I can prove I was framed, *with government help*, what would the *Mail* or the *Independent* fork out for that, eh?'

There was a silence, and Iain held his breath. Don't think, don't hope, just . . . he groped for the right word . . . *pray*!

'Iain, facts of life, okay? I've been with this paper for nigh on fifteen years. Last month, they cut my expenses to twenty-five pounds a week. That's a couple of taxis and a Big Mac, in case you're interested. You've got to understand – '

*Wrong!* Iain didn't have to understand anything. He slammed down the phone. Disgust showed in his breathing, in the way his mouth tautened into a snarl. He shoved the phone back in its drawer and tore the plug from its jack. He did these things unconsciously, as he used to hide his blade during that mercifully short stay in Albany, or sleeve a packet of fags to prevent a screw from getting his hands on it.

He went downstairs.

'Simon, I looked, but that intro tape's gone. What shall I tell them in the studio?'

'They found it while you were up there, actually. Sorry about that.'

Simon smiled up at him from his desk, but his eyes didn't quite meet Iain's. Somebody should have been sent to tell Iain not to bother searching any more, but it had been overlooked. That might have been an accident. It could have happened to anyone, in any office in London. In fact, it had happened to the ex-con.

A fuzzy band floated before Iain's eyes and he blinked. Get out. Take a break. Just . . . *go*.

'All right if I have my lunch now?'

'Certainly. Oh, and . . . thank you Iain. Sorry about that.'

He slipped out and lit a cigarette, but despite the nicotine and the fresh air the fuzzy, blinding band refused to go away. He began to walk, not knowing where. Then a voice said, 'Dad.'

He shuffled on, not associating the word with himself.

'Dad, it's me. Kate.' Someone slipped an arm through his. He stopped, for a second puzzled and afraid. He turned to look at his daughter. He knew he ought to feel something about this person, either positive or negative, but he did not know what he felt. An inner disturbance, a momentary shift of balance, that was all.

He smiled. Cause or effect, who knew? But – he felt glad to see her. She smiled back and he realized that, unlike him, she felt something elementary and good for the man she was learning to call Dad. This was his daughter.

'Hello,' he said. 'What brings you here? Thought you were supposed to be at college today.'

'Mornings only, Fridays. Fancy something to eat?'

'Why not? I'll get my sandwiches.'

'Save them for later. I'll treat you to the pub.'

154

Nagging words filtered upwards through his spine but he suppressed them. Maybe Alison had given her pocket-money, perhaps it had come from Darren, she could have stolen it. He didn't care. He wanted a drink.

'Okay,' he said.

They found a Victorian pub, recently done up with fashionable black paint and gilt window-frames and the original lanterns hanging from the outside wall. 'FINE WINES & SPIRITS', proclaimed one window, 'SALOON', said another – and: 'NO JEANS', ordered a hand-scrawled piece of paper on the door. But it was Clapham spit and sawdust, all the same.

She bought him a whisky and for herself a vodka-and-orange, ordering shepherd's pie for both of them. They took their drinks to a corner table and sat down, Iain keeping his face to the bar, out of habit. There was a TV at the back, the news was on. For a few moments the two of them sat there, digesting the latest from the Gulf.

'What do you think about it, then?' he asked her suddenly. 'This war?'

'What war?' She looked angry. 'There isn't going to be one.'

'Yes there is.' Iain nodded at the TV screen. 'We're going to fight for oil and freedom, in that order.'

'You really believe they'll fight?'

'Of course.'

Kate shrugged. 'That Saddam Hussein, he's all piss and wind, Darren says. When they bring in the nukes, he'll get out of Kuwait like a sprinter with the squits.'

Iain laughed. 'Hope so,' he said sourly.

'But you don't believe it?'

'No, my love, I don't, and it scares me. I've just got out, I don't want pictures of burning bodies all over my telly.'

There was a silence. 'How's work going?' Kate asked at last.

'It's okay.' He felt impelled to give her a real answer. 'Better than I expected. It's a routine. Having to get up in the morning.'

'You worked in prison, though, didn't you?'

'Joke.'

'Sorry.'

'No, it's not your . . .' He grunted. 'Talk about something else.'

'What?'

He thought. 'Your life. These past seventeen years.'

'You really want to know?'

He nodded.

'Hell. Lonely. Frightened. Bullied at school. Crying because I didn't have a dad, like the others. Tantrums. Swearing, smoking, boozing.' She hesitated. 'Whoring, I suppose you'd say. Some.'

He squinted at her sideways, then shrugged. 'It's your body,' he said. 'You want to use it as a protest march, I can't argue.'

Suddenly he shuddered, causing the Scotch to spill.

'What?' Kate said quietly.

He was thinking of Albany, that time the Bounty Bar had got him up against the wall, knitting needle to his chin. 'I'm going to fuck you,' BB had said. 'I'm going to chain you to the radiator and fuck your arse. Not today. Maybe not tomorrow. But soon . . .' And the screw ten yards away had turned his back, walking off because it was breaktime and he didn't want to lose a second of it . . .

Iain had got himself a blade, after that.

'What do you want out of life?' he said, showing by his expression that he wasn't going to answer her question. 'What plans you got?'

'I want to be a designer. Stage, I think.'

The school said she had talent. Alison always brought

156

him Kate's end-of-term reports and the kid was strong on art.

'Then go for it,' he said drily.

'No ifs or buts?'

'No. Stick to your values, no matter what.'

She laughed. 'You sound just like my dad,' she said, and then it was his turn to laugh.

'Tell you something,' he said, 'you turned up at the right moment, this morning. God, you did.'

'Thanks. I'm glad. I wasn't sure . . .'

'Not sure who I am, is what you're really trying to say. I don't know you, either.' He drained his glass. 'But I'd like to.'

'Really?' The word came out fast.

'I'm proud of you. You're not what I'd have wanted, in a perfect world. You don't dress well, or speak well, or even act soft . . . just sometimes. But in prison, you hear a lot about the other bloke's family. Most of them are nothings. Black holes.'

Kate sat in silence for a moment. She was about to speak again when the barman called their number and she rose to collect their food. When she came back with the plates she said, 'So I'm not a total let-down, then?'

'Not total, no.'

'You say what you think, don't you?'

'Mostly. Except when I'm lying in my teeth. Not much in between, I do agree. My glass is empty. You having another?'

She nodded. He went up to the bar, mentally counting his money. It had cost far more than he'd imagined to send pineapples and cigars to Powis. He'd thought about doing nothing, on the basis that Powis would probably forget, but he had too much to lose if his old boss decided to go to the police. Now he'd just enough for the drinks. Pay-day tonight; the notion put a smile on his face. He carried the drinks back.

'Ta,' Kate said. 'Thanks.'

'You're welcome.'

'Dad . . .'

'What?'

She pushed her plate aside. She took a sip from her glass, opened her pack of cigarettes. To Iain she seemed disorientated, all at sea. She lit up and exhaled past his left ear, her gaze almost meeting his, not quite.

'I do love you,' she burst out.

Before he could answer she had jumped up and was thrusting her way through the crowd towards a door marked 'TOILETS'. He felt relieved; guilty but relieved. Again, he was forced to vault over the gap where emotion ought to be. Open yourself to love, he told himself wearily. Tell Kate something, lie to her a bit . . . no, just go easy on the truth, no need to lie.

She came back wiping her face with a tissue, and shot him an over-bright smile. He waited until she was sitting down. Then he leaned forward so that only she could hear him and he said, 'Listen. I'll tell you what I feel, right?'

She nodded. *Go easy on the truth.*

'I've been numb, for seventeen years. I'm thawing out.'

He hesitated. She was nearly an adult, in the eyes of the law. And suddenly, to his surprise, he did feel something: an irresistible desire to be straight with her, to be up front in dealing with his own daughter, not because that's what you were supposed to do but because it felt *right*.

'I can't say I love you, or anyone,' he said. 'I'd be lying. Even Alison . . .' He faltered, and lit a cigarette from her lighter, sitting with hands on his knees and staring at the floor between the two of them. 'But one thing I can say,' he went on, with visible effort. 'I'm going to tell you the truth, Kate. About everything, all the time. And I haven't felt that about anyone since I went inside. And maybe to

158

you it doesn't seem like much, but by God! If you'd seen the things . . .'

He tailed off. She was looking at him with rapt attention, her eyes two shining stars. He looked at his watch, and he muttered, 'Time to make a move.'

As they went out together she once more put her hand through his arm, and began to prance. At first it irritated Iain. Then, somehow, he fell into the swing of it, and before he could quite register what was up they were lolloping down the road like a couple of kids fresh out from school.

'My God,' Kate said as they arrived opposite the gateway to Aural Sightings, 'but you'd be hopeless in a Mexican wave!' She was out of breath and flushed. Iain had never seen her look so healthy.

'Try me,' he said.

But instead she leaned forward to give her father a hug and a kiss on each cheek. 'Love you,' she whispered. Then she pushed away from him, turning her head so that he wouldn't be able to see if she cried, and ran off.

Iain waved, but she didn't look back. As he was going through the door, however, he heard her voice, chanting, '*Let's* do the *time* warp a-*gain*. *Let's* do the *time* warp a-*gain*,' and he smiled. The smile turned into a laugh. Is this what it felt like, he wondered, for a cardiac patient who woke up to find they'd fixed his heart?

'Iain – have you got a moment?'

He was still laughing as he walked into Simon's office. Then he remembered the two lunchtime Scotches he'd drunk and promptly rearranged his face.

'Ted's upstairs in studio one, with our Scopex.' Seeing Iain's mystified expression he went on hurriedly, 'A wavelength-measuring machine. He needs an assistant for some experiments and I said I'd ask you.'

'Pleasure.'

Iain leapt up the stairs two at a time. On his way down

the corridor he again passed the chairman's office, its door still open. This time, Linda, the Goldilocks Girl as he mentally called her, was on her knees in front of the safe, putting something inside. She looked up angrily at Iain; perhaps she thought he'd come to knock her off as well as the safe. The notion amused him so much that he blew her a kiss.

That safe, he reflected, was an insult to criminal mentality. A complete and utter doddle. Nick a few quid, why not; serve them right for leaving it lying about, and yet . . .

The money could come in handy. But he needed to think.

A thought tickled his fancy: maybe now was the right time to give a bell to that guy who'd given evidence about safes and codes at the trial. Said he was from Special Branch, but what a joke – MI5 or nothing! *He*'d have a good laugh about Aural Sightings' safe, would Terence Grindle, the second man on Iain's list of men to see.

# EIGHT

'That's Reggie Raj; you remember him,' Grindle said without preliminaries, as Martin Heaney came in. 'Recent. Some people never age. Bloody unfair.'

Heaney slid into a chair beside Grindle's desk and studied the black-and-white photograph his master handed him. A podgy Indian face looked out at him against the background of a grey one-storey building. The cheerful-looking subject wore rimless spectacles and sported the odd wrinkle, but yes, a youngster's face. That was what idealism did for you.

'Where?' Martin asked.

'Place called Samarra, according to MI6. Iraq's biggest pesticide factory.' Grindle snorted. He looked rather like Darth Vader minus his helmet – bald, wart-ridden, ugly – and the snort matched his appearance. 'Chemical warfare plant, of course. Raj has ironed out the symptoms of dioxin poisoning, apparently. His latest stuff doesn't leave a trace. Not one trace.'

Martin replaced the photo on the desk.

'Well,' Grindle said, with an attempt at joviality. 'Long time no see.'

'It's been a while.'

'I read your recent report on the Forward woman. Absolutely first class.'

Martin said nothing.

'She'll work on him, will she? Got the point, did she?'

'Hard to say. There's a chance.'

'You know her pretty well, of course?'

Martin sensed danger. Not all of his contacts with

Alison had fallen into the official category. At first, yes, he'd been under orders; but it had been many years since anyone told him to follow up Forward's wife. That hadn't stopped him visiting her, though. I wonder if she liked the Valentine, he thought. I wonder if she knew it was from me, if she realized I stopped coming because of the Valentine card.

'Mmmm . . .' Grindle pushed back his chair and folded his hands across his stomach while he studied a man he'd last seen some seventeen years before. 'How've you been keeping?' he asked.

'All right.'

'I've read a lot of your stuff. Absolutely brilliant. Most of it.'

Martin said nothing.

'And now Raj is back in the frame. Forward's back. Sonja's back.' He paused. 'You're back.'

'We should hold a reunion dinner.'

The two men considered each other in silence for a while. As serious chess players, neither expected the other to blink; they were merely curious to see what havoc time had wrought.

'Got a problem,' Grindle said at last, releasing his stomach from its protective caress. 'All hands on deck, and so on. Only friends need apply.'

'Need to know,' Heaney improvised. 'Strictly no passengers. National interest . . . how am I doing?'

Grindle flushed slightly. While he recovered, Heaney looked around this oak-panelled office, a last outpost of colonial methodology. He doubted if it had changed much since it was built in the 1950s. New paper for the rocker-blotter, perhaps.

'We are about to go to war,' Grindle said. 'Our alliance with America must be perceived as rock solid.'

'And Forward's unlikely to help, is that what you're saying?'

162

'I'm saying I need to know whether you're more cooperative than you were seventeen years ago. If yes, we can shift you out of combing transvestite bars for rural deans on an awayday.'

Martin took a look at Grindle's face and, with the realization that more than one war was brewing, felt his heart sink.

'I see,' he said.

'Some people believe that there was something fishy about Forward's trial.' Grindle leaned forward, seeking to draw Martin into his confidence. 'Some people say the trial was rigged, by us, to suit the Americans. We don't want them saying that at this juncture. Do we?'

Martin shrugged.

'No.' Grindle answered his own question. 'At the trial, nothing came out about Harchem's product ninety-three twelve, thank God, or Raj's involvement in it. There was circumstantial evidence against Forward up to here, and the moment he was arrested the leaks from Harchem stopped.'

'As they would have done anyway.' Martin endeavoured to keep the weariness out of his voice, but that battle in this war was a losing one. 'All consistent with a frame-up, as I pointed out then. The real spy, probably the same man as the murderer, preferred to sacrifice further profits in order to save his cover.'

'Oh, certainly.' Grindle waved an expansive hand. His smile, however, was chilly. 'All I'm saying is that the evidence formed a seamless web. Part of which evidence was that the spy-ring had a means of communication, a code for use between themselves, the Harchem insiders, and their customers on the outside.'

'The Sonja letters.'

'As you say – Sonja. And now we have word from over the water that Sonja is getting restless. He is starting to sell up, he is in touch with Verity Newland again.'

'How on earth can we know that?'

'The Americans have one of Occydor's Chinese employees on their payroll. He's the go-between who handles their correspondence, though not before he's dipped inside and had a look.' Grindle's words had become marvellously distinct. 'Over the water they are starting to muse about Sonja. "Here is someone who wants to make waves," they are saying to themselves. "This Sonja never formally quit our employ, we always thought Sonja was loyal. But now Sonja wants an early retirement, and is preparing to blackmail us for a pension."'

'However,' Martin said, and his next words were every bit as distinct as his master's, 'we don't have to worry, do we? Because the trial wasn't rigged, the evidence was sound, and Forward . . . was . . . guilty.'

'I had always assumed,' Grindle said, 'that Forward was guilty.'

Martin considered the implications of that remark. He was interested in Grindle's use of tenses.

'What about Raj?' he asked. 'That photo, it's not just one for the album, is it?'

'Raj surfaced a year ago, working for the Mandeville Place mob.'

'Sorry?'

Grindle sighed. 'I forget how long you've been out of touch,' he murmured. 'Fronts for Saddam Hussein, there's a nest of them in Mandeville Place. Raj's present employer is owned fifty-fifty by Occydor Global, for which read Verity Newland, and BCCI – you've heard of *them*, I suppose.'

'The crooked bank. United Arab Emirates, isn't it?'

'Well, at least we can agree on something. Yes, a bent bank. It's been supplying Saddam with French Roland anti-aircraft missile systems and Chinese Silkworms, among other things. Raj is in it up to his neck, and so's

Newland. As I said earlier, Martin: the gang's all here. The only things that have changed are the product and the wrinkles on our faces. Raj is a fertile little nuisance. He's moved on since ninety-three twelve. You read about the Halabja massacre?'

'That Kurdish village in northern Iraq? The one Saddam Hussein obliterated?'

'Spot on. All done with nerve gas made by Reggie.'

'And what am I supposed to be doing about any of this?'

'Damage containment,' Grindle replied. 'Publicity, like loose talk, kills. Let me put to you a scenario.'

'Shoot.'

'We are back in the year nineteen seventy-one . . .'

Too bloody true, thought Martin.

'Suppose that Raj, while still working for Harchem, had developed ninety-three twelve to the point where it interested the Americans, still embroiled in their wretched little Asian affair. Suppose Raj, let's say with assistance from Newland and Sonja, sold the product to the Pentagon – and Reynolds found out. Not only found out – was threatening to go to Anthony Powis with it, knowing he'd explode.'

'Possibly enough to make someone interested in silencing Reynolds.'

'Exactly.' Grindle leaned back, one thumb stuck in a waistcoat pocket, the other elbow poised on the arm of his chair, dangling his spectacles. He looked like a minister who'd just got his way in cabinet. 'Exactly.'

'The US government?'

'Why not? It wouldn't be the first time.'

'And our Sonja can prove that . . .'

'We don't know whether he can or not. Or how far it went. What if the US connived at framing the wrong man, and *that* came out now? What do you think would happen?'

Martin didn't need to think. 'It would be disastrous.'

'Take it a stage further. According to the latest information coming across from MI6, Saddam is topping off his Scud-B missiles with binary nerve agents. A refinement of the Soviet VR-55. Who procured it for Iraq? Guess.'

'Newland?'

'And Raj, yes.'

Another long hold in the conversation. Then Martin said, 'Are you saying . . . I'm not sure what you are saying, but . . . if the Americans *knew* –'

'– about Raj, and had financed him from the beginning, him and Verity Newland together, and were *still* financing them . . .'

'. . . Then Saddam's army is going to be killing our chaps with American-sponsored matériel.'

'Precisely.'

Martin Heaney took a deep breath. 'Ah,' he said at last. And there was this great big silence, the kind that generates its own white noise.

'Forward,' Grindle said, making Martin start, 'has been to visit Powis. As you know. Not at all the sort of thing HMG wants to see encouraged. Don't you agree?'

Martin found himself nodding.

'We are not interested in abstract truths, at this juncture. On the eve of a major war, abstract truths tend to become rather like abstract art.'

'Meaningless.'

'Precisely. Oh, very *good*, Martin, very good. Now. I'm forming a committee of one. Damage containment: that's your brief. You worked on the Forward case seventeen years ago, you're one of the old firm, and *I won't have any outsiders.*' He rapped on the desk. 'Clear?'

Martin considered the proposition, taking refuge in silence while he did so. He was being offered rehabilitation. This is how it felt when they came to you in north-east Siberia and they said, 'So sorry, the last twenty years were all a mistake, sign here, and you can move back to Moscow now. Oh yes, and just one other thing before you sell your thermal underwear . . .'

'There's more,' he said. 'Tell me what you've got planned for Forward.'

Grindle gestured with a dismissive hand. But Martin, teetering on the very threshold of freedom, poised to win (or lose) everything, still couldn't leave it alone. 'Seventeen years ago,' he said, 'a heavy hint was dropped – not, in fairness, by you – that Forward should meet with an unpleasant accident before he could be brought to trial.'

'Good God,' Grindle said, with a straight face.

'I refused to take the unorthodox course then. I'd have to refuse now.'

In the silence that followed Martin belatedly wondered how he could have been so stupid. To see a future come within, slip from, his grasp . . . *how could you?*

Grindle said nothing for a moment. His face betrayed neither displeasure nor approval. At last he raised a hand from the desk-top and brought it down again in a 'let's close' kind of way. 'That goes without saying.' A pause. 'Welcome home, Martin.'

# NINE

The Arabs flew in separately, never more than two on a particular flight: from Abu Dhabi and Dubai, Karachi, Kuala Lumpur, Los Angeles, from the four quarters of the globe they came to Singapore.

Emil Barza was last to arrive that November day, stumbling off Saudia flight 384 in the middle of the afternoon with two briefcases clutched to his chest and exhaustion etched into every line of his grey face. Verity Newland met him at the airport. She took him straight to her apartment, where the others were already waiting. She drove herself, not wanting anyone, even Steven Lim, her secretary, to know who was coming, or why.

She parked beneath the tower block off Fernhill Close and rode with Barza to the thirtieth floor, where she had her penthouse. The other eleven men were sitting or standing in the semi-circular main living room, with its breathtaking views of Singapore, Indonesia and distant, misty Malaysia. They remained silent, perhaps aware of being under scrutiny by the *amah*, Mrs Boon, who now caught Verity's eye and shrugged, as if to say that the silver was still in place but she couldn't answer for the cut glass.

'Coffee,' Verity said softly; and Mrs Boon left.

Verity helped Emil Barza down on to a sofa and tried to relieve him of his briefcases, but he clung on to them. He was sweating, she noticed; his right eyelid couldn't stay still. He stank of cigarette smoke and that deadly, bitter odour which attends the long-distance air traveller for hours after his arrival.

Verity pressed a button on a panel let into the wall. Curtains began to slide around the panoramic window, shutting out the view. She pressed another batch of buttons, flooding the room with soft light. Details which had seemed insignificant before assumed new importance: the blotters laid out along the coffee-table, the pens and pencils in silver holders, even the ashtrays, everything suddenly spoke of business.

The men took their seats, according to Verity Newland's directions. She sat at one end of the long coffee-table; Emil Barza clutched his briefcases at the other. Nobody spoke. Mrs Boon came in, carrying a tray of cups and saucers. A few moments later she returned with two electric thermos flasks; she plugged these into wall-sockets and left, closing the door behind her.

Emil Barza raised his haggard face and opened his mouth to speak, but Verity silenced him with a movement of her hand. Moments later they all heard the back door, the servants' entrance, close. Verity stood up and made a quick tour of her domain.

'We're alone,' she said, resuming her seat. 'Mrs Boon will not return to this house until I make a telephone call, summoning her. So. We await His Excellency's instructions. Emil . . .'

Barza struggled upright, letting his briefcases fall. 'Madame,' he said hoarsely, 'please may I have a cup of coffee, well sugared?'

She poured it herself and carried it down the table. Just before she reached him she held the cup to her lips and took a quick swallow, pausing slightly before handing it over. His smile showed he realized what her gesture meant: the cup hadn't been poisoned. There was a little light in his eyes now.

'Gentlemen,' Verity said. 'Be so kind as to help yourselves to coffee.'

They took this from her, as they had been taking it

these past fifteen years: not merely a refusal to wait upon them, but a disdain bordering on insolence for which most of these men would, in their own country, have killed any other woman.

'We have so much to do and so little time,' Verity said as they took their seats again. 'Emil, please . . .'

Barza set down his coffee cup. 'His Excellency is pleased to accept all your proposals,' he said.

There was a slight but perceptible release of tension inside the room.

'He wishes everything in place immediately,' Barza went on.

Verity inclined her head. 'It takes only the pressure of my finger on a few buttons to send the money. Delivery of merchandise will take longer, but there are ways of expediting it.' She smiled glumly. 'Rather expensive ways.'

None of the men laughed or spoke.

'We shall begin by exporting the companies, as outlined in my first memorandum.' She looked around the room, counting faces. 'All the directors are present, I see.'

Barza opened both briefcases and took out their contents: pile upon pile of documents, each prefaced with a checklist of formal requirements concerning dating, stamping, registration with local authorities, and deposit of copies, each list tailored to a different country of domicile. For forty minutes the unsmiling men signed and signed, until their signatures began to frazzle and fade. At the end Verity collected up the documents, checked them against her own schedule and said, 'I'll send the money.'

She slipped into the study next to her bedroom, closed the door and went across to her Dell 325D computer. She loaded a secure communications programme designed solely for use by the Occydor group, and retrieved a file she had prepared days before, in anticipation that Sad-

170

dam Hussein would rubber-stamp her design. For twenty minutes the Dell spoke via a modem to the satellites that circle the globe, issuing instructions for the transfer of funds out of the hands of infidels into Muslim safe havens. She had the computer print out a list of transactions and carried it in to her guests.

'You may have copies if you wish,' she informed them. 'At your risk.'

She saw only a wave of shaking heads.

'Very well. The second phase ... our shopping list. Emil, what instructions do you have for me?'

Barza opened a zipped compartment in one of his briefcases and took from it five sheets of A4, which he handed to Verity. She glanced through them and grimaced. 'Short notice.'

'You can do it, madame.'

Verity Newland raised her head to find, as she knew she would, twelve pairs of eyes locked on to hers.

'Naturally.'

One of her guests chuckled; the others smiled. All except Emil, who regarded the woman critically, like a man tasting wine.

'That's everything,' she said. 'I suggest you go down singly or in pairs, at ten minute intervals. Fahid ... Abdel ... your plane leaves first, so you should go now. Walk to the main road before picking up a cab, please.'

The two men nearest her rose and made for the door, wasting no breath on goodbyes. After their departure, silence descended on the room. Verity poured herself a cup of coffee. She carried it across to the window and stood with her back to the ten remaining men, sipping slowly. While the translucent curtains were designed to frustrate prying eyes (even though at this height there were none) she could nevertheless see the terrace outside, with its thick chrome safety-rail, and beyond that, the lights of the city. She diverted herself by placing the

171

brightest lights in her mind: the Shangri-La Hotel, Top of the M restaurant, Compass Rose . . . Every so often she would hear quick footfalls as another pair of Arabs left, without bidding goodbye, but she continued to stand with her back to the room, pretending to sip her coffee long after the cup was empty.

At last there was only one man left, and only then did she turn around.

'You are staying overnight?'

Emil Barza nodded wearily. 'I'm booked in at –'

'No!' She held up a hand. 'Better I don't know.'

He stared at her through haggard, half-closed eyes. 'It's that bad?'

She shrugged, and moved to put down her cup. 'Lim tells me we are under surveillance at the office. It's possible my home is watched, too.' She hesitated. 'Did you get in easily?'

'Yes. I was travelling on a US passport. Even so . . .'

She watched his face, noting the fatigue, the fear. 'Even so,' she echoed softly. Then – 'Come, Emil: dinner.'

She took him to Alkaff Mansion at Telok Blangah, perhaps hoping the Arab name would bring them both luck. As they mounted the steps to the brilliantly lit white house, constructed in classical Moorish style, she glanced at him sideways, noticing how his eyes bulged, and was pleased.

'The Alkaffs were fabulously rich,' she murmured, when they had taken their seats at a veranda table. 'But they sold to someone even richer. A couple. They run this restaurant almost as a hobby and, oh!, they run it well.'

A young Chinese waiter came to light the candle in its glass globe; she ordered two whisky sours, knowing Barza's tastes in drink, food, and even – she caught the look that flitted between her guest and the waiter – boys.

'It's wonderful,' he said looking around. 'The cost . . .'

'Was stupendous. Everything has been restored to per-
fection: a rich family's house overlooking the sea, with
priceless furniture and artefacts, and an atmosphere of
old-world prosperity that our nouveaux riches would die
for.' She glanced around at the palms, the terrace and
the high chandeliers in the huge room behind her, casting their glow over a wonderful buffet spread. 'I love it
here. It has a quality . . .'

She faltered. For a while they sat in silence, enjoying
the stately old-time melodies being played by two grave,
bespectacled Chinese on piano and violin. When the
waiter brought their drinks Barza knocked back his with
one swallow, a man lost in the desert who had found
an oasis. Verity ordered refills, along with a bottle of
Nuits-Saint-Georges.

'It's even worth drinking French wine here,' she said.
'They let it rest, after the journey, they serve it at room
temperature and they don't mark it up out of sight.'

A fragrant curry aroma wafted out to them, mingling
with the cool sea breeze and the scents of the garden's
night flowers. Fresh drinks came, along with the wine,
but neither of them showed any inclination to forage
at the buffet. Barza lit one of those fizzy, foul-smelling
Indonesian cigarettes called *kretek*, and leaned back in
his chair. Verity kept an eye on his profile, but it told
her nothing. Her own attention strayed. Far off to the
right, a beautiful old albizia tree crowned the top of a
low hill, its three-tiered canopy seeming to float upon
a velvet sea. They sat alone on the veranda overlooking
the terrace and they knew this would be the last
time.

'Is it that bad?' she asked suddenly, echoing his earlier
question to her.

His response was wordless but unequivocal. In a series
of swift movements he leaned forward to rest his elbows
on the table and cover his eyes with his hands; he looked

173

up to one side as if appealing to Allah; he shook his head and stared into the glass before him.

The young Chinese waiter seemed to have a thing about Barza. One of the many reasons Verity liked this place so much was the unobtrusiveness of the service. Tonight, however, this boy was perpetually hovering on the fringes of her vision, with eyes only for her guest. Now he came forward and poured wine for the Arab to taste. He reached out to take the glass; then, remembering, made a gesture in Verity's direction, smiling into the boy's eyes as he did so.

She sniffed the bouquet without bothering to drink and nodded.

'Emil,' she said quietly, as the boy once more took up station on the edge of their circumscribed little world, 'I need your help.'

He raised his thin eyebrows once and essayed a smile. He was a small man, much given to melancholy, but tonight his rounded features seemed to have shrunk beyond the bounds of possibility, enveloping him in a sadness that could not be lifted.

'I've had several letters from America,' she said. 'From Jay.'

Barza wriggled upright. His right hand strayed to the table-top, nervously rearranging the cutlery.

'He wants money,' she went on quietly. 'He thinks he knows enough to be able to get it.'

'From you?'

'From somebody. He'll be coming to Singapore soon.'

'He's said so?'

'Yes. And I have to stop him.'

His eyes assumed their hooded, secretive expression, probing her depths, giving nothing away.

'He's still got ten per cent of Occydor. He's dangerous for me because he knows such a lot. And . . . and dangerous in other ways.'

174

'Other?'

Verity hesitated. 'I've always been afraid of him,' she said in a lower voice. 'Of what he might do . . . if . . . if roused.'

Barza considered this for a moment. 'He's dangerous for Washington also,' he observed. 'A word in the right ear would put paid to Jay.'

'Yes, but I'm out of touch, I don't know who to contact there. And besides – do you think I want to bring myself to the attention of the CIA, at this time?' She paused, wrestling with the anger that was mocking her attempts at self-control. 'I think,' she said at last, 'that His Excellency would prefer me to concentrate my efforts elsewhere.'

A small sound escaped Barza's lips. It might have been heartfelt assent, or a moan, or a stifled cough. Actually it was stifled terror; she knew that.

'Why all this talk of the CIA?' he said, following on immediately with a jittery laugh. 'Jay sold for plenty of US government agencies, back in the seventies. I can think of half a dozen who'd be glad to put him to sleep.'

'Him . . . and me. It won't be long now, Emil. Your President will be at war, soon after Christmas.'

'No, no! The Americans will back off; all talk, all talk, the Zionists will capitulate . . .'

He drained away to silence and for a while she left him there, marooned in his own pathetic swamp with the beasts and devils who haunted it.

'Soon after New Year,' she resumed, patiently, 'there will be a war. In order to fight this war, His Excellency requires matériel on a vast scale; he also needs money, much money. All this I can supply; Reggie has been stockpiling for years. We knew this would come, you see.'

'You . . . *knew*?' His expression had turned through

one hundred and eighty degrees, to astonishment. 'How?'

She wanted to say, 'Because Hussein is mad,' but it was bootless to state the obvious and besides, she did not want to antagonize this forlorn little man, so instead she replied, 'I have made a study of history, Emil. Great rulers must always follow the call of their destiny.'

'Yes, yes.' His eyes flickered away for a second while he committed that phrase to memory.

'It is my duty, and my pleasure, to assist His Excellency to realize that destiny. But if someone should put me out of action, Emil . . .'

'Out of action . . . ?'

'If I were to be tortured, you know what the Americans are capable of . . . I am a woman, Emil, not strong, like you. If I were to talk about the companies that we control, what they've been doing these past dozen years, the deals with Dr Bull, with Brush UK, with Schaublin of Switzerland; and Petrochemical 3, your uranium-enriching programme; if I were made to confess about the chemicals, the gases, the locations of the plants where His Excellency is putting together his nuclear capacity, about Al Tarmiyah, and Babylon, and the G2 centrifuges . . .'

But Emil had got the idea. He used both hands to raise his wineglass to his lips and he swallowed the contents in a series of gulps. She watched his Adam's apple bob up and down, the sight nauseating her.

'Don't worry,' he said in a thick voice. But then he must have forgotten what he was going to say, for he repeated the phrase several times with a vacant look in his eyes; and Verity made a connection that had been eluding her until now, she realized what he reminded her of: a man who'd survived a bomb-blast but whose mind would never be the same.

'We'll find a way around this,' he said at last. 'No one's

going to take you out of circulation just when we need you most.'

'You will . . . take care of it?'

But he shook his head, reaching for the nearly empty wine bottle before the conscientious boy-waiter could move.

'I cannot take care of it in the way you mean,' he said at last.

She waited.

'As of last week all covert activity is cancelled, world-wide. A policy matter. From the very . . . the very highest quarters.'

'Why?' she breathed.

'No provocations. None.'

She had not foreseen that.

'Are you saying,' she grated, 'that you can't do anything?'

They sat contemplating their respective views of the tropical night. The minutes went by, until at last she realized that his silence was the answer to her question. So after a long pause Verity Newland heaved a sigh and said, 'Shall we eat?'

The buffet was sumptuous, but she did not feel hungry; Emil, she noted, reacted to the sight of all that food with the enthusiasm of a long-term prisoner. As she moodily circled the table, taking a little curry, a couple of oysters, satay, a teaspoon of rice, it occurred to her that she would need another string to this bow . . . The first of the most recent Sonja letters had reached her by the hand of a Chinese teenager, the nephew of Harchem's old care-taker. She had not reckoned on seeing the boy again, but now she had a use for young Robinson Tang, after all.

The two of them returned to the veranda to find the attentive waiter putting final touches to a refurbishment of their table: clean ashtray, old glasses removed, even the bill neatly rolled and inserted into its bamboo container. And a new candle, although the old one had scarcely burned a quarter of its length . . .

She loved this place.

*

The young waiter saw them seated, did a last, quick inspection of the table, bowed slightly and removed himself on soundless feet.

He passed through the kitchens to the left of the veranda where Verity Newland and Emil Barza were sitting, exited from the mansion and did a long circuit of the grounds, so as to keep well out of their sight. He scampered down a stairway cut into the side of the hill until he came to the driveway. There he looked left and right, scanning the line of darkened cars. Suddenly one of them started up and began to move towards him.

As it drew level, the waiter bent down. The driver, an attractive honey-blonde American girl, leaned out and said, 'Reception's A1, you don't need to make any adjustments.' There was admiration in her voice. 'Where did you put the microphone?'

'In the candle-holder.'

During this rapid exchange, the car had not stopped moving. Now it accelerated briskly down the hill towards the main road. The boy did not wait to see it go. He had work to do.

# TEN

Virtually nothing distinguished the man from countless other visitors who daily invaded the collegiate quadrangle of modern buildings in Washington DC's L'Enfant Plaza. He came past the fountain towards the north wing, his eyes distracted by the signboards: Comsat, US Postal Service . . . but he had no business with them, it seemed, for he headed towards the elevators.

Once on the third floor he waited while the other occupants of the car streamed out, leaving him to follow right at the end and so read the signs without hindering anyone.

He did not look the kind of man who wished to impede others. He was on the short side, maybe five feet nine, and slight of build, with little remaining of his dark brown hair: it had receded high off his brow, leaving only a few strands brushed straight back in a futile attempt to conceal his baldness. He was in his late thirties, with a sallow complexion, the kind that speaks of too much junk food eaten alone in a bachelor apartment and too little fresh air. His suit was blue. You looked at it and knew that his job required a suit but he owned only the one. His black loafers, however, glinted like the nearby Vietnam War Memorial: with squeaky-clean, dark pride. He wore a tiepin of genuine gold, which clashed cultures with his polyester tie. Most people would have classified him as a not very successful attorney (this was Washington) with few outside interests, a Type B personality and no Significant Other to enrich his life.

He walked slowly along the corridor until he came to

179

a reception area that contained one Old Glory, two black women behind a desk with a forbiddingly high raised counter, and a sign saying: 'OFFICE OF FOREIGN ASSETS CONTROL'.

One of the black ladies raised her head. 'Can I help you?'

'I have an appointment with a Mr Jack Magno. My name is Tony Cover. As in Dover, not lover.'

'Ah, he's expecting you. Right along the corridor, his is the door next to the water-cooler.'

He thanked her politely and went on his way. If, half an hour later, they had stood Mr Cover up against the wall with two other men, one of them Japanese, and asked the receptionist to identify him, she wouldn't have been able to. He went through life leaving less of a trail than a fish in water.

He found the door he wanted, knocked and went in. It was an ordinary office, with no Big Business touches to tell lies about its occupant's importance. The furniture consisted of desk, chairs, low table for conferences, picture of President Bush and two silver sporting trophies on a sideboard.

A man in shirtsleeves was sitting behind the desk, one hand on the papers in front of him, the other resting on his hip. He had one of those heads shaped like the top of an artillery shell – no neck, rounded cranium – and a seedy, sandy moustache almost the same colour as his skin. Now he stood up and offered a hand across the desk.

'Mr Cover?'

'*Co*ver. As in "Dover", with the accent on the first syllable.'

'Oh, I'm sorry.'

'I'm used to it. You're Mr Magno.'

'Yup. Sure am. Take a seat.'

Cover hung up his raincoat and sat. Magno seemed a

little embarrassed. 'Colonel Southgate speaks very highly of you,' he said at last.

Cover's smile widened a bit before gradually losing its elasticity.

'I'm not quite sure where to begin,' Magno confessed. He opened a file, closed it again, put it back on the heap, shuffled the heap. While doing all this he did not look at his guest.

'Colonel Southgate outlined the nature of the problem,' Cover said at last.

'Ah.' Magno paused. 'This is a new ballgame for me,' he muttered.

'But not for me. Continue.'

Magno heaved a sigh. 'Okay. This is how it goes. Two days ago, the UN security council authorized use of force unless Saddam Hussein withdraws from Kuwait by 15th January. He won't, so there's going to be a war with Iraq. How much more has Colonel Southgate told you?'

'He has reminded me that in time of war most everybody puts the national interest first, but that certain individuals will not. They will put selfish, or even enemy interests first.'

Magno nodded his head. 'Right,' he said, and – 'Right,' he said again, this time smiling in the special way that thanks the speaker for saying what the listener felt but couldn't articulate.

'Such people,' Cover resumed, 'have to be taken care of.'

'One way or the other,' Magno suggested.

'And I am the other. Yes.'

Magno's smile died right there on his face, in mid-arc. He stared down at his desk, a flush pervading his cheeks.

'Perhaps you might start,' Cover encouraged him, 'by filling me in on the operations of the Office of Foreign Assets Control. Then we could pass to ways in which I might be of assistance to you and, equally important,

181

how your Office might be of assistance to Colonel Southgate and his department.'

Magno made the effort to pull himself together. He
straightened up in his chair. 'Okay. Overview time.'

He leaned forward to rest his forearms on the desk.
Cover noted that he kept his hands clasped together and
that his knuckles were white.

'Saddam Hussein has been planning this war for a long
time. He's been arming Iraq. This is not easy, on account
of the various embargoes he runs up against. His solution:
dummy companies, welded into a worldwide network,
able to call on fraudulent banks and other sources of
funds, to provide false end-user certificates to arms
dealers, and to bribe or cajole or in some cases threaten
investigators into keeping quiet.'

Cover nodded.

'Many of his offshore companies are based in London.
Control of a substantial number, however, can be found
in Singapore. Intelligence agencies have been able to provide my office with a comprehensive list.'

Magno pulled the top file towards him and opened it.
He extracted a sheet of paper and gave it to Cover.

'We'll call that List A. Just the company names. List
B extends to the individuals that run them, addresses,
organizational trees, things like that. List B fills an eighty-
megabyte hard disk; how much of it do you want to
digest?'

'I'll consider that.'

'Okay. There is some immediate firefighting to do. At
the top of my ... my hit-list, is a man called Jay
Sampson.'

He hesitated. Cover, who had dealt with the earnest
Magnos of this world many times before, did not pressure
him.

'Sampson,' Magno went on, 'was once connected with
the Singapore end of the Iraqi operation: a group of com-

panies trading under the name Occydor. He set it up in partnership with a woman called Verity Newland, long before Saddam Hussein took power.'

'Let me stop you there,' Cover said. 'Is Sampson a US citizen?'

'Oh, certainly.'

Cover nodded and raised a hand, inviting Magno to continue.

'Sampson's career was an interesting one. Back in the late sixties he developed contacts with high-ranking members of the Estikhbarat, Iraq's military intelligence operation. Through them, he got in touch with a man called Hussein Kamel Majid, who fronted the Military Industries Commission.' Magno paused. 'Majid is Saddam Hussein's cousin.'

Cover pursed his lips and nodded.

'Sampson used Occydor to set up a variety of on-going deals with Iraq's military. But by the mid-seventies he'd reduced his participation in Occydor to a minority stake and come home. He's executed various commissions for the US government since then, some of which you'll need to know about. According to our sources in Singapore, Sampson is now trying to get back on the inside of Occydor. He's making trouble, and for reasons of our own we don't want that right now.'

'I see. How much trouble is he in a position to make?'

'Lots. As far back as the seventies, some ex-directory US agencies were already using Occydor to –'

'Shut up.'

There was an awkward pause. 'Excuse me?' Magno stuttered at last.

Cover leaned forward, clasping his hands between his knees. He stared into Magno's face for a few moments; then he said, 'You talk too much.'

'Uh . . .'

'You talk too much. You've admitted this is a new

183

ballgame for you; I've told you, it isn't for me. So here's the basic rule of the ballpark, Mr Magno: when it comes to the seventies and ex-directory government agencies, you don't tell anybody anything, ever, not even if he's the President of the United States . . . *especially* if he's the President. You *never* volunteer information, get it? You wait to be questioned. You refuse to answer, once, twice, three times. You make them turn up the heat, Mr Magno, until you burn. Your boss tells you to squeal; you keep your mouth shut. *His* boss tells you; you keep your mouth shut. Eventually, yes, you tell: but by then your loyalty is so fully documented, in triplicate, that nobody, Mr Magno, will give a damn; now have you got that?'

During this quiet, steely tirade Magno's mouth had dropped open. The silence in the office was profound. Cover slowly sat back. He unclasped his hands. His body seemed to shrink, until he was once again the tired and not particularly successful lawyer who had walked into Magno's office a few moments before. He smiled his neutral smile.

'Let me see if I follow you thus far, Mr Magno,' Cover said. 'It wouldn't suit us to have Jay Sampson talking about the good old days in bars.'

'That is . . . correct.'

'Sampson's address: you know it?'

'There's a file . . .'

'Send it to Colonel Southgate's office. Anything else?'

For a moment Magno did not respond. The flush had vanished from his cheeks, leaving patches of unnatural whiteness around the mouth. His lips had set into a thin line. Cover read the anger in Magno's eyes. 'Is there anything else?' he repeated.

'I wouldn't tell you if there was.'

Cover grunted out a laugh. 'That's very good, Mr Magno,' he said softly. He stood up. At the door he turned. 'See you,' he said. 'Maybe.'

# ELEVEN

Alison lay in bed, staring at the ceiling. It was one o'clock, her night off, and she couldn't sleep. All that supported her was a thin sheet of electricity, or so it felt to her exhausted body: a crackle of tension that jangled the nerves from the tip of her scalp right down to her toes. She wanted to scream. If she screamed, Iain, himself tossing and turning in a disturbed, surface doze, would awake. She couldn't face that.

She was worried about the coming war with Iraq.

Suddenly the world had lurched sideways, dislodging certainties, spilling convictions. Along with everyone she spoke to, Alison could not imagine what a war would mean. Did anybody seriously intend to unleash nuclear weapons over the Gulf? How many English troops would die, how painfully, how soon? *Could* those dreadful missiles, those Scuds, reach Europe? Everyone said no, but . . .

Alison clenched both fists until the nails dug into her palms. The pain merely added itself to her pile of afflictions, bringing the opposite of relief. She screwed her eyes shut and begged the Lord to send her blessed sleep.

She was worried about money.

The three of them had to live on just over fifty pounds a week. She was still paying off the mortgage on the house. With inflation over more than a decade the monthly payments had shrunk, but her other debts had grown. She owed money to the bank, the local Paki store, the milkman: not much, not enough to bring down solicitors' letters, but always there, like chronic indigestion. She owed her employers money, which she hated, *hated*, because some day one of them, both of them, might get her alone in the kitchen again; 'Money or sex,' they'd say, 'which is it to be, Alison? Money or sex . . . ?'

Iain was earning now, but he needed some cash each week and his wages didn't make much difference to the household budget. After years inside he had no idea of the value of money.

She was worried about the mail.

Most days she was the one who picked the letters off the mat. Kate and Iain left about eight thirty, often together now, she noticed. She, Alison, stayed in bed until two when she was doing night duty, and the postman came at around nine thirty. So she was the one who sorted the letters. Thank God.

Ever since that letter had come from America, with its double postage and the Buffalo postmark, she'd been dreading the postman's knock.

Today had been different.

She'd come down to find a thin white envelope with the building society's name overprinted on the back; her first thought had been, 'Oh God, not more arrears . . .' But it had been the wrong shape and thickness for that. Then she remembered: mum's nest egg.

Both her parents had died within a year of each other, in Singapore, not long after Iain's trial. Because she was working all hours to prepare the appeal, she'd missed her father's funeral; then, when her mother fell terminally ill, she hadn't the funds to fly out. Anyway, who would have taken care of Kate?

A few weeks after her mother's death a firm of Singapore lawyers had written to her out of the blue, saying that the hospital wanted paying and there was some suggestion of an estate; would she like them to pursue the matter? She never acknowledged the letter but they

186

wrote back anyway, saying the house had been sold and, after payment of various debts, there were a few thousand pounds left. She'd been too stunned to think. Her first reaction was to spend every penny on Iain's case: solicitors, QCs, oh God, even that awful little clairvoyant dwarf who lived by Lambeth Palace . . . But then she'd looked at Kate, and thought, No. I'm not going to touch this money for a long, long time.

But when Kate had to have a warm winter coat, because she'd outgrown the old one in a year, or new shoes, or some special book for school, Alison had dipped into the fund. A few pounds here, a few there: funny how it all added up.

So today the annual statement had come from the building society, and what it all added up to was two thousand seven hundred and eighty pounds. One day, that would stand between them and disaster; she knew it, she knew it. Iain wouldn't keep that job. He'd go on the dole. He'd be left with nothing.

She was worried about herself: the fabric of Alison Forward. She'd long ago moved on from the paint-and-a-thorough-weeding stage; her roof was falling in, every pane of glass showed cracks, wind howled like a banshee through each crevice. A haunted house, too, full of ghosts. One phantom in particular: a man who had loved her and taken love from her, long ago.

She would have given anything to be loved. Forget the wine and roses, what she wanted was for a man to get out of his clothes very fast and take care of everything. She could settle for lack of technique. She wouldn't care if he came prematurely, or was rough, or was slow, or grunted like a pig. They amused her, all those articles in the *Mail* about how to educate your man in bed; angered her, too. Other women wanted everything. She wanted *anything*.

A husband who wasn't impotent; now there would be

a start. Iain with lead in his pencil. She couldn't remember anything about that, although she'd been there when it used to happen; just as witnesses to a murder sometimes blotted out all memory of it. The last time they'd made love was in their Singapore apartment, the one the police had arrested him in next day. He'd complained yet again about the bed, she could remember his exact words: 'Whoever made this must think we're trying to give it up for Lent.'

Her eyes closed, but she could still see the ceiling. She knew that her eyes were shut, she could feel the cold ring of sweat around her throat where the nightie touched it; she was asleep and awake.

She was in a London street. It was night-time, winter. Her feet dragged her towards Gerry Reynolds' apartment, by the river. Gerry was Iain's boss; mustn't offend him, mustn't be late. The concierge was supercilious and cold; he looked her up and down as if not sure whether to admit her. She went up in the lift, seething. She walked along the corridor, almost there now . . .

The door was ajar. Gerry had forgotten to lock it, how silly. She pushed on the door. It gave. She went in. It was dark in the hallway. Another door opened. A voice said . . .

No. No. No.

*Stop it now.*

Quietly, so as not to disturb Iain, Alison went to the bathroom and splashed water on her face. She tiptoed back to bed and lay down again, praying that the dream would not return, and indeed, her brain was merciful. Pleasant thoughts began to swarm inside her head, busy bees of memory.

She was back in Singapore, where the sun always shone and people smiled. She was young. She had a career, a husband, a home and a future. Life was sweet. Fingers stroked her thigh. The part of Alison still in Clap-

188

ham fought them off (why did she do that?) and then realized that she hadn't moved, the fighting was all in her mind. So the fingers must be, too . . .

*      *      *

She was asleep and awake, lying in a room on the top floor of the Prince Hotel in Singapore, the water tanks above her head disgorging with a cantankerous roar every twenty seconds or so. She felt desperately tired, and could find no rest. She lay on the narrow bed, striving to relax: a paradox nobody can resolve.

She hated this room. Only senior staff were allowed to use it for their breaktime and there was supposed to be only one key. This was a joke. There were many keys, everyone used it: to smoke and sleep and, Alison strongly suspected, to make love. There was a sourness in the atmosphere, a certain dank limpness about the sheets, that she loathed.

Only desperation would have brought her to lie down here. She had four hours off and the thought of going home revolted her: the travelling, the heat, the noisy air-con unit at the Holland Village apartment . . . And she didn't want to be anywhere that might remind her of Iain, because last night they'd quarrelled, their spat overflowing into the morning. Not for the first time . . .

She jerked her head to the right, then to the left. She held a forearm to her brow, seeking to darken the room, which had neither curtains nor blinds, but to no avail. She began to review the quarrel: he'd said . . . she'd said . . . he'd sworn and shrugged . . . oh, *pointless!*

There was no telephone in the room, only a wall-mounted intercom above the bed. Every so often it would emit a series of clicks, as if about to trumpet forth the latest pearl from Big Brother. This happened now, jolting

Alison into wakefulness. Nothing happened. She waited, on tenterhooks. Silence.

She sat upright, sighed and reached for her handbag. Perhaps if she tugged a comb through her hair, took an aspirin, got a divorce . . .

'I don't *want* a divorce,' she said grumpily. 'I want a real husband.'

Yet Iain was all too painfully real. They'd been married for less than a year – good heavens, did she expect everything to come perfect at once? Her mother had actually said that to her, only a week ago, when she'd run off to the house in Changi for tea and comfort. Why, your father and I . . .

Alison screwed up her eyes and gave her face a good rub. These rucks in the cloth sometimes appeared early in a marriage, they took time to iron out. No, he hadn't got a colonial expat background, and so what? No, he didn't understand the Chinese; and who did? Yes, his table manners needed refining; whose didn't? My *God*, woman, have you no bad habits . . . ?

No, she had none.

Before, he'd been romantic; now he took her for granted – that was the trouble. He threw his underpants down and expected someone to pick them up, wash them and then put them away. Sometimes he said things that hurt, without thinking: 'I was surprised to hear your Ma say that, it was almost twentieth century.' Well, that was *her* phrase, after all; can't blame Iain for adopting it. *His* people were provincial, lower middle class oiks . . . well, they were! For every black there is white, *yin* begets *yang*. Petty, petty, petty.

He was such a rotten lover it had to be a joke. Please let it be a joke.

The first night in Tosca Road, she'd seen the signs and turned her back on them. Perhaps after going to so much trouble to get rid of Susie and Clara, the fussing around,

190

the scheduling and rescheduling, the dreaming and idol-
izing, she couldn't face the thought that she might have
been wrong. He'd apologized, saying he was tired, and
she felt only deep, intense sympathy for him; she
thought, how nice to find a man generous enough to say
sorry. She had assumed, in her innocence, that saying
sorry carried with it a determination to change, when
in fact all it meant was that he'd got into the habit of
apologizing. Even that stopped, after a while.

All the necessary evidence was laid out for her by
that first dawn, in Tosca Road. She'd misinterpreted it,
*chosen* to misinterpret it. He did not understand her
needs, and she had not the means of communicating
them. She'd told herself sex wasn't the be-all and
end-all. Well, well.

What a bummer.

The intercom buzzed, properly this time, and she
pressed the button.

'Telephone for you, Miss Alison.'

She liked it when they still called her that. 'On my
way. Put it through to number eight.'

She jumped off the bed and made her way along the
corridor to the housekeeper's phone. And then she
thought, What if it's Iain?

She paused. Either he'd still be angry from their quarrel, or this was an apology. Either way, she didn't want
to hear it: even if he said he was sorry it would only be
to keep the peace, to ensure that his bloody pants got
picked up . . . But she must take the call, now that she'd
said she would.

'Hello?'

'Alison! You're not working. Neither am I. Swim?'

She gasped with the relief of hearing Jay's voice.
'Where are you?'

'The Tanglin.'

'I've only got a couple of hours.'

191

'"A thousand ages in thy sight are like an evening gone", my dear; can't you make it longer?'

'Well . . .'

'I will await you by the pool.' And he rang off with a chuckle.

She skipped along to the lifts and stamped her foot in exasperation when one didn't come the moment she pressed the button. She didn't have a swimsuit with her, but Maisie at the Tanglin would always fit you up if you asked her nicely, and, oh, but she did want a swim! And to see Jay again . . .

Some Chinese god rearranged the board very quickly, like her own, experienced maître d' coping with a numbers crisis in the restaurant. A taxi came immediately, they were not digging up Scotts Road, even the lights opposite the Goodwood Hotel were green. She paid off the cab by the car park and skipped inside to beard Maisie in her office; sure enough, there was a swimming costume to fit her. She ran down to the poolside bar. No sign of Jay. With a pout of disappointment she went on to the ladies' changing-room. And then, as she was coming out, adjusting her cap, she saw him!

Jay was on the edge of the springboard with his back to her and to the water. He stretched out his arms, bending his knees. Suddenly, with a terrific upsurge of power, he leapt into the air, flipped over backwards and penetrated the surface of the pool with both feet locked together and his hands high above his head, vertical as a severed plumb-line.

'Bravo!'

As his head broke water, tossing left and right, Alison clapped her hands together and cheered. A few amused glances came her way; not many. Her exuberance would be cause for remark at the next film show, or whist drive. It would get round. Good, she thought. Good.

He swam over to the side and held on to it, smiling up

at her. 'Glad you could come. I haven't thanked you for that Japanese banquet.'

She flushed up to the hairline, down to the tops of her breasts. Yes, that had been a splendid evening: one when everything went right. So much of the business he put her way went right.

'Do it again,' she said. 'The dive, I mean.'

He laughed. 'You think I can duplicate miracles?'

'I know you can.'

He swam away. Alison decided not to swim at once – funny, when she remembered how eager she'd been a moment ago. Instead, she took a seat at one of the tables by the pool, on the tennis-court side, where she could watch him without distraction. She ordered a fresh lime juice from Little Johnny and sat back, crossing her legs; and as she did so she thought, I like my thighs that colour and I'm really glad I lost those four pounds . . .

He reached the ladder at the far end and climbed out of the pool, swishing his hair back off his face with both hands. Her throat tightened, forcing out a little gasp of air.

She had done business with him, drunk with him, eaten several meals in his company; she had joked with Jay Sampson, and smiled at his sallies, and even flirted madly with him when she deemed it safe. But she had not seen him wearing only a swimsuit before, and the skimpiest of swimsuits at that.

She cast a quick roving glance around the pool, at this time of the afternoon occupied mostly by matrons middle-aged and younger. Surely this was not quite the thing for a man to wear, what would people think . . . ? But those who noticed Jay at all followed him with their eyes, their enigmatic expressions indicative of nothing.

Alison's gaze reverted to Jay. He was darkly tanned. He padded lightly around the pool on the balls of his feet; Alison's sharp eyes could see the roundness of his arches,

193

how unlike poor, flat-footed Iain. His legs resembled beautiful young saplings: teak-coloured, sturdy.

Jay turned the corner of the pool and hopped on to the springboard. His arms were muscular and large, like his chest. A broad ridge of muscle descended from just below his nipples, a streak of black hair dividing it neatly in half, two deeply etched clefts on either side. He was beautiful, oh gentle God, he was.

He stood at the far end of the board, judging his dive. Until this moment Alison had been fooling around, pretending, and now she stopped. She looked at what all these blessed women were looking at: his crotch.

She could see, quite clearly, the rounded pouch at the bottom, where his testicles lay confined. Above that, thick and proud, something stretched the white material, dragging it out of shape. A real man, then. *Really* well hung. A whopper.

*'For God's sake,'* she hissed under her breath. Her heart had begun to thump and she felt exceptionally well, as if at the prospect of some grand excitement. She became conscious of the wetness between her legs; damn you, Jay, you've had that effect on me before . . . She saw another woman put on her sunglasses and also cross her legs, *bitch!*

Jay rose up on his toes, lowered himself again and repeated the series of movements. Then he ran forward, bounced high in the air and jack-knifed into the pool, disappearing beneath the surface with scarcely a splash.

Alison hauled in a deep, trembly breath. As she did so, she became aware of that other woman, the one with sunglasses, studying her from across the pool. Alison could not read her eyes, but the woman's fleshy lower lip was protruding slightly, perhaps in contempt, or perhaps . . .

'You okay?'

A shadow fell across her, cutting off the light. She

opened her eyes. He had come out of the pool and was standing in front of her, hands on hips. She could have reached out a hand and stroked the front of his white trunks.

'Yes,' she said. And then – 'You're strong.'

'I guess. I keep myself in shape. Rock-climbing, that toughens you.'

'Rock-climbing? You?' She had never associated him with any sport; but then, she knew little about him, except that he was gorgeous.

'In the Adirondacks; Whiteface Mountain.' He looked at her for a moment. Then he said quietly, 'Come home with me.'

She swallowed, wanting to laugh: indeed, only the realization that she would have hysterics prevented her. She ought to feel insulted, and to let him see she felt insulted. She wanted, needed, a man to come and say, 'Excuse me, madam, but is this person annoying you?' Iain, a voice wailed inside her head, Iain, where are you?

But Iain was at work and he'd stay at the office until six o'clock at the earliest, by which time she would be back on duty anyway.

'Yes,' she said.

'The car park. Ten minutes.'

'Make it five.' Her voice was shaky as an invalid's but he must have caught the message, for he nodded. 'Five, then.' Her courage needed renewing from second to second, if he wanted her he must hurry, oh yes he knew all that, he wasn't stupid, he's done this before, you silly cow . . .

When she settled into the front seat of his Aston she wanted to be sick but at the same time she wanted him, how she did! Sometimes it was vomit, sometimes butter-flies, during that endless, instantaneous journey to *Rumah Anggerik*, the House of Orchids. She wondered who had seen them. Someone always did, in Singapore.

Business, she would say, if they challenged her; we had business to discuss. And they would look at her in the same way that the woman by the pool had looked at her: with an expression that said 'Whore!'

She would deal with that another day. The car raced on, her future never more than fifty yards ahead of her, behind the green jungle wall.

His house was beautiful. She walked in with downcast eyes, aware that there must be servants; but if she did not see them, they would not see her, she would not be here, this whole misguided incident would not have occurred.

Somehow she was upstairs, in his bedroom, breathing fast. Her legs were shaking. She sat down on the edge of the bed. She wanted to say, No, this is a mistake, let me go home. But if she'd done that she would have looked a fool. Which was better: to take a dent in your pride, or become a slut? Oh, the latter, definitely . . . She was in too far, the waters were up to her neck, they were closing over her head. She was going to commit adultery, just because she couldn't admit she'd been wrong to come.

'Alison,' he said, and his voice was urgent; 'Alison, listen to me.' And then he was on his knees between her legs, looking up at her with anguish in his eyes. 'Alison,' he said again, 'I love you. I've loved you from the instant I saw you, you're my life, my soul . . .'

Her head was in a whirl. Love, who said anything about that? But then he was lifting her up off the bed and kissing her. A faint tang of cigarettes, but mostly fruity. Something had got into her blood, it felt like the Laurent Perrier champagne he always plied her with. She was tingling. In a moment she was going to let go, but for now she held on to the illusion of resistance, savouring her saintliness. He loved her. She would let him kiss her and then she would say, No, I'm a nice girl. *He loved*

196

*her*. She would enjoy his lips on hers, his tongue probing her mouth, and then she would, then she would . . .

He pushed her over, gently, on to the bed. There was a moment of awkwardness, of pinched legs and not knowing quite where everything ought to go. He lay on top of her, nuzzling the neck of this thoroughly nice girl, and his hands were at her breasts. She arched back, closing her eyes. His right hand glided down to her thigh, pushing up her skirt, and she jumped as if stung. Inside her, a thousand-megawatt alarm system sprang to life, lights flashing, buzzers sounding, juice pumping. Jay rolled the two of them on to their sides. Now his hand was on the zip of her dress.

Her pathetic pretence at defiance ended with frightful suddenness. It wasn't a decision to surrender, it was a rout. He *took* her. First she capitulated; then, following the ancient traditions of treason, she collaborated. She released the moan that had been building up within her chest. She let her hands play where they wanted to play, and yes, those lewdly tight white swim-briefs hadn't lied. And oh, it was fun! It was *wonderful* . . . because he loved her, you see.

He took her. That was the consolation, the excuse: she had no choice. What, you mean it was rape? Ah . . . But much later, when death itself seemed the only possible release from such paralysing pleasure-pain, she discovered that, like all good generals who suffer routs, she had a fall-back position.

She loved Jay and he loved her. Thus was victory snatched from the jaws of defeat.

\*　　\*　　\*

Alison lay on her bed, her hands clenched into fists, tight little balls of skin and bone, by her sides. She could feel his body on hers now, as if it had all happened that

197

afternoon, not eighteen years ago. He was *real*. The husband she shared this bed with wasn't real.

Jay fucked the same way as he loved: like he meant it.

Does he think of me now, sometimes? she silently quizzed the ceiling. Does he lie in some bed, awake in the small hours, uttering my name in reverence and agony? Yes. He does. I know it.

His latest letter had told her so.

'I must write to you,' he'd said back in 1972; and she hadn't wasted an ounce of breath on protest. It was mad, it was suicide, every letter fresh evidence of adultery, but she must write to him too, so to hell with it. And he had been clever: 'Change sex,' he'd said; 'I'll be Sonja, you be Johnny. If anybody finds one by chance, it's a mistaken address, or it belongs to a former owner — I won't date the letters. And if they're steamy, I'll stamp them double-value, so you'll know . . .'

All the letters had been double-franked.

Crazy.

'The Sonja letters', that's what prosecuting counsel kept calling them, at Iain's trial for murder. Like something out of *The Thirty-Nine Steps*. Sonja, such an alluring name, she'd thought when Jay first mentioned it, so romantic. In court number three at the Old Bailey it sounded like the tawdry alias of a Russian spy.

Nobody else in court knew that Alison, too, was on trial. Every day she sat there, head held high, while somebody or other quoted from this Sonja letter or that one, worrying away at the meaning of yet another steamy phrase. They contained the most powerful words she'd ever read, and in court they were just obscene. Coded messages, that's what the prosecutor said. She used to look down from the gallery while this barrister, in his starched collar and dark suit, handled the letters with impeccably manicured hands; and she wondered what he would have done if he'd known that sometimes Jay would masturbate and wipe his sperm on the letter before sending it to her . . .

And now, another Sonja letter. From nowhere, out of the blue, to stop her heart beating and make her hands go cold. She would lodge it in the bank, out of harm's way. Tomorrow. Friday. Sometime. Until then, she would keep it hidden. No one else would ever read it, not like those that had been desecrated in court.

Tomorrow she would deposit the letter in the bank, definitely. She already had it by heart. She began to recite the letter in her mind, and as she did so her hands slowly relaxed, and unfolded, and strayed to her breasts . . .

Do you remember, darling, *Ching Ming* festival of 'seventy-two? We were lying naked on the bed, you and I, with the fan going strong, your body tucked into mine, soldered by so many wetnesses: of sweat, and seed that had dissolved in the heat, and the juice from your insides all sticky and spent. My hand lay squeezed between your thighs and you pretended to be asleep while I worked . . .

# TWELVE

'There – see him?'

Jay's voice came to Neil Robarts as a soft murmur. They were standing in the cover of a big oak tree, about a quarter of a mile from the road that connected Eccles with Wyoming County Highway 39, at the point where fields gave way to the treeline fringe of Breaky Hollow.

'I see him,' Neil replied. 'Give me the glasses.'

Jay handed over the binoculars. 'That's the same red Ford,' he said. 'Three times last week cruising my neighbourhood. Then yesterday, out-of-state licence plate but same car. Must think I'm stupid, I guess.'

'Most government agencies think of the cattle as stupid,' Neil observed drily. 'I know, I work for one. What you going to do about this creep?'

Jay said nothing for a while. They continued to watch the red Ford, parked half off the road, a hundred yards or so away from Jay's Pontiac. The driver seemed to be asleep.

'Back up,' Jay murmured. The two men began to walk deeper inside the Hollow, passing between the 'posted' signs that marked the boundary edge.

It was the run-up to Christmas. All the leaves were down now, but the trees were dense and there was little fear of them being visible from the road. Twigs snapped beneath their feet, hidden from sight by a carpet of dead foliage. The Hollow smelled mouldy. Greyish moss coated tree trunks; here and there toadstools sprouted, their red and white caps enticing with corruption, like strip-club pimps. It felt colder than the thermometer would allow.

Winter came hard and sharp in upper New York state.

'Okay,' Jay said. 'What do you know about the guy in the Ford?'

'I don't *know* anything,' Neil replied.

Jay grunted. Neil Robarts had come up to Eccles for a Christmas vacation; the United States stood on the verge of war and it was sending one of its intelligence analysts on holiday. Although if the pedantry revealed in Neil's last answer was any indication, Jay could understand why.

'Best guess, then,' he growled.

'Know a guy called Cover?' Neil pronounced it to rhyme with Dover.

Jay stopped, frowning. 'Can't say I do.'

'He's been asking about you. Where you live, what you're doing.'

'So what did you tell him?'

'To get lost.'

'Thanks,' Jay said. 'You think that guy' – he tossed his head towards the road, where they had seen the Ford – 'is anything to do with Cover?'

'Could be. Is he why you brought me out here, to die of cold?'

Jay nodded.

'You think they've wired your house?' Neil's tone was subdued.

'Maybe. Used to be something in the constitution about that.'

'Play it straight. Just tell the local cops: Look, some fellah's bugging me.'

'I wouldn't get far. No, I'm going to run.'

'Run?' Neil stopped and grabbed Jay's arm. 'You mean it?'

Jay nodded. 'I'm cold,' he said. 'Tropical heat's what I need. Only, they won't let me go. Will they?'

Neil shook his head.

'That guy in the car back there . . . he's just the first.' Jay walked on, forging ever deeper into the Hollow. 'Now, it's watching. Soon, they'll visit. Friendly, sure. "Mind giving us your passport, Mr Sampson?"'

'So where're you going to go?'

'You know,' Jay said eventually, 'I'm not sure I plan on telling you that.'

'Thanks a lot.'

'What you don't know, you can't tell, even if they flutter you.'

'Even though I just found out where Newland's living for you?' Neil's voice was bitter. 'First treat me hostile, then treat me stupid. You're going to Singapore, aren't you?'

'Neil, listen —'

'I want my money. On the plane up here I figured I wasn't going to say that to you, but I'm saying it now. You owe me two grand. I want it today.'

Jay walked on at the same even pace, but Neil stopped. When Jay was about ten paces down the path from him, Neil shouted, 'I want my money, you son of a bitch!'

Jay halted. He sauntered back. 'I've got your money,' he said.

'Look, I didn't mean —'

'You didn't really want the money, you wanted to be loved, yes. I sold Sal's engagement ring, some of her other stuff. I'll be selling the house too, only I don't want to wake anyone up just yet. You sell it for me, Neil. When I've gone. Take whatever you think is right, I'll give you power of attorney; send me the rest.'

'In Sing —'

'Singapore, yes. I still own ten per cent of Occydor. Verity has the other ninety per cent. She'll have to buy me out.'

'Can't you . . . I don't know, can't you just take the

202

income from your ten per cent, or something? Why go stirring up a hornets' nest?'

'Because there *is* no income. She never declares a dividend on my shares and I can't force her to. When we set up Occydor in the Caymans we never thought it would mushroom like it has. The companies' constitutions don't help me one bit. Once I dropped out of active management, I effectively dropped all my rights. I lost interest, Neil, I drifted away.'

'So what's changed? Why should she do anything for you now?'

'*I've* changed. I've always had the power to bring her down, because of what I know. Before, I wasn't prepared to use it. Now I am.'

They stood in silence for a while. Then they walked on, only this time their bodies were closer.

'I can prove a conspiracy,' Jay said. 'A concerted effort on the part of the CIA and Britain's MI5 to prevent anyone discovering how the Pentagon acquired product ninety-three twelve. Ninety-three twelve, changed, hotted up, sold to Iraq along with God knows what else, Saddam Hussein's using its derivatives *now*. To do that, they framed an innocent man for murder.'

'You think Cover doesn't know about what you can prove? You think he won't do anything he can to stop you? Wise up!'

'I *am* wising up.'

'You're not! Listen . . .' Neil stopped and, when Jay turned towards him, laid a hand on his chest. 'It's cold out here – I don't mean Breaky Hollow, I mean where you are *at*. But there's still an invitation for you to walk right through the door, up to the fire, sit down, thaw out.'

'In Washington.'

'Sure, in Washington. The hub of the world.'

'In a jerk outfit specializing in frauds on the American people. Frauds paid for by my taxes.'

203

'You were happy enough to take your cut all those years. Travelling the world, peddling arms whenever business was bad, when you were stuck with some bill – '

'So I worked for them once. And I quit, right?'

'Can't you ever let up?'

'Not while I'm breathing.'

'Well maybe someone intends to fix that.'

Jay shrugged and walked on. After a while the men came to a path running between thickets of dense yew. Jay turned on to it. 'This'll bring us back to the road,' he said. 'We've got another ten minutes, maybe less, just two guys taking a stroll, so let me finish. No, I'm not coming in to work for any hick government agency, I'm going to find Newland and she's going to buy my shares in Occydor and set me up with enough for a comfortable old age.'

'And if she doesn't?'

'Then the British will. Or our State Department.'

Neil whistled and shook his head.

'But she will play. I've been writing to her and she hears where I'm coming from. She won't negotiate unless I come to Singapore, to talk. And she can't keep it out of her letters.'

'Keep what out?'

'Fear.'

The trees were falling away to either side of them, now; ahead they could see where the path came out into fields again, a pale grey-white wedge of daylight framed by branches.

'Don't go, Jay. I beg you: do not go.'

'I have to. She won't deal 'cept face to face.' He grunted. 'I wouldn't, in her shoes.'

They walked on in silence until they broke cover, emerging close to where they'd left Jay's car. There was no sign of the red Ford. They walked down a rutted track, ridged in the middle with thick weeds, until they came to the road, and Jay's Pontiac. He unlocked, then looked underneath, rising with a self-deprecating smile on his face, and Neil grunted out a laugh.

'Verity Newland's got plenty to lose,' Neil said as he got in the front seat. 'And a powerful friend.'

'Hussein?'

'Sure. She always wanted in to military procurement, didn't she? Well, she's come a long, long way. Forget about superguns disguised as oil-pipe. She delivers the gas and the bugs.'

'Seems incredible to me that nobody's stopped her.' Jay shifted into first. 'Wouldn't take much.'

'Do you know what it takes to get authorization for covert action these days? No, of course you don't ... well it takes around nine months. By the end of that time the mark's either skedaddled or died of old age anyway.'

'And we are supposed to be going to war. Read the latest Clancy?'

'Not yet. Why?'

'Kind of nice little note, at the beginning. Meant for our sort of people. "Would that America served you as faithfully as you serve her" – something like that.'

They laughed.

Jay swung on to Highway 39 and headed north. When they reached the house he did not park at once, but drove up and down one more time, looking for anything suspicious. There was no sign of the red Ford, so Jay parked the Pontiac in the drive. He waited for Neil to get out before closing his own door and locking it. As they walked up the driveway he reached for his latchkey, but his movements were slowing and he didn't know why. Then he did know why.

'Neil.'

One word, spoken softly; but Neil swung around at once, knowing its tone of old. Jay flicked his fingers open

205

once, and reverted to a state of utter stillness. Neil turned towards the house, surveying the front from left to right, up and down. He caught Jay's eye. Jay beckoned. When Neil was a foot away he moved slightly, forcing his friend to stand between him and the house, so that anyone inside couldn't see what passed between them. He swiftly handed over the back-door key. Neil glanced at it, jerked his head towards the rear of the house and received a quick nod of acknowledgement: enough to send him scuttling quietly around to the back.

Jay stayed where he was, giving Neil time.

They'd had visitors, while they were out. No, wait a minute . . . maybe they still had visitors . . .

Jay couldn't have said how he knew. The house was sending him a message in the way that familiar things can do: a curtain hanging not quite straight, a window left ajar that had been locked when you went out.

He approached on lithe feet, keeping the front door on his right; some people put a key in their own lock and got blasted away from inside, he'd known it happen. *What was it?*

Nothing obvious, that was for sure. The curtains *did* hang straight, the windows *were* all locked. Yet there was something . . .

He cocked his head, listening. No sound from Neil. Jay hesitated a few seconds longer. He turned around in a full circle, surveying the street, his lot, the neighbouring lawns. Everything looked, was, exactly the same. Except for the one vital detail that was *wrong*.

He crept up on his front door, inserting the key noiselessly in the lock and turning it slowly, so slowly. He stopped when the door stood open one inch, and he sniffed. Normal. No gas, no fire, no perfume or aftershave; just the faintest left-over smell of the chili wings he'd fixed for their lunch.

He glanced down, and there was the clue.

Beside the front door he kept a small Malay pot garden, a hangover from his Far East days. There were several dead ferns in dragon-pots set on two tiers of planks, with a number of trailing plants above, also dead. A few leaves, brittle brown crisps, had fallen on to the deck. Someone had cleared them away.

The leaves, lying in an untidy pile when he and Neil had left the house, were now shunted into the angle between wall and planks. Jay bent down, squinting at the pot. That, too, had been moved: he could see a small crescent, its inner surface bounded by the round pot itself, and an outer line of brown peat mingled with dust to show where the pot had been before. Scarcely noticeable, unless you were trained to see such things; but if you were, then as obvious as the World Trade Center on a clear day.

They'd been looking for his latchkey, supposing he might leave it there when he went out. The perpetrators had been brave. In broad daylight they'd stood at his front door, fiddling with his pots . . . amateurs.

Or professionals who'd been disturbed. Alerted by means of a radio signal, transmitted from a red Ford . . .

All these things went through his mind in the space of two seconds, the last of which he used to climb back up the steps. He pushed on the front door. It swung open. Jay crossed the threshold, sniffing again. Silent as the grave. He looked along the passage to the back of the house, caught a shadow as it flitted sideways in the kitchen.

'Neil,' he called.

For a second, no answer. Then – 'Secure aft,' someone said quietly, and Jay relaxed, recognizing Neil's voice. Now the man himself came into view at the far end of the passage, the back-door key dangling from one hand.

He pointed upwards with an enquiring tilt of the head. Jay mouthed 'No'.

Neil padded down the passage. There were two doors leading off into living rooms. He paused for a second outside each before opening the door with deft, controlled violence. Nothing. Nobody.

Jay waited for him. Together they moved to the foot of the stairs. Jay bounded up, Neil keeping a couple of treads behind. By now Jay felt sure that the house was empty. He barged through the upstairs rooms but he wasn't expecting trouble and he wasn't disappointed.

'Zilch,' he muttered.

'What made you think otherwise?' Neil asked.

Jay explained about the pot.

'What could they have been looking for?'

Jay shrugged. 'If somebody's interested, they search the file, they search your home, they end by searching you. Jesus . . .' He stared at Neil, face creased in a frown. 'The bureau . . .'

He ran downstairs, jumping the last four treads, and bounded into the living room. As soon as he entered he saw what he'd feared: his father's roll-top desk was open. He knew he'd left it shut, locked.

He shuffled forward, suddenly weak. A professional job, done with a key, no sign of damage, not even the smallest scratch. He sat down heavily, hands lolling between his legs. Neil came to stand beside him. He rested a hand on Jay's shoulder. 'What's gone?' he said softly.

Jay began to open drawers. He worked systematically from right to left, putting off the worst. A big roll of money lay at the bottom of one drawer, untouched. At last there was nothing left but the secret compartment.

He felt around the back of the upper left drawer, and a panel sprang open. He reached into it, going through

208

the formalities, but he was weary now, the game a burden to him.

The secret compartment was empty. 'Letters,' Jay said. 'Only letters . . .'

Absent-mindedly he peeled the rubber band off the money-wad and counted out two thousand dollars, which he then handed to Neil. 'Want interest too?'

Neil took the money, but only after a pause. 'No.'

Jay replaced the band and tossed the roll down on to the desk as if he were flicking a Frisbee. It landed with a thump. Neil sank down into the nearest chair. 'Tell me the worst,' he said.

But Jay remained lost in thought. The intruder, whoever he was, had been interrupted by their return. That much seemed obvious, because instead of photographing the letters, which was the plan, he'd stolen them. Brave and yet not so: the thief knew the letters' significance, which meant he also knew Jay could never report their loss to the police, so it wasn't much of a risk.

They would know, now, that Verity Newland was proposing a reunion, in Singapore: a date, a time, a place. They would deduce what he wanted, could put together by a process of reasoning what kind of letters he himself had written in order to provoke those replies. They would know he meant to implicate them, they would know themselves to be endangered.

They would come.

His brain hauled on the next link in his chain of reasoning and he closed his eyes. They had stolen the letters; he would find them missing; then he would know what *they* knew. So they would have to alter their plans. They would come for him tomorrow, tonight, now, *they were on their way* . . .

Jay involuntarily took a great gulp of air, making Neil start. He grabbed the money and stuffed it inside his jacket. He snatched a glance at his watch, his agitation in marked contrast to the stillness of a second before. 'Out!' he snapped. And when Neil opened his mouth to argue Jay didn't bother with sweet reason, he grabbed him by the shoulder and shouted, *'Now!'*

# THIRTEEN

December 21st: his first Christmas on the outside for seventeen years, and already Iain was hating it, the preparations, the false bonhomie, the faint air of burped-up booze and hypocrisy that infiltrated even Aural Sightings at this sentimental season. How he'd loathed prison Christmases! The screws put up a tree, some piece of moth-eaten rubbish knocked down cheap on the last Sunday before the holiday, and somebody would always 'accidentally' push it over. It would lie there for three days, looking pathetic; every time Iain saw that poor tree he would think of old lags' kiddies crying for their dads and he would want to cry too. He'd think of Kate, of Alison . . .

But this was all lovely, wasn't it? A real tree, fancy decorations, things in the shops for those with money to buy 'em. Drinks with Art and Brian and Chris and Dick . . . and Yohan and Zebedee too, more than likely. Not that anyone wanted the con, of course, but better include him anyway, can't have him getting violent and spoiling things for the rest of us.

He didn't know why he felt like this. Rotten way to start Christmas . . . it was three o'clock on Friday afternoon and Aural Sightings wouldn't be working on Christmas Eve, which was a Monday this year, so the staff were opening the wine now, getting an early start. Somebody pressed a glass of boxed Soave into his hand: 'Merry Christmas, Iain, and a very Happy New Year!' It was Linda the Goldilocks Girl, who detested him. Suddenly she raised herself on tiptoe and planted a kiss on his

211

forehead; everybody went: 'Ooh!' and 'Here we go, then!' Inside him there was this gallstone of unhappiness at not being able to feel happy, but there were tears in his eyes, too, just like when he was banged up, and, oh, but he felt so *muddled*. So damned muddled, and upset, because it was the season of goodwill to all, and why shouldn't they like him, he'd paid his debt to society, hadn't he? And didn't meek and mild Jesus, didn't he say to forgive everyone . . . ?

He drank some wine, smiled at Linda, his eyes bright with a prickly film of tears. Her own eyes crinkled in a parody of a smile and she patted him on the cheek before traipsing over to switch on the cassette-player. 'We *wish* you a Merry Christmas . . .'

There were about twenty people huddled in one corner of the downstairs open-plan unit and they were having a merry old time. They had streamers and crackers and those hooters that unrolled to tickle you with a feather. Some of them had got round to wearing their paper hats. Simon said, 'Listen everybody . . . what's got three legs and . . .'

Iain didn't hear the rest, because he'd slipped away and was going upstairs where he could mend his hatred and keep it in repair. But even that was difficult, because when he reached the back room, the one where he'd found the disused phone, the first thing he set eyes on was the little pile of presents he'd assembled for Alison and Kate. Nothing big or expensive: some perfume for his daughter, bath oil and a book for Alison; but sitting there on the desk, wrapped in their cheap red and silver paper, done up with a bow, their tawdry, look-at-me cheerfulness made him feel ashamed of his gall.

He pushed them aside and sat down with his head in his hands. He just wanted to be alone. This time last year, he'd spent twenty-three hours out of the twenty-four alone, and that was purgatory. Now he had people around him and he wanted to be by himself. No fun, being human.

Iain pulled himself together. He opened the bottom drawer of the desk and took out the thick manila envelope. In it were the passport the Guv had supplied him with only last week, a pair of contact lenses, some hair dye. Everything just as he'd left it. The chances of anyone finding his treasure were remote, but Iain still worried. This was the only place he'd been able to think of. At home, someone would be bound to come across it.

He must hang on to this passport. The prospect of being able to escape when things got desperate was what kept him in touch with his sanity. At least, that's what Iain told himself.

When he'd gone to collect his passport the Guv had brought up the topic of Bangkok again, and Iain had refused again; but as he was going out he'd turned to the Guv and said, 'Got anything going in Singapore?' And the Guv had replied, 'I'll look into that, Iain, if you want.'

Later, on the bus going home, Iain had regretted saying that . . .

He stuffed the envelope and its precious contents back inside the drawer. He collected his presents, carrying them tucked under his arm, and went out. The sound of revelry below became louder as he advanced towards the stairs. The MD's door was open, as usual. Iain paused. From where he was standing he had a good view of the safe.

There was a problem he wasn't supposed to know about, but your ears grew long in prison. On the day after Boxing Day there was going to be a party, with lots of local bigwigs and the major contributors of funds. The MD had done some deal with his brother-in-law's catering company, which wanted paying in cash. The banks were going to be tricky over the holidays, so they were keeping a lot of money locked up in the safe. A thousand pounds, maybe more, to take care of the party and end-of-year bonuses to full-time staff. For once, pay-packets were being left in the office overnight.

It wasn't a fortune. But you could buy a one-way ticket to Singapore for £365; Iain had seen the ad in the window of a travel agent's on Northcote Road. All he had to do was call this number in Deptford and have a couple of lads around with a bunch of skeleton keys; his cut would be half, and he'd see he'd got a perfect family alibi.

He stood in the corridor for a long time, staring at that blessed safe. It would be so easy; like taking money off a child.

Iain realized he'd descended into prison slouch. He straightened himself up. He shook his head and he turned his back on the safe, and he went downstairs.

They pressed him to have another drink but he refused, saying he'd like to get home before it got too dark. They smiled, and nodded; he saw how they exchanged glances, knowing their thoughts: first Christmas after all those years, must be a fantastic feeling . . . At the door he waved. He shouted, 'Merry Christmas, everyone!' and they replied in kind.

There was a bounce in his step as he turned down Lavender Hill towards the Junction. Red, green, blue and yellow lights twinkled in the gloom, all speaking the same message: Tidings of comfort and joy. As he meandered past the shops he was treated to different carols, Christmasy pop songs, even organ music. There *was* a future. It might not be very attractive, but he was part of it. He belonged.

As he turned right into Kelmscott Road he was mentally preparing his speech. He wouldn't make a big song and dance about it, but, by God, he'd get the words out if they choked him.

Alison was in the kitchen cooking supper while she listened to the six o'clock news on Radio Four. The Gulf Crisis: 'What does Mr Shevardnadze's resignation *mean* . . . ?' But seeing him come in with his brightly wrapped bundles she smiled, and lifted up her mouth to be kissed. He lingered over it, showing her he meant it, and she seemed pleased.

Iain switched off the radio. 'Don't listen to all that stuff,' he said sternly. 'There isn't going to be a war; I've decided.'

'Changed your mind, have you?' she teased him. 'Getting out of Kuwait after all?'

'Definitely. Can't stick the climate. Where can I hide these?' he murmured, laying his packages on the sideboard.

'On top of the wardrobe. Going to make us wait for Christmas Day?'

'You bet.'

'Good. So am I.'

'Hope you haven't spent too much.'

'Of course I have – what else is Christmas for?'

He smiled, feeling she was right. 'Is Kate around? Only I've got something to say – and that *can't* wait until Christmas.'

Her face tensed, she slackened her embrace. 'Oh.'

'Don't worry. Good news.'

'I'm pretty sure she's in her room. She was taking a bath earlier: one of those all-afternoon jobs.'

He went to the foot of the stairs and called, 'Kate! Can you come down a second?'

''Kay.'

She joined them in the kitchen a few moments later. She was wearing a very short, flared black skirt, a baggy white sweater, black stockings and trainers and, to cap it all, a huge scarlet ribbon, tying her hair into a clumsy ponytail.

'Do you have to go out like that?' Alison automatically clucked, and Kate pouted: 'Oh, Mum . . .'

Iain felt he was watching Pavlov's dogs do a demo for a visiting scientist. 'Hey,' he interrupted. 'I've got something to say.'

They looked at him expectantly. He gestured for them to sit down before going to fetch the bottle of sherry from inside the dining-room dresser. He poured three glasses. 'Happy Christmas,' he said.

'Oh, hah-hah,' Kate's drone had gone down a peg to winge. 'If that's it, then –'

'It isn't it. You shut up.' But he spoke the words so good-humouredly, as a real father might, that she took it. She even grinned sheepishly, and took a sip from her glass.

'It's not been easy,' he began. 'For any of us. I know that it's been bloody difficult for me, but it's been worse for you.'

Alison and Kate were both gazing at him now. He could smell their fear of what might be coming. 'I've done some rooting about,' he went on quickly. 'Tried to clear my name. Seen a few people. And what it comes down to is, I'm not getting anywhere. Not going to get anywhere, either. So instead, I'll have to make the best of things.'

Their rapt attention was starting to get on his nerves. 'Settle down. Make a few plans for the future. This house. This job.'

What more did they want, with their moon-like eyes and wet lips? Blood?

'This . . . family. My family. People I love.'

There was a silence.

'Have you been drinking?' Kate's question wasn't a joke, she sounded truly curious. But instead of getting on his high horse, Iain laughed. He felt good inside, all of a tingle.

'A bit,' he admitted. 'I've got a decent job now, love, and at Christmas they have an office party. I'm not drunk, though.'

He swivelled slightly, so that his gaze could embrace Alison. 'When I was in prison,' he said quietly, 'I used to think about you all the time, both of you, you and Kate. And I thought, When I come out, it'll be brilliant, you know? That's all I thought about, really, for seventeen years, all any of 'em think about. Any of *us*, I mean. But when it happened for real, I . . . couldn't take it.'

'Nor me.' Alison's voice was thick, muffled.

'So these last couple of months, I've been chugging along, you know . . . baffled. Like.' He was gathering momentum now. Maybe it was the wine and the sherry. 'You'd grown up without me, into people. Three-dimensional people, with lives I couldn't share. I should have been there, but I wasn't. Only now I can and I am.'

They continued to stare at him, like wax statues.

'So that's it,' he ended lamely. 'I'm going to make the best of everything. Mainly you. That's what I want to say.'

He drained his glass. He set it down on the table. After a moment he began to draw circles on the formica with the glass, staring at his own handiwork as if he'd stumbled on a hitherto unknown Leonardo da Vinci.

Kate stood up. She came to stand beside her father. She put her arms around him and rocked him gently to and fro. Suddenly she buried her face in his neck and began to shake. He felt wetness on his skin and clumsily reached up to stroke her hair. His fingers tangled in the ribbon. It came loose. He started to apologize, but she shook more vigorously and after a while he divined that she wasn't crying any more, she was laughing. Yet when she stood up her eyes were water-bright. 'You nerd,' she said, tossing her head. 'Nerdy, nerdy, nerdy Daddy . . .'

She flung herself into his arms and wept and laughed

and rubbed her tears over his face; and then she arranged herself on his lap and he cuddled her, smiling at Alison through his own tears while she wiped her face with a tissue, and: What a jolly Christmas, he thought, all tears and tissues . . .

'What am I going to do with this?' Kate said, peeling the ribbon away from her tangled hair.

'Well . . . you could use it to strangle the goldfish . . . if we had a goldfish.'

Kate flicked the ribbon at him with a moue of disgust before knocking her head against his chest. She sank into his arms and, to his surprise, began to suck her thumb without any sign of embarrassment.

'Baby,' he teased her. She shook her head, not taking her thumb out, and closed her eyes.

The doorbell rang. 'That's Darren,' Kate said, leaping off Iain's lap. 'Must go.'

'Why don't you bring him in?' Iain suggested. (It was Christmas, wasn't it?) 'Let's put this bottle of sherry to bed.'

Kate kissed him quickly on the mouth. 'Going to the flicks,' she said. 'Don't want to miss the start. We'll grab some Heinekens, bring them back later. Bye-ee!'

'What are they going to see, do you know?' Iain asked Alison as the front door banged shut behind Kate.

'*Home Alone*, I think. All about a little boy who –'

'– Who's left alone at Christmas and beats the villains and grows up.'

'Ain't it the truth,' Alison said.

'Ain't it just. Come here.'

She rose and came around the table to take her daughter's place on his lap, in his arms. 'We're home alone too,' she murmured.

'Mm. Nice.' He kissed her, and it was better than it had been so far; could she sense that?

'Must finish the pie,' she muttered. 'Got to go soon.'

218

He could tell how disappointed she was. 'Your last night,' he said.

'For a while.' The hotel was closed over Christmas, she'd have four days off. Iain suddenly found himself making plans for the holiday, grandiose schemes that involved borrowing Darren's van, pub lunches, walks by pounding grey seas . . .

'Have I got time for a bath?' he asked.

'If you're quick.'

He wanted to have supper with her before she left, so yes, he would be quick. He ran the bath before peeling off his clothes; by the time he got back to the bathroom it was full of steam and he had to add plenty of cold water before he could lower himself in, and even then his skin tingled pink.

He lay back with the water up to his neck and he thought: Christmas. I'm free. I'm safe. I don't have to worry that someone's coming through that door with a shiv, I'm not going to be banged up in solitary, I'm not on Governor's report. I have time off. A hot meal is waiting downstairs. I have a respectable job and I am definitely not going to burgle that safe. I have things that no other man has. I have a second chance. I am happy.

He felt something strange and raised his head a little. He was getting an erection. His hand went to the shaft that was stiffening as it lay flat on his stomach. He could lie here and rub himself, he could wank in his own bath in his own home, God, what a *treat*! He laughed out loud. His first erection in over a month, and a real one, not a piss-inflated one.

He closed his eyes. There she was, waiting for him: the woman. He looked closer. Alison! How funny, he'd been expecting Madonna, or Cher, or that Eurasian pin-up old Fuzzface had taped to the ceiling of the cell they'd shared in the 'Ville. Some wank-tank. And here was his wife. Younger, slimmer, but Alison, darling Alison . . .

219

'What were you laughing at, I . . .'

She'd come in without knocking. He jumped, shocked and a little angry: this wasn't prison. But then he relaxed. It wasn't his home, it was *theirs*. He had a wife who'd stuck by him for all those years, and now here she was, in the bathroom, smiling at him – a touch hesitantly, but smiling all the same. When she looked down he didn't feel embarrassed. His hand, temporarily paralysed, began to move again.

Alison sat on the floor and rested her arm on the side of the bath. She allowed her own hand to descend into the water, swishing it against his thighs. She did this for quite a while, smiling into his eyes. He loved that smile, he always had; but he knew there was a question behind it. He didn't know how to answer, because he was afraid. Since he'd got out, they hadn't made love, not once.

Her touch lingered against his thigh, stopped. Then he felt her hand move.

'Are you,' he said, 'attempting to take things out of my hands?'

She burst out giggling. He joined in. Then there was a tidal wave as he reared out of the bath, standing upright in every sense before her. She gazed at the evidence of his potency, newly established at eye level, and stopped laughing. Her lips parted. Slowly, very slowly, she leaned forward . . .

He stepped out of the bath, water sluicing everywhere, but she didn't protest at the mess, didn't protest when he picked her up and carried her to their bedroom, where he laid her on the bed and flung himself down alongside her, kissing her lips, her neck, her ears, hair, chin . . . He was sopping wet and Alison did not mind. He tore her dress, one of the few good ones she had, he hurt her when he stripped off her bra; nothing mattered. He had come home and she was waiting.

He slithered inside her. His slippery, moist body pounded against hers while he grunted out his yearnings. Alison laughed, she beat his chest, fought him with tears, passion, an upsurge of raw emotion she thought she'd never know again. He was coming now. She closed her eyes and reached up with her entire body, offering it to him, a sacrifice . . . and there was Jay, pumping himself into her like a hero from legend.

Iain came. He lay there not speaking, but breathing heavily. His heart hammered away so fast that she wondered if he might die. Somehow it helped, this hypothetical conundrum, and she allowed herself to dwell on it: first the ambulance, then the doctor . . . or was it the other way around? And who arranged the certificate . . . ?

Iain raised his head. He cupped her face between his hands, he tried to speak, but it dissolved into a weak laugh. At last – 'That was . . . fantastic,' he said. 'Thank you, thank you, thank you . . .'

She smiled. She did not tell him that she'd wondered if he might die, thus setting her free from her own life term, or that all the waiting had been for naught. No point in explaining that by making love to her he'd unlocked the truth: that he had survived to be reunited with a wife who no longer loved him, because she wanted her lover back. She needed Jay like her next breath.

'Yes,' she said. 'That was great.'

*

The evening of the third day after Christmas found Iain walking along Northcote Road. He'd just escorted Alison to Clapham Junction and seen her on to the train that would take her to work. She'd told him not to be so silly, but he'd insisted; they'd walked down the road together, arm in arm, like an old-fashioned courting couple. Now

221

he was on his way home, drawing up a mental inventory.

Christmas had been good, bloody good. He'd eaten and drunk too much. Kate's boyfriend Darren had come around a few times; Iain wasn't thrilled about that – the boy knew stuff-all and he liked to brag – but he seemed fond of Kate and she loved him and since there wasn't enough love to go round in this world, Iain was content to watch the situation develop in its own way. He'd spent odd moments jotting down ideas for streamlining Aural Sightings: nothing dramatic, just a few corners that might be trimmed. Satisfying, that. Made him feel not quite wasted.

Sex. Lots of it with Alison, at all hours of the day. Kate and Darren giggling, Kate ever more risqué in her behind-the-hand comments. Fucking, *loads* of it! He couldn't get enough of her. Alison, well . . . actually it was to be expected. She'd gone without for so long. But now she was doing good, as they said inside.

Which reminded him . . . New Year's resolutions. One. Do not continually and forever use prison slang, methodology, habits of thought. Get rid of them. You are an educated professional, remember that. Resolution two: contact the Institute, find out about re-qualifying. Lift yourself up.

It's beautiful, the free world. Don't leave it, ever again.

He reached the lights where St John's Road intersected with Battersea Rise and waited to cross. The last two days had been so good: a trip to Brighton, walks on the common, sex . . .

And another journey, a pilgrimage. He'd used a British Rail holiday bargain fare, and taken his family to Solihull, to visit his father. Old George Forward, 'Centre' to his friends, had been born in Fife; it was his idea to put a fancy 'i' into Ian when what turned out to be his only child was born. A schoolteacher, he'd moved south in 1956 when his wife Norma learned her sister was dying of cancer and wanted to be near her. At the time of his son's trial George had opted for early retirement and a life away from the world: Norma acquiesced, but it was she who'd come to visit Iain in prison, not George. She never spoke about why her husband didn't come. But when she hadn't visited him for over three months, and there'd been no letters, Iain, frantic, made enquiries through Social Services. She was in hospital. Blood pressure, they said; that and a weak heart.

They let Iain out for her funeral. George was at the graveside, supported by two friends. Afterwards Iain had wanted to turn away, too afraid of a rejection he thought inevitable, but George had called his name in a tremulous voice. They hadn't said much, but they'd shaken hands. His father started to write to him after that; once a month the letters came, assembled in shaky, outsize letters, frail but legible.

When Iain had written inviting him down for Christmas he'd replied that he didn't feel up to travelling. But Iain, suddenly ready, had taken them all up to Solihull. George was living in sheltered accommodation, hale enough for a man of eighty-one. They'd sat in his tiny room and talked about now. 'Then' had never happened. Iain knew that for as long as his father lived he was always going to prefer it this way. Deep down, he felt sure his mother had believed him innocent, whereas father feared him guilty.

'Hello, stranger.'

Iain, lost in memories of that day in Solihull, didn't turn his head. Then the voice repeated its greeting and a vaguely troublesome memory grated the back of his skull. He turned. A man was standing at his elbow, hands in pockets, his head thrust forward as if to be sure of identifying Iain in the light of the streetlamps.

'It is you, Iain, isn't it? Thought I recognized you.'

Iain stared at him. The memory, like a worm

burrowing its way to the surface, would break through any second now . . .

'Heaney. Martin. You remember.'

Then memory burst through like a whole can of worms: this was the man who'd interrogated Alison after the police had brought him back from Singapore.

'Remember me? 'Course you do.'

Yes, he remembered all right: Heaney had grilled Alison, and sometimes he had sat in on the others while they grilled Iain. A boy with a pained expression, as if he'd trodden in dog shit.

Heaney gripped Iain's elbow. 'See that pub over there? Buy you a drink, wish you a Happy New Year.'

'I don't want a drink.'

'Just the one. My shout.'

'I said, I don't *want* one.'

The lights changed. Iain shook Heaney off and strode across the road. But as he reached the opposite pavement his pestilence caught up with him. 'Now Iain,' he said, 'that's hardly friendly. Season of goodwill, you know.'

Iain marched on.

'Look.' Heaney fell into step beside him. 'We can do this the other way. Offices. Interviews, notes, tape-recorders. I'd rather not, honestly.'

'I've got nothing to say.'

'Spare me a moment. Please.'

Iain's head drooped. He had a serious criminal record. There were always going to be people with irresistible demands like this one.

'Keep it short,' he snapped.

The lights of the pub on the corner glistened boldly out of the surrounding darkness, welcoming them. Iain ordered a large Scotch, since the British government was standing treat. Heaney drank chilled lager from the pump: weak froth spilled down over the hand that carried his glass and Iain irrationally thought, Christ, what have we come to in seventeen years . . . ?

'How *was* Powis?' Heaney said, lighting up a John Player Special. 'No, have one of mine . . .'

Iain felt light-headed. He accepted the cigarette, knowing that tobacco wouldn't help, but he had to do something to cover the gap. Why be surprised they were following him? Here, just a mo, *where* had they followed him . . . ?

'He'd aged a bit,' he answered, trading Heaney calm for calm. 'Sad.'

'Very.'

Heaney took a long drink of lager and sucked in his lips, for all the world as if they were two mates discussing some old codger of an uncle.

'Pleased to see you, was he?' Martin said at last.

'I think so. He doesn't get many callers.'

After that they sat in silence for a while. The pub's evening business had got off to a good start, but that was Christmas for you. You get a lot of blacks in here now, Iain thought.

'What did you talk about, then?' Martin enquired. 'Old times?'

'Old times.'

'And the Guv? How's *he* getting along these days?'

'Very well. Thank you.'

Iain's cigarette was almost a butt before he spoke again. 'I remember you,' he said. 'Pretty well.'

'I knew it would come back.'

'Oh, it never went away. You interrogated Alison. And me. Funny . . .'

He stubbed out his cigarette, taking long enough over it for Martin to become uneasy about that dangling, final word, and say, 'Why funny?'

'You never thought I did it.' Iain jerked his head around. 'Did you?'

'What makes you say that?' Heaney's smile was intact again, but Iain had seen a momentary tremor.

'Can I talk to Grindle?' he asked suddenly.

'Iain.' Martin swivelled around until he could put his arm along the back of the banquette on which they were sitting. For a second his fingers gripped Iain's shoulder before scuttling away, and he said, 'Iain, that's the whole point. You aren't really supposed to talk to *anyone*.'

He stood up the second he'd finished speaking and went to the bar for refills. He knew his prey would wait. That infuriated Iain.

'The message from on high,' Heaney said as he sat down again, 'is that you should lay off. We gave you a little rope, fine, everyone's entitled to run around a bit when he comes out of clink. But enough is enough.' He raised his glass, eyeing Iain over the top of it for a few seconds. 'Cheers,' he said, and drank.

'Yeah.' Iain remembered his New Year's resolution. 'It's all right, I've got it off my chest.'

'Good. We thought you had, but when you went to see the Guv a second time, after I'd had my little word with Alison, we wanted to make sure.'

'You saw Alison?' Now it was Iain's turn to pull his body around, so that he could stare at Heaney. 'When?'

'She didn't tell you?'

'Of course she didn't, you dickhead, why would I pretend about a thing like that. *You saw my wife! Christ!*'

'Keep it low, eh?' Martin treated the pub's smoky interior to a quick scan. 'No one's business but ours.'

'*Ours?* Listen, mate, it's not your business, either. How dare you approach my wife. Eh? How fucking *dare* you?'

In the silence that followed his resolution came back to haunt him reproachfully; he was talking like the oldest of lags and he couldn't help it – 'I don't know what come over me, your Honour' – oh *fuck*!

'All right,' he said, holding up both hands, for he saw

226

that Heaney was about to speak. 'I'm sorry, I'm *sorry*, all right?'

He kept his hands up, to show he still needed a little time. Martin respected that. Martin had never been a bad sort.

'Please,' Iain said at last, 'don't do that again. If you have any cautions to utter, any advice to offer, please . . . come to me. Not her. Me.'

'Fine.'

'Only she deserves a break.'

'I agree.'

Iain breathed hard. He tipped the remains of his first Scotch into the new one and knocked the drink back. He put the glass down and wiped his mouth.

'I had this thought,' he said. 'I thought I might try and prove my innocence.' He laughed quietly to himself. 'Well.'

'All over now?'

'All over.'

'Good. You see, we're busy. It's manpower. You cost out London weighting, transport allowances, and . . . well, you don't want to hear our problems. The thought of you traipsing halfway round England, the world maybe, while we gird up the old loins to fight Arabs was enough to give head office a fit of the vapours, frankly.'

Iain scrutinized him. The pub was crowded now, with many talking, laughing couples and larger groups contributing to the uproar. But around the two of them there had settled a protective bubble of peace that sharpened his senses and readied him for an unknown off.

He must say nothing. He must not move. Softly, softly . . .

'Singapore, for example.' Martin Heaney was gloomily seeking inspiration in the ashtray. 'Send two bods out there, hotels, cars, equipment, air fares. Not funny. Not.'

Iain leaned his head nearer to Heaney's. The protective

bubble enclosing them screened out all but Heaney's words. He must not disturb it by so much as a blink, a facial tic.

'Verity and her Occydor empire.' Heaney's monotone continued to be addressed to the unresponsive ashtray. 'At least somebody did well out of your fall, old son. Not like me. Quite the little expert on Iraq; maybe they ought to give her a consultancy in Whitehall.'

Occydor ... Powis had said Oxyacetylene, Oxy-something damn stupid ... *Why are you telling me this?* Iain longed, longed, longed to put the question: the one question he must never ask. What was the point? If this were a trap, Heaney would scarcely be likely to tell him. If not, *why not?*

'Pity about Verity Newland, in a way,' Heaney went on slowly. 'She so obviously tried to help you, at the trial. Insisted on giving evidence for you, I do remember that: character stuff mostly. But you'll know better than me.'

*Why are you telling me this?*

'But they demolished her, in cross-examination.'

*It's true, it's true.*

'"Over-egging the pudding", wasn't that how the judge put it? Something like that.'

*You may feel, members of the jury – it is a matter solely for you – that Miss Newland's self-evident enthusiasm for the defendant rather got the better of her at times, leading her, it may be, to rather over-egg the pudding . . .*

'Something like that,' Heaney had said; but Iain knew he was quoting from the transcript of the summing-up, that he'd seen it, and recently, too.

*Why have you been reading the transcript, Martin?*

*Why didn't Alison tell me he'd come to see her?*

The bubble was dissolving. Three men came to take the next table, dogs at Wembley, starting-prices, oh God, shut up!

Heaney had helped interrogate him and at the end of

228

it he'd realized Iain was innocent. Iain remembered the look on his face, which as good as said so. And now here he was, insidiously whispering . . .

'Why?' he asked.

'Why am I doing this?'

Iain nodded.

'You got shafted. I got shafted.'

'What are you talking about?'

Heaney spent a long time weighing him up. Then he said, 'Know what I've been doing, these past seventeen years? Work that's about as useful as what you cons do inside.'

Iain stood up. 'If you're going to talk shit, I'm –'

'You're not going anywhere.' This time, Heaney's grip was surprisingly strong. 'We've had our formal chat, and now this is for me. Off the record. For *me*.'

His voice was as firm as his grasp on Iain's arm. Iain slowly sat down again.

'Seventeen years ago,' Heaney said in light conversational tone, 'I was asked to kill you.'

Iain opened his mouth, shut it again.

'Yes, that's right, we do that kind of thing. Still.' Heaney drained his glass. 'But I wasn't having any. So they shunted me into a siding and left me to rot.'

'Stop there,' Iain said. 'Did I kill Reynolds?'

Heaney held him with his eyes for a long moment. He shook his head.

'Right,' Iain said. 'Who did?'

'I don't know. I'd like to.'

Iain let out a sigh. He closed his eyes. 'Do your chiefs know about this?' he asked.

'What, that I'm talking to you? Yes, they told me to warn you off; I've done that. They don't know anything else.'

'Taking a bit of a risk, aren't you?'

'My risk, not yours.'

'Why bother?'

'I've told you, I don't like being shafted.'

'There's more. Come on, I know there's more.'

'Keep your voice down.' But Heaney's own voice was rising.

'I'll shout if I want to.'

'All right!' Heaney banged his hand on the table. 'But it's personal, see. There is another reason, and it's personal, and it doesn't affect you in any way, shape or form – now have you *got* that, sunshine?'

A number of heads turned to see what the row was about; the buzz of talk quietened for a few seconds.

'There are answers to be had,' Heaney went on, in a more moderate tone. 'Singapore. That's where you'll find out who killed Reynolds. Talk to the Newland woman.'

'Yeah? And how the hell am I supposed to manage that?'

But Martin had already stood up.

'Here, wait a minute,' Iain said. 'Suppose I need to contact you?'

Heaney shrugged.

'But you can't just –'

Heaney was halfway to the door.

'How the fuck am I supposed to get to Singapore?' Iain yelled, this time silencing the entire pub.

Heaney turned and grinned at him. 'You'll think of something,' he said. 'Knowing you.'

# FOURTEEN

Jay stood at the farthest extremity of Terrapin Point, watching the brown water flow down, down, down, inches from his feet. His hands were numb, despite the mitts he was wearing; his sinuses burned, his face ached. None of this mattered. For by his elbow Horseshoe Falls smoked lazily against the black-and-white snowscape of Niagara in deepest winter, and wherever he looked it was beautiful.

He slithered up the path towards the nearest mounted telescope and popped in a quarter. He could just make out Canada through the mists drifting up from the ravine that separated the two countries. Scarcely a figure moved across the frozen landscape, hardly a vehicle ventured forth on the deadly roads.

Jay exhaled, his breath coming out in a dense white cloud. He was the only person on Goat Island; the *only* one. Not a single tourist, no family up for a weekend vacation, not one soul.

Why, then, did he feel sure he wasn't alone?

The trackers were good. Brilliant, in fact. For a long time he'd not seen them, even though he'd tried everything he knew to flush them out. Then yesterday afternoon, by the shopping-mall opposite the blue glass Oxychem building, he'd thought he'd identified somebody looking too intently into a window, perfectly placed to catch Jay's reflection as he passed. But before he could react, a woman with a snivelling kid in tow came up to the guy, demanding how much longer he was going to be and did he know the thermometer was poised to drop through the floor . . . ?

The kid was a nice touch, how had they made it cry . . . ? Paranoia gnawed his brain like sexual jealousy. The family moved off, quarrelling. None of them looked back.

No, they weren't watching him. Couldn't be . . .

Jay snuggled deeper down into his overcoat and began to walk back through the woods, past the car park and the police station. Halfway across the bridge he stopped and rested his elbows on the balustrade. The water was shallow at this point, a side-stream, yet still it swirled and mashed in a fury of smoke. Far away to his left a great cloud-column reared up above the Horseshoe Falls, leading him to think, when first he'd seen it, that this was just one more chimney in Niagara's dire industrial hinterland, something to ruin a natural wonder instead of the wonder itself. Beyond that, the elegant Skylon Tower – Canadian territory. Ahead, the ugly observation deck on the US side. And Rainbow Bridge.

The words of Verity's last letter to him, one of those stolen from his house, thrust into his memory. January 18th 1991, that was the date she proposed for their meeting; somehow he had to get to Singapore before then and today was the 15th. She must have made contingency plans to leave before war broke out, so she was taking a gamble by fixing on the 18th: six days ago, the US Congress had backed Bush's decision to fight if necessary and, if Neil had it right, the US warplanes would go in two days from now.

Verity, the old house on the bend in the strait . . . unhappy memories, grey as the sky cloaking Niagara, deadened Jay's heart. Once he'd known warmth and wealth and love. Now he was a widower, on the run, with nothing but sorrows to call his own.

He knew that letting his thoughts run away with him

was merely an excuse for putting off decision. He pulled himself together and for the umpteenth time scanned the concrete grey sky, the dreary landscape, the unearthly beauty of the muddy-brown falls descending in a dense vapour of fog and spray. A four-wheel drive ploughed slowly down one of the few roads still visible as a dark strip against the surrounding white. Nothing else moved. Jay made his decision. For anyone wanting to cross the border into Canada, unseen, this was as good as it got.

Even as he knew that he was going to run, today, now, his heart started on a tattoo of fear.

He crossed from Goat Island to the mainland, turned left and began to stroll toward Rainbow Bridge. He forced himself down to a steady pace, wanting not to run, to seem natural, yet knowing the day was too cold for a saunter.

The watchers would see him whatever he did, however he did it.

Ahead of him he could see the squat US Customs and Immigration Service building. He crossed a car park, veering to his left, where a wooden signboard with an arrow on it said: CANADA. The path meandered around the back of the building, ending in a one-way turnstile. Jay pushed through it. He set foot on Rainbow Bridge.

No one in sight. But he wasn't alone.

He'd first known this feeling three days before, a week after he'd arrived on the outskirts of Niagara. The Blue Dolphin Motel on route 62 had suited him perfectly: an abandoned oasis of stuffy indifference where a man might play whatever role he chose. There were only four or five other guests. A few doors down from his room he could hear the tap-tap-tap of an unskilled typist working, erratically and without plan, on a document that had no end. Jay began to hope it might be a suicide note . . .

He was on the narrow footway, approaching the middle of Rainbow Bridge. Three flagpoles and a plaque indicated the boundary. He paused, as any innocent tourist might, to put a coin in the telescope and survey the river far below, sweeping both banks for signs of trouble. On the Canadian side he could see a group of six people, wrapped up like so many bolsters. They were moving away from him. As he watched, they split up; one of them bent to roll snow into a ball, which he threw at his nearest companion.

He trained the telescope on the road he'd walked earlier. Somewhere beyond it his car sat in a motel parking lot, dirty and forlorn beneath its off-white sheet of snow: abandoned. Near to the car, a suitcase, containing a few possessions: abandoned. All that was left ... abandoned.

His throat constricted. But then the quarter slipped through the trap, closing the shutter, cutting him off.

He damned himself for a sentimental idiot and stepped across the boundary line. He was in Canada.

Jay followed the sign at the end of the bridge and turned left through a swing door into the blessed, almost suffocating warmth of a passage heated at taxpayers' expense. Ahead was a waist-high turnstile, beside him, two change machines, one of them broken. He knew the set-up, he'd done his homework: his pockets were laden down with quarters, for admission to Canada through the turnstile, for telescopes. Jay put his coin in the slot and passed through into an office where a man in blue uniform was seated behind a desk reading a paperback.

'Howdee,' he said. He marked his place with a book of matches and stood up. 'Where you from?'

'US of A.'

'See your passport, please?'

Jay handed it to the immigration officer, who flicked through the pages and raised his eyebrows. 'When you going home, Jay?' he asked.

'Tonight. Just planning on a quick walk round.'

The officer slapped his passport shut. 'Don't freeze to the sidewalk,' he said, handing it back. 'Have a good stay, now.'

The beauty of it, Jay reflected as he ducked out of the warmth, was that you didn't have to show your passport stateside. Not leave a trace of your leaving, in other words. And Canadian immigration had no written record of his having entered.

He ran down two flights of steps into Niagara Parkway and turned right. Now the ravine was on his left. His homeland lay on the other side of it, scarcely visible through the mist. There was a paved park here: fir trees, well spaced out; neat, old, stone walls; more of the ubiquitous telescopes recessed from the road in bays overlooking the ravine. He was out, he was *free* . . .

And then suddenly his world focused. He could see nobody, but he was in the crosswires. He took a step forward. The sensation intensified. He looked up, down, in every direction. Nothing, no one, *danger*!

He stumbled on past the Skyline Foxhead Hotel, his fingertips tingling with shock. To his right a road led up the hill into a garish part of town: Jay caught sight of a wax museum, a vertical, red-and-gold illuminated advertisement for Guinness. And coming down the hill towards him was a man, his face hidden by the brim of a fedora hat.

Jay turned sharp left. He needed to climb that hill into the town, where he could pick up a bus for Toronto. Instead, he found himself blundering in the wrong direction. He turned his head to scan the main road, and there behind him was a second man, approaching from the direction of Rainbow Bridge.

Why did he suspect this pair of wanting to harm him? You're being ridiculous, he told himself. Now stop, turn around, walk up that hill . . .

He glanced over his shoulder. The two men had teamed up and were bearing down on him, now about a hundred yards distant. They were the only figures moving on the landscape, apart from Jay. The temperature had sunk below zero, but he was sweating. Suddenly he turned and set off at a trot.

He was heading south towards Horseshoe Falls, away from where he wanted to go. He passed the hydroelectric station on the left, the noise of falling water growing ever louder. Not far ahead he could see a low building: a shopping-store of some kind . . .

He ran up the steps and found himself entering a tourist supermarket that sold a mish-mash of gifts, toys, clothes, snacks and candy. The place was big, but almost deserted. He thrust his way past a couple of oriental teenagers, perhaps part of the group he'd spotted through the telescope having a snow fight. An exit sign . . . Jay ran towards it. As he passed through the door into a large foyer he looked back, in time to see the two men enter the supermarket.

Jay put on speed. But as he headed for the glass outer doors of the foyer, he saw a third man walk up to them from the other side and stand there with hands in pockets, gazing at him impassively.

Jay skidded to a halt. On his left, a wall; to his right, a sign: TO THE SCENIC TUNNELS.

No way out.

Keep moving. *Move!*

He ran up to the booth and bought a ticket for the tunnels. Tunnels, *shit*, what were they . . . ? Down some stairs, into a curious tiled area, like a swimming-pool changing room. A woman on the other side of a counter handed him a yellow plastic waterproof. He snatched it from her and followed the signs to the elevator.

In the elevator the attendant told him that they were going down one hundred and twenty-five feet through solid rock, but Jay wasn't listening to the spiel, he was working out how bad this could be.

Backtrack. Think.

He hadn't returned to his house in Eccles since he and Neil Robarts had skipped, just before Christmas. He'd fled with his wad of money and a wallet full of plastic, though Christ knew how much credit was left in those cards. Jay hadn't heard from Neil since and was deliberately keeping himself out of contact. As long as Neil knew nothing of his whereabouts, he couldn't talk.

Jay had kept on the move ever since, somehow resisting the temptation to empty his bank accounts, knowing they'd be watching the banks, the railroad stations, airports. He'd reckoned they would get tired, because no way could they monitor the entire US–Canadian border. He'd gambled on them believing he'd run as far from his home territory as possible before attempting a frontier-crossing, which is why he'd never strayed more than seventy miles from his house. *Yet they were here!*

Jay's heart was beating terribly fast. There was a way out, there had to be. *Just keep moving forward.*

The elevator slowed to a halt, the attendant slid open the gate. Jay stepped out to find himself at the start of a passage that forked almost immediately. Straight ahead, stairs led down through a short expanse of rock to an observation platform on one side of Horseshoe Falls. He ran down them two at a time, oblivious to the danger from their icy steps.

He emerged on to the viewing deck amid a boom of falling water. Steam boiled up around him, restricting his horizon to fifty yards. He looked to his left, seeking a path on the side of the cliff, but the face was sheer and smooth. He ran to the right of the deck, placing his hands on the green-painted rail. But for his plastic over-garment, he'd have been soaked. Directly in front of him

237

roared Niagara Falls: thousands of gallons of water tumbling every second to be lost in a maelstrom of ice-cold smoke.

His hands whitened on the rail. He mustn't be trapped out here. But as he turned away, something caught his eye.

The black cliff-face curved away from the deck, rounded a concealed corner and then ran behind the tumult of falling water. No way out there . . . but about twenty feet above eye-level, just at the point where the rockface disappeared behind the falls, he could see a hole like the entrance to a cave. A steady stream of water flooded out of it to join the massive flow, inches away. This was a place of great peril. Tongues of water detached themselves from the main fall, curling upwards and in towards the cliff; when a tongue had climbed far, far up the rockface it turned over on itself, like a wave collapsing, to rejoin the cataract: a continual loop of spray, wheeling up and over to destruction between water and rock. Jay's eyes narrowed. In the place where the water looped, the rock was rough, with plenty of handholds. But it was wet, slippery . . . and anyway, it led nowhere. *Get out!*

He ran back inside the cliff, up the stairs to the elevator landing. But as he reached it, he heard the car coming down again and he skidded to a halt. He had only one choice: to lose himself in the tunnels. He set off down the other branch of the passage.

The walls were smooth, like the concrete floor, and painted white. Orange bulbs in wire cages provided some light, not much. Sounds distorted badly in here. Every so often enough water seemed to accumulate, perhaps close, perhaps far off, to overflow with an ugly 'splat'. It was like being in a drain, a cleaner than clean sewer.

He took a few rapid steps along this tunnel and stopped to listen. Jesus, what a place . . . He shut his eyes in an effort to filter out lesser sounds. And then, yes, there was something: he heard the elevator door closing, and a voice, male . . .

He made off down the tunnel until he reached a junction. The tunnel went on ahead of him but he had the option of turning left. A sign on the wall told him that this was the way to Cataract Portal. He risked a look down the side-passage. Next second he had his back against the wall, fighting down bile.

A torrent of water was racing down the side-tunnel towards him. He was going to be swept away, drowned.

The fit lasted a second, no more. Then his heart dropped back into place, his throat opened again; he could breathe. He stood off the wall and looked, properly this time, down the shorter passage.

It was perhaps fifty feet long. At the end was a waist-high metal gate; beyond it, the falls: a swirl of whites and greys and silvery tints crashing down to dissolution in the Niagara River with the force and fury of a primeval god. So huge was this sheet of water, so quickly did it pass before his astonished eyes, that in a weird optical illusion it seemed to create a vast fountain, and it was this that had caused him to believe he was about to be flushed out of the tunnel like a helpless spider trapped in a lavatory bowl. And the *noise* . . .

He held his hands to his ears but the water echoed inside his head, unstaunched and unstaunchable, leaving no room for thought. An essential force of nature vented its wrath in a shriek, fifty feet away from him, and he was terrified.

Jay's heartbeat gradually steadied. He pulled himself off the wall, knowing he'd allowed himself to be panicked into a series of wrong decisions. Now he was bottled up like a rat in a trap. Essential not to panic any more.

He heard a noise behind him and turned with a start. Two black-clad figures stood at the junction of the

239

passages by the lifts. Third man upstairs, watching the elevator, yes . . . They stood there and looked at Jay. It was too dim to see their expressions, but they boded nothing good. One of the pair began to advance slowly while his comrade stayed on guard.

Jay stayed rooted to the spot at the intersection with the side-passage that led to Cataract Portal. He was damned if he'd show fear. He rested his back against the wall where it made a corner, and waited.

As the man advanced, he acquired a face. Pale, with shadows under the eyes, and a sharp-edged nose. Until this point he'd kept his hands in his pockets, but now he slowly removed them, lifting them almost to shoulder height. The message was obvious: I am unarmed.

Jay relaxed a fraction. Then he remembered: there were two of them; all they had to do was grab him, toss him through the cascade of water and that would be the end of Jay Sampson. No witnesses, no come-back. Guns were redundant here.

'Mr Sampson . . .' The voice resonated just above the level of the water's flow. 'We would like to talk with you a moment.'

Jay swallowed.

'This isn't comfortable.' The man's voice was slightly effeminate: it twanged, and the water took the twang, elevating it into a camp whine. 'Would you come some place quieter?'

Jay edged along the wall of the side-passage towards the cascading, grey horror. He saw how the man's expression changed to one of annoyance. He saw him look back to where his colleague must be waiting, by the elevators, eyebrows raised in query. It was as if a signal passed between the two pursuers. When the first man turned to face Jay again, there was new purpose in his eyes.

He took another step towards Jay. 'Mr Sampson,' he said. 'I'm with the FBI. My name is Cover. I'm going to lower my hands now and I'm going to reach inside my coat for ID. Okay?'

Jay fought to keep his breathing under control. He did not like this man whose name rhymed with Dover, and whose eyes glittered strangely in his gaunt white face. Neil had mentioned someone called Cover ... He watched while Cover's hand slithered inside his waterproof and he thought, This is it ... And all the while he was easing his way along the wall, towards the water, now less than twenty feet away.

A single orange bulb illuminated Cover's hand, holding out a laminated card. In spite of himself, Jay squinted down. As if it *mattered*, the guy wasn't really FBI, he was a killer ... He continued his slow retreat. Cover's lips moved, but here the noise of the water was deafening. It interfered with Jay's brain, rendering him drunk, stupid.

His eyes focused on Cover's face. The thin lips were twisting into a slow smile. Seconds away now ... the move that would shove him through the fermenting boil to mince his flesh and bones on boulders hundreds of feet below, he must think, the noise, try to *think*, the noise, the noise, *the noise* ...

There was a way out. One way.

He knew, now, the meaning of the ominous black cave in the cliff-face that he'd seen from the observation deck. It was Cataract Portal. He stood mere feet away from it, from that incessantly looping tongue of water ... and a rockface with handholds.

The ID card wavered. Jay's eyes diverted from it for a second, saw the gun coming up in Cover's free hand. He swung his fist off the wall: it landed awkwardly, for Cover had anticipated the move, but the feel of his knuckles against his opponent's skull was enough to bring Jay out of trance and into reality.

Cover lurched against the wall, sliding down it. He recovered enough to lash out with a foot as he fell; Jay went sprawling. Shock-waves radiated through his skull, blood was in his mouth. He dragged himself on to his knees. He crawled backwards, seeking to put himself out of Cover's range. As he came upright again, purple flashes exploded before his eyes, but desperation ruled him now – he vaulted over the low steel gate and flung himself to the edge of the portal. Cover shouted something Jay didn't hear. For a second he hesitated; then he spun around, dropped to his knees and lowered himself out of the hole.

A fatal mistake, he knew instantly, but one too late to rectify: he was dead on arrival in hell. Ice-cold spray drenched him, and that was only the slick of curling water, he wasn't in the falls proper. No good. Finish.

Yet somehow he hadn't died. If he knew he was frozen, that meant he was still alive. Slowly, perceptions and thoughts began to beat a way back into his brain. Come on, get a grip, *fight*!

The black rock was treacherous and refrigerated, but it was irregular too: there were ample holds for both hands and feet. Slowly, agonizingly, he stretched out his right hand and made contact. Now the right foot . . . that's it, that's it! Slide your left hand . . . left foot.

He was moving. He was soaked to the skin, colder than he'd thought possible, his gloves were already full of water, his arm-muscles screamed protest at the torture, but he was on his way.

*Make this fast, or not at all.* Already numbness was creeping along his arms, into his shoes; he had minutes left. He must not look down and he must blot out the noise of the water. Inside his head, Jay began to play the last movement of Beethoven's Ninth Symphony. When that didn't work he started to shout it out loud. Da-da-da-da-DA-d'da . . .

He would fall. He'd done rock-climbing at school, in Asia he'd become good at it, but that was then, this was now. And yet even as he moved across the rockface, things came back to him: memories of how to feel with a foot, testing for the safe hold, how to control breathing and panic . . .

The light was starting to go. He had minutes, minutes. He knew that Cover must be on the edge of the portal, looking for him; knew, too, that he would be invisible to anyone in that position.

He closed his eyes and prayed; he sang Beethoven; but he never once stopped feeling with his toes and his fingers' ends for the next precious hold that would save his life.

Hopeless. Failing. No strength left now. Too cold. Too tired, too afraid. He stopped singing. The water's roar defeated him. At his back loomed a monster with an appetite that never dulled.

He stole a glance to his left. It felt as if he'd come so far, but it was only a dozen feet. Don't look right. Don't know the worst. There is no worst.

Jay's body closed down. He stopped moving. He was, he realized, crying. Not from grief, but from sheer frustration. His muscles screamed at him to stop this madness and he obeyed. Fear got him in the guts: he knew he was going to fall and that meant death. A split second of terror before his head cracked open on the rocks, spattering them with brain and blood, as when the child Jay Sampson once used to be had dropped gulls' eggs on the sidewalk . . .

His right foot jerked sideways in a spasm he couldn't control. He'd iced up. Water of deadly coldness soaked his clothes, his skin, his innermost being, draining away sense, thought, life. His foot jerked again.

As if down a long, dark tunnel a thought came winding to Jay: the last thought he would know on earth. His foot was in contact with something soft.

He raised his head and opened his eyes, craning around

243

to the right. He'd made it to mere inches away from the knoll of grass and rock that supported the observation deck. One great final heave, and he'd be on it. Safe.

But he was locked. He couldn't move. All he could hear was the ever-present thunder of falling water. Suddenly he seemed to dematerialize and seconds later he was standing on the observation deck, watching himself: a fly, clinging to a vertical wall, ready to drop. *Pathetic!* He began to cry again, the tears dissolving into a veil of frigid water coursing down his face. To die like this . . .

No. You do not have to die.

The voice echoed around his brain; next second he was back inside his body, eyes wide open, staring at the coal-black rock just one inch away from his face. He forgot he was cold, soaked, exhausted. For the voice summoning him back was Alison's.

'Alison,' he shrieked, '*Alison!*'

His voice was lost even before it hit the air, but somehow he managed to kick with his right foot. Soft, definitely soft earth, not rock. He unclenched the rigid fingers of his right hand and slid it sideways. Left hand. Left foot . . . a spur of granite dislodged itself and he lurched sideways, down; '*Alison!*' he screamed again. His feet lashed frantically, but there was no ledge, nothing. He lifted his knee, found a bare inch of outcrop, rested his toes on it. Now or never.

His face banged forward against the rock, he tasted salty blood and cried out with shock. But he could see green, knew he was on the verge of the knoll: he drew down one long, deep breath, tensed every muscle in his body, and threw himself sideways.

He fell on his right arm. A lance of red-hot pain shot through his body. His jaw landed on rock, stunning him. He slipped downwards, fingers gouging at the soil, feet digging in hard, until he no longer moved.

Jay slowly turned over on his back and stared at the

sky. 'Thank you,' he said. He repeated it, several times. He raised his right knee. Pain shuddered through his frame. *Ignore it. Make yourself ignore it, if you don't want to die of exposure . . .*

Where would Cover & Co be? he wondered through a fog of pain, as he began to crawl up towards the observation deck. How long had he been hanging from the rocks? It felt like minutes, but . . . he looked at his watch. Broken.

He was almost up to the concrete base of the deck. He hooked his fingers over its top and pulled himself up. As his eyes came level with the floor he saw boots. Half a dozen people were standing there. The light was poor, but he could vaguely see Mongolian features. He stared up at them; they stared back at him. He heard a girl's voice, whispering and excited.

Jay reached up for the lower rail. A man ran forward to help him. He hauled himself over the fence and landed on the deck, to be surrounded by half a dozen whispering, enthralled Chinese students.

He stared from face to face, trying to picture himself through their eyes. He was soaked, shivering and bloody: a demon from another realm. A hand plucked his sleeve. 'Please,' a small voice said. Jay turned. Somewhere below shoulder height, a diminutive girl was holding out her camera to him. With her other hand she described vague circles in the air. She nodded encouragingly at him. 'Please,' she said again.

With that, she thrust the Nikon into his hand and ran back to the rail, where the other five members of the group joined her. They pushed back their waterproof hoods, and the boys adjusted their hair. They smiled. Jay staggered, his mind on the verge of giving way. He was dreaming, these people weren't for real; he'd all but died and they wanted him to take a group photo. Run for it. Throw down the camera, turn and high-tail it out of here

245

while you can. Then a brainwave flashed through his mind and he thought, Fuck it, why not?

He clicked the shutter. When the girl came over to collect her camera, bowing gratitude, he bowed back, not once but twice.

'Where do you come from?' he croaked.

There was an anxious whispered conference. The tallest boy stepped forward, appointed group spokesman. 'We all from ... ah ... To Lon To Un'vers-tay. Taiwanese exchange students.'

Jay did mental gyrations. 'Toronto?' he said. 'How d'you get here?'

Another whispered confab. 'Ah ... we have mini-bus.'

Jay was so groggy he could hardly stand. But on hearing the boy's words his heart gave a great throb of joy and he said, 'I need a lift into Toronto. Any chance?'

'Ver' good,' the boy agreed. 'We go now. Coal.'

'Very cold. Freezing.'

They started up the steps. Jay dug down in memory for fragments of the Chinese he'd learned in Singapore. He turned to the girl nearest to him.

*'Zai Toronto da xue, nimen dou xuexi sheme?'* he asked her. What are you studying at Toronto University?

She replied mechanically, in English, 'Physics'; then it dawned on her that he'd spoken in Chinese and she gasped. The others began to jabber at him in their own language. They had reached the elevator. They were *in* the elevator, rising to the surface. While Jay struggled to keep his head above water linguistically, the gates slid open. They climbed the stairs into the supermarket. And there, fifty feet away down an aisle, stood Cover and the two others he'd seen earlier.

One man moved quickly forward, but Cover as quickly gripped his wrist. Jay saw all this out of the corner of one eye, knew then for sure that Cover wasn't FBI, that Cover was fatally allergic to publicity and the light of day. Jay was at the exit, securely cocooned by his entourage. They were crossing the car park towards a mini-bus. They were getting in. The driver started the engine. A girl turned to Jay and asked, 'Where do you come from?' Receiving no reply she twisted herself down and around to see his face.

'He is sleeping,' she reported. 'What a pity.' And then – 'Why do you think he wanted to commit suicide?'

# FIFTEEN

'Kate . . . Ah, yes — Iain's daughter.'

But Simon kept his eyes on Darren all the while, as if afraid of being hit. Kate enjoyed that. She liked it when people let Darren see their apprehension. He had this loopy smile, one reason why he turned her on; sometimes men (usually it was men) thought him mad. Women looked at him differently, and that *really* gave her a high. Neatly coiffed women in designer dresses, who strode past building-sites with their tits up to their necks, they were the types who couldn't take their eyes off him.

'I think he's upstairs,' Simon said uneasily, continuing to gaze at Darren. 'In fact, I asked him to turn the lights out, we're the last, you see . . .'

Darren nodded dreamily, but said nothing. Half an hour before they'd been lying under a tree on Clapham Common, him and Kate, sharing a joint — 'gear', that's what Dad called it, funny name — and it hadn't gone down too well with his McEwans' Export lunch. Or with the White Dove he'd taken the night before; Ecstasy was never going to be friends with Darren, but he wouldn't learn. Kate hoped he wouldn't start a fight just at this moment in time. It had been her idea to collect Dad in the van, save him a walk home, since they were in the neighbourhood. He'd be pleased, she knew that.

Darren was pleased, too. He'd said so. He truly admired Dad. Seventeen-stretch for Em One: a hard man, was Kate's father, and Darren respected him. 'A face,' he kept telling Kate, 'your old man's a regular face.' Faces were successful, professional criminals, heroes to Darren. There was this mobster in Deptford who kept saying he'd introduce Darren to one, 'always in need of a smart young man,' but somehow it never seemed to happen. That pissed Darren off. He had a criminal's vanity, did Darren, and a criminal mind, i.e. small. He seriously wanted to get rich quick, but no one would put himself out to help.

He thought Iain was going to start him off on a life of big-time crime. At first, Kate had tried to explain that, in fact, actually, her father was innocent. This was unproductive material, leading nowhere, so she abandoned it. Now, whenever she particularly wanted Darren to be nice to her, she talked about fixing up a meet with her old Dad. Darren still fell for that. He was dumb, vain, malleable, constitutionally lazy and cruel. A man, in other words. Kate's man. She loved him.

'Upstairs, then?' Darren enquired, though it didn't come out quite like that. *Ussairs-en . . .*

Kate grabbed him by the hand. He snatched it away, but she managed to secure him second time around. Darren had started to sway rather, in the general direction of Simon, and his loopy grin was frayed at the edges. If his next line was, 'Stop looking at me,' they were in more trouble than she could handle. This was stuff that creamed her crotch, but only in the run-up. With Darren you took your fun on the foreplay, or not at all.

'Come on, luv,' she said quickly. 'Let's go find Dad . . .'

He didn't want to come but nor was he quite ready for a fight, so he compromised by making her half-haul him up the stairs. The corridor was dark. At the far end a shaft of weak light spilled out of an open door. Kate started towards it. Darren jerked his hand away and leaned against the wall, his jaw working.

'Darren . . .'

To her immense relief he said, 'Aw-rye', and came

249

upright. But then he caught sight of another door, also open, and began to struggle towards it. Kate seized him again. He fought her off.

'Dar-*ren*!'

He turned and with a lazy sweep of his fist batted her across the forehead. The blow sent Kate sprawling on the floor. He ignored her, pushing on into the chairman's office.

As Kate sat up another voice said, 'Who's there?'

She turned, still a little groggy but recognizing the voice. 'Dad?'

At first the corridor seemed empty. But then a shadow moved at the far end, somebody walked through the shaft of light, and she saw Iain.

He covered the ground between them swiftly. Only afterwards did she remember how quiet his movements were, so that he seemed to materialize at her elbow out of nothing, like a genie smoking up from his lamp.

'What are you doing here?' he asked, helping her up. 'What happened?'

'I thought I . . . we'd come to fetch you, we've got the van.'

'We?' His eyes darted to where Darren was stroking the office safe.

'Only . . . Darren's a bit drunk.' She essayed a laugh. 'He couldn't see where he was going and he knocked me over.'

'I see.'

Iain dematerialized again. In the time it took Kate to gather her wits he crossed the office. A flicker of movement danced before her eyes. Darren was up against the wall, Iain's forearm lodged in his throat.

'Come here, Kate.'

He spoke in a way she'd never heard him use before. Halfway between a whisper and a murmur, his voice came out clearly but low: she guessed that was how you spoke in prison when you didn't want to draw attention to yourself. She approached the two men hesitantly.

'Listen, dog's breath,' Iain said to Darren. 'I'm tired of you. You'll never amount to shit, know that? *Eh?*'

He shoved his forearm upwards and Darren squeaked.

'Say: I'll never amount to shit. *Say it!*'

Darren said it.

'You're a small-time thief, a liar, an arsehole. You're violent. But I'm more violent. See?'

Darren nodded.

*'Talk to me, dog's breath.'*

'I see,' Darren croaked.

'In prison,' Iain said, 'we used to boil people like you. Know what I mean?'

Darren shook his head.

'Scalding tea,' Iain explained. 'Poured over you. Slowly. "Boiled", see?'

Iain's face was a couple of inches from Darren's. Kate could smell Darren's fear oozing out of him like night stink from a marsh. Without moving his forearm, Iain reached up with his free hand and grasped Darren's nose. He used the nose to waggle Darren's head backwards and forwards a few times, as if testing his grip; then he banged the boy's skull against the wall. Darren crumpled.

'You don't touch my daughter in anger,' Iain said. '*Ever!* Now crawl, dog's breath.'

Darren crawled.

'When we come out of this building, Kate and I, we don't see you. Don't smell you. *Vanish.*'

They listened, father and daughter, while Darren groped his way down the stairs. It was possible to chart his progress by a series of thumps, chair-legs scraping on wood, and finally the slam of a door. After that came several seconds of silence, broken by Simon's anxious voice.

'Iain . . . are you all right?'

'Quite all right, thank you, Simon.'

Kate started. Her father had spoken in a professional person's voice. She looked at him, wanting to see again the hard man who'd come out of the shadows to vanquish Darren, but all she saw was Iain Forward, her dad, and he was smiling.

'We'll be down in a mo,' he called. 'Are you wanting to lock up?'

'No, no, I'm here for another ten minutes.'

They listened as Simon's footsteps pattered away.

'I'm sorry about that,' Iain said. 'But he's not going to knock you about while I'm around, not even if you beg him to. All right?'

She nodded. It was, she discovered, much more than all right. It was lovely.

'I'm glad you came,' Iain said. 'Been meaning to talk to you. It's difficult at home.'

'With Mum there, you mean?'

'Whenever she's there, you're not.'

'Sorry.' She hadn't meant to apologize, but somehow he'd commanded it and she'd obeyed. He had the most enormous presence.

'Come in here.' He led the way up the passage to where light was still shining through the last doorway. Kate stepped inside and looked around: a dusty office, filing-cabinets, boxes, on the desk, some papers . . .

She moved towards the desk but Iain forestalled her, laying his hands across the papers before she could take them in properly. Yet she saw enough to be startled: surely that had been a passport, its blue corner peeping out from the pile? And that narrow strip of shiny paper of a brighter blue with red lettering . . . what would her father want with an airline ticket?

'Dad,' she blurted out, 'you are happy at home, now. Aren't you?'

He stuffed the papers inside his jacket before answering. 'I'm happy,' he said abruptly. 'I like this job.'

'And the garden, you like that, don't you?'

She remembered guiltily how she'd laughed when he'd first brought gardening books back from the library. Roses: he said London air was good for roses on account of the soot.

Iain came to stand opposite her. He looked into her eyes and she felt a little of what Darren must have gone through, only there was no rage in his stare, just power.

'Kate,' he said. 'Do you know how much I love you?' Suddenly he put his arms around her and drew her to him. 'If anything happens to me,' he whispered, 'take care of your mother. Promise me.'

'What could —'

'Just promise, love. Please.'

'Of course I promise. But —'

'I know you're fond of Darren. He's a streak of piss, but he's *your* streak of piss.' He laughed softly. 'God, I understand. Just don't put all your money on him, okay?'

She nodded.

'I don't want to see you hurt. And he will hurt you, you know that, mm?'

Yes, she knew that.

'Which is part of the fun, but only you see it that way; he doesn't.'

She looked up at him, awed by his understanding. He squeezed her gently. 'God bless you, Kate.'

He kissed her cheek and she had never known a man touch her with such tenderness. She felt so safe.

'Will you be coming home tonight?' he asked her. 'Shall I see you tomorrow?'

She thought about Darren, what a louse he was. But . . .

'Don't shake your head, Kate. Speak to me.'

He'd said that to Darren. *Talk to me, dog's breath.*

'I don't think I'll be home tonight, Dad. Sorry.'

He held her from him, examining her face. 'You shouldn't say you're sorry,' he said. 'Unless you really are.' His hands dropped to his sides. Kate stared at the floor. At last Iain said, 'I've got a few things to clear up here.'

Kate raised her head. 'Don't be late,' she said mechanically.

Iain nodded. ''Night, then.'

''Night.'

At the door she glanced back. Iain was looking at her with such anguish on his face that for some reason she felt this to be their last goodbye, felt that she should run to him . . . fight for him. But then he lowered his eyes and the feeling left her; she hurried along the corridor, suddenly desperate in her need for another man's other kind of touch.

# SIXTEEN

Jay trudged into the terminal complex of Lester B. Pearson International Airport and made for Canadian Airlines' reservations desk. At six thirty in the morning, daybreak still seemed a long way off. There was space on flight CP1 to Tokyo and an onwards connection to Singapore: with war brewing there were seats on every flight. He paid cash, knowing that any credit card transaction could be traced; and anyway, he doubted if he had any credit left.

Check-in was easy, too. He had only hand luggage. He hurried through the gate early, wanting to test his passport against Canadian immigration's records, but no one stopped him.

He'd been lucky, he reflected as he handed his bag over to be X-rayed. Outside Niagara he'd asked the Taiwanese students to stop while he cleaned himself up in a diner's washroom. After that he'd bought some clean, dry clothes and treated his rescuers to coffee and donuts. He'd kept his eyes open, but caught neither sight nor sound of Cover.

Even so, Jay took one final precaution. He made them drop him off quickly at an intersection in Milton, before ducking into the shadows and waiting to see who followed him. No one did.

He thought about that, as he wandered through the brown-panelled, dreary terminal. He'd roughed up a self-proclaimed US Federal agent, and the Canadians, 'our good neighbours to the north' as the FBI sneeringly called them, should have known about it by now. There were

255

reciprocal arrangements, leading to extradition. Maybe he hadn't roughed Cover & Co up enough to warrant extradition; more probably, they were so illegal themselves they didn't dare try for it. Jay didn't know and he didn't care.

He bought a paper on his way to the gate. All the talk was of the build-up to Desert Storm, just hours away.

He found a phone booth and fuelled it with money. Neil Robarts answered on the twelfth ring.

'Hi,' Jay said.

'Where are you?' Neil's voice lost its sleepiness somewhere between the first and last word. 'Shit, don't tell me.'

'I won't. What's happening?'

Heavy breathing followed at the other end. 'Listen,' he heard Neil say, 'I'm scared. Really scared. *Don't* . . . say anything. Our associates have been keeping a close eye on Miss V and I've been keeping a close eye on them. Suddenly, you show up in the frame. Suddenly, *I* show up there, too. Like looking in a mirror. I'm being leaned on, Jay. Cover's definitely the name to watch for, Tony Cover.'

Jay laughed. 'Tell me about it! Go on.'

'No one, but no one, wants the past raked up and it's going to get terminal. Do you read me, Jay?'

Neil's voice trembled as he said that. Jay felt his guts clench.

'I read you. Listen, Neil: I called my lawyer and had him send you some papers; they should arrive in a day or two. It's a record of my time with Verity, the start of Occydor, everything. There's copy invoices, minutes of meetings, you name it: the history of how Occydor helped the Pentagon sell out to Saddam Hussein and the men who ran Iraq before he did. You're to hold them. If I don't check in once every seven days, publish them.'

256

'Got it.'

'My lawyer has the same instruction.'

'Man, you need more than a lawyer. God bless you!' Neil's voice resonated with anguish. 'God bless you, friend, and good luck.'

'Thanks. Listen: they're calling my flight.' He paused. ''Bye now.'

Jay hung up. For a moment he stood staring foolishly at the phone, disconnected like the line, ignorant of what to do next. His friend, his best friend . . . when would they meet again?

Suddenly he felt afraid to turn around. He would turn and there they would be, Cover & Co, smiles and guns all handy.

He forced himself to look over his shoulder. A few people walked here and there. No one so much as glanced in his direction.

Stop worrying, he told himself. Get to Singapore, go back to the House of Orchids, make a base there. That's your goal, the only thing worth thinking about. Forget everything else. *Forget it.*

He got to the gate just as it was opening. This was where the Mounties should stop him; they had the power to do that. But the girl was bored, not the slightest bit interested in him. *Why?*

She took half of his boarding-pass and dropped it through a slot and he thought, Yes, that's it, a lifetime trashed, that's me. He sat in the holding-lounge looking out, and all he could see was darkness.

*

As Martin Heaney entered his Mayfair office after lunch, the phone was ringing. He took off his jacket and draped it over the back of his chair before picking up the receiver, not expecting a catastrophe.

The operator said, 'This is a Q-seven call, logged at

257

fourteen-nineteen, sixteenth January, nineteen ninety-one. Identify.'

'Heaney, Martin,' he said, 'F section, nine-oh-five.' He pressed a switch to activate his on-line tape-recorder. 'Go.'

'Martin,' a woman said, and she was crying. 'I'm sorry, I know I shouldn't be doing this, I'm sorry . . .'

'That's why I gave you the number,' he said soothingly, 'so that you could use it. Alison, what's wrong?'

'It's Iain.'

'What about him?' But as soon as he'd heard it was a Q-7 from outside he'd guessed the worst.

'He's gone. And he's taken my money.'

'Start at the beginning, love. Tell me everything, as it happened.'

'He was so . . . so strange, last night. Came home late.' She was rising above the crisis now, the tears drying in her throat. 'Didn't speak much. He'd been so . . . so *good*, these past few weeks. He was into gardening, he read the papers, he was . . . he was coming alive.'

'Go on.'

'Then last night he was all silent again. Like when he first got out. He wouldn't talk to me. I went to work. When I got home, this morning, I could feel . . . something different. Bad.'

'Wait a minute. Was Iain at home when you –'

'No. But then he'd have gone to work. Just a feeling. I started to look around. A case had gone, a small suitcase. And a few of his clothes. Razor. Toothbrush.'

'Yes?'

'And then I felt danger. Like, you know . . . when someone close dies and you feel it, even though you're . . . And I thought, Oh God, the money . . .'

'What money?' A long pause. 'Alison, *what money*?'

'I have this . . . this building society account. Not much. And the book was gone.'

'The passbook? *Alison* . . .'

'Yes, the passbook. So . . . so, I hadn't even taken my coat off, I . . . I went round to the office and yes, there'd been a withdrawal. Two thousand pounds. Nearly all of it. I saw the manager.'

'What did he say?'

'She, it's a she . . .'

'*Alison!*'

'She said my husband had been in with an authority, my signature, definitely my signature.'

'And what did you tell her?'

'Nothing. I said, Oh yes, of course. But she must have known . . . she asked me if I wanted a glass of water, I . . .'

'When was this?'

'An hour ago. So then I went to the place where Iain's been working. He wasn't there. I said I'd come around to tell them he was sick.'

'Well done.'

Verity Newland, he was thinking. Just like I told Iain, all roads lead to Verity . . . *Good man, Iain!*

'Martin, what am I going to *do*?'

'Nothing,' he said.

'*Nothing?*'

'Alison, listen to me. There are things that we can do to help – *if* you cooperate.'

'Anything, I'll do anything.'

'Act as if nothing has happened. Iain is too sick to work. There will be a doctor's certificate, tomorrow, for his employers, I'll see to it. You go to work, as normal. Does Kate know?'

'Not yet.'

'Tell her Iain's had an offer of a better job but it means going up north for interview. You know her, you know what she'll swallow.'

'Yes.'

259

'I'll be around to see you, at home.'

'When?'

'When I know something. Now, have you got all that, Alison?'

'Yes.'

'I have to go now. Mustn't waste time.'

'No.'

'Alison.'

'What?'

He wanted desperately to comfort her. But all he could think of was a few lame words: 'It's going to be all right. It *is*.'

He jabbed a finger down on the cradle, was about to dial another number; then he paused. He rested his elbow on the desk and laid his forehead against the hand that was still clutching the receiver. Martin Heaney closed his eyes and faced himself.

He'd long ago lost his ideals. Not that he'd had many. When he took this job, though, he'd had some notion of serving the community, doing the dirty jobs that must be done. That was a long time ago – he'd aged since then, becoming less employable with every passing year. Which was why he'd been pussyfooting around, not wanting to be forced into a decision. He'd spoken to Iain, had a word with Alison, nothing on the record, all disclaimable. All stuff that could be backed away from.

Now he had to choose. He could find out what really happened when they framed Forward for murder. Maybe. Or he could sit here and rot until he turned sixty-five, in just under a quarter of a century from now.

He opened his eyes. He released the telephone-cradle and dialled an internal number.

'I need an appointment,' he said, the second someone picked up the phone. 'In thirty minutes' time.' And then, over a squawk of protest at the other end – 'Tell Grindle that Forward's done a bunk; he'll see me.'

He dialled again, long distance this time. The connection was made with surprising speed.

'Hello?'

'Sorry if I got you out of bed,' Martin murmured. 'Martin Heaney.'

There was a long pause. Then – 'What do you want?'

'A few words. Verity, tell me: when did you last see Iain Forward?'

*

There was severe turbulence over the North Pole, but Northwest Airlines' flight 17 to Tokyo rode serenely above it at thirty-nine thousand feet, the soothing hum of its engines lulling the passengers into stupor. The business class section of the plane was less than half full. Tony Cover had a window seat and nobody sitting next to him. He sipped club soda, part of his programme to keep bodily functions at maximum efficiency on a flight, while discreetly surveying the rest of the cabin. It amused him that business class seemed to be the one place where no business ever got done, except by The One. Every business class had its One: a man (always a man) who set up his laptop portable PC and dug himself into a pile of paperwork as high as the flight-path, as deep as the ocean.

They were preparing to serve a meal, but Mr Cover did not care for airline food, even when it was prepared to Northwest's immaculate standards. He took a couple of foil-wrapped packages from his briefcase. He unwrapped the first: tuna mayonnaise with cucumber and a paper twist containing salt. The second, he knew, would be his favourite cut of bratwurst. Beth had had a lot of practice at this, but he never ceased to marvel at her.

She was the mainstay of his life: had been ever since they'd met at college, when she was trying to organize a Bible-reading class and he'd signed on as her first customer. He'd courted her for three years before they could both be sure they were ready for the commitment, and in all that time he'd never slept with her, because he wanted to marry a virgin and so did she.

Tony Cover took a bite into his tuna on mayo and munched thoughtfully. A tad of salt . . . yes, better.

She would be at home now, preparing supper for Jody and Finch, their two children. She would be thinking of him, as he was of her. She would say a prayer for him and, in a while, he would take time to talk to God about her and the kids, setting things out with gratitude and love. Once she'd put the children to bed, she would start updating their mailing list. For years now they had dedicated their spare time to the anti-gun lobby, pitting themselves, body and soul, against the National Rifle Association of America. Tony Cover never felt so comfortable, so sure of his place in his Maker's world, as when he was engaged on this task, his wife by his side. He intended to die in an America where for an ordinary citizen to own a gun of any kind was a federal offence, and they were winning.

It did not trouble him that in the diplomatic pouch shackled to his wrist he carried two Ruger P-85 pistols with fifty rounds of ammunition. He was not an ordinary citizen.

Tony Cover finished his sandwiches, ordered another club soda and adjusted his seat to full recline. Another nine hours to Narita, where he would connect with NW7 for Singapore. So far, all was going as planned. Sampson had fled, just as they knew he would, as they wanted him to: for things could be done with quiet efficiency in the Far East that might attract unwelcome attention if done closer to home. Sampson was heading into the very same jungle that was Cover's natural habitat.

He resented the way this pursuit of Jay Sampson took him away from his family, though. With war only hours distant, a man's place was at home. But a little resentment was essential to Cover's work. Killing another in the name of justice required a sense of righteousness, and resentment.

*

Martin Heaney entered the outer office by one door just as Clarissa, Grindle's *chef du cabinet*, came in via the other. She looked down her long, Sloaney nose at him, as if surprised to find it was riff-raff day, but he had learned to live with that. Grindle adored Clarissa; everyone else ignored her.

'You can go in,' she said coolly. She did not tell him to wipe his feet, which surprised him, quite. If he needed confirmation that his decision to jump in and start swimming for dear life had been right, Clarissa embodied it.

'Yes,' Grindle was saying into the phone, 'yes, yes. And you'd better book a table at the Caprice. Ten o'clock. Oh, *yes*!'

He put down the phone. 'Guests,' he said dourly. 'Holloway's coming into Heathrow at six. Stipe's setting up an inter-service conference at seven.'

Martin recognized Holloway as head of the FBI's foreign liaison unit. But – 'Stipe?'

'Company man, here in London. I want you at the seven o'clock. Kick-off's at twenty-one fifty, by the way.'

It took a moment to register. 'The war?'

'The war.' Grindle nodded. There was silence for a moment. Then he went on, 'You will have to find Forward. Where do you think he's gone?'

'Singapore.'

'And why?'

'I've just spoken to Verity Newland.'

'*What?*'

'If my guess is right, he'll be heading straight for her. She remembered me, by the way. And you.'

263

'Why? Did you process her, back in 'seventy-three?'

'I sat in a couple of times. She's not the sort of woman to forget a face.'

Anger had temporarily faded from Grindle's face; now it flooded back. 'What possessed you to phone her?'

'A committee of one, remember? You asked me to contain the damage, gave me a free hand.'

Grindle pouted. 'What did Verity have to say?' he asked with bad grace.

'Iain hasn't arrived, though she says she's been expecting him ever since she heard about his release.'

'Has she indeed? Now what do we read into that . . . ? Go on.'

'She said to tell you: Sampson's due in Singapore any minute. Who is Sampson?'

The silence deepened. Grindle looked at the desk-top, avoiding Martin's eyes. Eventually he said, 'Why would Forward want to go to Singapore? Verity told you she was expecting him; why?'

'Before Christmas, Alison told me he's still desperate to clear his name.' Rapidly he outlined what she had said on the phone, half an hour previously. 'If he needs that much money it's because he's going abroad. He wants to talk to Newland, I'd stake my life on it.'

'Why wouldn't he have gone to America, to find Sonja?'

'Because he doesn't know who or where Sonja is.' Nor do I, Martin added to himself; but I'm going to find out. 'No, he's after Verity.'

Grindle seemed reluctant to accept this conclusion. 'Look,' Martin said, 'why not run it past Singapore Intelligence, see what their immigration computer turns up?'

'No.' Grindle frowned. 'Go to Singapore,' he said, after a pause.

For a second Martin felt light-headed. Mostly you planned and you schemed and nothing ever went right.

264

Sometimes, as now, it all worked out perfectly and it was too much to grasp. But Grindle was speaking again.

'There is one message I have to get across: you're to handle this on your own. Resist, at all costs, the temptation to seek help from the police, Special Branch, MI6 or Singapore Security – particularly Singapore Security. If there's going to be a party out there you will take charge of that party, mop up the mess afterwards, and leave, turning out the lights as you go.'

Martin had not been invited to sit, but he did so anyway. He crossed his legs and he said, 'Why?'

'Because I damn well *say* so!' Grindle had been fiddling with his paper-knife. As he spoke the penultimate word he slammed it down on the desk, jerking his blotter out of trim. Martin saw a man who had not slept much in the last week and thanked God for the British obsession with secrecy that prevented people from knowing how things were run on their behalf.

'We think,' Grindle went on, 'that Iraq has got the Bomb.'

Martin looked down at his hands. He could think of nothing to say.

'So if I come across as a bit . . . stretched, you'll forgive me.'

'Yes. Of course.' Martin hesitated. Better ask the question to which he already knew the answer; Grindle would expect it. 'Why must I go to Singapore?'

'To stop Forward making waves. The Yanks are chasing him, too; with a bit of luck you'll be able to just sit back and watch. Failing that, head him off. He knows you; from what you've been saying in your reports, he even likes you a bit. Maybe he'll listen to you. Make him see how important this is, the war effort and so on.'

'Do we know for sure that he's left the UK?'

'No. Not under his own name, anyway. There's an all-ports watch in force. But I'm accepting your analysis.

265

If Sampson has . . . All roads lead to Singapore. Just make sure you handle it yourself; no outsiders.'

'Even though I don't have any authority there,' Martin said. 'Not even High Commission back-up, is that what you're saying?' Suddenly he didn't feel quite so pleased with himself.

'High Commission?' Grindle essayed humour. 'What's a High Commission?'

'No calling-card to be left with Singapore Security . . .' Martin's alarm was mounting. 'Isn't this all just the teeniest bit iffy?'

Grindle drew a deep breath and leaned across his desk, resting on one forearm. 'Years ago,' he said, 'you were asked to provide a speedy and conclusive termination to the Forward case before it got to trial, and you turned that offer down. As was your right. As I would have done, in your place. Now you get another chance. You go, all by yourself, you stop Forward, you come home. You have no help, no fall-back —'

'And no chance.'

'— and an opportunity to rehabilitate yourself.'

'By killing Forward.'

Grindle gazed at Heaney. He was exhausted. It showed in the way he squinted, the angle of his head.

'Martin,' he said at last, and it showed in his voice, too. 'We've had this conversation before. Under no circumstances is anyone going to ask you to break the law. But take it from me: if Forward succeeds in uncovering what happened in nineteen seventy-three, England is going to die a lingering death. The alliance will crumble; this war will be lost. The Arabs will not deal with us, or with the Americans, ever again, not even after they've stopped laughing. And so, even though nobody will ask you to commit a crime, do remember that the Americans may not be so fussy.'

Martin sat up straighter. 'That's what you meant when

266

you said the Yanks were after him,' he said quickly. 'They're out to get him.'

'Yes.'

'Have him picked up in Singapore, then. Protective custody.'

'If he's arrested, he will talk – that's the one thing we can't afford. Get to him before the Americans, make him see there's nothing to be gained by staying in Singapore, less to be gained by talking. Scare the hell out of him, make him feel there's an assassin behind every tree. Do what you have to. I want your personal commitment, I want it now.'

Martin let him dangle for a bit. It wasn't only teasing; he had to look inside himself to be sure of what lay there, what had lain there for the past seventeen years. In the end it was Alison that decided him; strange, when you thought about it, that he was going after Iain for her sake . . .

'I can't force you to go,' Grindle remarked. 'But you're smiling: is that a yes?'

'It's a maybe.'

Grindle raised his eyebrows, waiting.

'I want to know the truth about Forward. All of it. In particular, who is Sonja? Who's Sampson?'

'You do not need to know.'

'Any more than I need to go to Singapore,' Martin said quietly.

There was a long silence. Then – 'What is truth?' Grindle murmured.

But Martin, unlike Pontius Pilate, stayed for answer.

*

To Verity Newland it was like being in some alien space city: half dream, half high-tech nightmare. She was driving slowly around Serangoon Central, a complex of Housing Development Board apartments to the

267

north-east of the city. On and on she drove, looking up at the numbers on the sides of the blocks, great yellow figures painted on black squares, every block the same as its neighbour. These buildings were not set out in neat rows, either, but at odd, awkward angles. She knew this was partly aesthetics, partly a computer-devised plan to catch cool breezes in the heat of the day; but in any case she damned the architect to hell. She was lost.

After her third circuit she found herself heading down a broad cul-de-sac. And there at last, yes! The number she sought. Verity parked in a vacant slot, careful to centre her BMW between the double yellow lines which Authority used, even here, to demarcate and control. As she got out her heel caught in the perforated concrete ecobricks. She swallowed the oath that rose to her lips. Circumspection was all.

Eleven o'clock at night. Yellow neon lights illuminated every crevice and dark corner: no room here for vandals, druggies or graffiti-artists. This particular Brave New World worked magnificently. She leaned against her car and surveyed the rectangular block towering above her. Sixth floor, ninth window from the left . . . lights were burning behind a rattan blind. Verity rummaged in her handbag and fished out a pair of opera glasses. It took her a moment to focus them and find the window again.

Each apartment came fitted with six aluminium pipes some nine inches long, set out of the kitchen wall at a slight upward angle. They were an important part of Singapore domestic life. People used them for drying clothes. They clipped their wet garments to bamboo poles and leaned out of the window to insert one end of the pole in an aluminium pipe. Sometimes they leaned too far and had to be scraped off the pavement for cremation at Bright Hill, but the papers did not dwell on such incidents.

Verity squinted up through the glasses. Four of the

six pipes set below the window that interested her were capped with orange plastic fitments – they too were standard. The first and third, however, held poles, one of which supported some white tee-shirts, the other of which was bare. That was the signal: all clear.

She put the glasses back in her bag and ducked inside her car for long enough to retrieve a gift-wrapped package. She made for the open area beneath the apartments where the elevators were. There was nobody about, but she became aware of a strange noise, realizing that it had been lodged at the back of her consciousness ever since she'd got out of the car. A disembodied, unearthly voice echoed up and down the stairwells. Was it a chant?

The lift delivered her on to a concrete landing outside the flat she sought. Its steel outer gate stood ajar. She rapped on the door. The occupant moved soundlessly: when the door opened she had no warning of his approach, and was startled.

'Hello, Robinson,' she said to the boy.

As she crossed the threshold she experienced a moment of curiosity, for this was the first time she'd entered an HDB flat. But the apartment seemed almost bare of furniture. Everywhere had been painted white, her favourite, with a honey-hued wooden breakfast bar providing the only splash of colour.

A small hallway gave directly on to the living room, with the kitchen an open-plan extension of that. Next to the breakfast-bar was a stool. On it sat a Chinese man, his legs crossed. He was smoking a cigarette, right elbow resting on his left hand, both supported by his knee. The cigarette stood straight up before his face, obscuring it, but she knew him.

'Uncle Tang . . .'

He nodded. His head seemed to be on a perpetual-motion spring, like one of those awful ceramic dogs you sometimes saw on the back window-ledges of cars, the downward nod more pronounced than its upward counterpart.

'Long time no see,' he said, through a gag of catarrh. 'Long time no see.'

True, she thought; he was on the payroll of an Occydor subsidiary, but he worked at Sudong and she hardly ever went there now. He did not change position as she approached. When she was almost close enough to touch him he lowered his cigarette and he smiled. His lips were so thin as to be almost invisible. That, and the scrawniness of his body, and the persistent, uneven nodding, brought into her mind the nickname by which everyone had known him: Old Turtle. A bad name, because to the Chinese it carried overtones of cuckoldry, but it fitted him perfectly.

Suddenly he seemed to become aware that all was not quite as it should be, for he slipped off his stool, offering it to her with a smile and a wave of the hand. Verity hesitated. Then, slowly, she hitched herself on to the stool, while Old Turtle and Young Robinson settled on the floor, folding their legs up into the lotus position. They sat there, Uncle Tang puffing away at his cigarette and the boy blinking behind his big, ugly spectacles, and she thought, My God, what am I going to do, *what* . . . ?

Old Turtle worked for Occydor's subsidiary as a care-taker. Before that he had been with Harchem. He'd always professed affection for Verity, although she had never quite trusted him. He liked to be told things. In the old days he used to ask questions all the time. She never replied, but somehow he'd find out the answers without any help from her, and then take delight in telling her so. Verity disliked Uncle Tang because she was never sure how much he knew. Yet beggars could not be choosers; she had to use him now.

The ghostly wail that had haunted her since getting out of the car could still dimly be heard inside. 'That noise,' she said.

'Singing.' Robinson cleared his throat importantly, as if called upon to give an exposition in class. 'Karaoke lady. *Chr-chr-de deng.* Great song.'

Verity stared at him. 'I can't hear any music,' she said at last.

'No music. Just words. "Waiting Foolishly". Movie song, wonderful.'

Verity had a sudden vision of this sad woman all alone on one of the uppermost floors, living her fantasies, hour in, hour out, oblivious of the neighbours who were trying to get to sleep. So selfish. So un-Singaporean. And so damned annoying.

Verity handed her package to Robinson. 'A present,' she said.

He jerked his specs back up his nose and accepted the package from her, unwrapping the paper with care. 'Wow!'

It was a lavishly produced coffee-table book: *Poisonous Plants of The World*. Robinson had become mad about poisons after his first visit to her office. They'd seen quite a bit of each other since then. The boy had all the makings of a top-class gofer.

Something fell out of the book. The boy picked it up. A photograph. He peered at it closely. 'Visual scanner,' he declared at last. 'Pretty good.'

'I want you to remember that face. Do you think you can do that?'

While he studied the photo she took the opportunity to glance around. They were good, these apartments; the workmanship might be slip-shod here and there, but this represented value for money. She guessed Uncle Tang had bought it as an investment. He would have lied to the HDB, of course, declaring he needed it for his widowed sister or some elderly relative, but that was all part of the game.

'I would know him, if I saw him,' Robinson said. 'Who is he?'

'His name is Jay Sampson. Can you remember that?'

'Sampson. Jay Sampson.'

'He will arrive in Singapore tomorrow morning. Turn over the photo; on the back I've written his flight number, do you see?'

The boy did as he was told, and nodded. Now Verity addressed herself to Old Turtle.

'Sampson's coming back,' she said.

Uncle Tang's genial expression did not change, but for a slow count of two his nodding stopped. He said, 'Coming back.' Once. Twice.

'We need to make certain preparations,' Verity went on slowly. 'So as to take care of ourselves.'

'Preparations. Care. Preparations. Care.'

'For this, I need the boy. Tomorrow is a schoolday. He must be reported sick; is that possible?'

'Possible, possible.'

'What should I do?' Robinson asked Verity.

'You must go to the airport tomorrow and wait for Jay Sampson to arrive. Make sure he doesn't see you. He will almost certainly take a taxi. Follow him, note the taxi's number. Uncle will be waiting for you outside, in a car. You will follow Sampson wherever he goes, and report back to me.'

Verity shifted her attention to the old man. 'He knows you, remember. So you mustn't let him see you. If he goes to an hotel, well and good. Make sure he checks in, that he doesn't just walk out through the back door, then call me and tell me where he is.' She hesitated. 'If he goes to the house . . . '

'Orchid House?'

'The House of Orchids,' she said. 'If he goes there,

you'll have to let the boy follow him. Sampson doesn't know him.' Now she turned back to wide-eyed Robinson. 'He'll be watchful. But the last person he'll expect to follow him is a schoolboy. That's why I'm asking you. Understand?'

'I understand.'

'You must stick to him like glue, Robinson.'

'Yes.'

'And I want you to understand something else. Don't try to be too clever. Find out where he goes and call me, that's *all*. Right?'

'Right.'

Verity slid off the stool. She picked up her bag and made as if to leave. Uncle Tang jumped to his feet with an alacrity surprising in one of his age and came with her as far as the front door. She reached out for the handle, but he forestalled her. Verity's heartbeat quickened; was this a trap? Ah no, he merely wanted to play the gentleman, as he'd been wont to do all those years ago when first dependent on her for his rice.

She looked down on him, a full head shorter than she was; she took in the singlet, faded-grey from too much cold-water washing, the creased green shorts, skinny arms and legs, tattoos scarcely distinguishable from so many bruises, the nearly bald head, the gold chain around his neck . . . everything just the same as seventeen years ago. Uncle Tang hadn't changed. But she was another person altogether.

'Be all right?' he quizzed her. 'All right?'

'If we keep our heads,' she replied, 'we shall be all right.'

As she went down to the lifts the ethereal woman's voice continued to haunt the darkness, like a witch from out of some nightmarish Chinese kung fu movie, and Verity inconsequentially remembered Robinson's translation of her song: 'Waiting Foolishly'.

# SEVENTEEN

Everyone else had only one topic of conversation – The War – but Kate and her friends lived inside a bubble. The War had broken out a few hours earlier, somewhere over in that direction. (Or maybe this direction . . . ?) Anyhow, a long way off. Some Arabs were fighting for independence and the fascists had gone to help out with atom bombs and suchlike. A few of Kate's fellow-students thought they'd be fried to a crisp sometime between now and the weekend, so they might as well get stoned. One boy said it was all Israel's fault, another opined that if they grew bananas in Kuwait, instead of oil, Bush wouldn't have bothered for two seconds. Somebody pointed out that you didn't grow oil. You know what I mean. You *do* grow oil: palm oil. Prat. Groundnut oil. Peanut oil, nerd. It turned out somebody had a bag of peanuts; they gathered around to share them. Kate did not have an opinion on The War, she just thought All Wars Were Silly, which formed the hub of a safe consensus. And anyway, today was Photography.

She took Darren along, largely for his muscle. This afternoon the design students were supposed to go out in pairs and ask people in uniform if they could photograph them. It didn't matter what kind of uniform: Traffic Warden, Fireman, Chef, even Pig. Just had to be a uniform, that's all. Kate wanted to do the Skins, but they charged a quid a time and she didn't have so many quids. But if Darren was with her, they didn't dare ask anything.

Darren worked as a glazier, on and off. That's where

Kate had first picked him up: on a building-site. One of her girlfriends had bet she wouldn't thwack his bum with a rolled-up *Mirror* as they walked by and she'd done it, because Darren had a lovely bum and she fancied a bit of it. Also, she could see he was weird, possibly psychotic, and on that account doubly desirable. But just now work was slack in the building and allied trades, so Darren was free and his boss let him have the van.

They covered Oxford Street and Tottenham Court Road; not bad. They were sitting in this little Eyetie caff, all stubble and steam, when suddenly Darren mumbled something to the table-top. What?

'I said, me bruvver's flyin' out today.'

Kate didn't know he had a brother.

''Course I do. Derek.'

Since when?

'Oh, come *on*! The soldier. His brick's flyin' out today.'

His prick's doing *what*?

Darren looked up from the table-top with an expression on his face that told Kate it was time to stop ragging.

'A brick,' Darren said, very succinctly for him, 'is what soldiers call their unit. Their platoon, see? And Derek's platoon is flying out to Saudi Arabia. Today. Right now, if you want to know. Which you fuckin' don't.'

'I'm sorry,' she said, stretching out her hand to cover his. 'I really didn't know you had a brother. You don't talk about him.'

He snatched his hand away. 'Elder bruvver,' he said at last, not looking at her. 'Sergeant, he is. Twenny-eight. Married. Baby.'

She realized, then, why he never spoke about Derek: another 'hard man', another hard act to follow. She struggled to remember snippets of conversation overheard, articles half read. 'He'll be all right,' she said lamely. 'They say it'll all be over in a few days. Honestly.'

'Yeah.'

Darren's mouth worked spasmodically, his mind else-where. She'd never seen him like this.

'The two of you don't get on,' she ventured.

He shook his head.

'I'm sorry.'

A long silence intervened, punctuated by the houghing and coughing of the espresso machine.

'He phoned last night,' Darren said at last. 'I was down the pub.' He wiped his nose on the back of his hand. 'Shoulda been there. Spoken wiv 'im.' He heaved a sigh. 'You wanna go home?'

*He* wanted to go home, that much was clear. 'Yes,' Kate said.

Darren dropped her off on the corner, saying he'd buy some fags and come up to the house as soon as he found a slot for the van. This street was one big car park, useful to commuters and residents alike. Darren had got done for illegal parking a few months back and his boss had made him pay the fine himself. He'd quit that job, but he was more careful now.

Kate slung the camera over her shoulder and walked up the road. It was a chill, dank day; she was glad to be coming home. As she reached the gate she saw, without surprise, that somebody had double-parked in front of their own house. A dark blue car, spattered with mud, its engine still running. She couldn't see the driver because the windows were of tinted glass.

By natural progression her thoughts turned to Darren's fine, and from there slithered to his hitherto unsuspected brother, Derek. What was it like, she wondered, to lose somebody you loved in war? Her grandparents would have known about that. She'd never met Alison's parents; they died while she was young. And Iain's mother had snuffed it while he was serving his sentence – of grief, perhaps? – so all she had to go on was a recent memory of visiting Grandpa George in Solihull, and he hadn't talked about war.

*What was it like to lose someone you loved?*

Her mind was still on this problem as she walked through the front door. She looked down the hall and saw a man in the kitchen. His hands were on Alison's shoulders. He was shaking her.

Kate screamed.

The man lowered his hands and turned, his face registering surprise. Alison took one look at Kate and cried, 'It's all right, close the door, it's all *right*, I tell you.'

Kate reached out behind her and slammed the front door.

'Come here, Kate,' Alison said. When she made no move: 'Come on, it's safe. I want you to meet somebody.'

The girl advanced slowly.

'This is Martin Heaney,' Alison said when Kate reached the kitchen. 'He was the case officer who . . . who interviewed me, after your father's arrest. He knows Iain's innocent.'

Kate's eyes swivelled. Martin nodded. 'Hello.'

'Why were you shaking my mother?' Kate blurted out.

'I was trying to make her see something. I got carried away. Sorry.'

'Who the hell are you, to make people see things?'

'A friend.'

'Oh yeah? Beat up all your friends, do you?'

'I wasn't –'

'Darren's coming,' Kate said to Alison. 'He can throw this bum out.'

'No,' Alison said firmly. 'Martin's trying to help.' She was on the verge of tears. 'Don't, Kate, I can't stand it.'

Kate felt a familiar grey veil come down over her head: the depression of guilt. But it was so unfair! It wasn't she who'd made Mum cry, it was this git, with his smarmy manner and cheap suit . . .

'Is somebody going to explain?' she asked in a small voice.

'Your mother's in danger,' Heaney said. 'So are you. Some not very pleasant people are determined to get to Iain; they're not above using both of you to do it. I want you to come to a place where no one will be able to find you.'

Kate looked at Alison. Guilt was expanding into fear now; it showed in her face. 'Hostages,' she whispered; 'is that what he means: we could be taken hostage?'

Alison nodded.

'Don't go,' Kate implored her. 'Say you won't.'

'I won't. He can't make us.'

'But . . . *why*?'

Alison said nothing for a moment. Then she heaved a short, sharp sigh and sat down suddenly. 'Iain's gone to Singapore,' she said.

'*What?* But you said he'd gone after a job . . . I mean, when, what's happening . . . ?'

'He's trying to clear his name.'

'So what's in Singapore to help him do that?'

Kate's mind raced back to the last time she'd seen her father, in the office at the end of Aural Sightings' corridor . . . a blue document, a ticket . . .

Alison rested her forehead against her wrist. She was crying, silently.

'Where did he get the money . . . ? Oh my . . . God.' Kate slumped down in a chair next to Alison's. 'He didn't? Mum, tell me he didn't.'

Alison nodded violently. 'Building Society . . . nearly all of it.'

'But . . . he'll come back. Won't he?' A long pause. '*Won't he?*'

'Who knows?' Alison hauled herself out of the depths, somehow. 'He said he'd given up trying to clear himself. He was lying.'

'Are you sure he's gone to Singapore? I mean, how *can* you be sure?'

Alison shrugged.

'Sonja's going there,' Heaney said. 'That much we do know, thanks to the FBI.'

Alison's lips tightened. She jerked around to look at Heaney. 'Is Verity still in Singapore?' she asked, after a long pause.

'Yes.'

'That's it, then. That's where he's gone.'

'Who's Verity?' Kate asked. 'Who's Sonja? I don't know why I'm talking to myself.'

Alison sighed. 'When your father and I were working in Singapore Verity Newland was Iain's boss.' She paused. 'He hated her.'

'You think she did it, this Verity? Framed him, I mean?'

'*He* probably thinks so.'

'But why would –'

'Oh, shut up.'

'Well thanks! All I'm trying to do is help.'

'Then be quiet and let me think.'

'What's there to think about, for Christ's sake? This gorilla's trying to kidnap you, Dad's done a runner, how much more –'

'I'm thinking about the *price*, you stupid little cow! *The price!*' And then, with shocking, unexpected violence, Alison reached forward and slapped her daughter's face. Not a token slap, but a hard show-stopper.

Kate gasped. She raised a hand to her cheek, now turning bright red. The pain grew in leaps and bounds. Alison's face hovered in front of her, contorted with rage: Kate knew the poison had not vented itself, there was more to come. Sober up, she told herself. Contribute. What was Mum saying, price . . . ? 'How much does it cost to fly to Singapore?' she asked. 'A thousand, or what?'

'Less than that,' Alison muttered. 'More than that.' There was a pause. 'I have to go after him,' she said suddenly. 'I've got to get him back. Stop him.'

'You can't. You know Dad: if he wants to do a thing, he will. Look, tell me, why are we supposed to be in danger?' Kate turned to Heaney. 'Come on, Mr Know-All, why?'

'People are trying to trace Iain,' he answered. 'People who want him out of the way. First thing they'll do is come here.'

'You make it sound like some lousy thriller,' Kate scoffed. 'Who is it – Fu Manchu?'

'Worse. Us.'

Kate frowned. 'Us?'

'The powers-that-be.' His lips twitched. 'The filth.'

Her eyes widened. 'Who are you?' she breathed at last. 'Really?'

'I'm from MI5.'

Whatever answer Kate had been expecting, it wasn't that. She looked uncertainly from face to face. Alison nodded. 'Iain knows things,' she said. 'Not his fault, but he does. He just does.'

'What things?'

'About chemical weapons,' Heaney replied, although she hadn't addressed her question to him. 'He can put a jigsaw together, if he thinks about it. Certain people don't want him to think too much.'

'Martin,' Alison said, 'does Grindle know you're here?'

'Yes. He approves. The last thing he wants is for the Americans to get their hands on you.'

'Grindle?' Kate put in.

'My chief.'

'Why should he care what the Americans do?' Alison asked.

'Because he's frightened of what may come out.'

'I don't get you,' Kate said coldly. 'You barge in here,

expect us to trust you when you say some Americans don't want this and that. Anyway, what makes you so different from them if your own boss is scared of what's coming out?'

'Martin believes Iain's innocent,' Alison said. 'I told you.'

'And so he's going to risk everything for us – oh, Mum, come *on*! He's a prat, surely you can see?'

But Alison ignored her. 'Martin, let me go to Singapore.'

He shook his head. 'Sorry, you and I have got to cover every inch of the ground. A long talk, that's what we need, Alison. Everything you can remember about Iain since he came out of prison.'

Alison thought. 'No,' she decided at last.

'Alison . . . '

'No.' She looked up at him sideways before rising and going to stand behind Kate's chair. She placed a hand on her daughter's shoulder. Heaney weighed them both for a moment. He put his hands in his pockets and smiled. 'I should have known,' he remarked ruefully.

He was like an uncle who could take liberties and get away with them; Kate saw how her mother smiled back at him, trustingly, affectionately even, now that she thought she'd won. Then he took his right hand from its pocket and after momentary suspension of belief Kate realized he was holding a gun.

'I did know,' he said. 'Actually. Right. Sorry about this, ladies. Alison, this isn't in the brief, but I'm doing it anyway. I'm going to prove that Iain was innocent. I don't trust Grindle. He's promised me Iain won't be harmed, though I only half believe him. And I wasn't telling the truth earlier: he doesn't know I'm here. So I'm taking you somewhere you'll be safe from him, as well as the Americans.

'There's a blue car outside. You walk out, down the

281

path, you get into the car, you don't look back. I'll be right behind you. *Now*, please.'

Kate felt betrayed when her anger abandoned her. While she was angry, she could cope. But her rage had slunk off, leaving her just a teenage girl, afraid, and suddenly freezing cold.

Alison's hand tightened on her shoulder. Somehow she was on her feet and walking down the narrow hallway. She could sense Alison, a step behind. She opened the front door. Four or five yards away, the muddy blue car she'd noticed earlier was still double-parked right opposite their gate, its engine running. Tinted glass. Just like the movies. Only real.

As she walked on, she saw something else out of the corner of her left eye. Movement. A person. But before she could analyse what was happening, an ugly sound cut into her brain and she heard a grunt. She wheeled around. Heaney was clutching both hands to his stomach, doubled up. Over him stood Darren, who now brought something metal down on Heaney's head. It connected with a thud, like the tamping of moist earth. Heaney sank to his knees. There was blood everywhere. Kate screamed.

Alison stood on the doorstep, watching impassively. Kate, frozen in mid-scream, stared at her mother.

Darren had got Heaney in a half-nelson. He hustled him down the path and wrenched open the car's front nearside door; Kate spun around in time to catch a glimpse of a pair of shoes lying soles outward, the driver . . .

'In you go,' Darren said cheerily. 'With your mate, then. You won't be wanting your shooter, will you? No? Ta, then. Bye-bye.'

He'd managed to bundle Heaney inside, on top of the driver. Now he came back up the path, tossing the gun from hand to hand.

'Didn't like that driver,' he explained. 'Give me lip, he did, when I told him to move on.'

'So you hit him?' Alison said, in a neutral tone.

'Yeah.' He grinned at her.

Alison nodded. 'Good,' she said; and while Kate was still struggling to come to terms with that, she went on, 'I need some dosh, Darren.'

# EIGHTEEN

There were seven people aboard Pelangi Air's morning flight from Kuala Lumpur to Tioman: three Japanese couples and a lone man. This solitary passenger sat well forward, just behind the two pilots, watching in fascination as they manipulated the heavy controls to put them on a course south-east from the capital before settling down to their newspapers. It was very noisy in the cabin: not only on account of the Dornier's engines, but also because the Japanese couples were happy. Thousands of miles to the west, a steel rain of destruction was falling on Iraq, mincing flesh and pounding buildings flat, but much they cared. They were on their honeymoons.

The flight was soon over. As the tiny plane banked sharply, heading in a steep dive for a landing-strip no bigger than a football pitch, the sons and daughters of Nippon scrambled to starboard, cameras at the ready. 'South Pacific,' a girl cried, and everyone aimed their lenses at that fabulous landscape immortalized by the fifties movie.

The sole passenger was last to disembark, his guts still churning from the hairy, turn-on-a-wing-tip approach. Tioman was nowhere near the south Pacific, he mused, but it was tranquil, and breathtakingly beautiful, and hot; and it was the same as he remembered it. For twenty years ago it was here that he had come, as the Japanese came now – on honeymoon. The two of them had sailed up from Singapore; and as their Malay crew hove into the wind, making ready to cast anchor, Alison had shaded her eyes to look up at the famous double mountain, and she had said, 'This isn't happening, *pinch* me, Iain . . .'

The Japanese lined up for the Tioman Holiday Resort Hotel coach, men in front, the women that dutiful three paces behind, all tacitly begging to be shepherded, given the treatment. As Iain Forward trudged past them he thought irrationally of Jews queuing at Belsen or Dachau, pictures from a bygone age . . . 'You will be taken to the showers . . . to the right or the left, as I signal . . .' It crippled him inside, this notion of war and atrocity, but it would not leave him; it stayed in his guts as he followed the beach road along to where he remembered the jetty to be.

Iain took a short-cut through the grounds of the new beach resort hotel. A Malay stood beside a tall Macarthur palm, holding a thin rope. Iain stopped, lowering his rucksack. The rope twitched. His eyes followed it upwards into the palm leaves, where a berok monkey was heaving on a coconut. With a squeal of delight the simian at last succeeded in freeing the nut, which fell to earth like a green bomb. A shower of tiny birds sprayed up out of the foliage and dissipated, along with the last of the early morning mist. When the Malay clicked his teeth the monkey came scampering down the tree-trunk. Iain caught the man's eye and smiled; the Malay grinned, the monkey swore, Iain walked on.

There was a golf course now, with sprinklers bursting across it at regular intervals, but there were few people about. Perhaps it was still too early. More likely, the war was keeping them at home. The flight to Bangkok from London had been nearly empty, and long – the airlines, not wanting to test air-safety over the Middle East, flew around it instead – so Iain had got a good night's sleep, stretched out over five seats in the 747's rear cabin.

He found a patch of shade beneath the jetty and settled down for a rest. Later the jet-foil would come, on its daily run up from Singapore. It would collect more passengers and return, creaming into Finger Pier four hours later. There, just another idle holiday-maker, a certain Marc Didier Cresson, would disembark, the stamps in his Canadian passport indicating that he had left Montreal a fortnight previously, en route to London . . .

Iain wiped the sweat from his brow. He had no idea if this was going to work, but it had worked damn well so far. He'd flown first to Bangkok, reasoning that they would think he was making for Singapore direct, and so would not watch flights to Thailand with the same intensity. From there, train to Kuala Lumpur, one human ant among many anonymous others. Plane to Tioman: no immigration formalities necessary, since he had already entered Malaysia at the border with Thailand: a much neglected, ill-guarded border. Singapore immigration still lay ahead, but at Finger Pier, not Changi airport; and later, much later, than they would expect him to come . . .

He did not know whether MI5 would have tipped off the Singapore authorities, or where he would stay, or how he would get to Verity. All that lay in the future. What mattered now was surviving.

He'd survived seventeen years of straight hell. He knew how.

A long-boat was being launched into the waves, not far from where he sat, ready to take a party of scuba-divers off for a morning's sport. He and Alison had snorkelled from a long-boat just like it, before returning to their rented hut, light lunch, heavy sex . . .

She was no longer the woman he had married; that was for sure.

*Do not think about anything at all.*

Alison was off-limits. His prison-trained mind saw danger looming and issued the order; Iain obeyed it. A glance at his watch told him to expect the jet-foil in another hour. He lay back beside a cool steel pile, tilted his straw hat over his eyes, and closed them.

\*

Robinson Tang raced along the front of Changi airport's terminal, frantically looking for Uncle. At last! As Tang Gui Wen pulled into the kerb, Robinson wrenched open the door and leaned inside.

'Sampson's taking the bus,' he hissed.

'You are sure?'

*'Yes!'*

'All right, you take the bus, too.'

'But Miss Newland said —'

*'Take the bus!* Meet you at the city.'

Robinson's mind was in turmoil. How to be sure of making contact with Uncle again? But before he could speak a traffic-policeman's whistle sounded, warning Uncle Tang that he had overstayed his welcome, and — 'Go!' he yelled as he reached out to slam the passenger door, almost severing his nephew's fingers.

\*

Jay was pleased to find only a few other passengers on the bus: some Australian backpackers with luggage and voices that took up a lot of space, two ground steward-esses going home, a schoolboy carrying a notebook who looked like an avid plane-spotter. Jay sat at the rear of the bus, one arm stretched along the seat-rest so that he could keep an eye on the road behind without appearing too conspicuous. Cars overtook or turned off; no one vehicle appeared to be following him. Jay knew that sur-veillance could be a lot more sophisticated than that, but he allowed himself to relax a little. He'd got away from the States, and Singapore was tugging at his heart-strings: everything different, everything just the same.

The bus roared down the East Coast Parkway, with

brightly lit apartment blocks to the right, parkland and the sea on his left. Jay felt happiness greater than any he'd known in years. He was back where he belonged. Nobody could touch him here, in his city.

He rubbed his eyes. Tiredness was getting to him. Of course Singapore wasn't safe – when had it ever been safe? *Wake up*, he told himself sharply.

Originally he'd planned to ride into town and flow with the crowds for long enough to shake off anyone who might be following him, then take a taxi to the House of Orchids where he could hide out. Of course the house would be a mess; of course it would, but it was secluded and safe and he could shelter there, just for the day or two he would need to get sorted out. Now he decided to insert an additional precaution into this schedule. A cab to the house wasn't such a good idea: taxis were easy to follow, and you were alone in them except for the driver. Another bus, that was the answer . . .

*

The suspect – for so Robinson Tang thought of him – got off the bus at the top of Orchard Road where it veered left and became Tanglin Road. Robinson followed hesitantly, but Sampson paid him no heed. The boy felt exposed: it was like one of those dreams where you found yourself in a sunlit street, stark naked, doing something awful. But once the pumping of his heart had steadied a little, he realized that actually this was easy. Sampson just kept hurrying on with scarcely a backwards glance. Only when he came to cross a road did he look casually over his shoulder: so casually that Robinson couldn't believe he was checking for tails.

The boy dared not take his eyes off Sampson. He knew he ought to be looking out for Uncle as well, but the scent of the chase was in his nostrils. Robinson trotted along some fifty paces behind the suspect, keeping his

288

eyes focused on those busily striding legs. Uncle would just have to make contact later.

*

By the time Jay picked up his last bus, a number 172, he was well-nigh exhausted. He felt a fool. No one had followed him from the airport, of course they hadn't. He glanced wearily along the faces in the bus, saw not one he recognized, and slumped down in the nearest seat. His head drooped on to his chest. He ought to sit at the back, check the road . . . In a minute, he'd move in a minute . . .

He woke with a start, to find the bus all but empty. It was bucketing along at a great rate through a thinly built-up area interspersed with long tracts of blackness, open countryside. Jay realized he'd been dozing. One old man sat at the front behind the driver, his grizzled head resting against the window. A bespectacled Chinese girl was the bus's only other occupant.

Jay moved forward, staggering as the bus careered around bends. The driver seemed surprised by his request. 'Don't know any Sarimbun Avenue,' he said. 'Soon be at Thong Hoe; that any good?'

More lights, more houses, up ahead. Thong Hoe village. The bus slowed. Jay caught sight of a hawker centre swathed in antiseptic white light, with a few late-night customers. *That* hadn't been there, twenty years ago. Great God, where had all these houses come from?

He stepped off the bus and looked around. Journey's end, sad and drab. On the other side of the road the hawker stalls were closing up for the night. Jay turned back the way he'd come. Two sets of headlights rounded the bend, bunched up close together: a taxi and a private car. Some hundred yards behind came a lorry, bouncing its noisy way along on depleted springs. The three vehicles passed by, heading north for the Strait. A motorcycle sped down the hill in the direction of Singapore city.

Ahead of him were the lights of a Housing Development Board estate. To the left, the highway, Lim Chu Kang Road, ascending the hill and lost to sight where the street-lighting ran out, but Jay knew it went on for another mile to the Strait of Johor. On his right, the road to Singapore City, along which he'd recently come. He turned around. For a few seconds, he couldn't understand what he was looking at. Then his bag slipped from his fingers.

The narrow, rutted road he'd known as Sarimbun Avenue was no more. Instead, a broad earth track led up an incline into pitch darkness. By the light from the housing estate he could just see that the earth was deep red in colour, and patterned by the passage of many vehicles.

What else would have changed?

He became aware of a set of headlights advancing down the track towards him and moved to one side. The lights heralded something that made a lot of noise. There was a sugar-cane plantation behind him and he retreated into it until he could go no further.

The lights were very close now. They swayed with the unevenness of the track, and Jay could hear how the engine complained when the driver shifted gear. No synchromesh. Then he saw it: a brown jeep marked with military insignia, containing two soldiers as well as the driver. The jeep bumped down to the main road. Jay waited until it accelerated away. Only when he could no longer hear its engine did he emerge from the depths of the sugar-cane.

What in hell was all this about?

He'd seen enough of the jeep's insignia to have his memory jogged. Those were SAFTI badges: but what business did Singapore's Armed Forces Training Institute

290

have here? This had never been military territory in his time.

Jay began to trudge up the track. In contrast to his earlier demeanour, he was watchful and alert. Soon he'd left the light behind. He'd had the forethought to buy a torch whilst transiting in Tokyo, reasoning that the house would lack electricity or services of any kind. Now it came in handy.

He'd walked less than half a mile when he came to the fence.

It glinted in the beam of his torch, away to the left. He ploughed towards it: ploughed, because here the mud was glutinous with recent rain and the track bore less evidence of maintenance. A chain-link fence, twelve or so feet high, with razor wire coiled along the top. Jay backed away from it. But even as he reached the track, he heard the sound of dogs barking furiously somewhere inside the perimeter and he broke into a run, not pausing until the fence was far behind him.

He dared not use his flashlight, yet without it he was doomed to blunder through thick undergrowth, at the mercy of ruts and roots alike. His skin leached sweat. He looked back once, catching sight of another torch-beam as it played along that ominous fence away to his left; he heard the dogs whine, and hoarse shouts of command.

As he pushed on into the snag of bushes and creepers and rotting, fallen palms, he was aware of a prickly feeling at the base of his skull that had nothing to do with sugar-cane leaves. Somewhere behind the wall of black that hemmed him in on every side there lurked a watcher. Not the army, not SAFTI. A spy.

*

Robinson was starting to panic. He'd all but run out of money and had no idea how he was going to get home. Not a sign of Uncle since Changi airport. The taxi-driver who'd driven him from town to Thong Hoe village had been unpleasant, frowning in the mirror, questioning him incessantly, threatening to report him to his high school principal for being out late. As if it was any of his business! Robinson was on a mission vital to the security of Singapore and must on no account be stopped. Well, perhaps not vital, and perhaps not for Singapore, but hugely important.

He'd begged the driver not to drop him off under the glare of the hawker-stall lights. By this time relations were so bad that Robinson felt obliged to resort to Western ways: he offered a tip. Surprisingly efficacious, Western ways: the driver not only did as he was told, he shut up. Robinson waited until the cab had breasted the hill on the other side of Thong Hoe village before having the man stop and let him out. He ran back down the hill, keeping to the right-hand side of the road where sugar-cane plants would lend concealment. But there was no sign of the suspect.

Robinson skidded to a halt at the crossroads and bent down to rest his hands on his knees. He was panting hard, his heart felt like it might burst. In Kipling's terms this was definitely high-disaster low-triumph stuff. He had no money, he was far from home, he'd lost the man he'd been detailed to follow. Worst of all, he had no idea what to do next.

He stood upright and studied the terrain. No sign of anyone by the housing estate, to the east. He'd passed no one as he raced down the north-south main road. That left west . . . the dark, semi-jungle area by Sarimbun reservoir.

Army training land. Robinson's heart gave an unpleasant jolt. There were big red-and-white boards up, he'd seen them often: live ammunition exercises, danger of death, an outline figure of one man shooting at another . . . Surely the suspect wouldn't have gone in there?

Nervously he approached the start of a just visible tamped-earth track. And yes! – there were footprints, recent ones by the look of them. The boy bent down. There was enough light to reveal one set of tracks leading away into darkness.

Robinson straightened his shoulders. He cast a despairing look down the main road, hoping against hope to see Uncle's car come around the bend. The road yawned back at him. Robinson heaved a despondent sigh.

He was on the point of starting up the earth track when he heard the sound of an engine and was blinded by headlamps, suddenly very close, coming out of nowhere.

He leapt to one side just in time to avoid a jeep on its way to the north–south highway. Robinson stood and watched it pass. One of the soldiers riding in the back seat turned and stared at him: a hard look that sent the boy's heart soaring into his mouth. The jeep stopped. For an instant he thought the soldiers would speak to him, but they drove on, leaving Thong Hoe village to the night.

He hesitated no longer, plunging up the track as fast as he could run, anxious to put a good chunk of darkness between himself and the streetlights. Once he heard dogs barking up ahead and he stopped, hardly able to breathe; but the row subsided and after a while he went on, only more slowly, taking greater care not to make a noise.

His sight slowly accustomed itself to the blackness. Ahead of him was a strip not wholly black: charcoal-grey, rather. That must be the Johor Strait. Far away to his left and behind, an orange glow signified the city. There was a moon, partially obscured by cloud, it was true, but casting enough light to distinguish the shapes of trees and keep him on the track. Although he had matches he dared not use them, in case the suspect should turn and see. So he couldn't even risk a smoke – and oh, how he was dying for one!

He walked on, stopping sometimes to listen, but the

night returned him nothing save the sough of the wind and the occasional scrape of a cicada. There's nobody here, he told himself. Turn around, go home. But he couldn't go home, he didn't have enough money. As long as he went forward he wouldn't have to face his problems, which was fine, because they were assuming hitherto undreamed-of proportions. His mother was going to crucify him – and that was on top of whatever Uncle decided to do.

His spirits sank down into his trainers, through the soles, into the bowels of the earth. At last his feet dragged to a halt. The track had petered out, leaving only thin paths striking off in all directions. He bumped into something hard; his hand told him it was a fallen tree.

Robinson sat down on the tree-trunk and, after a last, vain wrestle with his fear of detection, took out a pack of Marlboro Lights. Nothing mattered now, anyway. He lit up. The nicotine made him want to vomit, but he was damned if he was going to waste it. He sat with his elbows on his knees, all hunched up, and after a while his shoulders began to shake.

*

A tiny part of Jay's mind dwelt on the spy behind him. Only a tiny part: he was navigating by blind instinct now, drawn onwards to his old home by signals too ancient and primitive for man to understand. His flashlight kept him out of the worst traps: areas where creepers and roots and rotting branches had erected themselves into a screen, or where the ground dipped suddenly. He noticed many of these depressions. The army had been here. They had made use of the land, *his* land, scarred it and gone away. He prayed they hadn't left any mines behind.

He was forcing a path through something moist and tangled, with the sticky consistency of a spider's web, when his knee came up against a rigid surface and he nearly cried out. He stood still, gathering his wits, then reached out a hand. While it was still moving through space he guessed where he was; the hand made contact with a wall and he knew for sure.

The House of Orchids.

And then he couldn't think what to do. How stupid – to come home and not know what should happen next. One thing was certain, though: no one had the gin chilling in the ice-box, there wouldn't be a hot meal waiting.

He pulled himself together. First, ditch the spy, then dig in. The more he thought about that, the more he liked it. With the army nearby, and the jungle for cover, he could hole up here for as long as it took.

To seal his resolve he banged on the wall of his house. His fist punched a hole right through the rotten wood.

Jay risked another flash from his torch. It showed him a window-frame and two wooden pillars, broken glass . . . The House of Orchids was a ruin.

His hand shook, dropped to his side. Dig in, hole up here . . . what a joke. He'd known it would be a ruin, of course he had, in the part of his brain that still functioned right, but he hadn't been able to face it. He'd made this plan to hide out at the house, living there secretly, while all the time he'd realized there would be hardly anything left, no roof, scarcely a wall standing. Now he had to face the truth. He could no more stay here than on the planet Pluto.

But nor could be bring himself to go, not quite yet. It might be a ruin, but dammit, this was *home*! He had to take a look around now that he'd come this far, *had* to! He shone the light down and with its aid began to pick his way along the wall. Ah, yes – main living room! Keep going, keep going . . . front door.

The door, what was left of it, lay on its back, just visible beneath the growth of creeper that covered it. The house had been absorbed into the jungle but not wholly digested, like a goat in a python: the framework still stood, there were doorways and places where windows had once kept out the rain. With his feet he made a small clearing on the floor of what had formerly been the house's principal room.

He turned through a full circle, trying to orientate himself. Memory flickered into life. There a sofa, here the bar, the Chinese ceremonial chairs . . .

He had made love in this room, to a horde of women. One day he'd taken Alison on the floor. They'd flung cushions from the sofa on to the bare wood and she'd lifted her skirts like a whore in a hurry . . . Suppose Ibrahim had come in! She'd lifted her skirts and he'd ripped down her undies until he could stick three fingers up inside her, and she'd welcomed them with squirt after squirt of juice, as if she had a pump tucked away up there . . . he'd bent her over a chair and taken her from behind, not bothering to remove his trousers, one hand thrusting up under her blouse for the breasts while the other circled around underneath, seeking out her little nut of a clitoris, and she was too tall, he was standing on tiptoe and she knew it; suddenly she'd laughed, he'd laughed too, and then next minute the cushions were spewing all over the floor and he'd shoved her over, 'My love,' he'd moaned, 'God Christ, but I love you so much . . .'

Jay, overwhelmed by the brutal onrush of memory, collapsed on to the floor with a little sigh. One of the boards gave way; the hand he'd put out to balance himself went through into the cavity beneath. Something scuttled over it, he felt a bite; when he snatched his hand away and flashed his torch at it the skin seemed to be a living black sponge. Ants! He jumped up, shaking his hand like an epileptic. It came into contact with foliage and he seized a bunch of leaves with his other hand, using it to wipe off the oozy, living mess.

He'd dropped his torch.

He forced himself to stand still, not daring to move his feet. The floor was rotten, he'd already made one hole in it. Had he kicked the flashlight through the gap? Slowly, very slowly, he flexed his knees, hunkering down until he could grope around on the floor. But he was afraid of the termites and of snakes, his body wouldn't obey him. Cautiously he moved one foot through ninety degrees, dragging the other into place beside it, and began to search the next quadrant. Nothing.

He took a deep breath, forcing himself to stay calm. Patience . . .

His neck ached. In an attempt to ease it he twisted his head from side to side. As he faced front again he thought he saw a tiny light move.

He blinked. The distant red spot was still there. Insect? Some kind of bug that glowed in the dark? Funny how it hung around that one spot . . .

Somebody close by was smoking. The red spot he could see was the burning tip of a cigarette.

Jay's heart flushed up into his throat. He couldn't breathe. This person had followed him to the house: somebody so confident, so arrogant, that he could afford to smoke . . . why? Was he waiting for reinforcements, summoned by radio? Did he already *have* helpers, even now ranging themselves around the house?

Jay had to think as never before, and his brain was out.

The jungle stayed utterly silent. If men had been moving into position while he blundered around inside the house, they gave no sign of their presence. Whoever was out there couldn't be alone.

If he was surrounded and outnumbered, no point in delaying the worst. He wasn't a fighter by disposition or training. He had no weapons. And yet . . .

And yet, he had witnessed this situation before. He remembered how you had to deal with a man who knew

297

too much, a man who could not be allowed to talk . . .

The red spot continued to buzz to and fro, up to the unseen smoker's lips, down again. He needed to find out more about him. How?

Jay was, he now knew, seeing the glowing cigarette-tip through what remained of a window. As he moved, leaves obscured the light. He halted. Then as he took another step his foot knocked against something hard. Jay breathed in sharply. His torch!

With gentle, controlled movements he bent down and, gritting his teeth, felt around in the green stuff that littered the floor. His hand closed on the torch. Now he had light. What did the man outside have?

He advanced slowly. Every step he took seemed to generate enough noise to awaken Rip Van Winkle. He managed to find the exit without risking the use of his torch. Gingerly he felt his way through the opening. His feet crunched on undergrowth; surely the man outside must have heard?

Jay looked around. Yes, the red point of fire had vanished. God damn.

Perhaps the intruder was just going away? Maybe he didn't even realize Jay was here at all?

Suppose it was the police, the army, Singapore Intelligence? He couldn't beat *them*. No way.

Somewhere on his left, a branch broke.

He jerked around, striving to penetrate the darkness. Over there . . . but not enough light to see anything.

When Jay had lived in Singapore he'd always felt safe. This was different. This was him or me.

Memories ruthlessly suppressed for years siphoned up into his consciousness from whatever dark pit had held them prisoner. He'd once known another man who'd discovered too much and had had to be silenced. When it came down to the wire, you did what you must.

He adjusted his grip on the flashlight. It wasn't very

big, but it was solid, heavy. He began to grope his way forward. No need to over-react, nothing too violent, too . . .

Jay blundered into something soft. Something that squealed in fright. His torch hand lashed down, once, twice, three times; he heard a moan, then something struck him in the stomach and he grunted with pain. His left hand, flailing, touched hair. He grabbed it. He swung back the torch and delivered a violent horizontal thrust, praying he'd make contact. He heard a horrible cry, somewhere between a grunt and a whimper. From the mêlée of impressions that followed he understood only one thing. He was holding somebody up by the hair; if he let go, that somebody would fall.

Jay released his grip. There was a thump. His trembling hands wrestled with the flashlight. Broken. He flung it aside. He felt around, his hands swiftly making contact with something soft, and warm. Shirt, shorts . . . paper rustling. And that noise . . . *matches*! Thank Christ . . .

He felt inside a pocket of the shorts. Yes, a box of matches. He struck one. The flare blinded him, deepening the darkness around it. Then something white caught his eye and he squinted down to where several sheets of paper lay in the mud. He stared. Sheet-music.

Slowly he moved the match. As soon as he saw the trainers, he knew. A child. He'd fought with a child. Jesus, Jesus, Jesus . . .

He struck another match. Shorts, a white shirt, bloody face . . . two small black orbs, coal-dark and lifeless: two marbles that gave back the match's flare without responding. Dead eyes.

He lit another match, then another, each time praying to be wrong, each time focusing on a different pulse point, the wrist, the neck . . . finally he threw away the matches and began to pound on the boy's chest, seeking by sheer force to make his heart beat.

All in vain. Through a fog of agony he became aware that each time he pressed down the boy's head jumped disjointedly to and fro with a click. Broken neck.

He knew the truth, then. He had murdered a boy.

Through the darkness in his mind, a thought was percolating. He had seen this teenager before. *Where? Think!*

The boy with a notebook, on the airport bus.

He must have been following Jay. Now he was dead. But someone this young would have no reason of his own to follow him. He'd been put up to it. And whoever had controlled this boy, his employer, would want to know what had happened to him . . .

Jay raised his head. Grey light was already softening the landscape. He could make out trees, palms, jungle blooms. A long, thick rattan vine lay coiled over the branches of a nearby mango. Jay stared at it, wondering what it reminded him of. Suddenly he realized.

They hanged murderers, in Singapore.

# III

# NINETEEN

'Why Not Stay At Home?' was a jolly little dosshouse on Singapore's Serangoon Road. It provided shelter for an Indian gentleman who confessed to owning the place in rather one-sided partnership with the Overseas Union Bank; an unlikely border collie called Wuff-Wuff; several bronzed, antipodean girls doing the Orient on ten dollars a day; and Iain Forward. He liked the place, mainly on account of its ridiculous name, but also because it reminded him of prison's best aspects: he had privacy here, something he'd lacked in Clapham. His towel, washed to the brink of extinction, hung from a piece of twine extended between two nails on the wall above his truckle bed. A piece of soap was provided, though that too had been used to the point where you could read the *Straits Times* through it. There was a mosquito net for keeping insects inside the bed with you. And beyond the window, jammed permanently open, lay one of Asia's great cities, today giving off the strange impression of being under siege; for war had come to Singapore.

He'd checked in and imagined for a moment that he could be happy here. Clapham wasn't home, this was – the place where he'd been happiest without ever realizing it. The illusion lasted only until he went out, thinking to buy a bowl of noodles from a hawker stall.

At first Iain thought he must be suffering from delusions. The streets were all but deserted. Cars, yes, he could see cars and buses; but the buses seemed only a quarter full, and there were hardly any pedestrians. He saw scarcely one white face. The cheap electronics shops in Lucky Plaza were empty, or even in some cases shut. The Indian money-lenders sat there with lugubrious expressions on their faces and useless calculators in their hands. This couldn't be Singapore.

His favourite noodle place was gone. What had once been Killiney Market was now a hideous shopping complex called Orchard Point. He settled for a curry at a basement snackbar before slowly walking up Orchard Road. Everything was new. No more Prince Hotel, he noticed; now there was something called the Crown Prince Hotel, high and white and with a façade that curved impressively at one end. The Paragon, that was new, the Promenade also . . .

In the basement of the Promenade was a supermarket, doing only moderate business for late afternoon. Iain thought he would stock up with chocolate and biscuits; might as well conserve as much of Alison's nest egg as possible – no, don't think about that. Or *her*. He noticed women buying tins, and huge bags of rice. At the checkout, housewives talked in hushed tones: he queued behind a trio of them, 'nuclear bomb,' one of them kept saying, 'A-bomb.'

Her monotonous repetition – 'A-bomb, A-bomb' – suddenly reminded him of something. All Category A prisoners in England would be shot by the army in the event of war. Where had he first heard that? He'd listened to the rumour a thousand times since then, everyone inside believed it. He'd met a prison padre who believed it . . . Were they shitting themselves, even now, as they waited for the clang of the gate, the sound of boots on the tarmac, the grounding of rifles . . . ?

He'd hardly thought about 'them' since leaving prison. Yet now he felt a twinge of pity for his old cellmates. He wanted to tell them: You won't be shot. Surely they wouldn't . . .

As Iain came out of the supermarket he caught sight of a news-stand towards the rear of the complex. He bought a *Straits Times* and scanned the front page. There was a long article about the likely effect of pollution from Kuwait's burning oil wells on China's rice crop, on the monsoons, on the atmosphere of places as far apart as Tokyo and Karachi. Iain leaned against the bar of Deli France and read it. Then he casually turned the page and was looking at a photograph of himself.

Instinctively he rotated to face the wall. His mouth tasted of dry dung. The photo was small and poor in quality, but unmistakably him. He had to force his eyes to focus on the text. Iain Forward (he read) was a convicted murderer, recently released on licence. Then there was guff about the licence system, what it meant. Then, how he had broken the terms of his licence by going abroad without permission, and was thought to be in Singapore. And how he should not be approached, but the police must be alerted at once if anyone spotted him.

Iain folded up the newspaper and tucked it under his arm. He took a few unsteady steps, got into his stride, and went up the flight of stairs facing him.

He must keep moving.

The Promenade shopping-complex was arranged on several floors and there were the usual lifts and escalators connecting them, but the chief means of access was a walkway that circled around and around, bearing you up to the higher levels. Iain mechanically started to follow this. Some of the shop-fronts were of intriguing design, involving mirrors or curved glass, and he began to feel as though he were in one of Alfred Hitchcock's dream sequences. Everything about this Singapore was unreal . . .

Don't panic. *Think.*

He had a fake passport and a new face: a wig of thick black hair concealed his pepper-and-salt tufts, blue

305

contact lenses disguised his brown eyes. Already he had the beginnings of a beard. The photo in the paper was of the 'old' Iain, and besides, it looked fuzzy. The odds against a layman recognizing him were remote. But a policeman, any trained observer . . .

Verity would see this press-photo.

He must move to another dosshouse, must move every day from now on. Go out only at night . . . *No!* Idiot! Fewer people were on the streets at night, those who were became conspicuous; go out at noon if you must . . .

He gripped the railing on top of the wall that protected shoppers from the central well, gazing down. *He was the only person around.*

What if they cornered him here, in the Promenade?

Somehow he had to resume control of his destiny. How?

He was, he realized, facing a dress boutique. At the far end of the shop a Chinese man sat reading. There were no customers, no other sales assistants. Iain weighed things up. He had to get moving, *now*, and the danger quotient here seemed tolerable. *Move!*

He entered the boutique. A bell rang: not an electric bell but a real, clangy one, suspended from the top of the glass door on a ribbon. The Chinese looked up from his book, smiled briefly, and went back to reading.

Iain found himself inside an emporium fitted expensively with dark brown wood and hung with sexy designer dresses. He made a show of looking along the racks while he worked out how to make his request. He came to some rich leather goods: briefcases, wallets, and the like. They were gorgeous.

'Giulia Schmid', said a voice at his elbow, and he started. The Chinese had come silently to stand beside him; now he picked up a cigarette-lighter covered in the same rich-looking hide, and flicked the flame into life.

'Beautiful, aren't they?' he said, and then he sighed.

'Beautiful,' Iain agreed. 'Expensive, though.'

The Chinese nodded. 'Too expensive for this time.'

'The war, you mean?'

'Oh, yes. Things were all right before the war.'

'I've never seen Singapore so empty.'

'Me, too.'

Iain looked at him properly for the first time. The man, tall and supple, was about forty, he guessed, with thick, black-rimmed spectacles and a gorgeous crown of luxuriant hair showing just the faintest tint of red. His face wore the severe, Confucian expression of a scholar. He seemed rather an unlikely character to work in a shop.

'Is this your boutique?' Iain enquired.

'Not mine. I'm the designer.'

'It's very elegant.'

'Thank you. Also very empty. Such a nice change to see somebody in here. Can I help you at all?'

'Actually . . . yes. Look, would you mind if I looked at your phone-book?'

'Be my guest. Business?'

'And residential. Both.'

The Chinese disappeared behind a curtain, re-emerging a moment later with the two-volume Singapore phone-directory. 'Do take a seat,' he said.

Iain sat down on a sofa placed against the wall between two racks of dresses and looked up Verity Newland. There she was. He wondered why she hadn't gone ex-directory; but then, why should she? A perfectly respectable businesswoman need hide nothing, fear nothing. And the companies . . Occydor, Heaney had said, and there they were, a host of them.

He was about to ask for something to write with when a hand materialized in his narrow field of vision, holding a Biro and a slip of paper.

'Thanks,' he said. He copied down the numbers, office

and home, and tucked the paper inside his pocket.

'You're welcome.'

Iain stood up and smiled at the designer. He walked to the door, pausing again by the Giulia Schmid leather, and took a last look around the shop.

'The dresses,' he said awkwardly. 'They're great.'

The Chinese smiled shyly. 'Thanks. Perhaps you could bring your wife in one day.'

'Yes.' Iain shivered in the way as a man does when something walks on his grave. Without quite knowing why, he said, 'Are you afraid?'

A peculiar question; but the designer seemed to read his mind, for he said, 'Of the war?'

'Yes.'

The man screwed up his eyes in thought. 'No,' he said at last. 'It's so far away, isn't it?'

But he'd hesitated.

As Iain walked out of the Promenade into the clammy night, traffic noise from Orchard Road assaulted his ears, making him realize how quiet it had been inside. Singapore was holding its breath, waiting for the war to go away. Or to come.

He had Verity Newland's addresses and phone numbers. Now all he had to do was stay alive, stay free, long enough to make use of them.

He dropped his newspaper into a nearby bin. Keeping as far as possible to the shadows, he quietly joined the sparse flow of pedestrians and set out on the long walk to Raffles Place.

*

Verity Newland raised her eyes from the engraved business card and studied the man who had given it to her.

'Washington,' she said. 'I really don't recall meeting you, Mr . . . Cover, have I got that right?'

'Yes, m'am.'

'In nineteen eighty-six.'

'Yes, m'am.'

'A long time ago.'

'Yes, m'am. But that is your card, as you see.'

Verity swivelled the revolving chair a few degrees, transferring her attention to the black, starlit world beyond the office window. Lights lifted off from distant Changi, silent pinpoints; she watched them climb to the south-east. Australia. Perth, perhaps: a lovely place. Sunny, healthy . . . peaceful.

Cover had come armed with one of her own name-cards; on the back were written the words: 'A great audience! Thank you.' And the date. In what looked like her handwriting.

'I met so many people, that trip,' she said, turning back to face Tony Cover. 'I'm sorry, but . . .'

'That's all right, m'am. A stirring speech you made. Inspirational.'

Verity considered that. She had indeed made a speech, addressing a coterie of international bankers gathered in a private banqueting suite at the Four Seasons Hotel. Her theme: the need to provide infrastructure and encouragement to secular Arab peacemakers on whom the stability of the Gulf region — and, it followed, of the oil-price set by OPEC — depended. Peacemakers such as Saddam Hussein, even then engaged in a blood-draining war with Iran . . . She would have remembered Cover, had he been present, but he was not present, and so she did not remember him.

Somehow he had managed to get hold of one of her business-cards, and had then gone to the trouble of forging her handwriting on the back. Impressive. But why go to so much trouble?

'How can I help you?' she said.

'Basically, I'm in Singapore on business and I thought I'd look you up.'

Which is a lie, she thought.

Cover mentioned a name. 'He's with BCCI,' he went on, 'and he suggested you and I had areas of, ah, mutual interest.'

She wondered who her visitor really was. He wore a knitted tie of marginally the wrong colour to go with his fawn suit: someone who didn't usually dress up, perhaps. Or just another klutz . . . no, he was Law. Law had this distinctive smell. Law or not, though, he was an attractive bastard. Handsome, no: too small for that. But she'd always gone for assured men.

'Iraq's in trouble,' Cover said. 'Though it won't always be in trouble. At some point there will have to be a rebuilding programme.'

She gazed at him, meaning to outstare this dazzling, dangerous man, but his own eyes contained just enough of a disarming smile to defeat her.

'I, and my investors, wish to be founder members of that rebuilding programme. We believe you could help.'

'I don't think so. There are sanctions in force. Besides, I no longer have any business connections with Iraq. Not a lucky place.'

'I disagree. Look, why don't you let me persuade you, over dinner. I've reserved a table for two at Domus . . .'

Domus, the Italian restaurant at the Sheraton Towers on Scotts Road, was one of her favourites: all those mirrors, the discreet alcoves, wondrous flowers, attentive service . . . she had a passion for their glasses, so delicate-looking and yet so strong . . .

'Thank you,' she said stiffly, 'but I have another engagement tonight.'

'You're throwing away the opportunity of a lifetime. This is going to make you seriously rich.'

'I am momentously rich already.'

'I don't believe I'm hearing this.'

'Then let me spell it out. I am *persona non grata* in Iraq. I would not, under any circumstances, be granted a visa. I've no wish to discuss that wretched little country or anything connected with it. My only desire is that Bush should bomb it flat and then' – she rose from her desk and began to walk towards the door – 'rub salt in the ground. Goodbye, Mr Cover.'

He continued to sit with his back to her. His head was level, his shoulders straight, he kept his hands on the arms of his chair. He wasn't the least bit fazed. Under other circumstances she might have wanted to pursue matters of mutual interest with Mr Cover, but not this evening.

Cover stood up. He turned towards her. She imagined he would grin, make some inane joke to pass off the momentary awkwardness, and leave. What he did was come up fast until he was standing inches from her, and say, 'I'll give you one chance, and, believe me, you'd better listen. I need your input. I intend to have it at any cost.'

'Goodbye, Mr Cover.'

'*Any* . . . cost.'

'If you do not leave now, Mr Cover, I shall scream.' She kept her voice level, but it cost her an effort. 'When my secretary comes running in, I shall tell him you touched my breasts. In Singapore, that is a serious matter; you will be detained in a not very pleasant prison until your trial and after it, if you are lucky, you will be thrown out of the country.'

Cover ground his teeth. He was calling her bluff, she would have to carry out her threat, and she did in truth want to scream at the thought of all that would follow. But just as she was drawing breath he wrenched his face away and backed through the door. Verity shoved it closed with her foot and leaned against the wall. Her face felt clammy. The makings of a stormy headache simmered behind her eyes. Everything about Cover had turned bad so quickly, it left her breathless.

She came off the wall and went over to her desk. She picked up the phone. 'Steven, come in here.'

Steven Lim entered a few seconds later.

'That man,' she said. 'Find out where he's staying. Who made the appointment, was it him or someone on his behalf; what did he say; what do we know about him; what can we find out about him? If he leaves Singapore I must know where he goes next, understood?'

Lim nodded. 'Anything else?'

Verity rubbed her forehead. Her wits had temporarily deserted her, she felt so tired . . . 'No, I'm going home early tonight. I'll be in tomorrow morning at six thirty.'

'See you then, Miss Newland. Good night.'

Verity absent-mindedly opened a sachet and began to clean her computer's screen. No matter how many lint-free wipes she used, the smears refused to quit the glass. This simple task, normally so therapeutic, was beyond her tonight. She abandoned it, collecting her handbag and going out to the bank of elevators. As she waited for the lift to come she rummaged in her bag for aspirin, swallowing two tablets. The doors slid open. She stepped inside along with several other people, one of them a tall man who pressed 'G' and then smiled at her as if in recognition.

Verity's headache was gaining ground; what's more, she had had enough of strange men today. Yet something about this one was familiar. She'd seen him before, a long time ago though. And it wasn't just casual recognition: the sight of this stranger triggered alarm bells inside her already throbbing brain.

He wore white jeans held up by a black leather belt, pale green open-neck shirt, trainers. Not a businessman. Not a resident either, to judge from his complexion, which was pale and badly in need of a shave. He didn't

312

open his eyes fully, but gazed at her through half-closed lids, which gave him a faintly reptilian look. Wrinkled skin, but, she sensed, not as old as he looked; mid-forties, perhaps. Born when? Say, 1946.

The first tumbler of the combination fell into place. 1946, in 1973 he'd have been in his mid-twenties . . .

Iain Forward.

She'd been expecting him ever since she'd read that piece about him in the paper, but this couldn't be him: his hair and eyes were the wrong colour.

Disguise . . . ? Let him speak; then she would know.

The elevator eased to a halt at the ground floor. Verity went out, hurrying now, deliberately not looking at the man.

'Hello, Verity.'

She ignored him; but out of the corner of her eye she registered that he was keeping pace with her, silently, and she shivered.

'Iain Forward,' the man murmured. 'Remember me?'

She toyed with the idea of attempting to throw him off with a turn of speed then evading him, somehow, until she reached her car. No good. Ridiculous, apart from anything else, and she declined to appear ridiculous.

She stopped, and turned to face him. 'Of course,' she said, absently. 'There was something familiar about you. But your eyes . . . I remembered them as brown.'

Iain chuckled. 'Can we talk?'

He seemed friendly – but then, how else was he going to appear here, in the middle of the OUB Centre's foyer, surrounded by hundreds of people?

'I'd like that,' she said. She decided not to divulge what she'd read about him in the *Straits Times*. Save that for when it might come in handy.

'Here?'

'No, not here.'

'Perhaps we could go to your place? Fernhill Close?'

Her heart missed a beat, but of course, she was in the phone-book; she had nothing to hide.

'Oh . . . not very convenient, I'm afraid. What about your hotel?'

He laughed, and she remembered how she'd always hated his schoolboy laugh; it was the same now, but nastier.

'Where are you staying?' she asked.

'Here and there.'

'I see,' Verity said. Damn this headache. 'Feel like a walk? They've rebuilt most of Singapore since you were here – have you seen the new waterfront?'

'No. You lead the way.'

She took him out of the building, along Raffles Place as far as Bonham Street and thence down to the Singapore River. There was an open-air food centre alongside Cavanagh Bridge, built out over the water on stilts. She bought them each a beer and they sat at a table overlooking the Victoria Theatre.

'Changes,' Iain said. 'Lots.'

'You must hardly recognize the place.'

'Atmosphere's the same, though.' He sipped his beer, apparently disinclined to be rushed, while he took a long, comfortable look at the skyline. 'Well now,' he said at last. 'And how's Reggie?'

'Reggie?'

'Raj. Harchem's tame mass-murderer, *you* remember him. Still plays patience, does he, with that little mini-pack he always carried? Still visits the whore-house of a Friday?'

Verity swallowed more beer than she'd intended. The ache in her head was extending its tentacles down to her stomach.

'You get a lot of time to think, in prison.' Iain grunted out a laugh. 'Funny, I was saying that to Anthony only the other day. *Sir* Anthony; I beg his pardon.'

'Powis . . . How is he?' she asked.

'Very confused and decrepit – until he chooses not to be. Know the sort of old codger I mean?'

Verity shrugged. When Iain had said nothing for a long time, she asked, 'What do you want?'

'To clear my name. Prove I never killed Gerry Reynolds.'

'Why here?'

'You're here.'

'Me? What can I do?'

'Introduce me to Reggie. I've got new evidence, something that was deliberately kept secret at my trial. I need confirmation, and Reggie Raj's my first stop.'

'I've no idea where he is. Sorry.'

Iain drained his glass. 'Think again,' he said, putting it down on the table with a clang.

'Look, I –'

'You know where he is, because you and he set up together and you made a fortune. You developed chemical weapons, didn't you?'

'Insecticides. We made insecticides.'

'And you've been selling them to Iraq. Saddam Hussein used your insecticides to knock off a few thousand insects, yes? Kurds, they're called.'

'You're talking rubbish.'

'The Kurds died. Gassed. It's been in all the papers, recently. Mustard gas, cyanide gas and nerve gases.'

'I never had anything to do with that. As for Reggie, I can't say; I haven't seen him for years.'

'Symptoms.'

Her head was lurching from side to side in ever more brutal oscillations. 'Symptoms?' she said stupidly. 'I . . . don't understand.'

'The people who died in Halabja village showed a number of interesting symptoms. They vomited blood. Blood came out of their arses, their mouths, everywhere.

Like the Hmong, in Laos.' Seeing her face, he threw back his head and laughed. 'Yes,' he said, 'yes, Verity, I've been doing my homework. Abrin, remember? Abrin causes symptoms like that.'

She stared at him for a long time before shaking her head.

'Reggie was into abrin in a big way. And cryptopleurin. Pinene. Ricin. Verity . . . I was the bloody *accountant*. I used to sit down with Reggie and ask him, Why the fuck do you need a ton of bloody castor beans? And he'd ramble on about insecticides, and surfactants, and L-C-T fifty factors, and I'd get so bored that in the end I'd sign the frigging chit. Only now, everybody's talking about those things. They're in all the newspapers, ducky. And there's lists of names: companies that have been black-listed for assisting Iraq. Along with the names of their directors. And guess what – there aren't so many Reginald Rajs in this, God's earth.'

Verity felt as though she were swimming in a warm bath of sticky sugar that was slowly sucking her down to drown.

'You think Reggie killed Reynolds,' she said dully. 'Is that it?'

'No.'

'You think *I* did it.'

'Great God, no!'

She took in his raised eyebrows, his open mouth, and she thought, He means it.

'The government,' he said at last. 'The British government did me down, and I'm going to prove it. I was sacrificed, Verity. Look, this is what I believe . . .' He leaned forward to fold his hands on the table, bringing his face close to hers. 'Reggie had developed something really lethal, see? Powis didn't want to know, but the Yanks did, maybe a lot of other people, too. How to sell it? Some kind of dirty deal was stitched together, with

316

government connivance. Reynolds was in the way, had to be got rid of; I was fall guy.'

'But *why*? Why *you*?'

'Maybe I just blundered along at the wrong moment. But the key to all this is the product, the whatever-it-was that got everyone excited, back in the early seventies. So I need to talk to Raj.'

'I don't know where he is. Oh yes, we did work together. But he went off to Iraq last year and never came back. That's the truth of it, Iain.'

He searched her face but she regarded him stonily, untroubled by his intensity.

'Iraq,' he said; and then – 'Do you ever worry about him?'

'Reggie Raj ... was a grade one, top flight little *shit*.'

Iain laughed. 'He was that!'

'So no, I don't worry about him.' Verity hesitated. 'Suppose I help you,' she went on. 'Would you go away then?'

He glanced sideways at her. She hated those snake eyes of his. They were new. Prison, she supposed.

'Do you want me to go away?' he asked.

'Yes.'

'Why?'

'Because life is full of problems at present and I can't cope.'

'That doesn't sound like the Verity I used to know.'

'Verity the Viper,' she snapped, suddenly enraged. 'That's what you called me, wasn't it?'

She picked up the empty bottles and stalked over to the stall. When she came back with refills her face was flushed as if with fever.

'I want you out of Singapore,' she said as she sat down. 'You terrify me. You may not have killed anyone, but you're capable of it.'

'Yes. Prison is an interesting faculty of the university of life, my love. What can you tell me?'

'Raj invented something, back in 'seventy-one or so,' Verity said, pouring beer. 'Project ninety-three twelve. It started life as a defoliant, a perfect defoliant. It could strip a forest bare, not just the upper canopy, and Reggie fixed it so that it could kill people, too. It was the most terrific success with Washington. But by the time Reggie had finished tampering with nature, Vietnam was nearly over. Defoliants were out of fashion. Reggie wasn't, though. People knew about him by then. He had a name.'

'And so funds were made available; you went off with Reggie, and started making friends your mother wouldn't have liked.'

'More or less. Reggie became an ace on dioxin – you know what that is?'

He sneered and then, raising his voice slightly, he said, 'An impurity of 2,4,5-T, trichloro-phenoxyacetic acid – good, aren't I? It poisons land, it poisons people. Part of Agent Orange.'

'Yes. That was just the start. He pumped up dioxin, botulinum, anthrax, ricin, saxitoxin . . . the Americans used that in their suicide pills, they gave him some kind of secret medal, God help us.' Despite the tropical heat she shivered. 'He was a horrible little man, I hated him. Him and his whores.'

'But he made money.'

' "Where there's muck, there's brass",' she said with a bitter laugh. 'How many times did I hear my mother say that? Yes, Reggie made money.'

'And it all started when?'

'Occydor? About when you . . . when Reynolds was killed.'

'So there *is* a connection!'

'You say so.'

Iain banged the table with his fist. 'Well *tell* me!'

318

'There could be. Reggie and I were . . . negotiating by then, yes.'

'With who?'

'The Pentagon.'

'What, directly?'

'There was a go-between.'

And the funny thing was that suddenly her head became remarkably clear.

'There was a go-between,' she repeated with emphasis. 'His name was Jay Sampson, he was an American. You met him, with me, once.'

Iain frowned. 'The name doesn't mean anything.'

'One of Gerry's ghastly dinners. Sampson was my guest. The night Dolly Cartwright got thrown out of Singapore.' Verity paused for relish. 'Alison spilled tomato sauce all down her dress.'

Iain shook his head.

'Sampson owned the House of Orchids.'

From the way Iain jumped she knew she'd scored heavily.

'But at the trial . . .' he began.

'They referred to him as "the owner"; no name, yes, I know. Their case was that you used to drop off your coded letters at the House of Orchids, that "the owner" was a go-between about whom nothing was known, that he'd left Singapore in a hurry at the time of your arrest. Sampson. Jay Sampson.'

'Why didn't you say this at my trial?'

'I was never asked and anyway I couldn't see the relevance. Our deal went sour. I'd lost touch with him by the time your case came to court.' She hesitated. Then – 'He's here. Or he will be soon.'

*'Here?'*

She nodded. 'If you want to meet him, I can arrange that. Tell me where you're staying, and I'll fix an appointment.'

She waited in suspense for his reply. When he remained silent she shifted her gaze a fraction, to find him concentrating on something behind her.

'Don't look around,' he murmured.

'Police?' she said quietly.

He did not answer directly. Instead he rose, smiled down at her, said, 'Be in touch,' and quietly slipped away, towards the waterfront.

Verity picked up her handbag. She stood and turned. Sure enough, two policemen in dark blue tropical uniforms were strolling between tables. They passed her by. She followed them with her eyes, expecting to see Iain in the background, but he had vanished.

The thoroughness with which he'd dissolved into the night made her uneasy. She found herself hurrying back to where she'd left her car, every moment wondering whether he would step out from the shadows to lay a hand on her arm ... The notion alarmed her; by the time she reached the parking lot she was almost running.

*

Jay rode the bus into town. He sat at the back, holding a copy of *The New Paper*, Singapore's English-language tabloid. He'd been reading the same words over and over, but they made no sense to him. 'MISSING BOY PUZZLE DEEPENS,' that was the headline on page one. When young Robinson Tang did not return home after school yesterday (he read), his parents had become worried. Eventually they'd contacted their neighbourhood police post and a full-scale search had begun, but there was no sign yet of the missing boy.

What got to Jay was the last paragraph: the boy had been out that evening with his uncle but had left him, saying he would 'meet with some friends'.

Who was that uncle? Where had he been when Robinson blundered up the track which led to the House of Orchids, and death?

Had he been there, concealed in the jungle, watching?

Jay's hands fell to his lap, crumpling the paper. He stared out of the window, conscious of his own barely formed reflection against the darkness. He'd spent hours hiding Robinson's body beneath the rotten floorboards of the house and covering it with vegetation. God, but he weighed a ton! Who'd have thought that such a skinny little teenager would have been so heavy? And those eyes, those awful dead eyes, filmed with death . . . he'd wrapped one of his handkerchiefs around the boy's head to stop him staring, but the eyes were there inside Jay's brain, torturing him, no matter which way he turned . . .

Every time he touched the body self-loathing welled up inside, making him feel sick. Even the memory was enough to fill him with nausea. Like those other age-old memories of a heavy corpse, the ones he'd been suppressing for so long . . . it wasn't his fault, not that time, not now, not really his fault, it was an accident . . .

You have to pull yourself together, he told the stubbly man in the window. You've eaten nothing all day. Not hungry. Well, *be* hungry! Right now, you're holding the pass – just. You've changed your clothes, next you need to shower and shave. Health club, Mandarin Hotel, followed by Hainanese chicken rice at the Chatterbox. Don't be like that kid, *survive*.

Time you went to see Verity . . .

As the bus drew nearer town it was becoming more and more crowded. Jay, anxious to avoid being looked at, sought refuge in his newspaper. He shook it out and folded it to an inside page. A name caught his eye at once. The item was short, he devoured it in seconds: 'Released-on-licence murderer Iain Forward is now no longer believed to be in Singapore, sources said today.

Sightings have been reported from places as far apart as Bali and Adelaide, but UK authorities have diverted their search from the S.E. Asian region.'

Jay struggled to make sense of it. Iain Forward had gone to prison, yes, he was out, yes, but what was all this shit about him being in Singapore? There must have been an earlier item in the papers ('*now* no *longer* believed . . .'). There'd been an alert of some kind, maybe? But it had turned out to be a false alarm . . .

Jay's head was spinning. *Was* this a false alarm? He'd worked with enough agencies to scent disinformation when he encountered it, and that last phrase about diverting the search struck him as superfluous.

What could Forward want here, who might he mean to see?

The name Iain Forward had always made Jay yearn to look aside, evading a cuckolded husband's sad, accusatory eyes. While he lived in America it was easy to do that. But here, with memories coming at him from every tree and building and inch of road, he no longer had the option of looking away. He could remember everything, if he chose. And there were some things he could not choose to forget; like that day in the fall of 1972 . . .

\*      \*      \*

Beneath a louring sky pregnant with thunder, Jay paced up and down the terrace like a caged cat. He would glance at his watch too quickly to register the time, call for Ibrahim, then dismiss him as he showed in the doorway. Nothing relieved his frustration, fear, jealousy, rage; nothing, no mechanism, could manage his love.

'Where are you?' he muttered. 'Why are you late, what's happened, have you had a crash? Has *he* decided not to go on that business trip? Has he come back unexpectedly? *Have you found another man: someone younger, more handsome, better?'*

He was being ridiculous and he knew it; but when you were head-over-heels in love, mad about someone – such a great phrase! – you were mad. No cure known to man. What an asshole he felt himself to be, yet how absurdly like a king. His woman was on her way and he wanted to screw her, and to love her, and to let her hair fall through his hands in tresses of gold while he murmured adoration into her perfect, perfect, *perfect* ears . . .

A car. Far off, but he heard it. Jay stopped pacing. He stood on the terrace with his head tilted to one side until he was sure. *Her* car, he'd know the engine-note anywhere. He sprinted through the house and skidded to a halt beneath the canopy as she drew up outside.

Alison seemed to be wool-gathering; Jay could see how she looked around, as if for her handbag, maybe. He wrenched the car door open and she glanced up quickly, almost as if taken by surprise, almost as if she didn't recognize him. An icy shower fell over his heart.

'What is it?' he stammered. 'For God's sake, darling, don't make me wait; if you're going to kill me, *do it*!'

She smiled, but wanly. 'What rubbish you talk, sometimes.'

'*Say you love me!*'

'*I love you!*'

Alison got out of the car. When he put a hand on her arm she shook it off, not playfully, as she'd often done in the past, but with a purpose.

'Not here,' she hissed. 'Ibrahim . . .'

Then he was having to run after her as she marched inside with the speed and determination of one escaping from a downpour. Perhaps – hastily he looked up at the sky – that was the reason, yes, it was going to rain . . .

Indeed, as he joined her by the big back window over-looking the strait a thick grey cloud unfolded and unfolded again across Malaysia, coming their way. A few heavy drops pattered on the chick-blinds, advance guards heralding the arrival of the army. Moments later, the deluge began.

It was September, the rainy season still a couple of months off, but this downpour was so loud it made conversation difficult. Great knitting-needles of water threw themselves at the ground: bad-tempered rain this was, and destined to last for a long time. Normally he would have relished it – to lie in bed beneath the revolving fan, spent of energy and semen, listening to the splatter outside, that could be heaven. Today . . .

'I can't go through with it,' Alison said, in the same venomous hiss. 'I won't.'

'What are you –'

'I can't take the lying any more.' She'd been staring out of the window but now she whirled around to face him. 'Iain's a decent man, he –'

'You've told him?'

'*No!*'

'But he's guessed?'

'He hasn't.'

'But . . . did he go away? Tokyo, you said Tokyo . . .'

'He left this morning. Three days of meetings, just like I told you.'

Part of him, a tiny part, was aware of those meetings: Harchem was opening a plant in Osaka, the Pentagon had asked him to find out . . . *your woman is going to leave you and all you can think of is . . .*

'Then what is wrong, Alison? We arranged this a month ago, I've been counting the days.'

'You think I haven't?'

He grabbed her arm again. 'No, I think you haven't.' Jay had to raise his voice above the sound of rain, grown raucous. 'I think you came here to say goodbye.'

He dropped her arm. Suddenly weak to the point of

324

exhaustion, he groped for the nearest chair and lowered himself into it, no longer looking at her. He covered his eyes with a hand. Jesus Christ, he was going to cry. He'd never cried in his life.

Jay could not understand how he had sunk to this point.

It had begun well; brilliantly, you could say. Alison was beautiful, she was sexy and sex-starved, with a body to die for. She was another man's woman; Jay liked that. They'd spent afternoons in bed together, no hard feelings, no remorse: at first once a week, then more often. And more dangerously. Until at some indeterminate point he'd truly fallen in love for the first time; and now it was the autumn of 1972, he and Alison had been lovers for almost a year, and still he had no notion of where it would end.

'You promised you'd spend the night,' he said to the floor. 'You promised.' The kind of thing zitty kids said: a realization that hurt him.

'I wanted to.'

'Wanted: past tense.'

'*Want* to, then. Oh, you can be so difficult, sometimes.' She stalked to the bar. He heard the clink of glass on glass and stood up, going to join her. Alison quickly moved away, holding a tumbler half-full of brandy. He knew it was brandy, knew what she'd drink in any given mood. He poured himself a Jameson, straight up.

She was by the window, looking out, the glass held in front of her lowered face while she stroked her brow with her thumb. She raised her head in a jerky, bird-like movement, and brandy slopped from her glass.

'Fuck!' She spat the word out like a bit of bad fruit.

'Alison,' he said, speaking carefully. 'What has gone wrong?'

Her shoulders tensed, but other than that she gave no sign of having heard. Jay tried to keep his voice modulated low, but he was turning shrill again and there wasn't a darn thing he could do about it. 'You have to tell me,' he said. 'It isn't fair.'

'Life isn't fair,' she said, addressing her remark to the Strait of Johor, now invisible behind a bead-curtain of rain.

She pivoted away from the window and looked at him. Her eyes flickered to and fro, as if the sight of Jay caused her physical anguish. He read the yearning there and took a step forward, stretching out his arms to embrace her, but she cried, 'No! You don't understand . . . you can't ever understand.'

When tears jetted from her eyes she made no effort to wipe them away. She took a gulp of brandy from her glass instead, and choked on it. Jay put down his glass and ran to embrace her. Alison, in the grip of a coughing fit, tried to push him away, but there was no strength left in her and after a while she stood there listlessly with her head on his chest, coughing every so often, crying every so often, until at last she became calm.

Jay rocked her to and fro. Outside the storm raged on. A great flash back-lit the greyness with putrid yellow. Seconds later, thunder cracked like a whip before unpeeling itself into an interminable coda of noise.

'I love you,' he said to the window. No, that wasn't right. There had to be a formula, a spell that caused conviction to arise like a genie; but that wasn't it. 'I love you,' he repeated, feeling merely stupid. 'I *love* you . . . I love *you* . . .'

Her skin was warm against his own. She wore a delicate artificial fragrance, but what got to him was *her* smell, the aroma of her hair, cheek, arms, clothes, lips . . . the Alison smell. Love had come late, and wonderful: an all-conquering king. For this smell, he would die. Without it, he *must* die.

326

Normally he was good with words, was Jay, but her presence always befuddled him. Theirs were silent encounters. Words would have taken off the glow.

'Oh, God,' he moaned. 'I'm helpless.'

'I can't keep my hands off your flesh,' a tired voice said in his ear. 'I can't bear it any longer.'

'I don't want you to keep your hands off.'

'Singapore's so small. Everybody knows.'

'Nobody knows. And what if they do? Do you care?' He gently held her away from him, so that he could search the soul revealed in her eyes. 'Alison, dearest, tell me honestly: do you care any more?'

She would say no. He read it there, in her eyes, but it passed away. She nodded her head, slowly. She said yes, she cared.

'I have a husband,' she said, and her voice was no longer clogged with tears, it sounded firm. 'You've spent all your life living on the edge; danger's what makes your life worth living. You're infecting me, Jay.'

He made a face, indicative of distaste, but she laid a finger on his lips.

'You are contagious. You are. I can't take the risk any more.'

'Why? You don't love me, is that what you're trying to say?' He couldn't help laughing. The idea of her pretending not to love him, as a way out of their dilemma, flooded him with hilarity.

'No, I love you. Jay, I love you more than I love myself.'

'There, then!'

'But not more than I love my baby.'

His heart went on beating. Blood flowed in his veins. How strange, then, that he should have died.

'I'm pregnant. That's why I was late today, I'd been to the doctor's. There's not the slightest possibility of a mistake and I can't go on with you, not now.'

She gazed into his eyes with an intensity he'd never seen there before, not even at the height of their mutual passion. It moved him. She was a woman, she was going to have a child, her life had shed all the old meanings and now possessed but one focus. *One*.

He was out.

Jay staggered backwards into his chair, falling against the table on which he'd set down his glass, spilling whisky everywhere. He was going to have to live with this. All his life, he was going to remember this moment, and feel it, and endure it, over and over again. Hell on earth.

'The child,' he whispered. 'Whose . . . ?'

Her mouth twisted into something he didn't want to analyse; no, of course, stupid, dumb, idiotic, they'd been 'careful', wasn't that the word? And yet you heard things, you read about them . . .

'Whose child is it?' He made each word discrete and explicit, not wanting there to be any possibility of a misunderstanding, so that when she answered, he would know. No ifs or maybes; he would know.

'Iain's.'

This time, he did not lie down under it. This time he felt the stab of jealousy's knife, curare-tipped and agonizing. Jay burned.

'The . . . bastard,' he muttered. The effort took all his breath, he had to inhale, hard and harsh, to recover.

'Jay, don't . . .'

'I've lain awake here, thinking of you and him making love, fucking away, I've lain in that bed upstairs . . .'

'I won't listen.'

'. . . with my heart sick, my stomach sick, *pain* I'm talking here, Alison!'

'I have to go. I didn't want it to be like this. I suppose I was being naive.'

'And he's got your kid. Well I'll be damned.'

'I didn't want to phone you and say this, Jay. I came here, paid you the compliment of treating you like an adult. Don't do this.'

He stared at her, speechless.

'Say goodbye in a way you'll want to remember afterwards,' she said.

Jay burst out laughing. 'Don't give me that shit,' he sneered, once he'd recovered a little. ' "Say goodbye in a . . ." Jesus Christ!'

She flushed. For a moment he thought she would respond in kind and his pulse quickened, but she turned away.

'I'm sorry,' she said, in a low voice. 'You'll never know how sorry.'

'I'll bet.'

'I loved you. I . . . love you. More than Iain. Much more.'

Her mouth was open, her cheeks flushed, there was a mole on her neck and from it sprouted a tiny black hair, why had he never noticed that before? What kind of woman neglected herself to that degree? He laughed again, putting all the offence he could muster into it. And she hit him.

It was a devastating blow. She deliberately angled her nails to rake his cheek. He raised a hand to the source of his pain and he thought, My God, the bitch really hurt me. Then he acknowledged something he'd tried to evade until now: she could be violent. Sometimes the force of her love-making bordered on cruelty. But this . . .

When he removed the hand, it was bloodstained. He reached out to wipe it on her dress. She backed away, but he caught her with the other hand and he smeared blood on her dress, her neck, her face, went on smearing until the blood had dried. Then he pulled her towards him and when she struggled he seized her head between both hands and used it like a towel against his wound, scraping her skin against his torn flesh, and then he kissed her. When he tried to force his tongue inside her mouth, she let him. That surprised Jay . . . until she bit his tongue.

He squealed. For an instant he let her go. His mouth was salty and warm and it hurt like hell. He was holding both hands to his lips. Without warning he formed them into fists and punched forward. The double blow landed on the bridge of her nose; for a second he thought he'd broken it and was glad. The funny thing was, she did not cry. He was the one making all the noise.

He punched her again, on the chest this time, and she fell over. He threw himself down on top of her, but she rolled aside at the last moment and he landed on the floor, jarring his wrist. He snatched at her dress as she tried to wriggle away. It tore. Another peal of thunder coincided with the rending of cloth and smothered it. Her whole body was heaving with rage and fear, her breath came in a series of gasps, like a child with fever. He gripped one edge of the rent with his right hand, the other with the left, and he tore, leaving her dress in tatters. She darted a hand up to claw him again but he intercepted it and bent it backwards. She bit her lips, but would not scream: he saw that she would not give him the satisfaction of hearing her scream and doubled the pressure. Just when he thought her wrist must break, she squirmed her legs between his and tried to knee his crotch – unsuccessfully, but with enough force to tip him off balance.

He slapped her face. She spat at him. He wiped away her saliva with the back of his hand. He licked it off his skin, mixing her juice with his own, and spat it back in her face. She jerked her head up and he saw, just in time, that she meant to bite him. He dug his elbows into her breasts and pressed down with his whole weight. He

330

brought a knee up into her groin and levered himself upright a little, enough to slap her.

Her struggles became weaker. He tried to rip off her bra, but the material was too thick and she still had enough strength to stop him reaching behind her back. He left it. He wrenched her bikini slip down a few inches. Her legs flailed. He put his left hand under her chin and pushed backwards. This time she did let out a low moan. The sound excited him. He pushed harder.

Her panties split. He snatched them away. She was struggling less now. He stuck his first two fingers in his mouth to moisten them. For a few seconds he merely stroked her bush with them, enjoying the look on her face. Outrage. Yes.

Jay shoved.

He felt for the neck of her womb, the hard round knob lodged deep inside her body, where the baby was. She was so wet. But wet in a different way from usual. Normally she flooded him with a coating of warm, light oil. This substance was watery and lacked lubrication. It stank. Maybe the kid's fault.

When he raised himself to a kneeling position she lay there and looked at him. She did not move. He undid the buttons of his shirt and removed it. He unbuckled his belt. He lowered his trousers, letting them fall to his knees. His movements were unhurried and casual. He was an executioner with a victim who wasn't going anywhere. He lowered his underpants. He stroked his cock for a few moments while he smiled at her, because that's what medieval executioners did, they showed the prisoner the instruments and let them think about things for a while.

Alison rolled on to her side. He thought she meant to try an escape and his hands lanced out to pinion her, but she merely lay on her side with her legs drawn up.

'Look at me,' he said.

She closed her eyes.

'*Look at me!*'

She turned her head into the floor so that he could no longer even see if her eyes were open or not. Jay lay down next to her, shoving his left hand between her legs to open a path.

Her spring was so unexpected that for a second he just lay on the floor, feeling stupid. She was up and running before he had stumbled on to his knees. Where will she go? he thought. Naked, bleeding, what can she do?

Alison reached the centre of the room. Lightning scalded the sky, clothing her near-naked body with sickly light. She threw back her head, opening her mouth wide, and she screamed: '*Help!*'

At that moment the heavens above rent from hemisphere to hemisphere, smothering her cry. Jay raced forward to send her flying against the back of a sofa. He pushed her off balance, using the sofa-back as a fulcrum, and swung her legs up to rest on his shoulders.

He took Alison standing, with her sprawled over the sofa like a broken life-sized rag-doll, and with every thrust she moaned, but too quietly for his taste. So when he had started to come he withdrew, sending shots of white seed spattering over her thighs, and he pushed her back even further, enough to bugger her and then she did scream, yes, like a butchered animal, because although his penis was slippery with semen and juice it reared huge and he wasn't about to wait: but the storm abetted Jay, a fellow-conspirator entering into the spirit of the thing, and Alison's agony expired unheard.

He came out of her. His eyes were open but he could not see: streaks of purple and red and green banded before him. It took a while for them to fade. He leaned against the sofa and he realized that the noise he could hear was himself, bellowing. Eventually he lapsed into silence from want of breath: physical deficiency uncontrolled by will. He could claim no credit for falling silent.

There was blood on his hands, his legs, the floor. Blood everywhere. Looking at Alison's battered body, he realized that he could claim no credit for anything.

'Get a divorce,' he cried hoarsely.

She opened her eyes. She tried to speak, but her voice failed her and all that came out was a curious clicking sound. She swallowed. She licked her lips; but the thunder chose that moment to vent more rage and he could not hear what she said.

Jay bent down towards Alison. 'What?' And when she did not reply at once, he shook her. *'What?'*

'I said . . . all right.'

*       *       *

'We are arrived. *Excuse me! Sir!'*

Jay woke up. Or rather, he hauled himself up out of the deep, dark place where he had been lurking.

'Sir, we are arrived at Shenton Way terminal. We do not go any further.'

He turned, slowly, to find that the bus-driver was standing in the aisle, looking down at him with an inquisitive expression on his face.

'I'm sorry,' Jay mumbled.

He would have to pull himself together. The Mandarin Hotel was on Orchard Road, he'd missed his stop by miles, must have been dreaming . . .

When he stood up the driver made an odd sound. Jay stared at him. The man's eyes were downturned towards Jay's crotch. Jay followed their direction, and saw that if his erection grew any larger he'd split his pants.

He pushed past the outraged driver and jumped off the

333

bus. The moment his feet touched the ground he started running like a criminal in flight.

*

The drive home soothed Verity's nerves somewhat, though muzziness was building up inside her head again. She checked the encounter with Iain for flaws and could find none. She felt pretty sure she'd persuaded him that Raj was in Iraq. And the suggestion that Iain should meet Jay struck her as tantamount to genius. Two troublesome characters from the past, cancelling each other out, neutralized. Yes.

As the elevator carried her up to the penthouse she worried about whether she'd been right not to turn Iain in to those policemen on the waterfront. He was wanted by the authorities, she could have had him taken out of circulation, all it would have needed was a look . . . but no. That was a card to play later. Right now, she had other plans for Iain Forward.

She had other worries, too. The dial on her answering machine told her there were four messages. Normally she would have poured herself a drink and sat down while listening to them with half an ear, but this evening she all but threw herself on to the machine in her haste to press the play-back button. Let it be Robinson, or at least Uncle Tang, *please* . . .

She found herself waiting for the message that mattered, the words that would change everything. They must be there. *Must be!* But . . . an invitation to a charity do . . . her personal stockbroker, with a request that she call him back . . . the secretary of the company that managed this apartment-building, announcing the date of the AGM . . .

Her hands were clenched by her sides. Verity's head was pounding. She stopped breathing.

'Hello.'

334

The fourth message consisted of just one word. And the click of disconnection.

Jay Sampson.

As she'd entered the room she had switched on only a table-lamp. Now Verity hurried to the bank of switches and ran both hands down them, punching them, flooding the room with the light of comfort and security.

'Mrs Boon! Mrs Boon!' For an instant she failed to recognize the voice as her own.

The *amah* hurried into the room. 'What is it, Miss Verity?'

'Have there been any callers today?'

The woman gestured helplessly at the answering machine.

'*Callers*, you . . . foolish woman! Visitors! A Chinese boy, a teenager? An American man?'

'No, Miss.' Mrs ,Boon's face closed down, her voice turned smooth as polished ebony. 'There have been no visitors today.'

Or any other day, that's what she's thinking . . . *bitch! Just because I'm not a Chinese whore like her, with men, men, men* . . . Verity caught up with her thoughts, grabbed them, stifled them back into Pandora's Box.

'I'm so sorry,' she said. 'I have not been well today. I do apologize for shouting, Mrs Boon.'

'No problem.' The monsoon past, Mrs Boon's shutters went up and her face was open for business again. 'Like some jasmine tea?'

Verity shook her head. 'No, thank you. I'll see you in the morning.'

'Ho-Kay. I've cooked you some rice dish, left it in the ice-box. Cook it *hot*, kill the germs, or you'll get sick. Yes?'

Verity summoned up a smile from somewhere and nodded. Moments later, the servants' door slammed and she knew she was alone. She crossed to the bar and

335

poured three shots of Bacardi into a chunky tumbler, along with some unsweetened lime juice. She swallowed half, making a face, and went over to the picture-window. All of Singapore lay spread out beneath her. Amidst so many glittering needle-points of light, where was Iain, she wondered? Where was Jay . . . ?

Where was poor Robinson Tang?

She'd phoned his uncle, Old Turtle, who had sounded subdued and apprehensive. The boy's parents were making trouble. Stall, she'd told him; act natural. But Uncle Tang stood on the verge of panic, she knew.

Something bad had happened to the boy. Her instincts told her he was no longer alive. She took another quick drink in an effort to wash away the thought, but it refused to leave her. Who would have wanted to harm him? Surely not Jay? And yet who else could it have been? Suppose the boy had been clumsy and Jay had seen him, questioned him?

A shiver passed through Verity's body. Her face hardened. Even if Jay had grilled Robinson and the boy had talked, it didn't matter. She could still destroy the man who had left her for another woman, years before. She had nothing for Jay Sampson except revenge.

The doorbell chimed. Her thoughts froze in mid-flood. She wasn't expecting visitors. For a second it occurred to her, with a surge of hope, that this might be Robinson. But no, he wouldn't come to her apartment.

Then she knew who it was.

The hairs on her neck stood upright. The bell sounded again, and she half turned towards the door, before slowly pivoting back to the window; because after all, this moment wasn't going to come again. She sipped the remains of her daiquiri until nothing remained but the ice, and then she selected one of the cubes to suck, taking her time over it.

She had the power, now. Not like in the old days, when the man outside had owned her, body and soul. This visitor wasn't going to go away. Let him wait.

She had waited twenty years.

# TWENTY

Iain made a difficult left into Orchard Grove Road —
everything had changed so much since 1973, not least a
three-fold hike in the price of petrol — and cruised up
past the Shangri-La Hotel, getting the hang of his rented
Mitsubishi Lancer 1.5. It was still early. He planned to
take a look at the apartment block where Verity lived.

The road bore round to the left and began to climb.
Here, all was well-manicured gardens and dignified
houses, some of them original colonial bungalows. Ahead
of him, however, he could see a glass tower, tapering
slightly from base to tip, its concave frontage curving just
enough to capture and then please the eye. She occupied
one of two penthouses. To live thirty floors up in Singapore took serious money. Verity had done all right.

An electronically controlled gate, the kind of thing
found at the entrance to a high-security prison, barred
this glittering glass palace from *hoi polloi*. Iain slowly
drove past, eyeballing the tower's main entrance which
was set down below road-level. What he saw made him
brake sharply and pull into the side. A white BMW stood
on the forecourt. Because he had tailed Verity as far as
her office car park the previous evening, after she'd left
their riverside rendezvous, he knew she drove a white
BMW.

He got out and sidled along the verge until he could
look through the bars of the gate. Licence-plate the same:
her car. The driver's door was open, the engine running,
but there seemed to be no one around.

A concierge came out through the glass doors, holding

a briefcase. Verity followed a few steps behind. Iain ran back to his Lancer and got in. Moments later, Verity's BMW drove out and turned right, towards town. Iain followed.

He was cursing his luck. First, to discover she lived in a fortress, then to find she hadn't gone to work early, leaving him with a clear field, lastly the knowledge that she'd be heading for the city via the quickest route, Orchard Road, which meant that he'd have to buy a daily licence for the restricted traffic zone. But if he stopped to do that, he'd lose her.

So what?

Iain took his foot off the throttle. Why was he following her? He knew where she was going, and once she was there she'd stay locked up in her office for the next twelve hours or so. Waste of time when he had such a long list of other things to do. Find Raj, for a start.

And yet . . . what was this? Instead of making for Orchard Road she turned left, heading north for the junction with Stevens Road. Iain dropped a gear and picked up speed again. Interesting . . .

He'd had no experience of tailing someone in a car. He soon discovered it was bloody difficult. The longer he stayed glued to Verity's tailgate the clammier he became, until at last, in desperation, he put his foot on the gas and overtook her. He looked in his mirror. She maintained the same steady pace and Iain relaxed; until suddenly she made an unsignalled left turn into Jalan Jurong Kechil, leaving him to steam on along Upper Bukit Timah Road.

He put his foot down and roared up through Ewart Circus, taking the major artery, Jurong Road, which should eventually lead him to the northern junction with Jalan Jurong Kechil – or so some desperately dangerous map-reading suggested.

But he knew he'd lost her. There were no white BMWs on Jurong Road. He coasted past the junction with Jalan Jurong Kechil, but Verity had vanished. Iain swore, and banged the steering wheel with his fists. He pulled over and took a proper look at the map. The network of roads, most of them new since his time, meant nothing.

He was just folding up the map when a flash of white snagged his eye. He whipped his head around in time to see Verity cruising sedately along Jurong Road. He caught up with her just before she turned north. He adjusted his speed until he was far enough behind to be inconspicuous in her rearview mirror, and settled down to keeping the BMW in sight.

She led him all the way up the island, almost to the Strait of Johor; and there she posed a problem by turning left on to a track of tamped red earth, where Iain could not follow without making himself conspicuous.

He parked beside a group of hawker stalls and got out of the car. Verity's BMW was already disappearing over a rise in the track. He ran across the road and began to follow. The heat soon got to him, he couldn't keep it up. He slowed to a walk, wiping his forehead. *Shit!*

Then he saw her tyre marks, picked out cleanly in the ochre mud, and he untensed. She wasn't going anywhere he couldn't track her.

It was odd country. Ahead, the horizon was bounded by distant trees. To his right, scrub quickly gave way to jungle. A tall mesh fence bounded the track on its left hand side. Iain saw a sign: SAFTI. What could that stand for? Then he saw the representation of a man shooting and the crackle that had been echoing in his ears for the past few minutes jumped into focus. A firing range. He quickened his pace.

About a mile after leaving the main road, the track skirted what looked like a flattened building site. It was littered with untidy piles of bricks, rubbish, rotten planks and chopped vegetation. Iain could see no one. To his right was an old wire fence, much dented and, in some places, collapsed, but still evidence of a boundary. Beyond it lay *belukar*: secondary jungle consisting of palms, albizia trees, ferns, tall, untidy clumps of bamboo hung with creepers. A footpath, of sorts, led into this green chaos. Iain hesitated. There were the tyre marks; where was the car?

He pushed on along the main track, but within a few yards it turned one final bend and petered out in a clearing. Somebody had organized a bonfire here, and in the recent past, too: a thin trail of smoke still oozed upwards from the ashes. Suddenly a car-door slammed shut. Iain didn't hesitate: he dived into the nearest thicket. So *close*! How had he failed to see the car, the white car for God's sake, amid so much greenery?

He peered through some ferns. For a moment, the clearing remained undisturbed. Then he saw a clutch of low-hanging branches tremble and part. The BMW nosed through the gap. A woman's voice said something, but went unanswered. Iain raised his head a fraction. Someone, a man, was walking around the boot of the car, and the screen of foliage had fallen back into place: he must have been holding the branches aside to let the BMW through. Iain took a good look at his face but didn't recognize him. The man got in, his door shut, and the car slowly drove off down the track.

Iain waited a few moments before ducking beneath the branches that had concealed the car and taking a look around. He was in a glade of grass and sand that had the feel of a lovers' trysting place. At the back of this the grass had been trampled down into a path, barely discernible after endless days and nights of sun and rain, but there. And what was this, footprints . . . ? Iain began to follow the path. He proceeded with great care. Something worth hiding lay at the end of this quest, else why go to such trouble to conceal the car? And if the thing really was worth hiding, maybe somebody had been detailed to guard it. He didn't intend to blunder into an ambush . . .

He had been following the path for about a quarter of a mile, and guessed he was getting near the Strait of Johor, when he took a step forward and his foot kept going right on down, into the earth. Iain nearly fell. At first he could see nothing. Then what looked like a brick caught his eye, and he knelt.

The object was indeed a brick: part of a hollow pillar, obviously an artificial construction. Iain realized he'd put his foot into the empty space at the pillar's centre. He raised his head. A few yards away he saw what might be another of these oddities. Foundations. There'd once been a house here.

As he came upright he began to notice other strange features. Over to his right, vines cloaked a frame of some kind. A *window*, for God's sake! Rotten, broken, but a window nonetheless: there were shards of glass underfoot, they crunched as he moved.

Iain swung around in a circle. Now that his mind had made the necessary connection it all became clear: remains of a doorway here, more bricks and some tiles there . . . the shape of the dwelling dissolved out of the jungle like one of those optical puzzles, now you see it, now you don't.

About ten yards away, to the west, the jungle screen thinned to let in light. Iain, hot and claustrophobic, began to make his way towards it. The air smelled differently here, fresher somehow, and he knew he must be almost at the coast. He moved faster. A squabble of bulbuls rose up from a nearby seraya tree, cursing him, their fluttery wings standing for fists shaken in anger. Something bit his leg. He looked down. Ants: an interminable column of them. Iain leapt aside and pulled up his trouser-leg to see an angry pink swelling. Suffused with sudden rage, he stamped on the rolling serpent at his feet, scarcely denting it. The ants kept right on moving. He followed their progress with a malevolent eye, through the ferns and grasses, until the black army coalesced around something pale, half buried underneath a pile of branches. It looked like a shirt. Iain nearly decided not to bother with it. Then, for some unknown reason, he decided he would.

*

'I estimate it will take Forward a couple of days at the outside to trace Raj,' Verity said calmly. 'And once he's done that, we're dead.'

Jay sat slumped in the BMW's passenger seat, chewing a nail. He seemed not to have heard, but as Verity prepared to turn off the track on to the main road by Thong Hoe village he stopped chewing for long enough to say, 'Can't you get rid of Raj?'

'He's working flat out at the plant. BCCI's stooge virtually lives there, checking on him.'

'Nobody gets into Sudong without a pass. Do they?'

'No one.'

'So why worry about Forward?'

'You haven't met him.' Verity shivered slightly, a tremor that owed nothing to the car's air-conditioning. 'He's changed.'

Jay started on another nail. 'What if he does get to Raj? What if Raj does talk? He's got no proof of anything.'

She turned right, driving along the northern edge of Singapore island now. They were almost at Kranji Reservoir before she spoke again.

'Iain Forward's a violent man,' she observed quietly. 'He scares me. Terrifies me. Can you imagine what he'd do to poor Reggie?'

Jay grunted.

'He's got to be stopped,' she persisted. 'You do it. MI5

343

will thank you, the FBI will thank you. All the things you want, you can have. *If* . . . you get to Iain Forward first.'

Jay said nothing for a few miles. Then – 'Where are you taking me?' he asked uneasily.

'Ponggol.'

'Why, for God's sake?'

'Because you can get a boat across to Malaysia from there,' she explained smoothly. 'Safer for you.' *And for me*, she added mentally.

'I don't want to waste time in Malaysia.'

'Nor need you. But as a base . . .'

She let the silence work for her, knowing his thoughts. If Iain Forward uncovered the truth about his murder conviction he'd go public with it and Jay would lose all bargaining power. He must surely see the sense of her proposal.

'I'm not going to Malaysia,' he said suddenly. 'Period.'

'So where are you going to stay?' she scoffed. 'The House of Orchids?'

'I'll find somewhere.' He glanced at her out of the corner of his eye, a sour expression on his face. 'Perhaps I'll call on De Souza. Is he still fronting for BCCI here? Or Doc Rogers, if he's not too busy making Saddam's nuclear detonators look like cartons of ice-cream to fool the sanctions-busters.'

Verity smiled, but she understood the message well enough. Jay had done his homework, kept it at his fingertips. When he'd come to her flat the night before he'd brought copies of papers deposited with his lawyers in the States: enough to take out fifteen per cent of the Pentagon's entire class of '72-'73, she estimated, along with their political masters. How like the man she'd loved all those years ago! And she wasn't going to let him slip through her fingers again, oh no!

'I suppose . . .' She knew it was mad, and yet, and yet

. . . 'I suppose I could put you up. For a few days. No one would know you were there.'

As she waited out the silence she unintentionally counted her own heartbeats, one, two, three, and she cursed herself for the weakness that had nearly destroyed her once before. Jealousy. That slut Alison. She was the one who should have spent seventeen years in prison. *She* was the root of all evil.

'No,' he said, with finality.

'Aren't you even going to think about it?'

She hadn't meant to say that. She was out to destroy this man. But blood was fluttering in her cheeks, her vocal cords were taut and painful, her hands trembled, she could no more conceal her unwanted emotion than she could prevent the sunrise.

'No. There'll be people watching you. It was mad of me to visit last night; if there'd been any other way, I wouldn't have come near you.'

The words dropped into the car like lead shot, sinking her hopes.

Verity eyed him sideways. She'd been prepared for changes, and they were there. In the old days he had been a god, a bronzed and handsome he-man; now his rounded shoulders and sunken eyes framed in lizard-skin told her all she didn't already know about middle age. His face dropped, as if the flesh was too heavy for the bone beneath. He used to be so tall, still might be if he hadn't learned to walk with a stoop. His wonderful black hair was fading away, turning white here and there, but not in a way that made him look distinguished.

Yet he had . . . something. His big frame hadn't shed all its muscle. Despite a new tendency to flabbiness, his long face conveyed the old power, the intelligence bordering on craftiness that she remembered so well. The stern wedge of a chin still jutted. She looked at him and

345

knew why she'd wanted him, all those years ago. Still wanted him.

'Jay,' she whispered. And when he remained silent, she slid her hand on to his thigh.

He knocked it aside and wrenched his legs away from the central console. 'Oh, for Christ's sake,' she heard him mutter.

Raindrops splattered against the windscreen, harbingers of a downpour. Soon the windshield was a flowing screen of water but she gazed right through it, unblinking, her head held at precisely the same angle. Only when Jay reached across to switch on the wipers with a grunt did she come back to the present.

'Where do you want to go, then?' she asked in a small, flat voice.

'Ponggol. You're right.'

Despite herself, she felt a momentary relief.

'How will we stay in touch?' he asked her.

Verity pulled herself together and thought. 'Call me in the morning and again in the evening, every day, at ten a.m. and ten p.m. Use the number of my portable, it's tap-proof. But I'll set a meeting now, as fallback.'

'Give 'em the stuff I left with you last night. I'm not coming to any meeting. Too dangerous.'

'Then you can rot. You want the money, you meet with them.'

'They tried to kill me, back in the States. Why in hell do you think I'm riding around in this car with you instead of shacking up at the Hilton?'

'That was their patch. Here, they're powerless. And they want reassuring. Yes, they will pay, they've said that. But they have to be convinced that you're going to drop out of sight and stay there.'

He stared at her without speaking for a long time, long enough to make her wish he'd stop, let her get on with her life, just disappear.

'Jay,' she said suddenly, 'has anyone been following you?'

'No. Why?' There was suspicion in his voice and she cursed herself for being so stupid. That was no way to get at the truth about Robinson Tang. But oh, where *was* he?

'No reason,' she said, with an attempt at a shrug. 'Listen: you have to have a fallback rendezvous in case anything goes wrong. Three nights from now, be at the Kranji War Cemetery. Do you know it?'

He nodded reluctantly.

'The car park, at eleven. Call me morning and evening; if you can't contact me, just get to Kranji and wait.'

'Who else will be there?'

'I don't know yet. But I will be, and no one's going to try anything in front of a witness.'

'How do I know I can trust you?'

'You don't. But you need me, I'm all you've got. So choose.'

They were driving up the last of the long, straight stretch of road that led to Ponggol. She pulled in behind a couple of buses, beside the Chinese shrine with its weird, perpetually burning wooden statue, and got out. After a second's hesitation, Jay followed suit.

They walked down the road to a small pier. Across the Strait of Johor, flares burned brightly on the industrial hinterland; here and there a welding torch was at work on some construction project, sending its shower of Roman Candle sparks high in the torpid air. The water stank of sewage. Verity cast a jaded eye around at the dingy seafood restaurants with their tables laid ready for coachloads of Japanese, the gaggle of cats fighting beneath the tables, the smoke from the shrine, and she thought, God! Who in his right mind would come here to eat? Who in his right mind would come here at all?

But there was a pier, and even now a boat was

chugging towards it from the direction of Tekong Island. She waited until it had docked and Jay had gone aboard, before turning her back on the Strait, and her old lover and the sordidness of everything. She got into her BMW. For a moment she stared at the Gehenna opposite. Then she picked up the phone and dialled the Ladyhill Hotel, asking to be connected to room 615. Its occupant answered on the first ring.

'Heaney.'

'Yes,' she said, fighting back tears. 'Got him. Yes.'

*

Iain sat on a bench beside the Public Utilities Board's misshapen concrete headquarters, staring blindly at the passing pedestrians. It was lunchtime, the streets packed with giggling secretaries, harassed-looking shirtsleeved men muttering into portable phones, students, a few (a very few) tourists. He saw none of them.

There was a corpse, the body of a teenage boy, concealed in the jungle by the Strait of Johor. Quite a lot of it had gone the way of all flesh. Iain's stomach turned as he thought of what the ants were getting at. And Verity had gone up there to meet a strange man, taking precautions against being seen.

Was the man Sampson? Did he know about the body? Did she?

Why had she never mentioned her dealings with this mysterious Jay Sampson, when it might have helped him most: before his trial?

What was her game?

He stood up and began a slow walk down Exeter Road, unsure what to do next. He ought to change dosshouse. He moved every day, but now there was a new urgency to it. He was a lifer, an ex-con, a murderer, and he was in the vicinity of a corpse. What if someone had seen him? He hadn't noticed anybody, but – he shivered –

348

Singapore was full of invisible eyes. He remembered from the seventies how your neighbours always knew your business, concealing their knowledge behind a polished veneer of courtesy.

He couldn't bring himself to inspect the remains too closely, but he felt sure that death hadn't been natural. The body had been *concealed*, it hadn't just fallen down and lain in the open. Which meant the boy must have been murdered. And he, Iain Forward, was a convicted murderer.

People were inveterately lazy. Why bother to hunt for a real murderer when you had one neatly labelled and pre-packaged, ready to hand?

As he walked he found himself looking over his shoulder. Nothing about the street-pattern struck him as odd. That respectable matron over there, the archetypal *tai-tai* with her Louis Vuitton handbag and French-cut dress . . . was she with Security? Or the elderly Chinese gentleman walking with the aid of a cane? The little cluster of school-children in their well-pressed uniforms . . . Iain walked faster, in time to the beating of his heart.

On the corner of Killiney Road he stopped, waiting for the lights. Just up the street was the Comcentre, open twenty-four hours a day. The lights turned green, but he stood there, undecided. There'd be a security guard, of course, although he wouldn't be on the lookout for Iain. Or would he . . . ?

His feet were taking him up the pavement, in through the glass doors. The Sikh security-man glanced at him indifferently. Iain approached the desk. Suddenly he knew why he was here, what he wanted to do. He booked a phone call to England, handed over his twenty dollar deposit and went to sit in the corner until they called him.

Someone had left a newspaper on the seat beside his. He picked it up and began to idle through it, the words making scant impression. But then, right at the top of the page, he saw a photograph and the word 'Missing'. His hand paused. *Missing Boy's Parents' Distress.*

Impossible to match the clean-cut features with what he'd found in the ground earlier, and yet . . . Iain started to read the article. When the girl directed him to a phone booth he took the newspaper with him.

He dialled the number, dazzled by the speed with which London came on-line. He prayed that Kate, not Alison, would answer. But then came a click, and his wife's voice on the answering machine.

Iain heard the tone. He wanted to slam down the receiver, but something prevented him. Haltingly he spoke a message, in the artificial way people do when they're talking to a mechanical stand-in for somebody they love.

'Kate, this is Iain. I just called to say . . . I miss you. Love you, darling. I . . . I'm sorry, that's all, I'm very sorry.'

Slowly he laid the handset back on its rest and went out to pay. A word from his daughter, that's all he'd wanted: something to hang on to, something to keep him going on a quest that now seemed hopeless.

As he walked out into the harshness of a Singaporean afternoon, closing his eyes against its fierce light, he tried to think what his next step should be. Why had he come? To beard Verity in her lair, make her talk. Had he succeeded? No. Yet the answers were all here, in Singapore, if only he could hack a way through to them.

He must talk to Raj. He'd bluffed his way with Verity Newland, basing his reconstruction of events on memory, on what Powis had said, and thin research in libraries' newspaper archives before leaving England. Verity had confirmed some of it, not enough. Without input from Raj, he was right back where he'd started.

From what Iain remembered of the diminutive Indian

scientist, he wouldn't be likely to stand up to pressure. Seventeen years in prison had made Iain a past master of knowing where, how, to apply pressure. On the other hand, nobody was going to invite him to Occydor Pharmaceuticals' top-security plant on Sudong Island, which was where he felt sure Raj now worked. He couldn't *know*, but he'd have bet any money on it: Raj and Verity had been thick as thieves, she'd never have let him go. All that talk about him having disappeared in Iraq was bullshit.

Occydor Pharmaceuticals was listed in the Yellow Pages, along with the rest of the Occydor empire, so at least Iain knew its address. He had tried tracing Reggie through the residential phone-book, but Raj, R. was a common-or-garden entry; he could waste a lifetime checking every one, only to find that the man he wanted was ex-directory.

It had to be Sudong. A bus to Clifford Pier, and then see. Maybe he could bribe a boatman . . .

The terrible heat made his scalp itch beneath the wig he'd been wearing ever since leaving London. He felt ridiculous, yearned to take it off, but didn't dare. How much longer would he have to go on with this farce? No end in sight, no end to anything.

As he reached the bus-stop on Orchard Road, he remembered he was still holding the newspaper. He threw it in the litter-bin. The boy's face, crumpled now, gazed up reproachfully. How old would he have been? Fourteen, fifteen, a bit younger than . . .

Kate. Where had she gone? *Why wasn't she at home?*

# TWENTY-ONE

They sat on the bed, a foot of space between them, and, as if to symbolize such an unusual mother–daughter truce, they were holding hands.

'What are you going to do?' Kate asked.

Alison squeezed her daughter's hand. 'We must make a plan, yes?' But she didn't seem to have anything in mind, and silence fell once more.

They were occupying a small double room on the first floor of the Lido Hotel, in a narrow street leading off Beach Road. Their taxi-driver had recommended it, on the way from the airport. Even after paying two air-fares Alison had quite a lot of money on her, thanks to Darren. He hadn't told her where it came from, and she hadn't asked; he'd just driven them to Heathrow, helped with their luggage and waved goodbye. Going through the gate, Kate had looked back once, but Alison hadn't been able to read anything on her face. Does she miss him? she wondered. Would she die for him, as I would have done for Jay?

Things were rapidly catching up with Alison now. She'd quit her job and England on the same day, burning all her boats. She had to get Iain back: that was what preoccupied her waking thoughts, her night-time dreams. But it wasn't the whole of it. This was a place where once she'd been happy. After years of isolation and poverty, of going from Tesco's to Kwik Save to check the price of a tin of baked beans, suddenly to be transported to a land where bowls of scalding *laksa* seafood soup could be had for pennies meant heaven on earth.

Memories, memories . . . she had sat in the taxi, seeing *through* the changes, as if she had X-ray eyes; Singapore, her old, beloved Singapore . . .

And then there was Jay . . .

Kate interrupted her thoughts with a sneeze. She groped for a tissue. The Singapore Streamer, Alison thought sadly; hers is a cold that will run and run. Some things didn't change.

Suddenly she knew what she had to do, even if it sounded daft: 'I'm going to visit my parents' graves,' she said.

Kate gazed at her, goggle-eyed. 'You're going to do *what*?'

Alison went across to the wonky dressing-table and started to arrange things that didn't need arranging, with quick, nervous gestures. 'Father died after the trial,' she said to the mirror. 'Shock, as much as anything. Then there was the appeal, the petitions . . . my mother fell sick. Something tropical, I never did understand it. She got sick and stayed sick, and I . . . well, I just assumed she'd go on like that for a long time.' She paused. 'And she didn't.'

Kate looked at the floor. 'Sorry,' she muttered.

'They're buried in a cemetery, north of town.'

'I see.'

'You don't have to come.'

'I'd like to.'

'It'll be desperately hot.'

'I'd *like* to.'

Alison went back to sit by Kate. After an uncertain pause she took her daughter's hand again. Kate returned the pressure.

'Then Verity,' Alison said, in a kind of hiccup.

'Verity Newland?'

Alison nodded.

'She gave evidence at the trial, didn't she?'

'Yes. I keep forgetting, you've read the case papers.'

'Everything. Iain told me to. I don't like Verity.'

Alison had been staring at the floor. Now she raised her head to look at Kate. 'Why? She wanted to help Iain.'

'No, she didn't. She pretended to. But the barrister tied her up in knots. She was smarter than she let on. She should have seen where he was coming from. She *did* see. But she let him walk all over her. Why are you going to see her?'

'Because she's the person he'll make straight for.'

'And you think you can intercept him, is that it?'

'Sort of. Oh, Kate . . . I don't know what I'm doing, I know it all sounds so ridiculous, but I can't just sit at home, I've got to do something.'

Kate puckered up her mouth and thought. 'You're right,' she said at last. 'Look, why don't we go and see the graves? Then find this Verity horror.'

'We?'

'Of course.'

'You're not coming to Verity's, Kate.'

'Oh, don't be *stu*-pid.'

'You're not coming.'

'Listen, Mum: I don't go, you don't go. Got it?'

'I have to see her alone. She won't talk otherwise, I know her.'

'You know her?'

'From way back.' Alison's voice was bitter. 'Well enough to realize that my only chance with her is not to have a witness.'

'But it's dangerous.'

'Rubbish. What can she do to me, here in Singapore? She's a respectable businesswoman.'

'Mum, you're so naive!'

Both women were standing now, with more than just physical distance between them. There was a silence. Kate bit her lip.

'Look,' she said, in a quieter tone. 'Long flight, yes?'

Alison nodded wearily.

'So let's go and visit the graves. We'll talk it through afterwards.'

Alison managed a smile. There was nothing to talk about, but why make a fuss? Kate thought she was stupid; maybe she was, but when it came down to it she'd know how to give her daughter the slip.

\*

Verity had seen the red Porsche 944 several times over the past few days. It was a striking vehicle for Singapore, where import taxes more than doubled the cost of a car. The Porsche drew attention to itself. She saw it while driving to work, noticed it again going home. After she'd dropped Jay at Ponggol Pier, she'd glimpsed a brief flash of red in her rear-view mirror as she neared the city.

Until this morning, she'd been in two minds about it. Now she felt sure it was following her.

She'd chosen to drive west along Holland Road: not the fastest route, but more convenient for Jurong Town Pier. She'd been putting off a visit to Raj for too long. Verity had not been honest with Iain about Reggie Raj: he worked on Sudong Island, in a plant that once had belonged to Harchem and now was owned by Occydor Pharmaceuticals.

She made the turn south, to Clementi and Common-wealth Avenue, which would take her into Jurong itself. Because she was concentrating so hard on her mirror she nearly drove into the side of a green Mercedes; its driver hooted angrily and she stamped on the brakes. Her heart was beating faster than usual, her lips were cracked and dry. She had too much to cope with. But, yes! The red Porsche 944 was turning after her, keeping the same distance behind. One driver ... passengers? How many? *What did they want?* How far were they prepared to go?

The morning might be dull and overcast, but the thermometer told her that outside it was eighty-six degrees. Verity felt too cold for comfort. She jabbed at the fan-switch, turning off the air-conditioning. In less than a minute the car was a Turkish bath with leather seats. She boosted the air-con again, her attention still hooked to the rear-view mirror.

Now the Porsche was moving up. Fifty yards.

Ahead she could see the turning to the Chinese Garden. Turn south, for the pier, or keep going?

Keep going.

Bad move. *Bad.*

Her hands larded the steering wheel with sweat. Almost without realizing it she was through the not yet completed residential area of Boon Lay and on her way to the industrial hinterland of Tuas. Upper Jurong Road, the turning off to Nanyang University, options closing fast now; and there, in the mirror, always the red Porsche.

Tuas was the westernmost part of Singapore Island. It consisted of factories, refineries, ship repairers, some green-field sites as yet unbuilt on: a desolate, smog-shrouded industrial estate, featureless and bleak. Nowhere to hide, no exit. She was driving along Jalan Ahmad Ibrahim, God, there must be a way out! Raffles Country Club . . . keep going.

She found herself turning north-west, with the flow of other cars, on to the spur road leading to Tengeh Reservoir. On her right, the country club's golf course, to the left, Fraser & Neave's enormous factory, next to that the Tiger Brewery, all high-tech blue and yellow. The road itself was wider than a football field, deliberately made big enough for the air force to use as an emergency runway. Verity suddenly put her foot down. She did not know this area but now she had a chance, just one: the road was so broad she'd be able to turn around without reversing, double back, hit the accelerator and stay stamped hard down on it until she got to Jurong Town.

Half a dozen other vehicles were coming along the opposite carriageway towards her . . . let them pass, then . . .

But the driver of the Porsche had anticipated her. As she swerved over to the left, giving herself maximum room for the semi-circular turn, her pursuer roared up on her offside, forcing Verity even further left. She pounded the horn with her fist. The Porsche stayed glued to her flank, the two vehicles all but touching as they raced up the road.

Verity braked hard. The other driver peeled off to the right, turning on a rice-bowl: before Verity could reverse out of danger he had come up behind her, nuzzling with his forward bumper. The white BMW lurched forward under the impact. Verity wanted to scream, but this was beyond screaming. This was war.

She slammed the car into first and shot off again. She was running out of road. To the left she could see a bank of red earth, with distant buildings just visible through the murk, half a mile away or more; to the right, nothing but palm trees marking off the golf course from neighbouring land. Barricades, signifying a dead end, hurtled up to meet her.

Verity braked. She skidded, wrenched the wheel sideways, away from the red Porsche, which by now was again hugging her offside like a pilot fish with its chosen shark. She came to a halt inches from the bank of earth. For a moment she was too shaken to move. A sign in front of her swam into focus: 'McCONNELL DOWELL. A DEVELOPMENT FOR SINGAPORE BROADCASTING CORPORATION: TELEVISION WORLD.' Cranes, scaffolding, nothing live on the landscape. She could scream her throat in two, and nobody would hear.

A hand opened the door. She looked at the hand. Pale, with a coating of thin black hairs. Male. Gold Cartier Cougar, which frightened her: decent Singaporeans did not go in for displays of wealth, therefore the wrist attached to the watch was also attached to a gangster. And there was something familiar about it . . .

'One last chance,' said a soft American voice. 'I did warn you.'

Verity swung her legs out of the car. They were stiff and she staggered a little as she came upright, hoping Cover wouldn't notice.

'You did,' she said. 'And I told you I would scream, and say you'd touched my breasts.'

She could not understand why, but she was smiling at him and, even more surprisingly, he was returning her smile.

'I nearly did, and to hell with it.'

'Since I was going to say that you had anyway –'

'I might as well have enjoyed it. Yes.'

She read his eyes. They seemed immensely strong, brimful of character. You could not shake the owner of eyes like these.

'You're married,' she accused him, tersely. 'Lucky you.' And then, after a pause – 'Lucky her.'

He closed the door of the BMW and leaned against it, his arms folded across his chest.

'You're also very persistent,' she observed.

'Faint heart ne'er won fair lady.'

'"Ne'er"? Fie, Mr Cover, such language.' Verity glanced at the Porsche. 'You're alone.'

He nodded.

'Brave.'

'Discreet.'

'Oh, I don't think so, Mr Cover. Red Porsches, in Singapore, hardly rank as that.'

He laughed. 'Okay, so the auto's a giveaway. But it's me on my ownsome, and as a wealthy, young American tycoon, if I like to rent glitzy cars, that's my business.'

'But it's not, is it? Business, I mean . . . who are you with – the CIA? FBI? NSA? I can't keep track of you all.'

'It's hard,' he agreed. 'I'm here to stop the rot. Who needs know more?'

'And I'm the rot?'

'You're bait.'

'Whether I like it or not?'

'Uh-huh.'

'And whom do you want to trap, Mr Cover?'

' "Whom"? Fie, Miss Newland.'

She laughed out loud, and he joined in.

'Let's talk about product ninety-three twelve,' he said. 'And Jay Sampson.'

Verity took a few steps away from the car. He made no attempt to check her. She stared out over the scrub. A warm, wet wind dragged itself listlessly to and fro across her skin. The air, she realized, was thick with dust; she would need a deep cleanser tonight.

'I have to stop him,' Cover said. 'It's late, we are at war; there are things that can . . . *not* come out.'

Verity nodded.

'Until our boys went in, Sampson stood a chance. Now no.'

'And you want me to help you?' she asked, turning around. 'He could be dangerous.'

'Not how I read him.'

Verity hesitated only a moment. 'I hired a boy to follow Sampson,' she said. 'He's disappeared. He vanished so long ago that I have to assume the worst.'

'Dead?'

'It's possible.'

359

Cover whistled. 'And you think Sampson —'

'Yes. No.' She tossed her head in frustration. 'Who else could it be? I don't know why I'm telling you this. What do you want?'

He did not answer at once; the story about the boy troubled him, she could see.

'Here, let me show you something . . .' he said at last, going to his car and reaching inside the back seat. For a second it crossed her mind to jump in the BMW and run for it. Then she saw that the ignition was empty. Cover had taken her keys while she had her back to him and she hadn't heard a thing.

He came back with a cardboard file. She took it from him and opened it. Glossy black and white photographs fell out. Since Cover obviously wasn't going to pick them up she knelt down to retrieve them. As she turned the first one over she recognized herself, and froze at his feet, like a slave awaiting her master's pleasure.

'Tuwaitha,' he said. 'Saddam Hussein's nuclear research centre. That's Raj in the background on your left, of course. Al Furat . . . bomb design, centrifuge production. Al Qaaqaa, testing plant. Mosul . . . uranium enrichment. We project them as having four kilos of the stuff by now.'

The technical quality of these pictures, taken without the subjects' knowledge, was amazing. In one of the photos she looked a little pale, that's all, as if the shutter-speed wasn't quite right for the time of day. Yes, she remembered: 1989, the grand tour, she, Reggie and half a dozen others. Ten days in Iraq, seeing sights the tourists never saw. It had been Barza's idea, a kind of sickly reward for her efforts, parading what the Iraqi army had done with her help: for that was the year when Reggie finally cracked the big one, the problem that had bedevilled chemical warfare from the beginning, by rendering death symptomless, so that after 1989, nobody, no busybody UN observer, no Red Cross official, would be able to say for sure that mass poisons had been used. His greatest triumph, the culmination of a loathsome career. And then came the last evening, in Baghdad, with . . .

'Saddam Hussein, a bottle of J&B . . . and thou.' Cover sighed, turning over one photograph that had not fallen from the file. 'The Rubaiyat of Verity Newland.'

She rose, stiffly, and handed the photographs back to him. She got the point, but he was at pains to underline it anyway.

'In Singapore,' he said, 'they would require precisely ten seconds to determine what to do with you, after seeing these.'

Ten? she thought. Five. Two.

'American companies armed and financed Saddam Hussein with the Pentagon's connivance and Washington's blessing; you were in on the act, sometimes as principal, sometimes as marriage-broker. We do not wish our boys to know how we helped them to die. Nor do the British.'

'Bush would be out,' she said. 'And Major.'

'Dead and buried,' he agreed. 'So you'll appreciate the need to give me every assistance, because we know you supplied the matériel Saddam used to wipe out Halabja. You set up his chemical plant at Samarra. The Pentagon was happy to monitor the Kurdish massacres that followed, because live guinea-pigs are so much more satisfactory than, as it were . . .'

'Live guinea-pigs.'

'Correct.' He smiled thinly. 'In the, ah, changed circumstances, those same Pentagon officials would do anything to cover up their involvement.'

'And if they were prepared to wink at the deaths of a few thousand Kurdish villagers in order to check that the ninety-three twelve derivatives really did work, they're

361

hardly likely to worry themselves over the fate of Jay Sampson. Yes, I see.'

During the silence that followed she noted details. Cover was wearing neatly pressed cream slacks and a denim shirt open at the neck. He was sexy. He was. 'Are you going to kill me?' she asked, and she wasn't afraid, just curious.

'No.'

'Why not?'

'You kissed, but you never threatened to tell. Besides, your interests and ours are thought to coincide.'

She nodded. It made reassuring sense, even if she could not quite rid herself of the notion that he was lying.

'There's a problem,' she said. 'Sampson has kept a lot of paperwork. If he doesn't check in regularly, the papers become public property.'

'*We* know about that. The originals were with his lawyers; they're with us now.' His smile was arch. 'Much safer.'

'Copies? Who can know how many copies he made, or where they are?'

'We know. Anyway, if Sampson doesn't come forward to verify them we can live with a few copies: deny everything, claim it's all an elaborate fabrication. Nobody can contradict that.'

'Except the copies. What if he's had them certified?'

Cover shrugged. 'We know where the copies are and we're working on that. If we overlook anything, well, let's just say the rewards are thought to outweigh the risks.'

A policy decision, then. She couldn't argue with that.

'Where does Forward fit into your plans?' she asked.

Cover's eyes widened. 'Forward . . . *Iain* Forward?'

'You know about him, then?'

'Of course, he's part of Occydor's history, it's in the file.'

'He's here.'

'Here? That makes no sense.'

'Agreed. Interesting, though, isn't it?'

Cover shrugged. 'Not my assignment.'

Now it was her turn to be puzzled, until the obvious answer presented itself. 'Ah . . . Martin Heaney's in town: his department, not yours.'

'Heaney?'

'MI5.'

Cover's lips twitched, his eyes narrowed a fraction. His smile remained intact, but she had seen the momentary insecurity and was already working out how she might turn it to her advantage.

'Perhaps you should meet with Heaney,' Verity said slowly.

'Why?'

'Because he's been sent over here to kill Forward. Just as you've come to kill Sampson.'

*

There were things about the Ladyhill Hotel that suited Martin Heaney, and things that didn't. He liked the staff, he liked the spicy local food the chef did so well, it was fun to sit outside eating breakfast while little black birds buzzed the swimming-pool for an early morning bath. The layout was wonderful: three-storey buildings arranged in a rough circle along the inside of a one-way private road, so that you (and your visitors) could come and go at will without attracting the attention of the front desk or other guests. It was a good location for a spy.

But he didn't like being so far away from the centre of things, even though the Ladyhill sat in a quiet, wooded neighbourhood close to Verity Newland's apartment.

He did not like the telephone system. Martin was a connoisseur of echoing, breathy lines. Singapore Telecoms haunted his dreams, uneasy ghosts trying to make a connection, nearly there, not quite making it. You were never alone on a Singapore line. He could tell. He had an ear, in the same way that Masters of Wine have a nose.

He lay on the bed, trying to get this across to Terence Grindle, six thousand miles away in London.

'It's not very convenient to talk right now,' he said.

'Not to worry,' Grindle replied, 'I'll keep it short. Mr Perkins is on a business trip to New York, he's been trying to contact his home, but all he gets is the answering machine and what if he makes a complaint?'

'I could always have a word with the regional boys out here.'

'No.'

'They're frightfully good on anything electronic. Frightfully.'

'We don't want to get our lines crossed.' (My God but we don't, Martin thought feverishly.) 'The gut-feeling here is that regional head office might get a wee bit touchy if we did that. Best to by-pass, mm?'

Martin dropped a long, sulky silence into the transcript. Then he said, 'If you insist. But when I see Mr Perkins, what am I supposed to say to him? I mean, his is the largest account we've got in this part of the world.'

'Try to stop him making a fuss.'

'Promises or pressure?'

He waited while Grindle got a silken laugh out of his system. 'Up to you, old man,' he heard the disembodied voice say. 'Anything that's necessary. Absolutely anything at all. Oh, absolutely.'

'All right. By the way, Mrs Perkins sends her love. She's got the children with her – extended university vac, or something.'

'*Really?* Well, do give them all my regards next time you see them.'

'Of course.'

'And Martin – anything to keep that account sweet, eh? Over here we've managed to keep Perkins' name out of the newspapers; it would be such a shame to spoil it. 'Bye.'

Martin lay back on the bed, listening to the noisiest air-con system he'd ever endured, and he thought, So what have we got? Mr Perkins (Iain) was definitely in Singapore (codename New York): we can be sure of that, because he's contacted his home and left a message on the answering machine, and Technical will have traced the call. Grindle's managed to divert attention away from Iain ('kept his name out of the newspapers'), so the local police won't have been alerted. I'm not to involve Singapore security, I'm free to act as I bloody well choose, and if I'm caught I'll serve longer in Changi Jail than bloody Iain Forward ever did in the Scrubs. Great.

He wondered briefly if he ought to have informed Grindle that on the night of his arrival he'd established contact with Verity, that she'd told him Sampson was hiding out at the House of Orchids, that he had visited the ruin and found a number of interesting things.

Martin went over to the dressing-table and slid open the top drawer. He took out something long and thin, wrapped in newspaper. A battery-operated flashlight, broken. He frowned at it for a long time before wrapping it up again and replacing it in the drawer, glad, on the whole, that he hadn't told Grindle too much.

He wondered what he should do next. Waiting was always the hardest part. Perhaps he'd go and buy a present for April. She wanted a briefcase with combination locks, her old one had worn out through years of ill-paid Legal Aid work and she fancied something smart. He'd told her there wouldn't be time for shopping this trip, and she'd told him to come off it.

Maybe he'd run into Alison. Singapore was a small place and there weren't many tourists. God, what a daft

365

thought! But he wanted to see her so much, to make sure she was all right.

Go out to buy a present for April in the hope of meeting Alison. Yes, well. Don't think too much. Bad for the brain. He'd go out. Much better than sitting around.

He pocketed his key and had got as far as the door when the phone rang.

'Heaney.'

'Martin? Verity. Have you been to the House of Orchids yet?'

'Yes.'

'And?'

'No one there. Have to try again later.'

'I'm seeing Jay this afternoon,' Verity said. 'But we need to meet first.'

'Where and when?'

'Now. I'll come to you. Twenty minutes.'

Martin replaced the receiver. 'I don't know why I'm doing this,' he said to his reflection in the mirror. 'Curiosity, I suppose.'

Curiosity, he was discovering, could take you a long way.

*

The two women caught a bus to the Chua Chu Kang Christian Cemetery. Alison knew that if she stayed on this bus she would continue right past the house on the strait where she'd lived her real life before losing it. When the bus stopped at the cemetery she had to force herself to get off.

They walked through the cemetery, a peaceful, grassy spot, with rain trees, angsanas, Straits rhododendrons, roses of Sharon and countless other wild flowers to please the eye or soothe the troubled heart. Kate said she liked it because it wasn't fenced off from the road, and there seemed to be so much room. Alison had a little map, preserved over the years from when the lawyers had sent her details of her parents' last resting-place. They found the double grave at the end of Path Four.

Alison wasn't prepared for the wave of emotion that flooded through her. She sank down before the simple headstone, read the names, the dates, and felt her heart would break. It had been so long ago. She'd kept the knowledge of her parents' deaths pent up in her heart where, she thought, it could neither harm nor pain her. She was wrong. Now, faced with actual evidence of the gap they'd left, the hole that could never be filled, she had not tears enough to vent her grief.

Kate tactfully left her mother alone and wandered about the grassy cemetery, sticking to the shade. She couldn't share Alison's grief, not having known her grandparents, although she'd seen photographs of them. Their grave was on a par with the snapshots: flat, void of emotion. Historical records, that's all. So she mooched between the headstones, and asked herself what her mother intended to do, what *could* she do?

'Wish I'd brought flowers.'

Kate looked around to find that Alison had quietly come to stand by her side, so quietly in fact that Kate hadn't heard her approach.

'I'm sorry,' Alison went on, reaching for her daughter's hand. 'Not much fun for you.'

'Don't say that.' Kate squeezed hard. 'And don't worry about the flowers. After all these years . . . well.'

Alison felt a stab of pain. 'I should have come before,' she said shortly. 'That's what you mean, I suppose?'

'Don't be stupid.'

'Oh, I'm stupid now, am I?' And she began to cry again, softly this time, with none of the bitter violence of before.

'Not stupid . . .' God, it was embarrassing when your

mother cried. 'Just, well, you couldn't have done more, could you? With Dad in jail, and that.'

Alison held a tissue up to her face. She was shaking, riven with grief.

'Mum, stop it.'

But Alison continued to shake behind her paper mask.

'Come on, for God's sake. We've got things to do. This Newland person . . .'

'You're so damn . . . *callous*!' Alison threw the tissue to the ground. 'I suppose when I'm dead, when Iain's dead, you'll just –'

'Oh, *shit*!'

Kate stalked off. She did not look back, even when Alison screamed her name at the top of her voice. Alison shouted again. Kate broke into a run. Alison made an effort at pursuit, but then the heat got to her and she stopped, damned if she was going to waste her energies on trash like Kate.

Just as well. The memory of how she'd slapped the girl in front of Heaney that time rose sharp and clean before her eyes: a satisfying memory, too satisfying. As she sank down beneath a tree, it briefly occurred to her to wonder where Kate might be going. But no, why give a toss when she'd meant to give her the slip anyway?

She felt drowsy. Her eyes were closing. Suddenly she was back in 1973, the London street, everything real, everything clear. Alison moaned, clawing her way back to consciousness. But she was exhausted, the vision wouldn't let go of her.

It was miserable in London. Gerry's block of flats looked appalling: old and cold and dank and even a little smelly. The concierge eyed her as if she was some kind of tart. Now here she was, almost at Gerry's front door; Gerry was Iain's boss, mustn't offend him, mustn't be late. The door gave under her touch. She went in. What a funny room lay beyond the hallway: yellow walls with red stripes, and an odd smell. She started to look around. And a voice said . . . a voice said . . .

No. No. *No*.

*

Kate walked for a long time, trying to sweat the wrath out of herself. She knew she ought to feel sympathy for her mother, comfort her, offer support. Only actually she couldn't, because she hated Alison right now. After a bit she started to sing to herself. She came to a big crossroads with traffic-lights, but no buildings visible, just open grasslands, shrubs, mid-horizons of trees. Which way back to town? South . . .

No, she didn't want that. Singapore City was all noise, bustle, shops, cars, towering office-blocks. Out here in the country was better. She'd go back later.

North, then. She struck off up Lim Chu Kang Road. There was a bus-stop, but Kate didn't fancy the bus. She held out her thumb and waited to see what would happen. Perhaps the police would come and throw her in the hoosegow; think what a story *that* would make, back in Clapham! Maybe some Chinese playboy, bored with his current mistresses, would see her white face and say to himself, 'I'll have a bit of that.' Her skin tingled at the thought. But what if some soldiers picked her up, raped her and then dumped her unclothed corpse in some bushes? For a second her hand drooped. Then she marched on, still singing, thumb still held high. This was Singapore; nothing exciting ever happened here.

What actually happened was that a nice, elderly Malay gentleman driving a Nissan Bluebird pulled into the side so that his wife could wind down the window and ask, 'Where are you going, Miss?'

'North,' Kate said.

The woman turned back to her husband and muttered anxiously. He took off his spectacles, wiped them and

369

replaced them on the bridge of his nose, gazing across his wife at Kate. 'North?' he said uncertainly. 'We are going to Thong Hoe Village. Would that be of use to you?'

'Ta very much,' she said, and jumped in the back.

It was pleasantly cool in the car. Kate realized she'd been behaving like a complete cow. Poor Mum! She'd have a wander around, then go back to the hotel. Perhaps Alison was right to see Verity alone . . .

'You are from England,' the Malay gentleman asserted gravely.

'Yes.'

'Holidaying?'

'Sort of. Where did you say you were going?'

'Thong Hoe Village.'

'Is that near Malaysia?'

'It is quite near the Strait of Johor. But it is not possible to cross over from there, you must take the Causeway.'

Something stirred in Kate's memory. On the day her father got out of prison he had told her to read the trial papers, and since then she had read them countless times. The Strait of Johor. Sarin-something, now why did she suddenly think of that? Thong Hoe, thing moe . . .

'Do you know a place called the House of Orchids?' she asked.

The Malay couple shook their heads. 'Is it some kind of museum?' the wife hazarded.

'I suppose it could be, now. It used to be, well, just a house.'

'I have not heard of it,' the man said.

'At the end of an avenue. Quite near the Strait of Johor, that's what reminded me of it. Sarin Avenue. No, Sarin-something, only I can't think of the something.' Kate giggled.

'When did you hear of these places?' the man asked.

'Oh, this would have been a long time ago. Seventeen years, more.'

The woman tittered behind a politely placed hand. 'Nothing's the same,' she said. 'Not one leaf, one blade of grass.'

'I'll tell you what,' her husband said. 'Here is the Singapore Street Directory.' He reached into the glove-compartment and handed her a paperback book. 'Thong Hoe is on page two-eight-six, I do know that. Maybe it will show Sarin Avenue.'

Kate found Thong Hoe. And as her finger lighted upon it, her eye was inexorably drawn up the map by the word 'Avenue'. Sarimbun Avenue.

'Wow!' Kate crowed. 'Sarimbun, "m" for mother not "n" for normal.'

The woman took the book from her and regarded it doubtfully. 'But this is army land,' she said. 'Do be careful. They fire real bullets.' She handed the directory back to Kate with an anxious look. 'It's a training area.'

'Oh.' Kate sighed. 'Never mind, then.' But it would have been fun to recce the place, because she'd never seen a dead-letter drop before. That's what the prosecution had called the House of Orchids, the place where Dad had left his messages for The Other Side. Whoever they were. And the owner of the house was supposed to have passed them on.

They'd arrived in Thong Hoe; suddenly Kate didn't feel like walking any more. The car was so comfortable. 'I suppose you're not going back into town,' she blurted out. 'I mean, I could wait.'

But no, these people lived here. The man pointed out Sarimbun Avenue, a simple, unmarked track leading off the road into the countryside, and drove away. Kate waved until they'd turned the corner, then looked around. God, it was quiet here in the sticks. Capital letters Dumpsville. Still, since she was here she might as well take a look. The army could hardly pretend to think she was a threat.

She crossed the road and began to forge her way up

the red-dirt track. Ahead of her she could see a horizon bounded by trees and dense shrub, with the occasional palm to remind her she was in Asia. All that tall grass and lush vegetation: what was lurking behind it? Were there still tigers here? Kate didn't know, but she pushed on anyway.

She passed the SAFTI signs without giving them a thought. A jeep crossed the track up ahead, but no one showed any interest in her. After what felt like bloody miles, the tamped red earth degenerated to a path. She came to a clearing, with no obvious exit save the way she'd come. Kate rested against a tree, exhausted. What a waste of time!

She heard a noise behind her, something pushing its way through the grass, and quickly stood upright. *Were* there still tigers here?

The noise grew louder. Time to go, lady. She got as far as turning back the way she'd come before a hand closed around her wrist, and she screamed.

*

Jay had kept on the move, shuttling daily between Singapore and Johor Bahru, the town on the Malaysian side of the Causeway. Sometimes he took the bus or the commuter-train, and showed his passport; but there were sleazier ways of crossing the Strait, where money talked with its usual cogency.

He lived on tobacco, the strong Malay black coffee known as *copi*, and his finger-nails, never sure whom he feared most – Singapore's hangman or the former colleagues who had appointed Cover to be their representative, his Nemesis. He knew it was crazy to come back to the House of Orchids but he did, constantly, haunting it like a 'hungry ghost' of Chinese folklore. No one had found the boy's body yet, and every day there would be less to find. He had been starting to feel safe.

So today he'd gone to the House of Orchids and made his inspection of the thing the ants loved. Last night on the phone Verity had arranged to meet him in town this afternoon, wouldn't say what it was about, but if he was going to keep the appointment he'd have to leave now. He pushed his way into the clearing on the first stage of his journey back to Thong Hoe, and there she was, this beautiful, sulky teenage girl with an angry pout and the most assertive breasts he'd seen in years.

He didn't know why he grabbed her. Stupid thing to do. She wheeled around. He terrified her, he could see that, and for a second he couldn't think why. Then he got a glimpse of himself through her eyes and understood. He must have seemed like a rough type: Western, jeans, a dirty shirt, older. Really old, like fifty.

The girl tugged her hand free and retreated a step. 'Do you always come up behind people like that?' she demanded, fiercely enough to show how afraid she was.

'Only when they're acting strange,' Jay retorted. He looked her up and down while he waited for his heart to steady. Too much caffeine, too many cigarettes: the combination of poisons had left him groggy. Sometimes he felt he was floating away, out of his own body. 'Who are you?' he said.

'Madonna,' she spat out. 'And you're Sean Penn, right? Who are you, come to that?'

There was something about her eyes, odd and yet familiar. They burned like chips of coal, and when she narrowed them she became dangerous as an alley-cat is dangerous . . . as her question was dangerous. *Who am I?* What sort of person comes out into the Singaporean countryside? Tell her you're a botanist. No! You know nothing about plants, but what if *she* does?

The girl was already turning away. 'Don't go,' he cried.

He had to keep her here at any cost, prevent her from

373

alerting others to his presence . . . *Any cost? Like with that Chinese boy, you mean?*

'My name's Jay,' he called weakly after her. 'I'm . . . I'm a journalist.'

He didn't know the first thing about journalism but it was enough to stop the girl. She turned around and said, 'Why are you here?'

'I have a story to write,' he lied, his voice coming out in a stutter. 'About a house that once stood here.'

Her flickering eyes became still and glass-like. 'The House of Orchids,' she breathed.

She knew, she knew, *she knew*! And he'd thought he was being so damn clever . . . 'You've heard of it?'

She nodded. And then – 'What's the House of Orchids to you?' she demanded to know, with something of the old fire.

'I . . . I want to write up the story of a man who was tried for murder.'

She'd turned pale. Her mouth moved. Jay hadn't learned lip-reading, but you didn't need expertise to understand that she was trying to say, My father.

'Your father?' And when her eyes lowered he took a few steps forward, until he was close enough to lay his hands on her shoulders. 'You . . . you're her daughter.'

She looked up at that, vulnerable, puzzled, just a teenager with an attitude problem and wonderful breasts . . . Jay struggled for control. He removed his hands from her shoulders. He said, 'You're Alison's child.'

'You know my mother?' Silence. 'You talk as though you know her.'

'I used to. Years ago, she was working in a hotel . . . The Prince.'

Her face lit up. 'Yeah, right. Did you know my dad? Did you?'

She was wide-eyed and eager now. Jay shook his head. 'No.'

Suddenly he knew where he had seen that look, those eyes before. Jay took a deep, shuddery breath and the jungle penetrated his nostrils, so like the smell a woman exudes when on heat. He turned away, unable to bear her eyes on his any more. After a bit he said, 'What's your name?'

'Kate.'

'Your mother,' he said. 'Alison.' *What joy to speak that name again!* 'Where is she? I mean . . . right now.' An inarticulate pause. 'Today.'

He saw at once from Kate's face that he'd stumbled.

'What's your newspaper?' she asked.

'You won't have heard of it.'

'Tell me anyway.'

He delved into his memory, made a stab. 'The *Lancaster Chronicle*. Upper New York State.'

'Got a press card?'

'In my hotel.'

'Which hotel?'

'Holiday Inn. Johor Bahru, over on the Malaysian side.'

Convenient, her face said, how very convenient.

'What are you writing?'

'The story of the way they faked your father's trial.'

Retrieval. No, better than that — *bull's-eye.*

Kate swallowed. He heard the clicking in her throat. 'Yes?' she muttered.

'He was framed. People were dealing in chemical weapons, they had to have a fall guy. They chose your father, he was nearest.'

'What's your interest in all this?'

'We were friends, your mother and I. I never forgot the tragedy in her face, that time. I went back to the States. Then last autumn we started to hear talk about a war with Saddam Hussein. An old buddy of mine is with our government. He told me a few strange things about where Iraq bought her chemical weapons. I got interested when he mentioned a company called Occydor, 'cause I remembered it had been set up by ex-Harchem staff based in Singapore. And then I made the connection with your father, who was ex-Harchem too, and he'd been accused of selling secrets. The trail seemed to lead back here. So here I am.'

She weighed him through those luminous, peril-filled eyes, and to Jay the time seemed long. Eventually she said, 'Did you find the House of Orchids?'

He shook his head. 'There's nothing left of it. Just scorpions and snakes.'

A muscle twitched in her cheek and he prayed he'd said enough to stop her from exploring deeper into the jungle. 'What brought you here?' he asked quickly. 'Curiosity?'

'Sort of. Look, are you really a journalist?'

'I surely am.'

'And you knew my mother?'

'Yes.'

'All right, then you'll remember where she lived in Singapore.'

She was testing him.

'Holland Village,' he replied uneasily.

'What car did she drive?'

'A green Ford, I forget the model.'

'She had a special name for the car . . .'

'Sarah Jane.'

Kate seemed to relax. 'Okay,' she said. 'My mother's here, in Singapore. She's looking for my father. He ran away to try and clear his name.'

Alison was in Singapore.

Jay realized the girl had fallen silent and was gazing at him expectantly. He should say something, but what if he said the wrong thing? Because he was within minutes and metres of happiness, but he could so easily screw up;

376

and if he did, he could never recover from that, no, not in a dozen lifetimes.

'I have information,' he said guardedly. 'You, your mother, you might be interested to hear it. I'd like to contact Iain, too.'

'Tell me!'

'Better if I wait until we're all together, your mother and us, then I won't have to go over everything twice, okay?'

She thought about this for a second or two, but to him it seemed more like an hour.

'Okay. Oh . . .'

'What?'

'I forgot; I don't know where she is. She's planning to meet someone today. A woman called Newland, she was at Dad's trial, have you come across her?'

Jay stared at Kate. His head was going round and round, he desperately needed support if he wasn't to fall over. 'Alison is going to see Verity Newland?' he croaked.

'She's trying to, yes. Why, what . . . ?'

'Oh, Jesus, come on.' He grabbed Kate's arm and started to hustle her down the track, blind to her anger. 'I have a date with Verity,' he said. 'In an hour's time. Your mother mustn't speak with her – understand?'

'Why not? Let *go.*'

'She's dangerous. She knows about your father, too. The truth, I mean.'

'What *is* the truth?'

'I'm due to meet with Verity myself, at Clifford Pier. We have to get there, fast.'

'*Tell me!*'

He paused, seeing from her face that unless he gave her something to hang on to she wouldn't help him, might not even lead him to Alison.

'Verity Newland framed your father,' he said shortly. 'Now *move!*'

# TWENTY-TWO

Alison found the Occydor group of companies listed in the phone-book, a dozen or more entries, all based at the OUB Centre. She asked the hotel porter for directions and walked to Raffles Place, trying to reorient herself in Singapore. It all looked so different. She remembered the Fullerton Building, of course, and the Bank of China: staid landmarks on a fluidly changing map. Raffles City, with its huge silvery skyscraper, was new. And Singapore itself was bigger now: they'd reclaimed lots of land along Eastern Parade, pushing back the very frontiers. There were more people, but fewer old buildings, and there were no longer any telegraph poles supporting serpentine tangles of overhead wires.

She came to Raffles Place, slightly repelled by its artificially jolly air of being a high-tech garden of remembrance where no one was ever buried, and she thought, It smells the same. *Gan dou-fu*, fried bean-curd, with its wonderful pungent aroma of chillis and garlic, and chokingly awful taste. Curry. The clean-city scent of disinfectant, Singapore's hallmark. Petrol fumes. And here also, the mildest possible taint of corruption arising from the river, stagnant and oily in the afternoon heat.

She had forgotten how much she loved it. All cities should be like this, she mused, as she crossed over to the OUB Centre: clean, inhabited only by immaculately turned-out people with happy faces and short hair. Singapore was an architect's impression of a perfect place that had somehow survived transition from misty artwork to reality.

Alison took the elevator up to the top floor but one.

378

She rose; her courage sank. Should she have made an appointment? No: Verity might not want to see her. As the doors slid open she heard voices at the far end of the lobby: one of them she knew.

'. . . And put him off until tomorrow afternoon. Three, no four. And Steven –'

'Yes, Miss Newland?'

'I – damn, what was I going to . . . you'd better come down.'

A 'ping' had just indicated the arrival of another lift. Alison stepped into the vestibule, took a deep breath and ran along in time to plunge through the doors of Verity's lift as they closed.

Her heart beat fast. There were several other people in the car, but for the first few moments of the descent Alison dared look at nobody. After a while she regained enough courage to dart a glance at Verity, now deep in murmured conversation with a young Chinese, evidently the Steven she'd been talking to earlier.

Alison's glance turned into a gape. God, how she'd changed! Plumper, older . . . She must be nearly fifty, but looked a good ten years beyond that. Her mouth was shaped like a staple: lips straight, the corners turned sharply down, ready to puncture and hole. Alison had seen such women at her Earl's Court hotel, coming in with the salesmen after a hard day at the exhibition centre for spirits and fags in the basement bar, as a prelude to six-packs and shags upstairs.

This was not how Verity used to look. Back in the seventies she'd possessed a certain lean grandeur. All except that one, terrible time . . .

The lift arrived at ground level. In the lunchtime crush it was easy for Alison to follow Verity across the banking hall without being observed. At the main doors the two of them parted. Verity stepped out into the glare, donning sunglasses. Alison followed.

Her quarry set off across the plaza, shoulders hunched. Change Alley . . . Alison quickened her pace, for that would be a good place to accost Verity in the throng without drawing attention to herself.

Once before, just once, she had seen Verity looking as she looked now – harassed. Even in those far-off days Alison might have relished the sight; would have done, in fact, were it not for the circumstances. But as she pushed on, willing herself to ignore the heat, the noise, the crush of bodies, those circumstances leapt out of her memory with the pernicious skill of a prowler who stalks, and plays, and lets his victim sigh with relief in the second before he kills; and she knew that by accosting Verity Newland she must at last face what had happened that dreadful night in London, the night of Gerry's murder.

\*       \*       \*

Alison and Iain were staying halfway up the Hilton; if she craned her neck she could see the beginning of Hyde Park and all of Park Lane, but she spent as little time as possible in their room. With Iain at Harchem's head office most of the day, she felt a need to go out. It was early January, only just 1973, and cold, but Alison didn't care. Before the year was over she would have given birth to a child, Iain would have a new job; Singapore – and Jay – would be bitter-sweet scrapbook memories. So she walked in the park beside the Serpentine, and did the sales: Harrods, Harvey Nichols, Liberty's. She didn't need to buy, looking was enough. She would talk to the baby inside her stomach, sharing life with this new part of her, and wonder at the glory of it all.

They were here for Harchem's first ever global sales conference. Executives had come from the States, Europe, Asia, all over. Originally Iain hadn't been invited, but after Reynolds had been in England for the best part of a week he'd sent an urgent summons. Something's in the wind, he'd told Iain, something too big to talk about on the phone. Get over here. Oh, and if you bring Alison, tell her to pack for the North Pole!

Wives could not travel at the company's expense, and few husbands were prepared to cough up. Daphne Reynolds herself stayed at home, thus setting an example that most were happy to follow. Alison pestered Iain, however, until he agreed to take her. Not that he needed much persuading: like so many little boys who'd never quite grown up, he hated sleeping alone.

On the plane he'd said something that left her breathless: he was ready for a change. Too many Sundays spent in the plant at Sudong with Verity the Viper for malignant company, too few hours' sleep a night, the perpetual need for circumspection in a suffocatingly small republic that monitored its denizens closely ... these things could be endured for a year or so, but did not constitute a life.

Once Alison had recovered from the shock she convinced herself that this was an incredible stroke of luck and she was happy. She encouraged Iain to ring round the headhunters while he was in England. Like someone recovering from cancer, she marvelled at being given her life back. Was love-sickness curable? Yes! Walking the damp streets of London, she *knew* it was.

Iain's desire for a move had sharpened once they arrived in London. There was really nothing for him to do. Gerry Reynolds hinted that he needed to spend time with Iain alone, but Reynolds was tied up, day and night. He's worried, Iain told Alison; worried and depressed about something, but he won't tell me what.

On day three of their visit Reynolds had telephoned very late to propose dinner the following evening. Just Iain, not Alison. Iain showed up at the restaurant;

Reynolds didn't. After an hour, Iain left. Next day Reynolds came to the regional seminar looking haggard. During a break he drew Iain to one side and apologized. He suggested another meeting, this time at the apartment where he was staying.

A friend, holidaying in Morocco, had lent Gerry his flat in Whitehall Court, overlooking the Embankment. More out of the way, Reynolds said, but without going on to explain why he needed to be out of the way. Come at five on Thursday. No, better make that Saturday. But we're leaving on Friday, Iain had protested. Change the flights. Come at *four* on Saturday.

On Friday morning, Alison had taken two phone calls in their hotel room, both from executive recruitment agencies. Interest in Iain was building. She went downstairs feeling happy, even irresponsible enough to go out and buy an expensive dress. But as she was crossing the lobby she happened to see the concierge's sign: two seats for the Royal Opera House that evening. *Yes!* Somehow in her heart she knew that soon they'd be celebrating, so why not anticipate?

'What about Reynolds?' Iain said, when she phoned him with the good news.

'What about him?'

'I'm seeing him at four.'

'That's *tomorrow*, darling.'

'No, he changed it again. I haven't had a moment or I'd have told you earlier. I'm going at five this evening.'

'*Damn!*' She thought quickly. 'No, it's all right: bags of time. Curtain-up's not until seven thirty.'

'I still say it's cutting it a bit fine. Suppose the meeting drags on?'

'Don't let it.' There was a silence which she broke by asking, 'What's wrong?'

'It's Gerry. This morning I told him I'm going and he's furious. He says he won't release me from my contract.'

'*What?* But he can't do that.'

'He's going to fight me all the way. Look, about tonight: we'll meet at Covent Garden, and you leave my ticket at the box office in case I come late.'

'Oh, darling, *please* . . .'

But another phone was ringing off the hook, he had to go.

Alison felt crushed. How could Gerry be so vile? Suddenly the day that had begun so brightly seemed grey and miserable. She couldn't think of anything to do. In the end she walked to Selfridge's, where she bought herself that expensive dress, and a coat. She wasn't going to need the coat in Singapore, but that was another reason for buying it, a kind of good-luck charm that Iain would defeat Gerry and win his release. She had a sandwich and a hot chocolate in the cafeteria, before crawling back through the park for a bath and a lie-down. She hadn't meant to sleep, but she did; and she dreamed of Jay.

He was standing in the garden of her parents' house in Singapore, shouting over the fence at somebody she couldn't see. At first this amused her, but then it became wearing and she told him to stop. When he wouldn't, she went over to him, and he began to shout at her. He was angry because she had lied to him, that day of the storm when he'd beaten her and taken her like some seaman's whore. She'd told him she was pregnant, when she wasn't.

Alison woke up then, feeling terrible. It was lonely in bed, and the room-temperature had dropped dramatically. Outside, darkness had already fallen over London. She pulled the covers over her head, but the awful feeling wouldn't go away.

She *had* lied to Jay. Why? Because she'd foolishly imagined it would help both of them make the break. But then she had to go and tell him she'd get a divorce from Iain. She'd meant it, at the time. Afterwards, they'd made clandestine plans, she'd got as far as consulting a lawyer, who had warned her of what lay ahead. She thought she could face it. But one day she'd written to Jay saying it was over, there was nothing to resurrect, he must forget her. And why had she done that? Because by then she'd discovered she really was pregnant, and the child was Iain's. The lie she'd told Jay had become truth.

But now, lying on her bed in the Hilton, Alison knew that she still loved Jay and was always going to love him; that all this nonsense about new jobs and fresh starts was just that: nonsense.

She got out of bed and went to sit at her dressing-table, feeling sick. She was going to have to get a divorce, after all. Oh this is ridiculous, ridiculous! You've been putting it behind you, you're going to begin over with Iain, move to another country . . . what is wrong with you?

Her reflection had no answer to give, not even when she said, out loud, 'You're going to have a baby, have you thought about that? What would Iain say if you tried to take his child away from him?' She burst into tears. She couldn't stop. She rested her head on her arms and wailed.

Once she'd cried herself out, she became half-practical again. It was getting late. A quick shower, that's what she needed, and a slow drink. There's always tomorrow. Get through this evening. Sleep on it. Think again in the morning, but give it a rest now.

Why did Gerry have to be so cruel? Now, more than ever, she needed to escape from Singapore . . . from Harchem. From Jay.

She struggled into her new dress, decided she hated it, but wore it anyway. At least the coat was a good buy. Somehow she'd made up time, and was too early for Covent Garden. She consulted her A to Z of London. Now here's something interesting, girl: if you were to walk to the Opera House you could almost pass by Whitehall Court. But it's a long way. Well, you have a long time to wait. But it's cold. Stay here, in the warm, drink yourself silly . . .

Alison thumped the dressing-table. Her stomach felt awful, she had a headache, alcohol was the last thing she needed. She held a palm to her forehead. She was starting a fever. Not used to the winter weather . . .

She would go to Whitehall Court and argue with Reynolds until he capitulated. She didn't care what she had to do, she wouldn't leave his flat before he'd allowed Iain to quit Harchem.

Alison put on her coat and went out into the cold.

There was a brisk wind at her back that night; it blew her along the pavement, needling in through what had seemed like thick clothes when she put them on. She wondered if Gerry Reynolds would mind her coming; he was Iain's boss, mustn't offend him. Then she thought, To hell with him, it's freezing out here, I'm not going to die for Gerry, and anyway, I mean to have one hell of a row with him. Then Jay came to her and would not go away. More tears pricked the backs of her eyelids, but she was resolute now, and ordered him out. He wouldn't go, though. Don't give me a hard time, she begged Jay; I've had more than enough. *Please!*

The further she walked, the more her hatred for Gerry grew. She'd never liked him, never! He was a swine, a bore, a cheap jerk who had no more business sense than a grocer's boy. She'd let him have it, she would!

It occurred to her, as she ploughed on through London's streets, that she had come to the end of her happiness and life stopped here. There was nothing to hope for, nothing to dread. She would have children and keep the homefire if not exactly burning then at least alight, like that awful dreary woman in *Brief Encounter*. Not Rachmaninov, however; she did laugh at that, too loudly, causing people to turn and stare. The Beach Boys, yes.

Whitehall Court struck her as the sort of pile where a Russian dissident might spend his first night in prison. There was a porter on duty in a cubbyhole beyond the heavy doors. When she asked for Mr Reynolds' flat he looked superciliously down his nose at her and pretended to consider the request, making her wonder what could be the matter with him. As she was about to knock on Gerry's front door it came home to her, hard: the man thought she was a tart. Her hand froze. She was wearing a new coat, an expensive dress underneath; this was, she instinctively knew, the sort of place where businessmen kept 'a little place in town'; she'd been branded a whore.

Well, *fuck* Gerry! All because of him, she'd been made to feel like a shoddy call-girl picked off the street . . . You bastard, she whispered to herself, I'm going to have you . . .

Jay came to stand between her and the knocker. He said, 'Well, aren't you a whore? Do nice married women like their stud's sperm sprayed all over their faces?' And she said, Yes.

Alison burst into a fit of sobbing. She could not stop. She leaned against the door and felt so stupid when it gave beneath her weight. How dreadful, she must stop crying, *somehow* she must find a way to stop before Gerry and Iain saw her.

She entered a dark, poky vestibule. Beyond that she could see a strange room. Such weird decorations, yellow walls streaked with red. Red that moved, she suddenly realized, this can't be right. She took a proper look, then, and saw that somebody had flung a pot of red paint at the walls; how careless, and what a funny smell. Of course, she knew it wasn't paint, but she wasn't going to acknowledge that, no, not yet . . .

Bit by bit the room came into focus. Gerry sat against

the far wall of what had once been a living room and now was a dying room. He had a look of surprise on his face: mouth open, eyebrows raised. The knife in his chest had already sunk down and sideways, like a spoon stuck into ice-cream.

A woman was standing beside the corpse. When she raised her haggard face Alison recognized Verity Newland. Verity stood there, distraught, breathing heavily. 'You!' she cried. And then her face dissolved into a trembly smile; 'Never mind,' she said, 'what's one more?' Her voice rose: 'Get rid of the bitch, do it, do it, *do it*!'

'No,' said a man's voice. Jay's.

\*     \*     \*

Alison leaned against a stall selling fake Benetton shorts. She felt sick. Ahead of her she could just make out Verity Newland arriving at the top of the stairs that would take her down to the Change Alley aerial walkway's harbourside exit. She must catch up. She drew in a deep breath and held it, letting it out slowly through her nose. Better. She walked on.

Yes, Verity looked unwell, but not as bad as on that night, eighteen years before, in Whitehall Court. Don't think about all that rubbish. Concentrate on now. Where's she off to, who's she going to meet? Come on, hurry!

Alison came out at street level in time to see Verity halt by the bus-stop, looking at her watch. Now, got you, Alison thought as she hurried on. I want a word with you, Miss Newland . . .

There were ten yards between them when suddenly Verity swivelled and from the way her shoulders straightened Alison knew she'd seen whoever she was expecting. Oh no, she muttered, *damn*!

But then a strange thing happened. Verity turned back

the way she had come and stalked away. She passed within inches of Alison but did not see her, did not see anyone: she was pale, her mouth moved soundlessly, she was gripping her bag hard enough to make the tendons rise along the back of her hand like steel cables.

Alison stared after her. What could have caused this transformation? She turned around and bumped into somebody. She was about to apologize when she realized who it was. For a moment the other person kept his eyes glued to Verity's departing back, but then he looked at Alison. Like two statues they stood there in the lancing sunlight, and it was not them at all, not separate people but a couple: lovers who had never been sundered, always one.

Jay reached out a hand, but shakily, as if unable to believe what he saw. He laid his palm against Alison's cheek. He stroked it. She gazed into his eyes. She saw the love, knew that it was mirrored in her own. She wanted to cry, and laugh, and shout for joy, and weep . . . and did nothing.

'Hello,' he said.

'Hello.'

'It's been a long time.'

'Yes.'

'Sorry.'

'Why?'

'Because I can't think.'

'Me too.'

There was a long silence.

Alison said, 'Are you talking to me?'

For a second he didn't get it, just for a second; but then his eyes flickered conspiratorially, right, left, right again. 'Do you know,' he whispered, 'I rather think I must be . . . don't you?'

She cried at that, with immense dignity, the tears rolling down her otherwise impassive face. At last she became aware of an insistent voice summoning her through the ether. She wished it would go away, but . . .

'*Mum!* I said, what *is* it? Are you deaf, or something?'

She awoke from the dream that was no dream. She glanced sideways and said, 'Oh, Kate, I didn't see you for a moment.' And then she did awake: 'What are *you* doing here?'

Kate stepped back. 'I could say the same thing about you,' she flared.

'I was trying to speak to Verity, I . . .' Alison turned on Jay a face full of confusion. 'Were you supposed to be meeting her?'

He nodded.

'*Mum!*'

Alison somehow suppressed the agitation Jay's nod had provoked. 'What?'

'Do you know this man? Is he straight up, or what?'

'I . . . know him. He's a . . . friend.'

'He says he's a journalist.'

Alison stared into Jay's eyes, trying to read what she was supposed to say.

'New set-up,' he mumbled. 'Got a job working on a paper.'

'Ah yes,' she improvised. 'I remember hearing, from . . . from somebody.'

'Mum, he says he's got info about Dad. Mum, are you listening?'

'Yes, of course I . . . yes. What information?'

'Look,' he said, 'is there somewhere we can talk?'

Alison thought, He doesn't mean talk. He wants to be alone with me, that's all. 'Our hotel, I suppose,' she said slowly.

They continued to stand in the same relative positions, staring at each other. Even when speaking to Kate, she continued to look at Jay, although she was vaguely aware

389

of her daughter's annoyance. Why was she annoyed? Oh, at being excluded – Kate always hated that.

'You can't take this man back to the hotel,' Kate exploded. 'You can't! I won't let you!'

'Kate, please listen . . .'

But still she could not tear her gaze away, not until it was too late. For when she did finally manage to parry the force streaming from Jay's eyes it was only to see Kate striding up the pavement towards Queen Elizabeth Walk without a backward glance.

# TWENTY-THREE

## THEIR NAME LIVETH FOR EVERMORE

Tony Cover stood at the foot of a shallow flight of steps, looking up at the inscription on the side of the severe white altar. This place impressed him. Kranji War Cemetery housed the remains of men from many nations, who had died in the South-East Asian theatre of operations during World War II. This being Singapore, everything looked immaculate. The cemetery was empty, except for two Malay gardeners wearing maroon overalls and pointed straw hats, and Tony Cover.

To his right was a well-tended lawn, slightly set apart by a low hedge. It housed two graves. One of them belonged to Enche Yusof bin Ishak, first president of the republic, the other to Benjamin Sheares, the second president. Cover had already examined them, finding the layout strange: how many presidents did Singapore intend to cater for in this field the size of a skating-rink?

But the more he looked around, the more he came to respect Newland's suggested venue. This was the place, all right.

In order to mount the steps leading up to the altar he had to pass between two square, brick constructions resembling sentry-boxes. They seemed neither ugly nor out of place in this, a war cemetery, serving rather as a reminder that all who rested here had given their blood in freedom's name.

As he came level with these two low buildings, Cover glanced sideways and saw something that interested him.

He approached the left-hand one. Set into a niche was a small metal door, rather like the door of a safe, but unlocked. He opened it, to reveal a cavity the size of a case of wine. Inside was a typewritten card: '*For administrative reasons, the Book of Remembrance has been temporarily removed. Persons desirous of locating a grave are requested to contact the Cemetery staff. Inconvenience regretted.*'

Cover closed the door, his face thoughtful. After a while he climbed on, skirting the white altar, and so came to the graves.

There were many of them, ranged up the side of a gently sloping hill, each a rectangle of white stone with a curved upper edge to soften the heart-rending impression of the spectacle. So many names, Cover mused as he walked on up the slope; so many dead, *pro patria mori* . . . The grass was short, even at the base of the stones, where the gardeners had planted many small bushes and flowering shrubs. He came to the top of the hill, standing between neat lawns alternating with beds and borders, and paused for breath. The afternoon mugginess, trapped beneath a low, soft-grey sky, was oppressive. Cover turned to find himself looking across the graves to the field where the presidents lay, beyond which were only trees. Truly, a place to rest in peace.

Behind him was the monument itself, and to this he now reluctantly turned – reluctantly, because if there was one thing to criticize in all of this beautiful place it had to be the monstrosity on top of the hill. Cover was a fan of the Vietnam War Memorial in Washington; for him, Maya Lin's design epitomized the meaning of the word nobility. Kranji's testimonial just mystified him.

Facing Cover now was a long, low construction of stone. It looked like a one-storey building that had had its front and back walls knocked out, leaving the partitions standing. All the divisions thus created, a dozen in number, were exactly the same. Towering above the central 'cell' was a conning-tower, the kind that might have graced a nuclear sub; and on top of that, to complete the illusion, was a cross that could easily have housed a periscope.

Cover looked at his watch. He'd been here over an hour but no one else had come to disturb the louring afternoon tranquillity. The two Malay gardeners continued their work, oblivious of him. At dusk they would close the gates, but the cemetery was bounded only by hedges, and hedges were penetrable. Through a clump of trees on his left he could just make out the red-tile roof of a bungalow, presumably where the supervisor lived. Would there be a patrol? Somehow Cover doubted it. Experience suggested that after about ten o'clock that red-tile roof would be sheltering a tired man nodding off in front of the TV while his wife did the washing-up.

He carried a Polaroid camera slung around his neck. Now he shot his way through two cartridges of film, covering the site from as many angles as possible. Only when he was sure he would be able to find his way around in darkness did he make his way down towards the exit.

As he passed between the two 'sentry-boxes' at the foot of the hill he paused, frowning at the heavy metal door just visible in its niche, and wondering what it was about it that intrigued him.

Then he understood. He looked around, keeping his movements casual and unhurried. The gardeners had moved on, up the slope; they had their backs to him. Cover hesitated, weighing the risks.

He went back to his car and opened the glove-compartment, locking the Polaroid inside along with the prints. For a moment he sat in the passenger seat, staring through the windshield and wondering if the ploy that had occurred to him was brilliant or outstandingly stupid.

One thing he knew for certain: Newland had been right to choose Kranji. And another thing he knew, too: he did not trust Verity Newland further than he could levitate.

That decided him. He got out of the car and set off back to the cemetery. This was consecrated ground, like a church, and, just as he would have done in church, he meant to leave an offering.

*

Verity passed through the outer office, vaguely aware of her staff clustered around the TV set, watching CNN. They hadn't expected her back so soon. Normally when she caught them out they panicked, but today they scarcely gave her a glance. She reached the haven of her private office like a thief claiming sanctuary and sank down in her chair. Things presented themselves to her through a blur of tears.

On impulse she snatched up the remote control and switched on her own TV. Footage of missiles and planes unreeled before her tired eyes. The producer cut to a correspondent standing in front of some palm trees. Baghdad.

The statistics of death were terrible. More shaky footage, the quality poor, as if photographed off a television screen: some government building went up in a pillar of smoke. Verity had not thought it would be like this. She'd allowed herself to be convinced by Saddam's rhetoric, reinforced by the terrible fire-power assembled north of Iraq's capital: the enhanced Scuds, the weapons-grade uranium, the super-guns, and the poisons . . . she had financed their purchase, she had bought them and sold them, and they were useless, useless.

As she pressed the 'Off' switch the phone rang, making her jump. Was it Jay calling . . . ? How could he turn up to their appointment with his tart in tow, such a slut, you could see it; scarcely out of school. *Oh, how could he do that?*

She picked up a pencil and pulled the diary towards her. She must reorganize her day, she must . . . the phone rang again. Perhaps it was news of Robinson Tang, perhaps it was Old Turtle, she must answer. She picked up the receiver. As she said 'Yes?' there came a sudden crack. Verity looked down and saw, somehow without surprise, that the pencil she'd been holding in her other hand had snapped.

'Yes?' she repeated.

'I have a call from a Mr Forward on one.'

'Put him through,' she whispered.

'Verity.' His voice sounded distant, quiet. 'What do you know about the House of Orchids?'

She'd been anticipating many things, never this. 'I . . . nothing. What do you mean?'

'Did you know there's some interesting remains on the site?'

She struggled to grasp his meaning. 'No. What kind of remains?' But the silence just went on and on. 'Iain, where are you?'

He laughed.

'Iain, I think you may be in some difficulty.'

'Oh yes?' He sounded bored.

'You remember what we were talking about the other day when we met? Your project here?'

'Naturally.'

'Well . . . there's a US dimension. There always was. And it's resurfaced, as I said it would. The man responsible.'

'Sampson, you mean?'

'Yes.' How easy treachery was, when it came to it. 'He owns the House of Orchids, and he's back, and he's the man you should talk to.'

'When would be a good time?'

'He's giving a supper party this evening, quite a small affair; I'm sure he won't mind if you join them.'

'Who else will be there?'

'Raj.' She waited for his reaction, but heard only silence at the other end. 'Is that convenient?'

'Where?'

'The best thing would be for us all to meet somewhere central. I know – Kranji War Cemetery. It's sort of mid-way for everyone.'

'That's a funny sort of –'

'Sorry, I've got an overseas call on another line. So shall we say eleven?'

He said nothing for a few seconds. She realized he didn't trust her and for a moment believed she had failed.

'Right,' Iain said; and the line went dead.

\*

Alison and Jay walked slowly back to her hotel. Singapore's skies had cleared; the sun beat down on their unprotected heads like the wild and hostile force it was, and they scarcely noticed. People swarmed around them on their way to Raffles City, or the Marina, but Alison and Jay did not notice the people any more than they felt the sun's rays.

'Where did you meet Kate?' she asked. Her voice sounded timid; she was afraid of the answer.

'At the house.'

'*What?*' But then, yes, it made sense. 'She ran away, we quarrelled . . . we'd gone to the cemetery, I wanted to see where my parents were buried.'

'That's quite close to the house.'

'Yes.'

'To where the house used to be.'

She looked at him. 'Gone?'

Jay nodded abruptly, once, letting her see his pain.

'She must have remembered reading about it,' Alison mused. 'The trial papers . . . she read them all.'

'She's a bright girl.'

'Mm. Difficult, too.' Alison managed a smile. 'What they call "her own person".'

'I saw. Alison . . .'

'Yes,' she whispered.

'What are you doing here?'

She thought: How funny; just then, a second ago, I felt sure he was going to say: Alison, I love you; I always have, I always will. And then she thought: Do I want him to say that? Truly? And *then* she thought: He's not interested in me any more.

'Looking for Iain,' she said. But no, don't monkey with the truth again. 'As soon as I heard you were coming here, I knew I had to come, too.'

They'd reached the hotel. With only momentary hesitation, she took him in. The desk-clerk looked like one of those humourless cadres you see in Associated Press pictures faxed from Beijing, standing in the background somewhere between Deng Xiaoping and a foreign dignitary. His spectacle frames were black, heavy and square, matching his expression. When he saw the two of them enter he rose an inch from his chair, and nodded. Eighteen years before, Alison could not have brought herself to enter a hotel with anyone other than Iain. Now it meant nothing, nothing.

They climbed the stairs together. She let him into the room and went across to lower the blind. The light softened to a pale, dull cream. He sat on one of the twin beds. She did not know where to put herself, so she stood by the window, watching him.

'There's something I have to tell you,' she blurted out. 'I've been wanting to tell you for years, confession I suppose, something like that.'

He waited.

'I lied to you,' she said. 'When I told you I was pregnant that time. I wasn't. I just wanted to end it . . . us . . . that's all. And I'm sorry, truly sorry, it's haunted me ever since, so rotten, so . . . so *cheap*.'

He lowered his head. 'It doesn't matter,' he said. And then – 'I forgive you.'

She waited for the thing she dreaded, his question about Kate, but it never came. He seemed . . . what was the word? . . . *overwhelmed*.

'Does Iain think he can clear his name here?' he said at last.

'I don't know what he thinks. He promised me he was going to stay, settle down. But . . . something must have happened.' A frown creased her face. 'I've been trying to work out what it was. I can't.'

There was a silence. Then she said, 'I'm so worried about Kate.'

'She'll be all right.'

'You don't know her.' She manufactured a smile, gold spun from less than straw, and said, 'What are you doing here, anyway?'

He grunted an unfunny laugh. 'Fleeing.'

'From?'

'Them. Me. Mostly me.'

'Still the same old Jay, then,' she said, looking away. He did not answer. After a while they both began to speak at the same time, both fell silent.

'You got my letter?' he asked.

'Yes.'

'You never replied.'

Alison shrugged. 'What was there to say?'

'That you loved me. Still. For ever.'

'Oh, Jay . . .' She looked down. 'Nothing's for ever.'

'We are.'

She raised her head and said, with a hint of a smile, 'How many others have there been, since me?'

'One. Sal. The woman I married.'

Alison said nothing.

'It wasn't love, if that's what you're thinking. It was . . . convenient. A shelter from the cold.' He paused. 'She died last fall.'

'I'm sorry.'

She saw the flicker of pain in his eyes.

'I love you, Alison, only you. No. Don't look at the floor, look at me. Come here.'

Like a woman in a trance she obeyed. When she was inches away from him he slowly raised his arms and put them around her waist, burying his head in her skirt. She felt his hands clench over her buttocks and something jangled inside her. She stroked his hair, the back of his neck, his shoulders. Slowly, very slowly, she lowered her head, until their lips could meet.

They stayed in that awkward position for ages, while the tiger of desire circled around them, biding its time. She felt, as she had never felt when they were together, that he needed her comfort: an extraordinary change. She wanted to give him comfort. She wanted to satisfy him in every possible way, because then she too could be satisfied.

He lowered his hands to the hem of her skirt and gently began to raise it. She squeezed his head and laughed. All around she could see only unbroken jungle. The tiger had fled.

She did not push his hands away. Instead she cupped his chin in her hands and lifted it, so that he could see her tender smile. She kissed him again. It was friendly, warm, void of passion: the best kiss she'd ever take from him. And the last.

When she pulled away he tried to hold her close, but she sensed the uncertainty in him, the weakness, and found it easy to disengage.

'I want you,' he murmured.

'And I you.'

'Then let's –'

'No.'

'But *why*?'

She held his hands, gave them a squeeze, and said, 'I love Iain.'

'No. You never did.'

She shook her head, breaking into a smile. 'You haven't been through what I've been through these last eighteen years.'

'I've been through it, too.'

She shook her head again, and because this time her eyes were half-closed she looked beatific. 'I loved you,' she said simply. 'Once.'

Then, suddenly, it was all too much to bear. She turned her back on him and walked out of the room. He could never know how much that cost her, or how she was doing it for him, only for him, so that he might go on. She walked away from Jay for the second time, ended her life for the second time. It was not fair, being asked to do this twice.

She walked for a long time, seeing nothing, hearing nothing. She had no sense of time. Eventually, however, she realized that the afternoon had imperceptibly shaded into twilight. She came to herself a little, then: enough to recognize her surroundings, the Shaw Tower, she could find her way back from there. The Shaw Tower, which had still been under construction the day she last left Singapore, thinking it was for ever. Yes.

She crawled back to the Lido to find the bedroom empty. She did not know how long ago their encounter had taken place. It might have been a few hours, or days, or reincarnations ago. She lay on the bed, sipping water, and her mind felt like a slate wiped clean.

When someone knocked on the door she did not hear, at first. The knocking repeated itself, louder this time.

400

Alison thought: that must be Kate. My daughter, Kate; I must let her in. She managed to get up. She went to the door and opened it.

Martin Heaney was outside, leaning against the wall, hands in pockets. He said something to her but she did not hear it. She was navigating on autopilot and her autopilot was wonky. She wanted to cry, and could not. She swayed. He reached out to catch her. He got her into the room and supported her over to the bed. He refilled her cup of water.

'What have you been up to?' he said as he sat on the bed. 'It's too hot to go running around for the hell of it.' He chafed her hands gently, and she let him. 'You should know that.'

Yes, she should. She ought to have let Jay stay in this room, this sordid little room, as he'd wanted. They could have lain on the bed and made love. They would have been young again, and beautiful. They would not have seen each other as they really were, but as they remembered themselves. It would have solved everything; alternatively, made things ten times worse. One or the other.

But, oh, it would have been sublime.

'Martin,' she whispered at last. 'I don't know what to do. I thought I'd find him. I thought I could set everything right. But I've lost him. I've lost Kate, Jay, everyone.' Her face squeezed itself into a ferocious mask, her cheeks turned red; tears flooded down her cheeks. 'Oh, Martin . . .'

He put the cup of water on the floor and held her tight until the storm had blown itself out. She cried almost silently, holding everything inside. He waited until dusk was falling and he had no more time; even then, he gave her precious minutes more. But at last he raised her gently and he said, 'Alison . . . you've got to help me. Then maybe I can help you.'

She looked at him through red eyes, and he smiled. 'Last time I tried to help you was in Clapham, remember? I wanted to take you away somewhere safe, my dear — oh yes, that was the truth I told, at the end. It didn't work out too well, did it?'

She wiped her eyes, even managed a wan smile. 'I'm sorry about . . . what we did,' she whispered.

Martin grunted. 'Just a headache,' he said. 'Whoever hit me wasn't very scientific.'

'No, he . . . he isn't. Not very.'

'Alison, I'm not allowed to ask the police for assistance. I don't know where Iain is. Newland's been helpful, but only up to a point. She's frightened. She's playing games with me; not only with me, I'm afraid. There are wolves in this forest, you know. Big, bad wolves. We need to get to Iain very fast.'

Her eyes slowly focused. 'He's in danger?'

Martin nodded. 'He got out of prison at the worst possible time. He's a bomb waiting to go off, is Iain. And he's coming out of the woodwork tonight.'

She sat up. 'Tonight?'

'Yes.'

'How do you know? Where? What time is he —?'

'He's been looking for a man called Raj. An Indian scientist, you'll remember him.'

'His name, I remember his name . . . Harchem's head of research and development?'

'Right. Verity Newland's told Iain he can meet Raj tonight. She's doing it to flush him out; Raj won't be there, of course, she's got him walled up in Sudong. So Iain's been told to be at Kranji War Cemetery, at eleven o'clock.'

'How do you know?'

'Newland rang to tell me.' He paused. 'She thinks I'm here to kill Iain.'

'And are you?'

'No.'

'Why are you here?'

'Officially, to head Iain off. Make him go home quietly and not make waves.'

'And unofficially?'

'Because I'm tired of not meeting my own eyes in the mirror. I know pretty much what happened back in nineteen seventy-three. Iain's innocent; take it from me.'

'I don't have to. I've always known.'

'And he's dead right about one thing: all the proof is here, in Singapore.'

She stared at him, not sure whether to believe. 'What's Verity getting out of all this?' she asked.

'Safety, she hopes. Protection.'

'From what?'

'If, when, Iraq loses the war, there are going to be some post-mortems about where Saddam got his arms from. She was in it from the start. If the papers get hold of it she stands to lose everything. So she's cooperating – at least, on the surface. But Iain mustn't go anywhere near Kranji Cemetery tonight, because it's a trap. So tell me, Alison, and I've come to ask you for the last time: can you think of anywhere Iain might be?' He shook her gently by the shoulders. 'Anywhere.'

Alison looked down at her hands, clasped in her lap. 'No,' she answered in a low voice.

'Could he be with Verity?'

'He could find her office easily enough. And . . . where does she live?'

'Fernhill Close. Does that mean anything to you?'

She shook her head.

Heaney paced restlessly up and down, lost in thought. When neither of them had spoken for a while, Alison said, 'I'm worried about Kate. I'd forgotten all about her. It's so late now . . . where is she?'

Martin stopped pacing. 'Does she know where Verity lives?'

Alison stared at him. 'What? Why do you . . . ?'

Martin wanted so much to comfort her, but . . . 'I have to go,' he said.

'Yes.'

'Wait for me. Keep the door on the chain.'

'I will.'

She listened to Martin's feet padding down the uncarpeted corridor. She thought back over what he had said and suddenly she knew where Kate was, knew she had to get to her daughter right away, now, before it was too late.

# TWENTY-FOUR

During the early evening a depression drifted south-east across Malaysia, bringing storm-force rain and a dramatic drop in temperature. By ten o'clock it had passed on to Indonesia, leaving Singapore dripping and pleasantly cool.

Jay stood in the shadow of a tree beside the highway, checking for the last time that no one had followed him. He waited until a solitary pair of headlights had vanished around the corner and struck off up the narrow road signed 'Kranji War Cemetery'.

For the first few minutes he moved fast, anxious to gain the security of shadow, but once he'd left the lights of Woodlands Road behind him he slowed down. Speed equalled noise. As he walked up the road, letting his eyes accustom themselves to the darkness, he tried yet again to justify this folly. He was here because Verity Newland had set up the rendezvous as a fallback, three days ago, and thanks to Alison he'd missed their appointment this afternoon. He had no choice but to be here. Yet he knew with as much certainty as he knew his own name that he was walking into a trap.

So why come?

I come, my friend, because a loser like me has no other shots to call.

After five minutes his eyes had acclimatized enough for him to deviate off the road, where the shadows were deeper. Suddenly he stopped and raised his head. Not far away, a dog had whined with excitement. Jay listened. A yelp, another eager whine. Over . . . *there*. He swivelled

405

right. In, or near, the cemetery. He waited silently for a few minutes. There was no more noise. Push on.

He walked slowly now, anxious to do nothing that might disturb the dog. Anyway, moving slowly made it easier to navigate. In his pocket he had a small torch, bought that afternoon to replace the one he'd lost on his first visit to the House of Orchids. Every so often he used it to check his position, but he was worried it might give him away. Fortunately his instincts and eyesight were both good.

The road was rising more steeply; ahead of him in the glare of spotlights he could see the cross on top of the monument. Jay rested for a few moments, trying to calm himself by concentrating on the imminent negotiation. His terms: no prosecution; one hundred thousand US dollars in cash; acknowledgement that he'd keep evidence of Western complicity in the arming of Iraq until after his death, when it would be destroyed.

It wasn't worth that much, what he had to sell. Immunity, yes; a small pay-off to stop him talking about how Pentagon observers had flown in the Iraqi planes when they sprayed Iraqi Kurds with lethal gas. He could name the officers and their units, he even had photographs of them sitting with Saddam Hussein over Scotch and dry ginger. He'd brokered the deal personally, using Occydor as one supplier; the photographs belonged to him because he had taken them himself. It would be worth a little effort on the part of the State Department to stem that dam, plug that leak.

In his heart, Jay knew that his was a story that would one day come out by itself. His silence had a value, yes; rank above rubies it did not.

He started up the hill again. Think of something else.

It worried him that he'd missed his appointment with Verity, earlier that afternoon. She'd said it was important. If only he hadn't run into Alison . . .

Be positive. He would get Alison back. She was his, she loved him, he had seen that love blazing in her eyes. She'd said no and meant yes. She was here in Singapore because he had come to Singapore; also, she had come to find Iain, but Iain Forward didn't want to be found, so she'd be leaving with Jay Sampson.

The three of them would be leaving together. Alison, Jay, and . . . and the girl, Kate. No, don't go down those paths, my friend, not yet, that can wait.

He chanced another flash from the torch. Its beam showed him that he was almost at the cemetery gates.

He'd visited this place once during his Singapore days, when an Australian business contact had asked if he could help trace someone thought to be buried there. He'd had no luck, but he remembered coming here and it couldn't have changed that much. The main gates were shut. Off to his right somewhere was a kind of *padang*, where they buried their political hotshots. Maybe that was the rendezvous.

His skin turned cold. He hadn't thought to ask Verity to be more precise; the War Cemetery, she'd said, and he'd just assumed that there would be someone here to meet him. *Suppose this wasn't the place at all.*

He'd reached the parking lot just beneath the gates. Not a single car was to be seen. Jay turned through a full circle. No one.

He glanced up through the gates. For a second he couldn't grasp what he saw. Then he realized someone was standing in front of the altar, a tall shadow in the reflected glare of the spots that illuminated the monument. As Jay shrank back the figure moved to his left, disappearing into the darkness.

Jay retreated silently. *This is silly*, he told himself; *you came here to meet a guy, there he is, go to him.* But he needed more time, needed a tighter grip on himself. So he kept

407

right on moving, away from the cemetery, until he was almost at the parking lot again. There he stopped, and considered.

His heart was beating fast, his mouth was dry; go on, face it, *you are scared*. He took half a dozen deep breaths, holding each one down in the nethermost reaches of his lungs, exhaling slowly to a count of six. He lectured himself. You have come a long way for this, thousands of miles, across continents; you've killed for this moment, God help you. *Yet you are here!*

Next step. Get inside the cemetery.

Jay struck off to the right. With the help of his torch he found the field he'd remembered from his first visit. He skirted it cautiously, making for the hedge that separated this area from the cemetery proper. The hedge was thin, threadbare in places; he forced a way through without too much difficulty. He emerged on the other side, scratched and panting. The main gates lay at a lower level to his left, the monument was on his right. Which way?

The man he'd caught a glimpse of was by the altar. So go down to it.

Keeping the hedge on his left, Jay quietly began to make his way towards the altar. Cold sweat soaked his shirt, his skin. When his foot lodged in a root he whimpered and froze, praying no one had heard. He crept on.

Ahead of him loomed a square building, some kind of gatehouse, with its twin on the far side of the entrance. The altar stood empty under the light. Jay squeezed his eyes shut and opened them again. Had he imagined that figure?

No. Impossible. Be careful . . . but keep going.

He reached the square edifice and rested one hand against the stone. It was sticky; he jerked his hand away. He took another step forward, into the light. A voice from

408

the shadows said, 'You're early, Sampson. Stop right there and hands on your head.'

*

Iain had left himself plenty of time to arrive at the rendez-vous before the other participants; he was in no hurry. Kranji possessed its own parking lot but Iain didn't intend to risk leaving his car there: too obvious. As soon as he saw the sign to the cemetery he pulled on to the verge of Woodlands Road and got out. There was nothing coming either way. He darted across.

The easiest route was along the side-road that led to the cemetery, but he avoided it. Other people were expected tonight and Iain saw no point in attracting their atten-tion. He hugged the open grassland until he reached the hedge demarcating the presidents' burial ground. Iain knew where he was, because as soon as he'd finished his phone call to Verity that afternoon he'd come on a recce. He also knew where to find gaps in the hedge. Before long he was inside the cemetery.

He didn't like this place.

Nothing to do with so many corpses beneath his feet; Iain wasn't superstitious. What haunted him was fear of exposure. The main entrance provided lots of cover, and up at the memorial building a man could always put a wall or the crown of the hill between him and his enemy. Too much middle ground, that was the trouble. The graves were on a slope between the memorial and the entrance gates, and their stones were only a couple of feet high, so unless you lay down flat behind them you were going to be visible in the spotlights.

Iain found a big-boled tree and rested against it. Except up by the memorial itself there was plenty of darkness. He'd have preferred a few more of those good thick walls that made up the memorial building, though; walls stopped bullets, darkness didn't.

Keeping to the shadows by the hedge he climbed up a level or two, the graves on his left. Once he heard a noise. He dropped to a crouch and listened. Apart from a lazy cicada somewhere nearby, nothing more sinister disturbed the stillness of the night.

He advanced slowly, relying on touch to keep out of trouble, but the going was hard. Every minute or so he sank down and flicked his disposable cigarette-lighter into life, but it dissolved only a small patch of black around him. The choice lay between brilliant radiance at the memorial on its hilltop, pitch darkness around the graves, and lesser illumination by the front gates below.

A dog barked. Panic twittered in the pit of his stomach. Iain dropped on one knee. Three feet away, no more, light from the memorial lost its power, giving way to dense shadow. He was safe, but only just. The dog whined, barked again; he could hear it scratching against something hard.

There was a caretaker's house tucked away, he remembered it from his afternoon reconnaissance. A caretaker, a dog: logical. Iain held his breath. The dog whined excitedly one last time and fell silent.

Iain knelt down and rested his hands on his thighs. He was breathing badly; *get a grip on yourself*. As his heartbeat slowed back to normal, other night sounds filtered through to reassure him: something rustled in the long grass, a bird squawked and fell silent, everywhere the drip-drip-drip of water from trees.

He gave the caretaker's house a wide berth. Before long he'd reached the top of the hill and was running down the far side, away from the main gate, until he once again found himself under cover of darkness; only then did he circle back towards the entrance. Now the full expanse of graveyard lay between him and the hedge through which he'd entered. He kept going down. If there was to be action, he'd find it at the gates.

He was within a hundred feet of the nearest 'sentry-box', which is how he thought of the two square stone buildings that flanked the gates, when he heard a noise.

Iain shrank back deeper into the shadows, his eyes darting this way and that. Disembodied sounds were the devil to place. That bloody dog, whining again? No, similar but not the same. A kind of . . . squeak. Like a heavy iron gate with a rusty hinge. And yet from where he crouched he could see the gates, and they hadn't moved.

Iain cocked his head and strained to listen. But the sound wasn't repeated. What did that mean? An early arrival at the party. Not a careful one, though; not a *fearful* member of the band.

What to do – stop, or go on? He decided to go on, moving as quietly as the landscape would let him, because he'd got the advantage over whoever had just given away his presence by making a noise. But he felt uneasy now, and kept looking over his shoulder. Was the noise bait to lure him into a trap?

Iain drifted further to the right, away from the gates, away from the sentry-boxes. He sneaked a look at the luminous dial of his watch. A quarter to eleven: still fifteen minutes before the appointed time.

He glanced back at the altar and now there was a man standing there, motionless, his face concealed by shadows.

Iain ventured forward a few steps, knowing the darkness enshrouded him. Verity had said on the phone that Reg Raj was going to be here. He tried to marry this man's physique to what he could remember of Raj. It didn't fit. Reggie had been slight of build, thin, with hunched shoulders, and he was a nervous fidget: if deprived of a pack of patience cards, his substitute for worry-beads, he would be constantly shifting weight from one foot to the other, rubbing his leg, scratching an ear. This man was calm, stolid, altogether different.

411

Even as Iain strained to see him more clearly, the stranger moved. For a few seconds Iain had no idea where he'd gone. Then he heard soft footfalls, and knew that the stranger was approaching across the lawn.

Iain's heart stopped beating. The man must have seen him, was coming to make contact. *But it wasn't Raj!*

Verity's turned me in, he thought. Verity the Viper. You bitch.

Then the stranger passed in front of a light, just for an instant, but long enough to show Iain that he was still some fifty feet away and moving at a tangent. If he'd seen Iain, he gave no sign of it.

Iain waited until the figure was again enmeshed in darkness and slipped away, up the hill. He'd been right about one thing: the action was going to happen by the main entrance, at the gates. From where he was hiding he couldn't see them well. He had to position himself more centrally. That meant penetrating the forest of gravestones.

He edged back until he reckoned he was about a third of the way up the slope. A swift glance showed him that the area around the gates was empty; no sign of the stranger. Right. Chance it . . .

He dived for the nearest file of tombstones, coming to rest on his stomach behind them. Not a sound disturbed the stillness. Iain cautiously raised his head. Altar, sentry-boxes, gates, all visible, no human shapes anywhere.

He wriggled his way along the wet grass in a monkey-crawl, with tombstones to right and left. There were no raised graves as such, the sward was perfectly flat except for the upright steles, so it wasn't too difficult. Before long he was within striking distance of the central aisle that led up from the altar to the memorial itself. Iain risked another look down. Some eighty feet to the entrance, he judged. Not a sound, not a movement. *Where was the stranger?*

A movement caught his eye, but in an unexpected quarter. Somebody – not the stranger – was over by the left-hand sentry-box, the one furthest away from where the stranger had disappeared. Then this person stepped on to the outer fringes of light and Iain saw his face; in the same instant an American voice called, 'You're early, Sampson. Stop right there and hands on your head.'

A shadow excised itself from the right-hand sentry-box. The stranger! He approached the altar, holding out something – presumably a gun, because the man by the left-hand sentry-box, the man addressed as Sampson, raised his hands. When the stranger was a dozen feet away he said, 'Up the hill.'

Sampson slowly turned and began to ascend the central aisle between the graves, with the stranger behind him. Iain rolled as close as he could to the nearest row of stones and buried his face in his arms. Don't look up, your eyes might reflect light, that or your pale skin; *be still*.

But as Sampson drew level with the file of tombs one level down from where he was lying, Iain heard that same American voice say, 'Hold it. We have to collect your friend.' And then – 'On your feet, Forward. *Up.*'

*

Alison changed into clean clothes. She put on some make-up, wishing her eyes didn't look so dead, and tidied her hair. As she descended the stairs, all the arguments against what she was doing crowded into her mind. None of them counted, because ever since Martin had put the notion into her mind she'd known one thing with gut-certainty: Kate, perverse as ever, was making a beeline for Verity.

How to find her? was the question on the top of her brain as she stepped into the lobby. Martin had mentioned a Fern-hill Close. The desk-clerk would be able to help.

'Excuse me . . .'

The hatchet-faced cadre looked up from his newspaper.

'I wonder if you could help me find an address, please?'

'He already has,' a voice said behind her.

Alison turned to face Kate. 'I'm so glad to see you,' she said tonelessly. But then emotion overwhelmed her and she rushed forward to take the girl in her arms.

'I thought you'd gone to Verity's,' she said, through tears. 'All alone, I . . .'

'Stupid!' Kate's voice wasn't pleasant. 'Why think that?'

Alison shook her head, suddenly fed up with doing all her crying for Kate. 'Oh, forget it.'

'I got this Newland woman's address, Mr Chen gave it to me.'

'Mr Chen?'

Kate jerked her chin in the direction of the clerk.

'Oh.'

Kate showed her mother a slip of paper. 'It's not far. Let's go.'

Alison dabbed at her eyes with a handkerchief. 'I'll see her by myself,' she said. 'I've told you that already.'

'You can't. What if she's got minders, or something?'

Alison laughed. 'Don't be ridiculous. And if she had, would you be any good against a couple of . . . of Chinese Triads?'

'Darren's taught me how to handle myself.'

'Oh, Kate!'

'Look, I don't want an argument, I'm coming, see?'

'You're not.'

'I am so!' With that Kate snatched the paper back from her mother and ran down the steps to the street. For a few seconds Alison was too shocked to react. By the time she'd collected her wits enough to give chase, Kate was already climbing into a taxi.

Alison stood in the middle of the pavement holding

both hands to her face. The thing she'd feared most was happening, and all because of her own folly. 'No,' she whispered. *'Please . . .'*

*

Iain raised himself on to one knee, feeling stupid. Fuck the bastard, *fuck him!* Bad luck, that's all; you did your best. Now concentrate on surviving for long enough to find out what the hell's going on.

He stood up. 'Who are you?' he said.

'It doesn't matter. This gun is loaded; if you doubt me, try me.'

But Iain had no doubt. He looked to one side, where the third man still had his hands raised. 'Fancy meeting you here,' he said. 'You were with Verity Newland, up Thong Hoe way. The House of Orchids . . . Sampson. Jay Sampson. Yes?'

Before Jay could answer, the man with the gun said,'This isn't a Democratic Convention. Introductions are scarcely necessary. Move up the hill, both of you, and keep moving until I tell you to stop.'

Jay said, 'And what if I say no?'

'I'll shoot you here,' Cover said in a flat voice. 'It makes no odds.'

'You wouldn't dare.'

'Why?'

'I have everything lodged with my lawyers. You're too late, my friend – it's all documented, sworn to, sealed.'

'Ah, yes . . . your lawyers.' Cover recited the name of a firm, followed by an address in lower Manhattan. 'They've been relieved of one almighty responsibility, Jay. They're no longer keeping anything for you. Nor is Neil Robarts. Shouldn't have made that call from Toronto airport; we'd been listening to Neil's phone for a long time. Ever stop to wonder why it was so easy for you to get away from the States?'

Jay said nothing.

'Because we wanted you to make that call. If you'd done it a couple of hours earlier, you wouldn't be here. But you are here. So move up the hill.'

Iain could not see Jay's face through the gloom, but from the way the man's shoulders drooped, the way he hung his head, he knew that Cover held a fistful of trumps. He started to laugh. Jay Sampson looked at him as if he'd gone mad. The expression on Cover's face was more one of curiosity, mixed with mild irritation.

'Unbelievable,' Iain managed to say at last.

The gunman did not speak, but he cocked his head on one side, as if inviting an explanation.

'First I come,' Iain obliged. 'Then *you* come, friend. Then *he* comes. And now the other guy behind you . . . frankly, it looks exactly like a Democratic Convention to me.'

The gunman laughed politely, as if boy, was that a good one. He was still laughing when Martin Heaney leapt up from behind and knocked him flat.

*

Alison paid off the cab and walked to the forbidding steel gates that guarded Verity Newland's apartment block. There was an intercom; when the concierge answered, she gave her name and was admitted at once. The porter indicated the elevators with a smile, almost as if he was expecting her. On her way up to the penthouse, Alison had time to brood about that.

She had her explanation as soon as Verity opened the door. Beyond her, she could see Kate sitting on the edge of a white leather sofa, a glass in one hand and a cigarette in the other. Of course, somebody would have warned the concierge to expect a second mad Englishwoman. Verity, or even Kate herself. It would, Alison thought savagely as she stepped across the threshold, be just like her daughter to do that.

'Welcome,' Verity said. She put breathy emphasis on the first syllable, loading it with sarcasm. 'Alison, my dear, you haven't changed a bit.'

She was wearing an emerald green skirt beneath a tailored white silk blouse; her fingers glittered with precious stones, her eyes with malice. Alison looked at Verity, at the deep, powder-encaked canals on her face, and she would have liked to clean them out with a nail, a sharp, rusty nail.

'What has she said?' she asked Kate, moving quickly to sit down beside her. 'What's she told you?'

'That I'm pretty. Well, I knew that. That I'm like my father.'

Alison saw how Verity's lips twitched with amusement when she heard Kate say 'my father'. She also noted that Kate was already tipsy.

'She's like you, too,' Verity said. 'I didn't notice the resemblance this afternoon, but I see it now. No wonder Jay picked her up.'

'What have you given her?' Alison demanded, and Verity laughed.

'What I'm having,' she said. 'A G-and-T, a Dunhill. Where's the harm in that?'

'We're leaving, Kate.'

'No.'

'*Oh, for God's sake, Kate!*'

'I said no. She's interesting.' Kate took a sip from her glass, though her eyes never left Verity's face. She said, 'I want to hear about the old days.'

Verity glided over to the console by the window and pressed a switch. The curtains swished back to disclose half of Singapore spread out below like an Aladdin's Cave of twinkling, illicit treasures.

'The old days,' she said dreamily, turning back into the

417

vast room. 'What fun we had, then. But do tell me, Alison' – a gesture at Kate with the hand holding her cigarette left a wisp of smoke in the air, like an evil genie's trail – 'she does *know* Iain's not her father . . . ?'

# TWENTY-FIVE

'Right, gentlemen,' Martin Heaney said. 'Up, please. Nice to see you, Iain.'

Iain gawked at him. 'How the hell . . . ?'

'Verity Newland wants to swap info for immunity, so she told me about this jolly meeting, no doubt in the hope I'd polish you off and save sunshine here' – he prodded Cover's inert body with his toe – 'a lot of potentially embarrassing trouble. His name's Cover, she says.'

Cover groaned and twisted around on to his side. Martin pocketed his gun and knelt down to frisk him, standing up again with a Ruger pistol in his hand. 'On your feet; I'll take care of this for you.'

'And is he really Sampson?' Iain said, pointing at Jay.

'Also known as Sonja.'

Iain stared at Jay. '*You* wrote those damn letters?'

'I did.'

'But then . . . who was Johnny, who were you writing them to?'

A silence. Then Jay said, 'It's not important.'

'Did *you* kill Reynolds?' Iain asked him.

'No.'

'Who did?'

Cover chose that moment to rise on all fours, groggily shaking his head. Suddenly he vomited and the three men surrounding him stepped back. Heaney grasped his shoulder and dragged him to his feet. Cover brushed his hand away. Heaney retreated another few paces,

419

levelling his own pistol. 'Knock it off,' he said quietly. 'Or I'll knock off you.'

'Who killed Reynolds?' Iain asked, with increasing urgency. 'Tell me.'

'Save it,' Heaney snapped. 'We're going back to the car now, all of you in front of me: down to the main gates. Iain, you and Sampson take the lead; Cover next. Go.'

Iain and Jay set off. They skirted the altar to its right; Cover went left.

'Cover!' Heaney barked. 'Follow the others.'

But Cover kept walking. Suddenly he broke into a run. Heaney dropped to one knee, getting off his first shot as Cover disappeared into the shadow of the nearest sentry-box.

Next second, Iain heard a familiar noise: the squeak that had disturbed him during his earlier recce. An unoiled hinge, that was it! And then a metallic slam, the sounds a postman made when emptying a pillar box.

Heaney fired a second time. Another gun answered from the squat brick building where Cover had disappeared. *He was armed again!*

At the first sound of firing, Iain and Jay had flung themselves down behind the altar. Now Iain raised himself on his elbows and wriggled around until he was on Heaney's side of it, keeping the stone between himself and Cover. Heaney crouched in the light, exposed and vulnerable. Even as Iain got his first proper look at him, another shot split the darkness and Heaney grunted, clutching his shoulder. He rolled down the steps, cannoning into Iain; the two of them lay in the angle between the altar and the ground.

'Hurt bad?' Iain whispered.

'Graze. I'll live. Where did that gun come from?' Martin swore. 'He must be still groggy from the bang I gave him. He wouldn't have missed otherwise, I was in the light.' Martin lowered his head into his arm for a moment, wiping away the sweat. 'Got to get him out in the open.'

'Will anyone have heard the shot?'

'Bound to: there's a caretaker here. Police already on their way . . . *shit*.'

'Thank God.'

'No, Iain, not thank God. The Singapore police don't know I'm here. Unless we can finish this quickly, we'll all three be up for murder.'

Another shot rang out and instinctively the two men ducked.

'We've got to rush him, from three different directions.'

'You've got his other gun,' Iain said. 'Give it to me.'

Heaney hesitated only a second. He reached into his jacket pocket and handed over the Ruger P-85, setting the safety to off. 'Aim lower than you think, it'll jump. He'll have fiddled with the trigger pressure, so be careful – it may be on a hair.'

'What next?'

'You and Sampson, around the other side of the altar. When I whistle, go straight forward. Fire, keep firing, don't stop, *don't* drop the gun. Sampson sprints right, towards the road; I'll be circling left. I'll give you thirty seconds from now to brief Sampson and position your-selves. Okay?'

'Okay.' Iain shuffled backwards on his elbows to find Jay sitting against the altar, head resting on his knees. He swiftly explained the plan. Jay said nothing. He sat there, limp and helpless as a rag doll. Iain shook him. No response. Then Heaney uttered a high-pitched whistle.

Iain leapt up and ran towards the sentry-box. The gun jumped and spat in his hand, funny, he couldn't remem-ber pulling the trigger; he heard other shots, an endless fusillade, he crouched, he darted from side to side, but above all he ran as he'd never run before.

He ended up flattened against the side of the sentry-box, cramming in huge breaths. His whole body was shaking. The terrible noise had stopped. After a few seconds he felt strong enough to risk a glance around the corner of the building. His head was out for scarcely half a second, but that was enough to show him a pair of legs flat on the stone, beneath the lights.

'Martin,' he called hoarsely. 'Martin, where are you?'

'Over here,' said a voice. Iain hesitated. Had that really been Heaney's voice. Then – 'It's okay, Iain, Cover's checked out.'

Cautiously Iain put his head around the corner again. The legs were still there. Another figure crouched over them, and with ineffable relief Iain recognized Martin Heaney.

'There's a sort of cavity in there,' Heaney said, nodding towards the sentry-box. 'For the book of remembrance. Our pal must have been expecting trouble, he'd left a spare in it. He probably knew Verity as well as we do.'

Iain wanted to ask: which of us killed him? Pointless; neither of them could ever know. He'd spent seventeen years in prison for a murder he hadn't committed, and now . . .

Martin stood up. 'We go. Where's Sampson?'

Iain made a big effort to dispel the sombre thoughts crowding into his brain. 'Don't know.' But as he spoke, a shadow arose at the far end of the altar. Nobody said anything.

'We go,' Heaney repeated. 'How did you get here?'

'Rented car. It's parked off the road.'

'Sampson, what about you?'

'Taxi.'

Heaney made a face. 'Hope the driver's got amnesia. Now, *hurry*.'

As he led the way down to the main gates Iain asked, 'What's going to happen about Cover?'

'Nothing. Officially he wasn't here any more than I am; disclaimable, disposable, just another motiveless murder.'

'And the guns?'

Martin stopped short. 'Thank Christ you remembered – here, give!'

Iain handed over the Ruger.

They had reached the gates. Martin pushed one of them ajar. 'We split,' he cried. 'You two take Iain's car, we'll meet –'

Even as he spoke, they heard the first high-pitched squeal of a siren, still far away to the south. Heaney set a harder pace. As they sprinted across Woodlands Road he managed to pant out loud enough for Iain to hear, 'Meet at the Lido Hotel, Beach Lane, turning off Beach Road.'

'Why there?' Iain gasped.

'Because that's where I left Alison. Now *run!*'

*

Alison sat on the sofa next to her daughter. Kate refused to look at her. Alison knew it would be futile to take Kate's hand, which is what she most wanted to do. She took a tissue from her handbag and dabbed her eyes. She said, 'Iain is your father. No one else. Iain.'

Somewhere behind her Verity chuckled. Alison heard liquid splashing into a glass, followed by the clink of ice-cubes. She forced herself to be calm. She said, 'I warned you: this woman is dangerous. All she wants to do is harm us, for pleasure. I know the truth, and I'm telling you: Iain is your father.'

Kate looked up and stared into the distance, still ignoring her mother. 'You said she knew the truth,' she muttered, after a long pause. 'Maybe she does. Maybe that's why you were so keen I shouldn't meet her.'

'Oh, I'm sure she wasn't.' Verity stalked back to stand in front of the two women. 'Poor baby,' she crooned, 'must protect baby from nasty people.'

Alison ignored her. 'You came to get the truth,' she said to Kate. 'Let's start with me.' She drew a deep breath. 'I had a lover, here in Singapore.'

Kate turned pale. She looked down at her fingers, knotted in her lap. 'Go on,' she said, her voice scarcely audible.

'His name was —'

'Jay Sampson. He was *my* lover, too, until your mother stole him.'

Kate looked up at Verity. 'You cow,' she said. 'You shut up, will you.'

Verity laughed, and once again moved across to the picture window. Kate faced her mother. 'This Jay . . . he's the same man I met today, right?'

'Yes. Jay and I . . . made love, several times. Your father never suspected. I knew it wouldn't last, I wanted to . . . to protect him.'

'Thing I like about you,' Verity observed to the glass, 'is you know how to make up a great story.'

'So I never told Iain, then or later. And because I knew it wouldn't amount to anything, I made sure that nothing we did could result in my getting pregnant.'

Kate made a face. 'You mean, you were on the pill.'

Alison shook her head.

'So what you're saying is that you split with this Jay character more than nine months before I came along.'

'No.'

'Then you can't be sure.'

'I can, because I was always in charge of things like that, and he . . . Jay . . . let me.'

'But it's true that you and Dad . . . you waited a long time, you tried to have me for ages before you did . . . oh, *shit*.'

'It's true. None of that alters anything. Now Kate, listen to me. We're operating in the big grown-up world now. Nasty place. You hate it; so do I. But I want you to listen.'

'Tell her about London,' Verity suggested. 'Tell her how you found Gerry's body. Go on.' She reverted to sarcasm: 'Kate's a big girl now.'

'*You* found him . . .' Kate, startled, reached for her mother's hand. 'I never knew that,' she said in a hushed voice.

'Iain and I were going to the opera that night. Your father had a meeting with Gerry, at his flat. I thought I'd pick him up there and we'd go on to the theatre together. When I arrived the door was on the latch. I pushed it open.' Alison hesitated, grappling with her memories. 'It was like a butcher's shop inside. She was there.'

'She . . . ?'

'Newland.' Alison half-turned in her chair, for the first time giving vent to her feelings. 'That bitch, there.'

Verity, her back to the sofa, looked down into her glass and up again: the only sign that she'd heard.

'Later, I found out why they'd killed Gerry. They told me why: she, that woman, she and Jay were up to their necks making poison gas for the Pentagon, using Harchem staff and facilities and their secret formulas, too; and Gerry found out. He worked away at it until he had the whole thing, and then he made the mistake of telling Verity. He planned to have a confrontation, with Iain there as his witness. So Verity tried reasoning with Gerry, or maybe even buying him off. But Gerry wasn't having any, so there was a row. It got out of hand. Gerry died. Then I blundered in.'

Kate gave her mother's hand another little squeeze. Her face had turned deadly white.

'I blundered in, and she wanted to kill me. They'd got rid of Iain because they knew he was coming and Verity'd met him on the stairs and told him the door was locked and she couldn't make anyone hear; so Iain went away with her before I arrived, but Verity came back a few minutes later. And when she got into the flat, that second

425

time, she must have forgotten to lock the door. That's what they worked out, while I sat there, shivering. Verity wanted to kill me, but then she had a better idea; and she said, No, we'll kill her *and* her child if she ever opens her mouth to say one word about this. She claimed to have a poison that couldn't be traced, to have several, and because Raj was so good I believed her. And that's when I started to cry, I think. I just kept having this awful picture of my baby, dead . . . so I swore I wouldn't say a word, and do you know, I went to the opera that night, like we'd arranged. Don't ask me what we saw, I sat through it rigid, with my dead baby in front of my eyes. She was bleeding. I knew it was a girl. I knew it was you.'

'Stop it.' Kate tore her hand from Alison's and began to rock to and fro on the sofa, with her hands over her ears. 'Stop it, stop it.'

'But the police were good, you see. They began to find out things, about the chemicals and gas and the horrors. They found some of Gerry's notes. So they came to me and said, we need more.'

'The police said that?'

'No. They did.'

'Who's *they*?'

'Oh for God's sake tell her,' Verity put in. 'If she hasn't got the sense to work it out for herself.' She wheeled away from the window and came to stand in front of the sofa again. She looked at her watch. 'I'm expecting a visitor soon,' she said. 'Once he's wrapped up a few fiddly little loose ends.' She rested her elbow on her free hand and smiled at them over the glass. 'Such as Iain,' she said, before draining it.

*

'What do you mean, she isn't here?'

For a moment Iain thought that Heaney was going to

lean across the desk and haul the clerk upright by his arms, but somehow he restrained himself.

'She went out,' Mr Chen said. 'She and Miss Forward together.'

'Where did they go?'

'I've no idea.'

Martin grunted out a sigh of exasperation, dabbing his grazed shoulder. He'd stuffed a handkerchief over the wound, but a bloodstain showed beneath his shirt and it was obviously causing him pain.

The desk-clerk looked sullen. Iain could see how Heaney had ruined everything by his show of temper. Lessons long forgotten flooded into his mind. 'Excuse me,' he said in a soft voice. 'I'm sorry to be the cause of so much trouble, but you see I'm Mr Forward, the lady's husband. She and my daughter are in trouble, I'm desperately worried for them.'

Because he never once took his eyes off the man's face, he could not look at Heaney. He was aware of him fiddling in his pockets, however, and for one terrible moment he was afraid the MI5 agent meant to try a bribe. He forced himself to keep his voice low, and continued, 'Is it possible that you could think where they might have gone? Did they perhaps ask you for the number of a bus, how to get to a particular area?'

The clerk hesitated. 'Well,' he said at last. 'The young lady did ask me to look up an address in the phone book.'

Iain's heart fluttered into his mouth. 'Yes?'

'But I don't discuss guests' business with strangers.'

Iain reached into his memory and dredged up Verity Newland's address. 'Can you at least tell me this,' he went on, in the same patient tone. 'Was it a house, an apartment, just by Fernhill Close?'

The clerk pursed his lips; then he nodded.

'Verity Newland, was that perhaps the name?'

The Chinese nodded again. Once Iain's softly-softly technique had breached his outer defences, he seemed to swing the opposite way; now there was no stopping him. 'The two ladies were rather unhappy. Fighting. They ran out. I think the young lady caught a cab, not sure.'

'And the other lady . . . my wife?'

'She walked away, sir; I couldn't see. Sorry.'

'That's all right,' Iain said, 'you've been most helpful. Martin, let's –'

'Just a minute.' Heaney held something out to the clerk. 'Is this one of your room-keys?'

The man peered at it suspiciously. 'No,' he said, with finality, before shifting sideways and busying himself with some receipts.

'I thought it wasn't,' Martin muttered. 'Right, Fernhill Close.'

As he unlocked the car, Iain asked, 'What was that key you showed him?'

'Tell you later. Quick, in the back.' Martin nodded at Jay. 'I want you to keep an eye on him.'

Throughout the conversation with the clerk, Jay Sampson had been standing to one side. He looked whipped; but Iain had a funny feeling that this was a front, that he meant to do a runner and was just awaiting the right opportunity. Heaney must have thought the same.

'Don't you think it's time you came up with a few explanations?' Iain said to Heaney as they drove off. 'Like why you're doing this, for a start?'

Martin scowled. 'Lots of reasons,' he said eventually. 'None of which stand up, actually, not from where I'm looking right now. I was angry at what they'd done to me, yes, and to you. And I was bored. Bored rigid. I kept looking at the future, and I kept thinking . . .'

He fell silent. After a few moments he seemed to make an effort to pull himself together; he sat more upright and he said, 'We don't have much time, but here's what

428

I think. At the trial, they had five major items of evidence against you.' Heaney began to count them off on his fingers. 'There was your thumbprint on Harchem's tech safe, to which you had no access – or so you said. Second, your prints were on the dagger that killed Reynolds. Third, money in a Swiss bank account. Fourth, the Sonja letters. And fifth, the fact that major industrial secrets were missing from the safe. Plus you had no alibi, but you did have an appointment with Gerry Reynolds before he died – Verity Newland saw you at his place, you and she left together, you both agreed on that – but that doesn't mean you killed him, all it means is that you had the opportunity. That was the whole of the prosecution case; agree?'

'Yes.'

'Right. Take the Swiss account. Anyone could have set it up as long as they were prepared to forge your signature, offer some ID, anything, a driver's licence.' Martin glanced in the mirror. '*He* did it, probably.'

But Jay merely continued to stare out the window.

'Verity could have borrowed your driver's licence for long enough to let Sampson, Sonja, whatever you want to call him, pop into the bank's local branch and do the necessary. What's more, Verity could have stolen – and did actually steal – the industrial secrets.'

'How do you know?'

Heaney smiled briefly. 'We know.'

A suspicion had begun to darken Iain's mind. 'When did you find out?'

'I plead the fifth. That leaves the letters and your thumbprint on the safe, the print on the dagger. Now there was a funny thing about those prints, the defence made a lot of it, do you remember?'

'There should have been more than one print on each object; it wasn't natural to find only one.'

'Yes, that, and also the prints were smudged: there was

429

barely enough to support a comparison. All of which the prosecution countered by saying you'd tried to wipe off everything and done a rotten job. Balls. Those prints had been planted.'

'Planted?'

'Forged. You were set up.'

'But you can't forge a fingerprint!'

Martin smiled. 'It's about as hard as forging a fiver,' he said. 'You lift an original print off something nice and solid, say a glass. The tame expert spends a lot of hours copying it, twirl for twirl, whorl for whorl, on to fine wax. Next, you reverse it, negative-positive, on to something no more elaborate than a latex fingerstall. You rub the stall against your skin, to pick up some grease, and then you stamp exhibit one with the only hallmark of guilt nobody questions, ever.'

Iain turned to face out the windscreen. He felt winded.

'They didn't have time to do a wonderful job on you; that's why the prints were smudged. Because forensic testing wasn't up to much in those days it didn't matter, but even now, who'd question it? A print's a print. Today, if someone *did* challenge it, it would show up like a shot, because the skin grease on the print wouldn't match yours. Worth thinking about, isn't it? And since we've got so far with Verity, it isn't hard to go the extra mile. She worked alongside you. A coffee cup with your thumbprint on the bottom . . .'

'Who planted the murder weapon in our apartment?'

'Ask Sonja. Come on, Sampson – tell us how you did it.'

Jay swivelled his head away from the window. He gazed at Heaney for a long time without speaking. Then he said, 'We've arrived.'

The car pulled into the kerb. The three of them got out. Iain saw that they were a few hundred yards away from the tower at the top of which Verity had her eyrie.

'I don't think we want to be announced,' Martin said. 'So leave this to me.'

He marched to the intercom let into the wall beside the gate. Iain heard him say something; the gate swung open, Heaney disappeared up the driveway. What seemed like a long time went by. Then Heaney suddenly re-materialized in the space between them. 'Come on,' he said.

They all proceeded up the drive to where the glass doors yawned open, letting an air-conditioned blast escape into the night. There was no sign of any porter, but Iain knew better than to ask questions. He was making for the lifts when Heaney called him back.

'Through here,' he said, indicating a door behind the porter's desk.

If the decor in the front hall was sumptuous, here things degenerated swiftly. Whitewash had been slapped carelessly on the walls, there were concrete-droppings on the dirty tiled floor. At the end of a short corridor they found a goods lift, its interior lined with sacking. Martin shepherded them inside and pressed the top button.

'You asked about this,' he said.

Iain looked down. Heaney was holding a key, the one he'd shown the hotel desk-clerk earlier.

'Cover had it. I'd a hunch then I knew what it was.'

Iain saw that the key was a Yale. 'What's it for?' he asked. But Heaney only smiled.

The lift clanked and groaned its way to the top. They emerged into a bare passage similar to the one downstairs. Halfway down was a door. Heaney approached it, with Iain at his heels.

'Now,' Heaney whispered, holding up the key, 'let's see if I'm right . . .'

*

431

'And then there had to be a fall-guy.' Alison's delivery was picking up speed by now; the words cascaded out of her like water over a dam. 'The police narrowed it down, you see, somebody inside Harchem, that's what they said, an insider. So after that, Verity meant to get Iain. She was frightened for her own skin, and besides, she'd always hated him. When she found out the police knew about his appointment with Gerry that night it must have seemed like a gift from heaven. The first thing was, they forged his signature on a power of attorney and made me open a Swiss bank account in his name.'

'Made you?'

'She'd kill me and my baby, that's what she kept on saying, over and over again, kill, kill, *kill*. And in the end, I said yes. I'd do it. But even that wasn't enough. They needed to plant papers on him. So I put papers in his briefcase for them. And the dagger in our apartment . . . and . . .'

'The letters,' Verity said. 'Let's get to the *fun* part, shall we? Tell her about the letters.'

There was a long silence. Verity prowled over to the bar and poured herself another gin. She cut up a lemon and dropped a slice into her own glass before coming back with the bottle to top up Kate's. The girl drank; because she was trembling some slopped over the side, but that only made Verity laugh.

Kate took a tissue from her pocket and began to dab at her wet jeans. Then, as if struck by the futility of this social gesture in the circumstances, she flung the glass on to the floor. To her surprise, Verity said nothing. Kate looked up and found the older woman's gaze levelled at the window. She swung around. The lights of Singapore were visible and, in the foreground, so was the thick chrome rail of the terrace's outer wall. Nothing struck her as odd. But when she turned back again, Verity was still staring at the window.

Kate blindly stretched her hand along the sofa until it made contact with Alison's. 'Mum,' she said quietly. 'I'd like to hear about the letters now.'

Alison's hand lay in hers for a long while. Then she pulled it free. She said, 'It'll hurt.'

'What *could* hurt any more, after this?' Kate's voice went from whisper to wail in a single register.

Alison took a long breath. 'Inside our house,' she began, 'the flat we rented, here in Singapore, there were some letters. Jay had been writing to me. We knew it was insane, we couldn't help ourselves. They were . . . explicit. Love letters. Right at the start when our . . . when we began, he'd written to me and signed himself "Sonja", I was to be "Johnny". I kept them in a hole in the floorboards, underneath the carpet. He never dated them: if ever Iain found them, I could say I didn't know anything about them, that they must belong to someone who'd lived there before us. Oh, I was mad! I should never have let him . . .' She broke off, tried again. 'Love is pathetic, you see. To the people involved it's like living inside this glorious bubble of champagne, but outsiders never see it. Jay, well, I . . . I just loved him.'

'More than Iain?' Kate asked, after a silence.

There was a long pause. Then Alison nodded: three heavy movements of the head. Her eyes were closed, but tears still managed to force a channel between the lids.

'Anyway . . . anyway.' Alison wiped her face with the back of her hand. 'The Singapore police were asked to search the flat. They found the knife, and the letters, and took them away. And then, in London they started to say that the letters were evidence of a conspiracy. That they were in code. Iain was Johnny, some big spy or other was Sonja, he owned the House of Orchids, and he'd vanished. They made it work, somehow. At the trial they called a man to say he'd analysed the code, and it meant this, that and the other.'

'Grindle.'

'Terence Grindle. He went on and on, about how when Jay had written my eyes were like two smouldering candles in some dark temple, it really meant, "Deliver the goods Thursday", and oh, it was terrible. Sickening. But because they did it so well, the jury believed everything.'

'Surely Dad's lawyers could have called a code expert to show it was a lie?'

'Oh, yes, they did. But Verity had been smarter than that! Jay'd brought in help: Grindle, the CIA, I don't know ... They'd got Jay to write some more of those letters, ones I'd never received, and they'd made me put them with the others, the real ones, before they were found. And when Iain's expert witnesses read those other letters, they agreed: yes, there was a code, just like Grindle said. And after that it was hopeless. The jury loved it: you could see it in their faces, every day. They were just waiting for the end, so they could find your father guilty and go home.'

And now, for almost the first time in this meeting, Alison lifted her gaze to Verity. She examined her enemy carefully. She said, 'I don't want Iain to know any of this. He's coming to find out the truth, and he mustn't. Ever.'

Verity's face was impossible to read.

'Because I did what you asked. I did what I had to, to save Kate, and I've lived with it ever since, minute by minute. So now you've got to promise me that he'll never know.'

'And if I don't?' Verity lit another cigarette, inhaling deeply. She said, 'Go on, Alison, tell me what's going to happen if I don't. I want to hear it. So does Kate, poor luvvy.'

Alison sat on the sofa, twisting her hands together. She spoke some words in a low voice. Verity bent down closer. 'What?'

Alison jerked her head up. 'I said, don't push me.'

'*Push* you . . . my dear, I wouldn't dream of it. And anyway, Iain won't ever know, I can promise you that.' Verity stalked over to the windows and stood with her back to them. 'Iain's dead, darling,' she said. 'He's been dealt with, just as I dealt with poor old Gerry Reynolds.'

From the look of triumph on her face, maybe she expected Alison to break down, to crumple; but Alison surprised her. What she said was: '*You* . . . killed Gerry Reynolds?'

'Of course it was me. Oh . . . I see. You thought *Jay* had done it.' Verity laughed out loud. 'He wasn't capable of hurting a fly! He wasn't capable of *anything*. If it had been left up to him, we'd have sunk without trace. His friends were useful afterwards, I will say that: forging Iain's signature, manufacturing his prints, that kind of thing. But *I* killed Reynolds; I'd do it again today without a second thought. Reynolds is history, and now so is Iain, because somebody's come to take care of everything . . .' Languidly she reached out a hand to press a button. The glass door behind her slid open silently. Verity half turned her head. 'Haven't you, Tony?'

There was a silence. Alison and Kate were both staring at the terrace. Simultaneously, they rose. Verity saw their faces. Her own smile slipped a fraction. She began to turn towards the terrace door, but a hand gripped her ear and twisted it, wringing a scream from the depths of her throat, and then the same hand banged her head against the wall once, twice, three times, before letting her collapse on to the carpet.

'Tony won't be coming,' Iain said, wiping his hand on his slacks. 'But he lent us the key to your back door.'

Martin Heaney and Jay Sampson followed him over the threshold. As Iain advanced to the middle of the room he removed his wig and tossed it aside. Alison stayed rooted to the spot, but Kate rushed forward to fling her arms around her father. He clutched her tightly,

435

stroking her hair, but his eyes never left Alison's face.

'You heard?' she mouthed.

He did not speak, he did not nod; he continued to stroke his daughter's hair.

Alison's eyes slid sideways and encountered Heaney. She shot him a brief, gritty smile. 'Funny,' she said. 'Funny, I nearly told you, several times. I knew you never believed all those lies in court. I don't know what stopped me telling you, really. Kate, I suppose. Who'd have looked after her?'

'I would.' Iain's voice was ragged and dangerous. 'I'd have taken care of her. I might even have taken care of you. The police would have sorted this trash' – he jerked his chin at Verity – 'and we'd have got on with our lives. Stop your lying *now*.'

They could all feel the danger radiating out of him, it was almost a visible aura, but Alison knew it to be focused on her. He would ignite her if he could.

'You did it for him.' He pointed at Jay. 'Because *he* was there, in Gerry's flat that night, *he* was going down for murder unless you saved him, *he* was the reason for everything.'

He reached into the hip pocket of his slacks and pulled out an airmail envelope. Alison happened to be looking at Jay. She caught his expression and knew that he was experiencing the odd feeling that steals over a person who sees a letter he wrote in another's hands, so crimped and used; and she felt sympathy for him, none for herself.

Iain took a sheet of paper out of the envelope. He began to read, only he wasn't really reading, that much was obvious from the way he held his head, he was quoting from memory.

'Do you remember, darling, *Ching Ming* festival of 'seventy-two? We were lying naked on the bed, you and I, with the fan going strong, your body tucked into mine, soldered by so many wetnesses: of sweat, and seed that had dissolved in the heat, and the juice from your insides all sticky and spent. My hand lay squeezed between your thighs and you pretended to be asleep while I worked . . . but then you amazed me and my hand stopped, for you had quoted poetry in that quiet murmur of sated love which always made my limbs burn; you said this . . .

"The moon over the royal palace looks down
    upon their parting
The parting of those who go to the east.
From those who go to the west."

And in that moment I knew you were sad beyond expression, because you loved me . . . as I loved you, but there was a parting, a separation, to be endured. We both believed it would be days. And see how the days have become years.

I love you now as I loved you then: beyond the line that makes us rational and human. You will know the things that are happening to my body as I write to you, just as I know the effect my words will have. Yin and yang do not change – the spear's work is to thrust inside, the body's to open, the lips to yield . . . so it will always be, my love, my dearest love.

"Every banquet must end", your last words to me. Every day I speak them aloud, with bitterness and sorrow. But there is another banquet. Those who go to the west sometimes return.

Count the days.'

Throughout the reading Alison continued to stare into Iain's eyes. 'You found it,' she whispered when he had finished. 'That's why you ran away . . .'

'After Christmas. I had time, then. Prison habit: you

437

always search, because maybe someone's dumped something in your cell and you have to find it before the screws do. After Christmas, when I'd started to fuck you again, and was jealous enough to search your drawers, your cupboards, everywhere, everything: that's when I found it.'

'So you knew . . . I'd had an affair.'

'Or was having one still. A Sonja letter, "Darling Johnny . . ." God! And yet how could I suspect you, the loving wife? D'you remember me telling you how they cheered me off the landing, at the Scrubs, when you came to visit? "She's there, mate", they'd shout. And they'd clap, they'd hoot, and you know why? Because you stuck it out, through good and bad, you stuck in there, faithful, loving, *loyal*. You bitch. You fucking bitch.'

She expected him to strike her down. She wanted him to do it. But he would not give her the satisfaction of touching her in anger.

'I wouldn't believe ill of you, not at first. I thought: this is Heaney and his crowd, planting evidence again, just like before, they think I'm a trouble-maker, I'll talk, so they're out to fix me . . . Better believe that than be ungrateful towards you. Better believe that than the truth, eh?'

For the first time his clear brow creased in a frown, moral certainty deserting him. 'Why didn't you go off with him?' he whispered. 'With your lover. Why didn't you?'

'With a murderer?' she replied.

'You believed that, did you?'

Alison lowered her eyes. 'Even if Jay wasn't the killer he was there when it happened; he didn't stop it,' she said. 'He and Verity were the only people who'd been in the flat that night, apart from you; and I knew you could never have killed Gerry. So what was I to do: go off with a spy, possibly a murderer? And my guilt? No, Iain – better to settle for just the guilt.'

'And the charade,' he sneered. 'Pretending you loved me, why go on with that?'

'Charade?' A look of intense pain flitted across her face. 'Well . . .' She broke a long silence by heaving a deep, shuddery sigh. 'I went on, because I wanted to prove your innocence.' Her voice lifted. 'Which I have done.'

She picked up her handbag from where it was lying half-open on the sofa. She took out a small tape-recorder. She wound back the tape a few revolutions and pressed 'Play'.

The quality was far from perfect, but they all heard the words: *'Iain's dead, darling, he's been dealt with, just as I dealt with poor old Gerry Reynolds.'* And then Alison was saying, *'You . . . killed Gerry Reynolds?'* A pause, some laughter. *'Of course it was me. Oh . . . I see. You thought Jay had done it.'* More laughter. *'He wasn't capable of hurting a fly! He wasn't capable of anything. If it had been left up to him, we'd have sunk without trace. His friends were useful afterwards, I will say that: forging Iain's signature, manufacturing his prints, that kind of thing. But I killed Reynolds; I'd do it again today without a second thought. Reynolds is history, and now so is Iain, because somebody's come to take care of everything . . .'*

Alison tossed the tape over to Heaney, who in his amazement nearly dropped it. 'This isn't quite how I thought it would be,' she said, with an attempt at humour. 'Anyway.' She turned to Kate. 'Iain's your father,' she declared abruptly. 'You can be sure of it.'

'No.'

Jay hadn't spoken before. Now, every head turned to him.

'She's mine,' he said softly.

'You're going to hurt yourself,' Alison warned. 'Leave it.'

Jay shook his head. 'No.'

Alison briefly closed her eyes and opened them again. 'That last time at the house,' she said. 'When you raped me. There was blood, yes?'

Jay was staring at her, she could see the anger on his brow but something else too, a waning of confidence, a doubt. As if mesmerized, he nodded.

'You thought it was because you were so violent, you apologized.' Alison laughed unpleasantly. 'You grovelled, perhaps you don't want to remember that. But it wasn't you, it was me.'

By now his face had turned pale. 'You're lying,' he breathed.

'I was bleeding anyway.' Alison stood before him, implacable as Fate. *I was having my period. That's how I know Kate wasn't your child.'*

She half turned to Iain. 'I would have gone away with him if I'd thought Kate was his. She wasn't.' She wiped her forehead. 'I'm so hot,' she said. 'Going to be sick . . .'

Too stunned, too ashamed, too overwhelmed with grief or anger, none of them moved in the time it took Alison to walk on to the terrace, clamber over the rail and drop.

A second passed; the still-life tableau dissolved in a blur of movement. Iain was first at the chrome rail, his wife's name on his lips, though whether he cried for loss or in anger no one could say, not even him; Martin followed; Kate shrieked *'Mum!'*, Jay sank down on the floor. Verity Newland joined the others at the rail. Thirty floors below, beside the swimming-pool, they could see a pale shape halfway in shadow; somebody was already creeping out to investigate . . .

'Damage control,' Heaney said crisply. 'Iain, look after the girl. I'll keep that tape. I want you and Kate out of here faster than fast.'

Iain hesitated; then he took Kate's arm and gently

440

started to pull her away. Kate, too numb to protest, let him. But Jay had clambered up. Now he barred their way. 'No,' he said.

Heaney stared at him, not understanding.

'Earlier this evening,' Jay said, 'you killed someone. You and Iain Forward. A man called Tony Cover. I was there. I saw it.'

'And how did we do that?' Heaney's voice was light, but there was a dangerous edge to it.

'You shot him.'

Heaney spread his hands. 'Where is the gun?' he asked. There was a silence.

'You rode with Iain to the Lido, in his car,' Martin went on. 'I joined you there. I'm being kind, I'm giving you a clue. Where, do you think, is the gun that killed Cover?'

They all saw the doubt gather in Jay's face. For a moment he remained silent. But then he said, 'Okay, so you ditched the guns somewhere the police won't find them. What about poor Alison, lying dead, thirty floors down?'

'What about her?'

'Verity and I saw you kill her.'

Martin laughed. 'Iain and Kate saw that I didn't.'

'Oh yes? And which of us has the conviction for murder?' Jay laughed. 'Martin,' he said, 'you'd better re-think this.'

Iain and Kate stared at Martin Heaney. His face was impassive, but they could feel the tension. 'You can't,' Kate breathed, not sure who she was talking to. 'Can't, can't . . .' She turned to Verity, meaning to plead with her, but as she did so they all heard the sound of police sirens in the distance, and the words froze on Kate's lips.

'Well,' Verity said, 'I don't know about you, Jay, *darling*, but I could fancy another drink.'

She moved languorously across to the bar. As she

441

reached it Martin said, 'Jay, I'll give you a choice. You can tell the truth about Reynolds' murder. Or you can hang, here, for the murder of Robinson Tang.'

Verity dropped a glass and leaned against the bar for support. Jay stared at Martin. Then his legs gave way, he sank down on to the nearest chair.

'I'll be back shortly,' Martin said. 'Got to get rid of Iain and Kate first. Some advice: be here, both of you, when I get back.'

Martin hustled Iain and Kate through the servants' entrance, along the corridor to the small lift. While they descended he uttered crisp instructions.

'At the bottom, turn right, go out the back door. I'll buy you time, not much. Get out of Singapore any way you can, I'll contact you in London.'

'Martin . . .' Iain suddenly grasped his hand. He tried to speak, had no luck, tried again. 'Thank you.'

The lift eased to a halt, the door opened. Martin said, 'Think nothing of it. You'll need a lawyer in England, but my guess is, he'll have the Home Secretary refer your conviction to the Court of Appeal to consider fresh evidence. I'll be there to help see he does.'

'But . . . will that tape-recording Alison made be enough, by itself?'

'It won't *be* by itself. Trust me.'

'But Jay's threatening to frame you for Alison's murder.'

'There won't be any signs of violence on Alison's body; it's a clear case of suicide. And you needn't worry about Jay: leave him to me.'

'Martin . . . Why have you done all this?'

'You know why.'

'I know what you told me, in the pub, in the car tonight. A load of bullshit.'

'Yes. You're right. I did it for Alison. There. Satisfy you?' Martin patted Iain on the back, but his smile was shaky, lopsided. He saw the questions gathering in Iain's eyes and said, 'No more time. *Go!*'

As Martin pushed them through the door into the lobby they caught a glimpse of alarmed occupiers, some in their nightclothes, starting to assemble. Then Iain took his daughter by the arm again, and together they ran in the opposite direction, towards the rear of the building.

The first police car was zooming into the drive as Martin headed back upstairs in the lift. At the door of the apartment he hesitated, fighting down nausea. Don't think about Alison, there'll be time for that later, time to mourn. Just do right by her, build a monument . . .

He entered the apartment to find Verity at the bar, Jay on the sofa. Verity was hacking away at a lemon, slicing it up with vicious slashes of a small, pointed knife. Hearing Martin come in she turned her head and looked at him through eyes of terrible coldness. Martin gazed first at Jay, then at her. He knew he had five minutes, less, in which to carry off the biggest bluff of his life. There was no time for subtlety; dive in, head first, *now*.

'Even before I came to Singapore,' he said, 'I'd contacted Verity. She was frightened, wanted immunity, all kinds of things. After I got here she told me that Jay Sampson was in Singapore and haunting the House of Orchids. By then I'd managed to find out that Sampson was Sonja; Grindle told me. So I went to the site of the old house, thinking I might find him. Instead, I found the corpse of the missing boy who's been in all the papers – what was left of him – along with a broken flashlight. Black, nine inches long, two Duracell Gold batteries.'

Verity's upper teeth showed on her lip, the skin around her eyes tightened. She went to sit on the sofa beside Jay, sipping her drink without a word. All the colour had drained away from Jay's face. While Martin was talking the hand holding his glass had slipped off his lap, on to the sofa; now the glass toppled over, sending a cascade of gin over the fabric. Neither he nor Verity noticed. But Martin noticed; and in his heart he rejoiced, because he knew then for sure that the torch he'd found belonged to Jay, and would have his prints on it.

'That torch is . . . safe. It won't take half an hour to put it back at the scene of the crime and make an anonymous but helpful phone call to the police, who will find your fingerprints – quite genuine ones, this time – on it, along with blood of Robinson's type. So here's what you'll do, Jay. You'll make a statement, accusing Verity of Reynolds' murder. You'll implicate yourself as an accessory, but I can't help that. You and Verity will be extradited to England. Assuming you do that, I'll lose the torch. Eventually. After you've both been convicted, in England.'

The long silence that followed was broken by a pounding on the door. Martin stood up. 'They still hang murderers here,' he said quietly. 'Oh yes, and one more thing: Alison Forward committed suicide. Remember?'

In the second before he opened the door he heard Verity mutter: 'Say *nothing*.' Several uniformed policemen quickly came into the apartment without waiting to be invited, followed by a tall Chinese wearing a suit.

'I am sorry to disturb you,' this man said. He did not look particularly penitent. 'A woman has died here. She fell. Do you know anything about this?'

During the long silence that followed, the uniformed police went about a swift search of the penthouse. At last Martin spread his hands and shook his head in denial. The Chinese scrutinized him with a frown. 'You have hurt yourself,' he said. 'Blood.'

'I grazed my shoulder when I was looking at my car's exhaust.'

After a mistrustful pause the Chinese said, 'I am Inspector Ma of the Criminal Investigation Department.' He

444

turned to Verity. 'Do you know anything about this death, madam?'

'No.' The word was spoken in a whisper.

'Sir?'

This was addressed to Jay. For several moments he stared up at Ma without speaking. Then he said, 'I wish to make a statement.'

'*No!*'

Verity was staring at Jay. When he did not respond, Ma reached into his jacket pocket and drew out a notebook. 'A statement?' he said. 'About the woman who died? What was her name? How did she –'

'About her, yes, and about . . . a murder.'

'Jay.' The hysteria had vanished from Verity's voice; to judge from her tone she might have been about to offer him some sound financial advice. 'You're making a mistake.'

'A murder,' he went on, ignoring her, 'in nineteen seventy-three.'

Verity's attack was so quick, so malevolent, that for a second no one moved to intervene. She threw herself on Jay, a small metal object uplifted to catch a glint from the lamplight. Crimson jetted out across the carpet as Jay went down under her weight. Next moment she was on the floor with two policemen pinning her arms behind her back. Beside her lay the fruit-knife she'd been using to slice the lemon.

Inspector Ma hadn't moved while his men restrained Verity. He waited impassively as Martin fetched a towel from the bathroom and used it to bind up Jay's hand, wounded when he tried to deflect the blow. Only after that did Ma shoot back the cuffs of his jacket with slight, controlled movements and say, 'A murder, in nineteen seventy-three . . . ?'

Jay drew a deep breath and nodded. 'This woman . . .' He gestured wearily down at Verity. 'Killed a man. His name was Gerry Reynolds. I . . . was with her. I saw it. I was part of it.'

Inspector Ma sat down and uncapped his pen. He glanced at his watch, made a note of the date and the time, and he said, 'Continue, please.'

*

As father and daughter stepped into the garden and the warm, moist night, Kate began to cry, very softly. Iain braced her up, until by the time they reached the gate in the fence he was nearly carrying her. With his free hand he unlatched the gate, already hearing the commotion begin behind him, the sirens, the shouting, a woman having hysterics.

'Dad!' Kate held him back. 'We can't just . . . *leave* Mum like this!' Tears were streaming down her cheeks. 'I must . . . *see* her.'

'No, Kate. It's part of the price. Come on.'

When he drew her gently to him, she had not the strength to resist. He held Kate tight while he stroked her hair, and he knew that a lifetime of paying the price lay ahead of them, that they would have to find a way of coming to terms with this, and it would be harder than death. They would do it. Together, they would.

Iain gave Kate one last squeeze. He hurried her through the opening; but, between closing the gate and speeding her away, he found time to plant on her forehead a long, tender kiss, and say, 'I love you.'

# Fontana Fiction

Fontana is a leading paperback publisher of fiction. Below are some recent titles.

- ☐ BLOOD RULES John Trenhaile £4.99
- ☐ PRIDE'S HARVEST Jon Cleary £4.99
- ☐ DUNCTON TALES William Horwood £4.99
- ☐ FORBIDDEN KNOWLEDGE Stephen Donaldson £4.99
- ☐ TIME OF THE ASSASSINS Alastair MacNeill £4.99
- ☐ IMAJICA Clive Barker £5.99
- ☐ THE WINDS OF THE WASTELANDS Antony Swithin £4.99
- ☐ THE HOUSE OF MIRRORS Michael Mullen £4.99
- ☐ TYPHOON Mark Joseph £4.99
- ☐ SEMPER FI W. E. B. Griffin £4.50
- ☐ CALL TO ARMS W. E. B. Griffin £4.50
- ☐ A HIVE OF DEAD MEN Geoffrey Jenkins £4.99

You can buy Fontana Paperbacks at your local bookshops or newsagents. Or you can order them from Fontana, Cash Sales Department, Box 29, Douglas, Isle of Man. Please send a cheque, postal or money order (not currency) worth the price plus 24p per book for postage (maximum postage required is £3.00 for orders within the UK).

NAME (Block letters)_____

ADDRESS_____

_____

While every effort is made to keep prices low, it is sometimes necessary to increase them at short notice. Fontana Paperbacks reserve the right to show new retail prices on covers which may differ from those previously advertised in the text or elsewhere.